NOVICE DRAGONEER

BOOKS BY E. E. KNIGHT

The Dragoneer Academy series

NOVICE DRAGONEER

DAUGHTER OF THE SERPENTINE

The Age of Fire series

DRAGON CHAMPION

DRAGON AVENGER

DRAGON OUTCAST

DRAGON STRIKE

DRAGON RULE

DRAGON FATE

The Vampire Earth series

WAY OF THE WOLF

CHOICE OF THE CAT

TALE OF THE THUNDERBOLT

VALENTINE'S RISING

VALENTINE'S EXILE

VALENTINE'S RESOLVE

FALL WITH HONOR

WINTER DUTY

MARCH IN COUNTRY

APPALACHIAN OVERTHROW

BALTIC GAMBIT

NOVICE DRAGONEER

A DRAGONEER ACADEMY NOVEL

E. E. KNIGHT

ACE
NEW YORK

ACE
Published by Berkley
An imprint of Penguin Random House LLC
penguinrandomhouse.com

Copyright © 2019 by Eric Frisch
Penguin Random House supports copyright. Copyright fuels creativity, encourages
diverse voices, promotes free speech, and creates a vibrant culture. Thank you for buying
an authorized edition of this book and for complying with copyright laws by not
reproducing, scanning, or distributing any part of it in any form without permission. You
are supporting writers and allowing Penguin Random House to continue to publish
books for every reader.

ACE is a registered trademark and the A colophon is a trademark of
Penguin Random House LLC.

Library of Congress Cataloging-in-Publication Data

Names: Knight, E. E., author.
Title: Novice dragoneer / E.E. Knight.
Description: First edition. | New York : Ace, 2019. | Series: A Dragoneer
Academy novel ; 1
Identifiers: LCCN 2019014387| ISBN 9781984804068 (paperback) |
ISBN 9781984804075 (ebook)
Subjects: | BISAC: FICTION / Fantasy / Epic. | GSAFD: Fantasy fiction.
Classification: LCC PS3611.N564 N68 2019 | DDC 813/.6—dc23
LC record available at https://lccn.loc.gov/2019014387

First Edition: November 2019

Printed in the United States of America
3rd Printing

Interior map by Eric Frisch
Book design by Kristin del Rosario

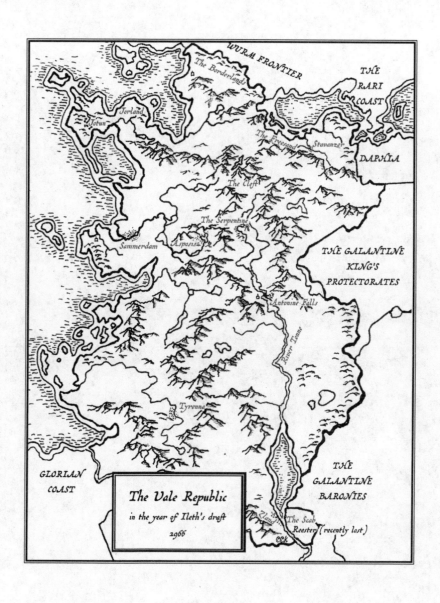

WURM FRONTIER

THE RARI COAST

The Borderlands

Jotun

Jorland

The Freeland

Stavanzer

DAPHIA

The Cleft

The Serpentine

Asposisz

Sammerdam

THE GALANTINE KING'S PROTECTORATES

Antonine Falls

River Tonne

Tyrenna

GLORIAN COAST

THE GALANTINE BARONIES

The Vale Republic
in the year of Ileth's draft
1966

Zland

The Scab

Reester (recently lost)

For Miriam-Rose and Rachel
Sisters in Terpsichore

NOVICE DRAGONEER

The slight girl swinging an empty bucket hiked down the seaside ruts in the early morning, only her shadow, the sun, and the breeze keeping her company. The shadow, because of the angle of the sun and the fact that she held the bucket in both hands, looked bent and afraid as it followed her along what passed for a road. But the seven-year-old girl's face showed no signs of fear, just a lipless determination to make it to the well.

Ileth was her name. She liked watching animals eat, the smell of pine trees, and climbing just about anything for the exertion of it and a chance to be alone with the view.

She had a view now. Out on the bay the fishing boats were already at work. You could see them gently rocking on the white-flecked sea, some near, some indistinct on the horizon, casting nets and pulling up traps. The cold air pouring down the mountains chilled her just as it no doubt did the men on the boats, but there was sun for a change this morning, and sunshine always cheered her.

She would have been smiling, except for the awkwardness of carrying the bucket. Who wouldn't rather be out in the sun and fresh air, even with a cold wind off the glacier-choked mountains? Anything to get away from the Lodge, with its stuffy cabbage smells and last night's stale tobacco.

She clomped up to the well in her scuffed, too-large shoes, not looking forward to the trip back up to the Lodge with the bucket full and at least three more trips ahead of her. The Lodge did have its own water pump, but it was out of order. Again. She should hurry. She'd already been warned about being poky this morning. They only warned you once.

A shadow flashed across the road, quick and vast, startling her. She looked up and froze in her clompy shoes, gaping.

A dragon! And so close!

It bore a rider, and the town watch-bell wasn't ringing, so that meant a Vale Dragoneer. Silver scales gleamed in the sun against the banner-blue sky. The dragon had some difficulty as it descended in its turn and set down fast and hard enough to raise dust, skidding and counterbalancing with its long tail whipping like a fleeing cat taking a corner. Its claws scored the earth into plowshare furrows. Bigger than a horse but smaller than a whale and mostly made of wings, it had a powerful neck supporting an armored wedge of a head and a long tapering tail, both fantastically flexible, that balanced the front and back ends of the muscular torso.

She'd known they were big, and seen them twice before far off, riding the air like eagles, but even her seven-year-old imagination couldn't have given the dragon's tendons and muscles their power and weight, its eye the intelligent cast as it glanced up and down the road, or its wings their washing-line rustle as it settled and folded them. She decided the dragon was long enough to wrap itself around almost any house of her little town and touch its own tail on the doorstep, shading the roof with its wings.

The dragoneer jumped off the saddle, all boots and sheep hide and gauntlets and scarf. The rider took off a wind-cutter helmet and the girl with the bucket saw fine, sharp features and hair wound up and pinned tight.

A woman!

She'd always imagined the dragoneers as men. Lone riders, in her vast experience of being seven and allowed trips into town for errands, were always men. The Republic's couriers bringing the mail were always men. Hunters, men. Traveling tinkers and pack merchants, men. Drovers, men. Stern, black-clad commissioners, men.

The dragon approached the well. It coughed. "Water," it said thickly, in the girl's own Montangyan tongue. Most people in the Vales spoke Montangyan, and everyone could understand it. Salt dusted its skin; it must have been flying close to the water for some time. The speech startled Ileth. A part of her knew dragons could talk, even learn human tongues, but it still seemed like an entertainer's trick.

The rider threw down and drew up the well bucket on its good rope and well-oiled spool. The people of the Freesand on the North Coast were nautical and knew good rope from bad. They'd never let a public well line fray.

The dragon drank. The girl watched it lap up the water like a dog, its tongue a blur, then the neck muscles ripple in fast succession as they sent the water down the muscular neck. The girl swallowed experimentally, feeling her own throat work.

Farther down the road, townsfolk emerged from behind their colorful doors—the people of the Freesand made up for their drab little salt-bleached houses with elaborately painted doors—suddenly having business on their doorsteps, but really to look at the dragon. They kept their distance. The beasts were unpredictable and didn't like crowds, and everyone had heard the story about the time the tanner's son had both his legs broken when he was caught by the tail of a dragon when it startled and turned.

But the girl with the bucket liked animals, the bigger the better. Especially tall, proud horses that swished their tails. She walked up to the well with the fearlessness of seven.

The dragon had infinitely more tail than a horse and its tip swished impatiently as it drank. Ileth tried counting the scales but it was an impossible task, especially on a moving tail. The dragon cocked one eye in her direction and finished the bucket, smacking its toothy mouth in satisfaction.

Its rider—no, his, only the green dragons were female, all the others were male—*his* rider inspected *his* left wing.

"The stitching popped," the dragoneer said. "No wonder we nearly plunked." She spoke well, what the stricter of the two teachers who sometimes came to the Lodge would call *best correct*. The dragoneer went to her saddle, opened a leather case, and produced some white line the girl with the bucket couldn't identify. It looked a bit like cording, only thinner.

Mechanically, as if there weren't a dragon just on the other side of it, the little girl drew up water and filled her bucket, watching the dragon while she worked.

The dragon sniffed the air about her. The girl watched his nostrils take in air, like a landed fish gulping. A forked tongue flicked out and back, so quickly she wasn't sure it had even happened.

"Agrath, don't do the thing with your teeth," the dragoneer said, extracting some bits of frayed line from the creature's wing. "She's just a child."

The seven-year-old forgot her bucket and ventured out into the open before the dragon.

"The th-thing with y-y-your teeth?" the girl said. She didn't like to talk because of her stutter, but how often could you ask a dragon a question, anyway?

The dragon stared straight at her, extending his neck a little so he slowly, serpentlike, came closer to her face. He had numberless tiny facets of polished silver metal scale in fascinating array all over his face, going down to the leathery spiked fans behind his jaw. You could get lost tracing the intricate patterns. With a suddenness of a curtain snapping in the wind, the dragon pulled back his lips and revealed a mouthful of gleaming teeth. To the girl there seemed to be hundreds of them lined up in his mouth like fish packed in oil. All long as boat-nails and sharp as daggers.

She squeaked in shock and jumped back.

But it was so funny!

"Again!" she squealed.

"If I do it again you have to clean them," the dragon said.

The girl nodded in agreement. They looked clean anyway.

Down the slope, anxiety worked on some of the watching faces, but the girl had eyes only for the great silver creature.

"If you want to be helpful, come over here," the dragoneer said.

The girl wanted to be helpful. Very much. Forgetting her bucket and her warning about being poky, she ventured over, sliding under the wing, noticing that it was thin enough so you could make out the shape of the sun on the other side, until she stood next to the dragoneer.

The dragon had a tear taller than the girl in one of the wide, sail-like expanses of wing-skin. The dragon had helpfully angled its wing so she could work.

"Wh-What are you d-doing?" the girl asked, though it was obvious that the dragoneer was setting about to sew the rend back up.

"Fixing some shoddy stitching," the dragoneer said. "What's your name, girl?"

"I-Ileth," the girl said.

She worked the dragon's leathery wing with needle and thread. "Ileth. Fine name. She was a queen in a far-off land, did you know that? Well, Ileth, my dragon, Agrath—"

"Your dragon, Agrath," the dragon said, shaking his head at the sky. "How come you're never 'my human, Annis,' hmmmm?"

"The noble Agrath—"

"That's better," purred the dragon.

"—has an injury that opened up again. Those grooms, what are they about? Here, Ileth, let me show you." She stitched back and forth quickly. "I do it two directions, like bootlaces, crossed over. Stronger that way."

Ileth was fascinated by the translucent skin of the wing, more so than learning that she shared a name with a long-ago queen. The dragon's skin was here, and she could touch it. You could just see blue veins running all through it. She tested it, seeing if she could feel a lump where the vein ran. She couldn't.

"D-Does it hurt him?" Ileth asked. Meaning the stitching, not her touch.

"No, not at all."

"Tosh," the dragon said. "I just endure, or we'll never get anywhere."

The dragoneer worked at a speed Ileth wouldn't have thought possible with such a large needle. "This is why we also have women dragoneers. It's not just about holding a crossbow steady. We women are careful. We are quick. And . . . we . . . are . . . thorough. Done."

A neat line of stitching ran up the dragon's wing. Just like bootlaces.

"You're . . . not any-anyone's m-m-mummy?" Ileth asked.

The dragoneer lifted a corner of her mouth.

"Not as such. You see, Ileth, I couldn't be a mummy."

"I'm s-sorry," Ileth said. She wasn't entirely sure how it all worked, but she knew some women didn't get to have babies and you felt sorry for them. Others, like her mother, died in the process and the babies ended up in places like the Lodge.

"It wasn't for me, you see?" she said, sitting on her haunches close to the girl, putting the big needle away in a special slot on the leather shoulder pad of her upper arm. Ileth could have spent a whole afternoon just studying the stitching and design of the armor. "I believe in the old wisdom. I think we each have an animating spirit putting life and purpose in us. Some people are earth," she said, picking up a handful of dirt piled up against the wall of the well. She made a fist around it and let it trickle into the fresh Freesand breeze. "They are strong, and once they find something they love, they protect it like a wall and shelter it like a brick house. They make excellent mothers. Others have a fire in them. A fire to light the way for others, show them the right. Fire to scare the wolves away or warm a room. They make wonderful mothers too. There are those infused by water, who bring peace and refreshment with their touch; they are a river that carries good things to people and sustain us and smooth our journey. Maybe they're the best mothers of all."

The dragon inspected his wing repair as she spoke. The dragoneer concentrated on Ileth.

"But I've always been of the air, my little queen. I need light. I need to wander, always headed for a new horizon. Most can't bear my storms, when they come. I'm only really at home when I'm up there."

"No doubt you're at ease in the air," Agrath said, itching behind his ear with a rear claw. "I'm doing all the work."

She splashed a handful of water from Ileth's bucket at him. "Irreverent cur! I'm just reciting your kind's old legends. Anyway, the clouds . . . they aren't such a good place for a mother."

She brushed hair out of Ileth's eyes. "What do you suppose you are, Ileth? What is lighting up those bright eyes?"

"I-I . . . d-don't kn-know."

"Do you have a stutter, dear?"

Ileth nodded gravely. Now the pitying look would come. The suggestions. The odd trick that cured their cousin when he was nine. *Don't worry, dear, you'll find a place.*

The dragoneer smiled. "Well, that's interesting. I'll bet that means you have all the spirits in you, just like a dragon. They're always fighting to get out and show the world who they are."

No one had ever spoken about her stutter like that. Her eyes went wet.

Ileth's lip trembled. She fell toward the dragoneer, hugged her. She smelled like old leather and lamp oil, and a hint of the sea. She'd probably bathed in salt water recently.

"Aren't you sweet," the dragoneer said, patting her head.

"Can I go with you?"

"No, moppet. I am on a commission. But how's this," she said, taking her by the hand and leading her to the dragon.

"Annis, I'm not a barnyard pony," the dragon said. But he didn't move to avoid the girl.

"You love it, you old incendiary."

She looked down at Ileth. "If you can climb onto the saddle, you can sit on him."

Could she! Ileth jumped and scrambled up like a cat chased into a tree, using straps, buckles, and cases as purchase. She arranged herself in the saddle. She'd been on a saddled horse and knew her way about, even if they had to hitch up the stirrups. There were reins threaded through the dragon's pitcherlike ears, which were made of the same sort of skin as the wings, it seemed. But she didn't pick them up. She didn't want to pull incorrectly and hurt the dragon.

She was higher than any horse could get her.

"Like the view?" the dragoneer said. "I do too."

"Would you like to go higher?" the dragon asked. For someone who didn't like being a pony, he had a kind voice.

"Yes, p-please please please!"

The dragon rose up on his hind legs. Ileth's stomach lurched and she held on to the saddle with white fingers. But she closed her eyes for only an instant. The dragon gently flapped his wings.

Ileth had no words for how she felt; she just hung on and looked all around until the dragon settled on all fours again.

"Awww," she said.

"How old are you?" the dragoneer asked.

"Seven."

"Well, you're halfway there. Can you read and write?"

She nodded. Well, she could write her name and add the date if someone told her what the date was.

"Math? How are you at figuring?"

"Add and subtract," Ileth said. "Ten percent of a hundred is ten," she added, although she still had no idea what *percent* meant, other than something grown-ups complained about when talking taxes and excises, whatever those were.

"Excellent. Keep at it. When you turn your apprentice age, in seven or eight more years, you come see me. The Serpentine, on the Skylake. Ask for me. My name is Annis."

Apprentice age was something for boys, but she made an effort to burn it into her mind like engraving on silver.

The dragoneer asked her to climb down herself. For some reason, she made her climb down on the opposite side, but Ileth didn't ask questions, she just did as told. A weapon hung there. It was a device that she knew was a crossbow. The boys often spoke of them, but she'd never seen one like this. It had extra levers and bracing. She knew, in a vague sort of way, that they were too expensive for any of the hunters or fishermen in the town to have. She scooted under the dragon's neck as Annis took her place atop Agrath.

"Must be off. It was lovely meeting you, Ileth. I hope we meet again. Remember, apprentice age! Watch your eyes, dear, his wings throw up a lot of dirt. Whenever you're ready, old scout."

The dragon rattled out his wings and flapped. How the pebbles did fly! Ileth crouched out of the way but risked a gritty eye to watch him take off. The dragon gathered himself and jumped like a cat. Unlike a cat, he stayed in the air. He went off over the angled, snow-shedding rooftops, wings cracking like whips, heading for the Cloven Cliff. She'd seen birds above sailing with wings unmoving on the air currents. The eagles were circling there now, as a matter of fact, with the sun warming the air.

Sure enough, the dragon, aided by the air at the cliff, rose in a series of corkscrew turns. The eagles scattered. The dragon and rider flew off into the clouds over the snowy mountains to the west. Ileth ran over to the pieces of broken wing thread the dragoneer had yanked out of the beast's wing. She carefully wound two of the longest ones she could find around her elbow, then pulled her sleeve down so they were hidden. She could braid them together and make a bracelet.

She wondered how tall she would be in seven more years, and if she could get her foot into a stirrup the way Annis had. She'd beg for an extra glass of milk tonight.

Seven years. An unimaginable distance in time. But maybe she could find out where the Serpentine on the Skylake was. The Captain had many maps in that chest with the thin drawers. If she was careful and quiet, she could look at them with no one knowing.

Ileth picked up the bucket. The walk back up to the Captain's Lodge didn't seem such a distance, now. And carrying water would make her stronger, strong enough to cling to a dragon in the wind. Her imagination caught fire at the thought.

She'd get a hiding for being poky, sure as sunset, but meeting Agrath and Annis was worth a hiding. Ten hidings, even.

PART ONE

THE RED DOOR

Fate takes wing
when character meets chance.

—SAYINGS OF THE SERPENTINE

1

Night, wind, and fog above, puddled road and wet meadow beneath. Trotting between them and well coated with elements of both, a youth, still more girl than woman, puffed as she ran. A riding cloak, heavy with rain, dragged at her. Adding to the mess was blood from a still-seeping cut on her chin.

A fierceness on her gashed, freckled face under a sloppy sailor's hat suggested she ran as the pursuer, rather than the pursued.

Ileth no longer felt the blood running from the cut, or the pain in the assortment of scrapes and bumps that had accumulated on the run since she realized that those louts at the brewery had sent her up the wrong road, apparently as a joke. If a little blood on her face and clothes was the only price she'd pay to reach her destination in time, she'd gladly let the wound drip.

The fortress she ran toward, a great pile of stone and slate roofs sprawled across a rugged peninsula like a sleepy cat on a branch, comforted her with its lights. The lights gave her hope ever since she first distinguished the impossibly bright beacon of the high lighthouse shining through the drizzle. She could have become lost in this dark, after all, an easy thing in the fogs of the Winderwind Valley girding the Skylake. The riding cloak was wet and heavy and dragged on her like guilt, but if she dropped it she'd never find it again in the dark. She'd slept in it these last two nights and might need it for a third if they denied her entrance. She had no idea of the hour, for the faint bells and chimes of the town beneath the fortress had been ringing in celebration of the Midsummer since sundown. Bonfires burned on the surrounding hillsides.

She splashed through a deep puddle and tripped on a treacherous submerged rock. Her forearm took the worst of the fall this time. She climbed back to her feet; took three deep, restoring breaths; and ran on. The way here was more puddle than road, thanks to the rain that had dogged the last leg of her pauper's journey to the Serpentine gate, the advertised entry point for admittance of would-be dragoneers desiring a berth at the Academy.

The oilcloth sailor's hat had kept her hair dry, but she was wet from nose down, muddy from her boots up, and tired every which way. Ileth allowed herself to imagine a hearthside chair and maybe even hot soup waiting for her within the Serpentine. Fourteen years of life in the Captain's Lodge had taught her over and over again not to waste energy on hope, but sometimes you needed to draw from the well of imagination to keep sore feet in motion.

She willed her body to run on. It wasn't so much of a run as a lurching series of forestalled collapses, but it got her to the approach.

The road rose, widened, and improved all at once. She made out something ahead through the rain, a wall and a decorative dragon-wing arch framed against the faint light from within the Serpentine proper and its jumble of windows, rooftops, and towers on the other side of the thick walls.

The dragon-wing arch marked the gate. On a night such as this the moist air made the decorative wings slick, and they reflected, in a silhouette of faint traces, the lights from the other side of the wall. The dragon wings just touched wingtips at the top and spread in a fanciful design, shielding those on the wall above the gate. The wings angled out, as though to spread and reach into the world beyond the gate.

Gulping for air and wobbly-legged, she realized she'd arrived. The moment she'd been imagining, preparing for, ever since her wellside encounter with the silver dragon and his dragoneer—resolved into fact: no longer a *someday*, an *if-then*, but a *now*.

Her stomach made a sour growl. She shouldn't have imagined that waiting bowl of stew in so much potato-filled, meaty detail.

Breath coming easily now, she had no idea what to do, having spent all her mental energy trying to arrive without much considering the arrival itself. The notice she'd seen, and, when she had a chance, stolen, simply said applicants to be dragoneers were to present themselves on Midsummer's Eve at the Serpentine Academy on the Skylake. What should she do? Announce herself and beg entry? Demand it? Wave the wet, creased, and frayed bit of placard she'd stripped off that notice board?

She stepped under the shelter of those road-spanning wings. She rehearsed her call quietly, under her breath, to warm her tongue. Three more breaths gave her enough wind to shout.

"Hello the—hello the gate!" Blast her stutter. It would betray her just now. It was always worse when she was tired and anxious.

It was northern phrasing. The Serpentine no doubt had formalized military ways to call out to the gate-watch that must exist in such a fortress, but they must expect strangers when they opened to applicants and posted notices.

Only the wind and a racking cough from above answered her. She made out two heads separating from the arch-pillars, wearing narrow fore-and-aft-style caps.

A voice said something that began with *stranger*, but the wind carried the rest of it away.

One of the figures put a speaking-trumpet to his lips. "The gate's shut for the night. You missed it."

"I wish to apply to the . . . to the Academy as a . . . a novice dragoneer."

"Do you have a letter of introduction or acceptance?"

"I have this," she said, waving the placard.

"Then I'm sorry for you, girl. As I said, you missed it."

"I-I-I'm bleeding," she said. Frustrated tears filled her eyes, but she blinked them back as she wiped blood onto her palm and held it up for the gate-watch to see.

"How old are you, girl?"

"Fourteen years. Fourteen years and one quarter," she said, the answer coming so automatically she hardly stuttered. The night felt cold for a Midsummer's Eve, though she was a week's hard travel south of the Freesand.

"You aren't. You look younger than that."

Ileth had no answer for that. She *was* small for her age, and for all that puberty savaged her innards, her complexion was still that of a child. "My-My birth's . . . recorded."

"You are alone?"

"Yes. O-Only—Only the . . . the applicant, your notice says." She extracted the folded placard and read from it: "N-N-No guardians, s-servants, or tutors ad-admitted." She hoped she said that as though she'd left anything like that behind her at the Captain's Lodge.

"Is there anyone who traveled with you to look after you? In town perhaps?" a different voice asked.

"No. Just me."

The figures bent to each other in conference, mirroring the wing-arch's peak above for a moment as their caps touched. A third crossed over to them from the other side of the gate.

The speaking-trumpet passed to the new silhouette. "I have the duty," a reedy voice said, amplified through the trumpet. "The gate doesn't open at night. Unless"—the voice turned hopeful—"unless you have the password."

Ileth shook her head. The reedy voice seemed far, far away as it finished, her body weightless. If her head broke free of her body and floated off, she wouldn't have been much surprised. She had never fainted in her life but once, and she clenched her torso muscles from neck to groin to halt her blood. It occurred to her that such was the dark, they might not be able to see her. "No," she said, stepping forward in case the light wasn't sufficient.

So, so far, and with nothing left to get anywhere else. She was half-starved even now, standing at the locked gate. And she couldn't beg a refuge, not at a fortress.

"Is a dr-dragoneer named . . . named Annis here? She rides a s-silver dragon named Agrath. She told me to ask for her."

"No. Are you a relation, by chance?" the voice called back.

Oh, if only she had been. Maybe the Captain's Lodge would have been different. "No."

They didn't reply to that.

"I am resolved to be a dragoneer," she said, taking a few more steps forward. There was still her age and her sex, unprotected in the night, and the Republic's Dragoneers had their reputation for gallantry. Maybe if they could see the mud, the blood, and her lack of any baggage beyond a blanket-roll, they'd bend the rules. "It is still Midsummer's Eve. Could you ask . . . your superiors to admit me?"

The speaking-trumpet passed yet again.

"Try the side door, girl. There's a path to your right. It begins at the base of the wall just where the road comes under the gate. Watch your step, it traces a cliff and the rocks are wet. Have you ever crossed a cliff?"

Before she could reply, the speaking-trumpet passed again.

"You should just go back to town," the reedy voice said. "Have someone attend that cut. Looks like it needs sewing up."

"Could you ask whoever is in charge of such things to give me the password? Then I could give it to you and you could open the g-gate."

The three heads froze in silence for a moment. She thought she caught the word *Midsummer* as they talked.

"Go back to town," the reedy voice with the speaking-trumpet said.

"Knock on the side door," the older voice boomed. "Keep knocking until they let you in."

"Don't be stupid," the first man who'd spoken to her called, though which of the other two options presented was stupid it didn't say.

The men above could talk as if she had options, but Ileth had made her choice when she deserted (as it had no doubt been called) the Captain's Lodge. Well, if she was going to fool about with a cliff on a dark, wet night, she would have to prepare.

The flickers of light coming over the wall and through decorative gaps in the gate gave her the ability to take off the too-large riding cloak and wind it about her blanket bag, which she then retied. Thanks to the wet, it made a heavy burden. The bag's rope would hold, but even doubled as she'd been taught, it dug into her shoulder painfully. She checked her knots. She had quit the Captain's Lodge with few happy memories but a certain amount of practical skill, and one was some knowledge of lines, loads, and knot work. A poor knot even around a sack of potatoes could tip the Captain into a rage.

She glanced one more time at the three faceless silhouettes. She grudged them the knowledge of her decision. She considered walking up the road and then circling back just so they'd wonder, but let the notion go. There was always the chance that they were more sympathetic to an unchaperoned girl than their orders allowed. Perhaps one would arrange for a better reception at the side door.

The path was there, just as the older man said, matching another one going in the other direction along the base of the wall. It wasn't much used, just a stretch of muddy gravel. She reached out and touched the fortress wall, its stones beautifully cut, laid, and finished. Nothing in Freesand had anything like these great carved boulders.

The cool, smooth stone settled her, drawing out some of the sting of finally arriving at the Serpentine and being refused entry. The wall—solid, tangible, cool—reassured her. She'd reached her destination. The dragons she'd risked much for and come far to be among lived on the other side of it. The stones made her feel less like a gambler who'd potted her entire purse on a throw only to see the dice come up blanks.

A dissonant chorus of voices who'd advised her against this journey repeated prophesies of failure:

You think those silk-sashes will let you join them?

They'll smell the gutter on you like gamehounds.

No family of a decent name would have a trip-tongued fool like you as a maid—you think they'll give you a dragon to ride?

The wall followed the contours of the peninsula, in this case a slight downslope. She sensed the vastness of the bay ahead and could see the lights of Vyenn, the town on the lakeshore, through the fog as a ragged spiderweb of yellow smears.

The wall of the Serpentine bulged out here and the track she walked narrowed to the point where she would hardly dare to herd mountain goats along it. Below, the Skylake produced no surf; it just seemed a vast emptiness beyond the cliff. Keeping her hand on the wall now for physical comfort rather than emotional, she negotiated the fortress corner. Her hand found a rope tied to a series of ring-bolts set into the stone, and she happily made use of the guideline.

Once around the tower the guideline ended and the path widened again but became harder to walk, as the ground sloped away from the wall sharply. The wall here wasn't quite as high as on the side of the gate but still formidable. The wind blew against this side of the fortress, bringing with it a low susurrance of the big lake lapping against rock below.

The lights of the Serpentine gave her some idea of the peninsula's size. From this outlook she could see the famous lighthouse beacon at a high point of the peninsula, supposedly the brightest light in the Vales. It rested on a dome built on living rock. It was a famous outline; Radiia the printing-house used it as their sigil on their books. Under better conditions, the Serpentine would be starkly beautiful, set high between blue water and white-capped mountains across the lake. She'd once seen a painting of it hung on the wall of a priest's house on one of the Captain's rare social calls.

It was two hundred paces or more before she made out a sort of knob growing off the fortress like a tree root sent down the hill. The path headed down to it. She guessed it to be the location of the door.

Ileth shifted the pinching rope of her blanket-bundle and approached the threshold, telling her sore feet to be patient for just a few more steps.

Whoever designed this fortress didn't care for visitors or much want to impress them. The doorstep was unsheltered and unmarked, lit by a single blue gas-flame. She looked in vain for a bell. The walls seemed placed to channel the mountain lake-wind across the threshold; the cold and wet passed untroubled through her layers of wool and linen and went straight on through to her bones.

The wooden door, painted with a dull red color made duller by rain and dark, felt like a cheat to Ileth. Though wet right to her sheath and tired, she still had enough perspective left to appreciate the irony of a fastness of famous heroes and infamous dragons closed off by planking more fit for a toolshed.

The flickering blue flame, a little brighter than a candle, hissed in an unfriendly manner as it illuminated the threshold. She reached up and warmed her hands by the flame. She'd heard of such innovations, but this was her first experience with a gas-light. The flame muttered at the mouth of a bent iron tube, crude as a share-farmer's pipe, indifferent to the wind, the weather, and her presence. But her fingers were grateful for its warmth.

It cast just enough light for her to make out the device on the center of the door, a sort of arrowhead design that she recognized as a dragon scale. A large and thick one, in a dull red that matched the door. It was hinged, and she realized it was a door-knocker.

She paused on the threshold to arrange her blanket-roll and dab the blood from her face. It had finally stopped bleeding. She took a deep breath, preparing to knock, but the chill mountain air drew forth a rattling cough. She prayed it was just her lungs cleaning themselves of the damage inflicted by that last, long run to the gate. This was not the time or place for illness.

The watchman had told her to knock. She explored the rugose surface of the dragon scale for a moment, thrilled again in the connection to the great creatures she'd come so far to live among. She lifted it, saw an orb of what was probably lead that matched a socket on the door, and let it drop. It gave a distinct but hardly impressive tap; a man with steel-shod boots would probably make more noise stamping on the step.

"Stranger at the door," a watchman called from a corner of the fortress wall above. It bulged out in such a way that it had an excellent view of the threshold below. No doubt he'd seen her long before she knocked but waited for her to trigger Serpentine routine.

A light glimmered and grew on the other side of the door. The door didn't need a peephole. The gaps in the planking were such that they afforded an adequate view of arrivals. She didn't know fortifications, but the door didn't look as if it would hold up long to an experienced axeman, never mind a team of attackers with a battering ram.

She heard a strange, dragging step inside.

"State your business," a raspy voice said from the other side of the door, somewhat muffled.

"My-My name is Ileth," she said, letting the words out slowly. "I-I w-wish to-to apply to the Academy as a . . . as a dra-dragoneer."

"Too late, girl, and I'm sorry for you. All the applicants are inside. We shut the gate at sundown."

Suddenly overcome by emotion, she stuttered out something about having traveled for days alone. It wasn't persuasive.

The raspy voice cut her off. "Don't take it hard, we'll kick a good quarter of them out again in a few days. You're lucky, you'll have a jump on them at the Auxiliary house in town. Vyenn has all sorts of drum-beaters looking for apprentices. If I were you, I'd join the Auxiliaries, if you want dragons. They have a few."

She had excuses to fill a book, but too much pride to be a beggar at a door rattling off a list of misfortunes.

"By the calendar it's still Mid-Midsummer's Eve." Her stammer always grew worse when she was overwrought.

"Have you a letter of introduction? An acceptance?"

The Serpentine had its routines, it seemed. The same catechism as the gate-watch.

"No," she managed to say, after a brief struggle to get the word out, knowing what the reply would be. "One of your placards. A dragoneer named Annis . . . met me years ago. She encouraged me to—"

"I am sorry. Annis Heem Strath and Agrath fell in the Galantine War. Just before the armistice. Go get under a roof. This is no night to wait on the steps."

In a way, the news of the death of the dragon and dragoneer was worse than being denied entry. She'd thought of them constantly these seven years, imagining a reunion: *I remember you, Ileth, and all grown up into a young woman,* Annis would say, smiling, the dragon above cocking its head, birdlike, for a better look. *Oh, that girl from the well, hullo there,* he'd say, then she'd tell him she'd made a silly little bracelet out of the cording that had come loose from his wing. She felt sick and tightened her stomach muscles again. The old trick to steady herself worked. She felt more than she heard the presence at the other side of the door start to depart. She pounded again, setting the boards a-clatter.

"Could I j-just get out of this wet? I'm very tired. I'll sleep in a stable. A pen."

"Go back to town. There's a poor lodge if you have no money for the inn. If you were my daughter, I wouldn't want you to try it, but the boatmen's dormitory is cheap and clean. I've heard they give a bed and a dinner for a song well sung."

"Please," she said, reaching up and pulling at the gap in the planking so it squeaked and rattled. She'd gone a bit mad.

A sharp rap on her fingers stopped her from trying to pull the door off its hinges. "Don't try that again or we'll empty night soil on you. Understand?"

She nodded. The personage on the other side of the door departed.

She turned a circle and blinked away frustrated tears. At least they wouldn't show on her wet face. She hated to be caught crying. Dragoneers in the songs and poems didn't cry—unless their dragon died.

Finally, she sat down on the steps, head in hands, failure sitting next to her on one side and misery on the other pressing close, no doubt winking at each other behind her back.

The cold stone leeched heat from her flesh and she realized she should have put down her bundle and sat on it, but she'd sunk to a place below such cares.

She wasn't sure what she had expected out of a reunion with Annis, Dragoneer of the Serpentine, but the silver dragon and his rider had occupied so much of her thoughts over better than half her life that the loss felt momentarily unbearable. Tears blended with the drizzle on her cheeks. What had she wanted? Certainly not a substitute mother. Her life had been a series of *I'm not your mother, dear*s from everyone from laundrywomen to shepherds' wives. Annis had just been one more not-mother, more poetic than the rest with her talk about being of the air spirit. All she knew was that she was counting on a reunion, imagining kind words about how much she'd grown or that she took good care of her teeth or a long welcoming hug and a job polishing boots and saddle.

A few deep breaths and a wiping of her eyes that was more habitual than effective left her able to consider.

Bone tired, with nothing but roadside berries in her since yesterday, she reviewed her options. Her flight from the Captain's Lodge had been such that she'd left without much other than her small necessities bag. She wanted to confuse matters on her disappearance, leaving behind even the brush and comb the Captain had bestowed on her when she turned twelve. She hadn't left a note when she slipped ship, as the Captain was probably styling it even now with a disgusted shake of his head. She had nothing to make camp, no barn loft where she might sleep dry, as she'd found the previous night. She could use the gas-pipe for a light, but she had no fuel for a campfire and she doubted there was any to be found on this rocky peninsula.

She coughed again. It came from an ominously deep inner pocket of her chest. The phlegm it brought up was real enough that her fancies about just lying down to die on this doorstep became an awful possibility of illness teaming up with exposure to take her young life. Perhaps she should go down to Vyenn and throw herself on the mercy of the poorhouse, as the doorman suggested.

Maybe the priests were right. You did get punished for your sins in this life as well as the next if you didn't immediately offer up an atonement. She'd defied the Captain, lied, even stolen from farmers' fields on her journey. It had all come so easily to her in her zeal to arrive at the Serpentine. Even worse, she'd proved good at it. She hadn't confessed or offered atonement for any of it yet. Perhaps she was naturally bad, after all. She'd been told often enough that she'd been conceived in sin. That old witch the Captain employed to keep night-watch over his charges had told her that the disgraceful circumstances of her birth were revealed by her stutter. *Sure sign that a child's been conceived with coin for payment clasped tight in the whore's hand . . .* Then there was that gaunt teacher with the badly fitted false teeth who told the children of the Lodge that evil nature could be inherited, like her freckles, and that she would have to pay for her mother's grievous faults, as her mother had died before setting the balance right. He'd taken the Lodge children to the altar-house, lining them up along a bench on the back wall where they wouldn't be mistaken for belonging to the respectable town families, and made disagreeable droning noises through his nose whenever the priests talked of faults being passed about like contagion.

She coughed again. This one was worse. It hurt. Then she retreated into herself and fell into a half sleep, a talent she'd learned on nights outdoors with the Lodge's chickens after they lost one to a fox or on long winter nights when she was punished by keeping the fires up. The great central fireplace towered over her early years even more than the Captain. Sitting before it, she'd developed a knack for dreaming without actually sleeping. The Captain would beat you for sleeping on duty, and he liked to sneak up and terrify you by choking you awake. He'd then tell you a ghastly tale, his breath reeking over his black-traced teeth, of entire crews who'd been gutted and strung up in their rigging by pirates because the watch fell asleep.

Motion at the base of the stairs roused her back to wakefulness as though she'd heard the Captain's heavy boots. She blinked crud out of her eyes and shielded them so the light from the little gas-flame didn't spoil her vision.

A short, fat man in a thick sheepskin vest and a muddy overcoat was leading another girl of her age behind him, tied together about the waist like mountaineers. The girl was in a heavy boat cloak and looked as though she'd been caught in a mudslide, making Ileth feel a little better about her own bedraggled appearance. The girl was saying something about the gate but stopped as soon as she caught sight of Ileth. The short, fat man straightened and let out a long, relieved breath.

"Appearances, miss. We're here," the man said, wheezing as he untied the line from the girl's waist before stepping out of his own much wider loop. The Captain would have offered a few blistering words over the condition of the rope and the knots.

The girl tossed the line away in the manner of one used to discarding tools for which she had no more use.

Ileth doubted their last meal was a handful of berries from the roadside. They both looked like hot breakfasts with a choice of honey or fruit mash.

The girl had a face that was mostly chin and cheekbones, with the deadly sort of prettiness of an ornate dagger. Her outer eyebrows were subtly shaped and ended with something like pen art, the way a manuscript illuminator might add an artful flourish to the beginning and end of a letter. Ileth idly wondered what it would be like to spend an hour having art drawn at the edge of each eye.

"Another miracle," the new girl said in an urbane accent. "Thank you, Falth. Mother chose well when she named you to see this through."

"You're very kind, miss. I hope if you write her an account of your trip, you'll repeat that."

"I'll begin it with that, Falth, and mention it again as a postscript." Ileth marked the girl's tight-clenched hands. She was human enough to be anxious, then.

"I'm sure—" the servant began.

"I'm sure I want to get under a roof."

Obviously a Name, that one. Ileth was northern-bred and had seen only one city, and that from a distance, but she'd still lived in the world enough to tell a Sammerdam hothouse tulip from a pasture-wall morningeye.

The servant moved to help his charge up the stairs to the threshold, but she waved him off. "Stairs I can manage."

The Name gave Ileth just long enough of a stare to categorize her as nothing having to do with the fortress. "I suppose you want to clean my boots and dry my cloak."

"Boots are—Boots are my specialty, miss," Ileth said.

The Name offered a tired smirk. "Here's a suggestion, meant kindly: at least get up off the ground when conversing. You'll find yourself with more work if you exhibit some manners."

Ileth didn't mind the correction. She was relieved not to be asked about her stutter, for once.

With that business concluded, the Name reached up and tapped the dragon-scale knocker. It amplified her genteel rap admirably.

"State your business," the raspy voice said, so alike to her own attempt at the red door that it might have come from her memory.

"Santeel Dun Troot, arriving," the servant Falth announced.

"Has she a letter of introduction?"

"It was sent and accepted this spring," Falth said, displaying a sort of folded letter-and-envelope in one with a wax seal and a bit of ribbon.

The young woman dropped her heavy cowl. The doll-like arrangement of hair and lace collar stole Ileth's breath. Her skin was a ceramic white. Straight hair powdered white save for two black strands descending either cheek framed her face from precise bangs, as though serving as no purpose other than a frame for the chalky complexion untouched by dirt or weather.

The Name made a little dip of an obeisance to the unseen presence on the other side of the red door.

It occurred to her that perhaps she should have played the part of casual servant better as the bolt slid open. Once within the fortress, she might get a chance to join the other would-be dragoneers.

"You're welcome to the Serpentine, applicant," the warden said. Ileth leaned a bit but couldn't make out more than a shadowy shape thanks to the glare of the gas-light. "No guardians, consorts, companions, tutors, servants, or pets, though. Your man will have to leave you here."

Though weary, Ileth wondered at that order. Did it reflect how hard it was to part an applicant from their household? And she felt a minor flutter at the use of the word *consort*. She knew they existed, but she'd never met a professional consort. Just amateurs. How many apprentice-aged youths even had such associations?

"Yes, I am aware of the Academy's rules." Santeel Dun Troot turned to her servant. "Falth, thank you." She walked back down the stairs at a careful, measured pace. "I was hoping they'd at least shelter you until dawn."

"Oh, no matter, miss." Ileth wanted to rub herself against his soothing tone like a cat; she couldn't recall ever hearing such a melodious voice. Falth handed over a beautifully woven tapestry that had been turned into a clasped bag with a leather shoulder strap. "I would hang that cloak to dry first and then beat the mud loose. Who knows what sort of laundry they have here."

"Never mind the cloak. You get a good room at the inn. Sleep in. Stay tomorrow night too, with plenty to eat and drink in between.

Bring in the local doctor if you have stiffness, you might need a liniment. Don't even think about what Mother would say about the expense. You've earned it after all this."

"I'm sure I will be fine. You'd best be off. He's waiting for you at the door." Falth was too well bred to point with anything but his chin, but the gesture toward the door couldn't be mistaken.

Santeel Dun Troot cleared her throat. "Please, Falth, some of those things I said to you over . . . well, I didn't mean them. Forgive me."

"I don't remember anything to forgive, miss. I was busy coping with that dreadful mud."

"Still, it was wrong of me to speak that way, whether you say you heard anything or not."

"Thank you, miss. Eyes ahead, not behind, as your father says. Good luck to you at your examination. I'm sure you'll do the Name Dun Troot credit."

Said Name took a deep breath and hurried up the steps, clutching her fine bag with straining fingers. The door shut and a bolt slid home.

So easy, with a Name and letter.

Falth took out a fine handkerchief and wiped his face. He looked at the soil that came off with distaste. "Now why couldn't all this have been handled at the gate? *You must apply at the door.* Dragoneers. Fah. I suppose they just fly in. Who needs a proper path for that?" He resettled his own, smaller traveling bag across his back and only then looked down at Ileth.

"Aren't you cold, out here in the wind?"

Ileth just nodded. It was better than stuttering.

"You're not pennymonging, obviously. Are you an applicant?"

This time she paused for a moment before nodding. The admission made her miserable.

Falth stepped up to the door and peeked about the edges, showing a lightness of foot and a grace that surprised her in such a stout man.

"You must be about her age. If they do let you in," Falth said, his voice measured to just overcome the wind, "I'm sure the Dun Troot family would be most grateful for news, especially if she isn't doing her utmost. It's important, supremely important, to her mother and father that she at least earn her apprentice sash. They would be intensely interested if anything stands in the way of that, either in her behavior or in the actions of others. Can you write?"

"Yes."

"Would you be willing to be a friend to the Name Dun Troot inside the Serpentine?"

Ileth tried to clear the fatigue and disappointment from her mind. What was he after? Better yet, what was he offering? She'd be no use to the *Name Dun Troot* sitting outside the shabby red door.

"Why—Why me?"

Falth smiled a practiced smile. He waved his hand at the doorstep as if to say, *Behold! All the choices I have, rank upon rank of them!*

"Maybe if we'd arrived with the others when the gate was open I would have made the offer to another. You're a northern girl by accent. You northern types don't accept commissions lightly and are generally reliable once your promise is dragged out of you. And forgive me if I tread heavily, but someone of your age and sex who has found her way here on her own and is quietly sitting in the dark and the wet must have a certain amount of wit and will. More than one boy on his way to the Serpentine has found himself waylaid and forcibly joined to a bargeman's crew or a mine or a lumber camp. As for girls—well, either you are too innocent to understand the risks you've run or you've lived in the world and anything I might add would just be insulting to the courage that brought you this far."

She shrugged in reply. Handy gesture: citified enough to show that she wasn't just out of the sheep pens, yet noncommittal. The Captain found shrugs objectionable—he liked direct answers in a firm voice— and she was still fresh enough out of his Lodge for its use to thrill her.

"I've not m-much hope of being admitted, sir."

Falth extracted a purse and scriptbook from a hidden recess in his cloak.

She held out her hand. "I won't be paid to spy on someone."

"I wasn't going to. The friendship of the Name Dun Troot can't be counted in coin such that I'd carry. I have three preaddressed, taxed, and carriage-paid packets. You'll find ample blank space for any message you wish to write; simply fold them back up as you found them and seal with whatever candle is handy. Three in case one goes amiss. I shall reply with other blanks. Write me in charcoal if you can't get a quill and ink. But do write."

"Even charcoal pencils cost," Ileth said. He'd identified her as a northerner; she might as well act the part.

"I can offer you something more valuable than a few figs.* I've spent some time learning what I can of the dragoneers and their ways. I'll offer you my intelligence for yours. The better your intelligence, the better my replies will be. I may even be able to help get you on the other side of that shabby little privy door up there, in exchange for your promise."

She gulped. "You—You—You have my promise. My name is Ileth, of the Freesand on the North Coast. I will post you those three bulletins."

He handed them over to her with a distinct bow of his head—but his head only. Still, the novelty of having a full-grown man make even a perfunctory obeisance gave her a tingle. She felt oddly heartened. If she did make it into the Serpentine, she'd receive such compliments as a matter of course. From the mannered, that is.

He leaned close, his voice a reassuring caress. "Then here is my intelligence: you never know what the dragoneers will consider as a test or illustration of one's character. Always act as though you are being examined by a jury." He gestured at the wall above with his chin, much in the same manner he'd directed his charge.

Ileth glanced up. All she saw was the Guard above, a silhouette with that vaguely fore-and-aft-rigged hat of the dragoneers. The sentry didn't appear to be making any effort to listen to what they were saying, or even watch the interplay between man and girl.

Falth read the confusion that must have crept over her face and continued: "I'll give you an example: there was one of your age, an

---

* The Republic's smallest coin depicts a fig tree and its fruit. The first luxury-good commerce with the miners and trappers who explored and settled the region was in dried figs and preserves, as fig trees would not grow in the Vales.

apprentice by the name of Sabian, traveling with a pair of dragoneers and their dragons in the Hierophant's War. They operated out of some small mountainside cave above the tree line in the Ludium, I suppose, as that's the only range of that height in that war. As usual, while one dragoneer scouted the area, the other hunted until they had sufficient game for a hearty meal for the dragons—dragons must be well fed to fight properly, I'm sure you know—and they left Sabian to dress the game and hang it properly. Their commission went badly. Both dragoneers were killed, one of the dragons was grounded, and in the following efforts to come to the aid of the injured dragon everyone simply forgot about the cave and Sabian.

"The war dragged on and the dragon who hadn't been injured remembered Sabian. At the first chance he flew to the cave with his new dragoneer. Sabian was still there, after a fashion. They found him seated just outside the cave, frozen like a winter pumpkin, with his still-cocked crossbow across his lap."

Falth shuddered in the light of the little gas-flame.

"Sabian could have abandoned the cave and found his way back to people, sheltered in a monastery or whatever you find in those mountains until some sort of accommodation was reached and he could be returned to the Serpentine, but he stayed at his post. The Dragoneers have made sure Sabian will never be forgotten again. They commissioned a statue from Therace Apitmothees himself—do you know the man's work?"

Ileth indicated she didn't with a shake of her head.

"Well, he's been dead longer than you've been alive now, but even then, his work commanded immense sums. *Sabian's Vigil* it's called. Based on how they found him. It's in the Serpentine somewhere, I believe. I should think you'll hear the story if you ever get inside. The point is, Sabian was given orders, and whatever happened to him—I suppose starvation and the cold are the most likely explanations—happened because he'd been given a commission and died rather than fail in his duty. Thought it might give you heart for whatever the Fates have placed on your road, Ileth."

"I don't—I don't see how this helps me. I'm not even inside yet."

"The Republic's Dragoneers make a certain fetish of willpower in carrying out one's duty. So keep trying to gain admittance. They might be wondering just how much grit is in you. Admittedly, there's some uncertainty, as you haven't made it across the threshold yet or taken your oath. They're still dragoneers and I only know their habits from dinner-table talk and drawing-room entertainments. I've never even conversed with one until today."

She nodded. At the moment, she didn't see how Falth's story would get her anointed by anything but the night's rain. But she could consider it at leisure. It looked like she had a cold, uncomfortable night ahead of her.

"I sincerely hope you make it in. Not just for the sake of the Name of Dun Troot, Ileth. For you to be sitting here in the wet with a cut-open face, either you have left something much worse behind or you have your eyes fixed on your fate-star. Maybe a little of both, eh? Well, I've done for you what I can. Make the most of it."

With that, he turned and stepped onto the path leading back to the cliff's edge and the road beyond. She envied him his easy life. Coin in his purse for all the food he might care to eat—just imagine, being able to sit down in an inn or tavern and have the owner's people bring you as much as you like!—and if the coin ran out, or was stolen, fill your purse at a banking house by scribbling your name down on a draft.

Envy comes easy when you're hungry and cold. Awful of her. She was becoming quite the collector of sins since she left the Lodge. She thought of an illustration in a copybook they'd been given to work from when she'd first learned her letters; there was an engraving of a hunched-over, evil-looking man with sins written on rolls of paper and stuck, bloodily, into his back with pins the size of knitting needles. *A PAINFULL TALLY* read the bold-lettered legend.

"Make the most of it," she repeated. "Get up off the ground when conversing."

Stuff the Dun Troots and their Name.

Tempted to hurl the addressed letter-envelopes off the cliff and into the sea, she sat back down to fight the useless impulse. Naturally someone with a Name would still be admitted. There was probably some kind of contract between the Serpentine and this Santeel Dun Troot's family, with plenty of connections to make trouble if a daughter of the Dun Troot family didn't have her chance to become a novice over something as minor as a delayed journey along the road from Asposis or Sammerdam.

Why such a girl would want to leave the undoubtable comforts of her home and station was more of a mystery. Ileth knew her own reasons the way she knew the shape of her hand but wondered why a Name would attach such importance to their daughter being taken in by the Serpentine. A marriageable daughter with both beauty and money would be more of an asset to the family than someone apprenticed to the dragoneers. At least that was how she thought matters stood with such families. Even in the north, when two famous Names were joined through marriage, there was talk about what each gained from the transaction. Maybe this Santeel was difficult, and the family had decided that a term of service collecting dragon manure or whatever they called it would do her some good. Or maybe Santeel Dun Troot had seen a dragon in a grand review, decided she wanted to sit astride such a commanding creature in a parade down the Archway in Sammerdam, and demanded that her family make it come true for her. Ileth, in a mood to think the worst of the girl, settled on that explanation.

The only dragon Ileth had ever seen up close was the one at the well. But one was enough. She wished, hoped, and planned to be among them since that meeting. Work with them. On a commission of importance, not parading down a street wide enough to be a river while cheering people threw flowers. From that meeting on, a new light shone into her life and she kept her face to it, like a sunflower following the sun. Duty, reputation, responsibility for the awesome power of a dragon—that was the dragoneer ideal she'd hugged in her thoughts in her lumpy, wool-sheeted bed at the Lodge.

She settled back down into her chilly half sleep, warmed by the toasty old imaginings. She let the sound of the wind and the faint echoes from the lake below tranquilize her. The philosophers said that babies in the womb probably heard something like it as they floated in their mother waters, waiting for their entrance into a new world.

The remainder of the night passed with only a messenger arriving, less muddy than she or those of the Dun Troot Name. Judging from his attire, he'd ridden. Strange that they made even messengers negotiate the cliff's edge. It seemed like an unnecessary risk. Suppose the rider was exhausted; both he and his message could end up at the bottom of the cliff. He, too, was admitted, only to emerge within an hour wiping something that was probably deliciously warming from his lips. He smelled of sweat, both his own and his horse's, and wet leather. He gave her one quizzical glance but otherwise ignored her.

Blearily, he marked the first hint of dawn. The clouds must have broken up a little overnight and the fog departed to wherever fog goes, for she could make out stars and the outline of white-hatted mountains rising steeply on the other side of the vast lake. Three of those mountains were somewhat larger, the White Sisters, she knew they were called, and their silhouettes huddling together reminded her, oddly, of the three watchmen she'd first talked to at the gate.

With that vague thought, she fell back into a deeper doze until the sun struck out from the serrated skyline. She'd missed her first dawn over the Skylake. The water below her was the blue she'd heard described as *deep* and *gemlike* and *brilliant*, and it proved beautifully true. The waters on the North Coast always looked foamy; they rarely stood still. The Skylake was as different from that as a polished stone is to sand.

The sight gave her some satisfaction. Even if her journey came to naught, she'd seen the waters of the Skylake. How many grandmothers up in the Freesand had done as much as that?

Thanks to the growing light she could see the lakeside town beneath the Serpentine. Most of the buildings were white stucco and tarry timber, and there were little flecks of color about that she assumed were planters and flower boxes. Inland, fields and grazing lands were jealously guarded by a rock wall, with a pair of stout, old-fashioned circular towers protecting the road entrance. The towers were overgrown and sprouted wildflowers at the top like close-cropped hair.

The fishing vessels had already put out. Ileth knew a fishing boat at a glance and watched them with some interest. They looked to be round-bottomed, unlike many of the boats on the Freesand, which had to be built with unweatherly flat bottoms to make it over the many bars and snags of her home bay. Bigger vessels, coasters carrying cargo, were tied up to the wharves. Only a few stragglers and small boats on other business remained near the docks and wharves ringing the town in a lopsided horseshoe shape.

Vyenn, it was called. Formerly Vyenn on the Godspring, and before that something else she couldn't remember that had to do with salt. What education she had mostly came through tales told by the Captain's visitors and guests, shipmen or boatmen all. Several had been to Vyenn and she'd done her best to draw them out over the years without seeming *too* interested, asking about the differences between river trade and coastal sailing.

With her spirit rallied by the sun and view, she tried the door again. Three successive knocks, each louder than the last, elicited no response.

She let out one stammering "Hello" up at the wall and gave up. The Guard looking out over the entrance didn't even pause in his pacing. Perhaps the night watchman had given orders that she was to be ignored. She didn't have night soil dumped on her head, anyway. The single call had managed to wake her appetite, too, and she was ravenous from her exertions and the cold night. With stiff, reluctant legs she tried the cliffside path again with the help of daylight and saw a treacherous ravine leading down to the lakeside. She managed it without too much difficulty. She noticed that the bottom of the cliff was strewn with broken barrels, rusted iron framing, and other odds and ends you tended to find on a lakeshore near a town, with a stave or reinforcement bar or two projecting out of the water like an accusing finger.

She followed the path back to the gate. This time there were no calls or orders from the watchers, who couldn't have missed her as she negotiated the hand rope around the south tower. She was in front of the gate in a moment and took it in.

The gate, seen in daylight, was much more impressive than it had been at night. There was a low sort of ditch, a dry moat, before the wall bridged by the road. She'd missed that completely in the dark. The gate itself was more of a grate or a fence, made of thick woven iron sheets laced in an elaborate pattern that must have been fantastically difficult to fashion, with wooden paneling behind, grain beautifully finished and gleaming. The design probably signified something, but she had little knowledge of art and less use for it, at least up to now. She doubted it had ever had to withstand a siege. She knew from tales that there'd once been warfare in this valley, but that was in the murky past before the Republic or even the Dragon-Troth. The bridge over the ravine looked as though it could be pulled up by removing the timbers from their rests.

A bell rang out, three deep, distinct *bong!* signals sounding within the Serpentine. They were answered, faintly, by another one in town—the bell ringer below probably took his cue from the fortress.

Her empty stomach heard the bells and her hunger rallied and gnawed at her. She could bear hunger; one of the Captain's favorite disciplines was deprivation of meals for a day or two. She could assuage it easily enough if she just had some water.

She waited another minute to see if the tolling of the bell might bring an opening of the grate-gate. But the entry remained closed and the road to the Serpentine deserted. It would be a warm day, she decided, judging the sun and the clouds scattering before like white dustballs swept off by a broom. She would have to find some shade; she'd been warned that skin scorched easily up in the mountains.

Standing in the shade of the wings, she traced the meeting of the two halves of the gate with a forefinger, imagining some magic that would open them. *Get me inside, fate, and I will prove myself a great dragoneer . . . dutiful and skilled and kind like Annis.* All she learned was that the woven steel looked as though it parted at the center, where multiple plates of metal met like interlaced fingers. The gate edge, where it met, was fitted into some kind of channel and each side had a wheel that ran in an arced groove, but she saw no other mechanism for opening it. She liked devices and had once gotten into painful trouble for taking apart an old sun-measuring device of the Captain's that had a broken handle and a degree-arrow that spun so freely it was useless.

Dragons and clever machinery. She longed to be inside, learning the secrets of the Serpentine. She wondered what the applicants who'd managed to make it inside the gate yesterday were doing. She heard vague sounds of activity within, shouts and calls, but it was far off and faint, like farmers singing out in the distance as they raked and stacked the hay.

A watchman pacing back and forth between the dragon wings ignored her. But another figure could just be seen around the nearer of the two arcing dragon wings. In the light, she could see he had a gleaming badge on the long fore-and-aft-rigged hat of his. Perhaps the hats symbolized dragons, thin at either end and thicker in the middle. No wings, though—unless they were hidden earflaps.

"Gate won't open until market day," the one standing still said. He had thick lips and was handsome in a well-fed way. He knew just how loud to make his voice clearly heard without shouting. "Four more days."

That would be five days without food, and seven without a bed. Unless she took the advice of the man at the red door and retreated to town. No, she'd see her siege through. One fourteen-year-old against the Serpentine.

She filled her lungs. "I'm an applicant to the Academy," she shouted.

"Then you should have been here yesterday." His head disappeared, then reappeared. "I'm sorry," she just caught over the wind.

"Could I take some water?" she asked. "I'm terribly thirsty."

"There's a cistern up the road."

Cruel. Even the lowliest posthouse would pass a bowl of water through the door if you asked. Water wasn't scarce anywhere in the Vales.

Damp, hungry, and tired, in roughly that order, she considered her options. Something must be happening with the applicants who'd been admitted, and the chances of her joining their ranks fell with each hour that passed. She should have pressed Falth for ideas to gain entry. Her remaining coin wouldn't buy more than old bread and maybe a cheese rind, or she'd have dined on something other than roadside berries yesterday. If she became desperately hungry there was always the lake.

She glanced up at the green hillsides sloping up from the Serpentine. There were encampments dotting what looked like a pasture, probably family of some of the applicants, waiting for the testing to be finished. They'd have picked over everything nearby. A roadside sculpture of some kind under a wooden sheltering roof was probably the cistern the watchman had mentioned.

She wished she had a belt to tighten. Well, the next best thing to a meal was a drink and a wash, and she could manage that at the cistern. Maybe there was some secret tradition: you weren't admitted if you couldn't be bothered to wash your face.

She followed the puddled road—how easy it was to negotiate when you weren't running in the dark—up to the cistern. It was a simple thing, an all-purpose cement trough fed by a small trickle. There was some slimy growth in the cistern, slick green stuff such as you could find clinging to the lee sides of river rocks. A clever sort of metal screw-plug set into a fitting would allow the trough to fill. Fascinated, she closed the plug and the flow of the water from the trickle increased.

She drank, which brought on another coughing fit; washed her face and hands and drank again; then opened the screw-drain and sure enough, the flow tapered off to the trickling flow from before. As she turned away from the cistern, she spotted a flash of red in the drainage ditch downslope of the road. She investigated and found a cast-off material that she assumed was a scarf, about a third of it soiled with mud. It was a good weave of dyed wool and smelled distinctly like horse. It had probably fallen from some mount or carriage.

Clutching her find with the first sense of satisfaction she'd felt since arriving at the Serpentine, she washed and wrung out the scarf at the cistern and carried it back up the road, swinging it about in the sunlight to dry it and using it to stretch her shoulders behind her. The brightness of the red somehow encouraged her and she wound it about her neck. It itched but it was warm.

Refreshed, she had the confidence to go back along the cliff and bang on the door.

"Just to let you know, I'm st-still here," she said. The call drew out a racking cough, but she felt equal to even illness in the morning sun.

The red door didn't care either way, and no voice responded from behind it or on the wall. She felt a little let down. She was in the mood to shout defiance and argue. She did notice that the pipelike gas-light fixture had been turned off. The metal was still a little warm.

She hung up her cloak on it to dry in the wind and sun. It was a good riding cloak, sized for an unknown girl a little taller. She'd had to sell her own coat from the Captain's. The riding cloak had been given to her by a kindly butcher's wife who'd pitied her shivering in the mountain air as she sold her some tripe and hoof gelatin. Slimy stuff but it kept one going for next to nothing. The riding cloak was old and frayed here and there and stained and the buttons didn't match, but it kept you warm, even when wetted.

Nothing to do but sit and wait, coughing occasionally and feeling headachy from hunger. She tried to keep her mind occupied so she wouldn't think about her stomach. Odd that she hadn't seen, heard, or smelled a dragon all this time. In her imagination they were always alighting and taking off from the Serpentine like birds about a pool. She set about trying to guess at the cargos of the barges and boats in Vyenn below. Fishing seemed to be the principal industry. She watched a coast-barge creep right past the town without bothering to stop; it just turned and started circumnavigating the Serpentine's peninsula, its sails skillfully worked by what she took to be two men and a boy, until the boat passed out of sight. The day passed slowly, marked only by the progress of the sun and an occasional sounding of loud signal-whistles from inside the Serpentine. Once she heard a sharp, whip-crack-like sound that startled her from her musings.

The day grew decidedly warm and she dozed, head pillowed on her little bundle bag and the recovered red fabric wrapped about her throat.

Traffic on the steps woke her. A man in gray plainclothes beneath a short vivid red cape, an ivory sash, and a single, beautifully wrought shoulder pauldron more decorative than functional—the uniform of a dragoneer—hurried up the steps, holding his sheathed sword so as not to let the scabbard bang on the steps. He was unshaven and he had a bit of what she guessed was meat sauce on his lips. He ignored her as though she were one of the lichen-covered rocks littering the cliff. The door opened for him without his even having to knock. By the time she was fully awake and on her feet the door had closed again.

She rushed up to it and shot the timbers. "Hello?"

"You're still here?" the gruff voice from the previous night asked. She could just make out the loom of a figure, not quite as tall as the Captain, on the other side.

"Is it possible for me to have a hear-hearing?"

The figure slowly turned away, then turned back.

"Part of the challenge, girl, is to be here on time," the gruff voice said, in the harsh tone of a schoolmaster with a miscreant. "I don't know what kind of education you have or haven't had, but the phrase *too late to make a difference* haunts many an old battlefield. Money can be reaccumulated. Losses, even of a dragon, can be replaced. But once an hour is gone, no worldly power can restore it. Understand?"

She nodded.

"Remember that, wherever you fetch up."

With that, he departed the door again. She wondered if he'd dropped her a hint, to see if she had the wit and determination to make use of it. *Wherever* certainly included the Serpentine.

She sat on the step again, feeling oddly lonely. She'd been on her own, more on her own than she'd ever been in her life, for the last twelve—no, thirteen—days, but she'd never felt so apart from everything. She was like a shipwrecked mariner with her bare few possessions. The people of the Serpentine and Vyenn were going about their lives. She haunted the edge of their routines like a ghost, able to observe but not interact.

The sun was already falling behind the mountains to the west. It would grow cool soon. She retrieved her coat, now mostly dry, with the remaining damp in the lower third where it would do the least harm. But it wouldn't remain so for long; the clouds were thickening.

Sitting on the stones drained life and heat from her. If she was to spend another night on the doorstep, she should fashion something to get herself up off the ground. She thought about the shoreline. You could sometimes find odds and ends washed up, if you were willing to get wet and dirty in the search.

Well, if life was a test and time couldn't be retrieved, she'd best get to it. The light was fading.

She'd marked the ravine leading down to the lakeshore on her previous trips and decided to explore it while the sky was still light. She disturbed some young grasshoppers but had no luck catching one and missed an easy snack. Though she preferred them toasted over a fire and drizzled with a little honey, she was now desperate enough to eat one raw.

She made it to the lakeshore, coughing with the exertion, and explored the spot where she'd seen some birds poking around. The birds meant there might be a consistent current bringing food in. There was some driftwood and darting tiny fish, but nothing she could sit on. Moving a little out onto the peninsula, she recovered a possibility at last, a torn-up basket that might have been used for laundry. It was made from basket-reeds and wouldn't support her weight if she turned it over and sat on it. Still, it would be insulation of a sort. She smashed it in such a way that it folded, then folded what was left again into a square about the size of a chair cushion. On the way back out of the ravine she seized a big snail off a rock and sucked it out of its shell. Where there was one, there might be more, and Ileth hunted about and found three others, smaller but no less disgusting to extract. They were slimy and revolting and wiggled when they went down her throat.

Five minutes later she felt a little less light-headed from her hunger. Whatever good they did her was probably used up in the climb back to the door.

The broken carrier crackled under her as she sat, with her hooded cloak ready, and waited for the rain. Sure enough, it came, the same heavy drizzle as the previous evening on her last stretch of travel. Probably some working of summer sun, the mountains, and the giant lake. She drew the hood of the cloak close, picked the most substantial trickle off the wall, and refreshed herself with the rainwater. Then she marked how the water ran off the Serpentine and settled herself to be out of the worst of it.

Unlike the previous night, the rain passed after an hour or so, but she heard the ominous sound of thunder and caught a flash of light illuminating the cloud line inland. She hoped the storm was moving away.

She could just see a fringe of light around a mountainous cone of rock that sat astride the peninsula. She imagined it must come from the famous lighthouse.

As she searched the landscape, motion caught her eye. A dragon passed overhead, a high shadow, mostly wings and tail. The familiar thrill she always experienced when seeing one of the great, rare beasts warmed her like a hot drink.

The dragon passed directly over the Serpentine and began a long, sweeping turn, riding the wind with the grace of a petrel despite its size. The darkness obscured its color. It dropped from sight behind the fortress. A whistle trilled from the fortress. Its long blast cut through the stiff wind remarkably well, then two quick shrieking hoots that sounded metallic and mechanical. She wondered what two blasts of a whistle meant when a dragon came in for a landing.

Faint, shouted orders came over the wall. It must have landed. She wished she were on the other side again, not because she'd be fed, or dry, but just so she could watch a dragon come in for a landing and see the people attend to it. She wanted to watch its wings fold, its tail curl as it settled so the rider could dismount, then hear it speak to the staff.

She imagined the activity of the dragon's landing. Too bad there were no trees on the peninsula, so she could climb one and look over the wall.

"I'm going out, blast you," and a sudden clatter broke her thoughts.

A youth made mostly of arms and legs threw open the door and exploded into the night next to her. He made it to the bottom of the stairs and continued going down even though the stairs stopped, sinking first to his knees before he went on all fours. He gave a great doglike heave and the contents of his stomach struck the little landing with a *splat!*

Ileth's empty stomach gave an upward lurch in sympathy.

The youth rocked back on his haunches and wiped his mouth on the sleeve of his rough work shirt. He wore loose-fitting canvas clothing that wouldn't have looked out of place on the sailors of her own northern coastline, right down to the loop-and-peg that you could use to close the collar tight. If she'd greeted him at the Captain's Lodge she would have taken him for a young visiting shipmate. He had a plain white sash wound about his waist and tied tight, which sailors didn't, and he lacked the various rings and bracers and even tattoos sailors often wore to record their travels and adventures.

"Are you all-all right?" she asked. In her concern for him the words flowed out easily enough.

He didn't seem to hear her for a moment, then slowly turned his head.

"I ask myself that more and more," he said.

She was rehearsing words again when a coughing fit struck.

"And you, are you all right?" he said in turn. He stood and, stepping toward her, pulled a handkerchief from his pocket (a sailor wouldn't have a pocket handkerchief either), glanced at it and thought better of it, and shoved it back into his clothing.

She stood and backed away a step. "Best keep away. Might pass it to you," she stammered, and half willed up another cough as if to illustrate her illness. Everyone knew coughs could be passed around like gossip. Most homes in the Freesand had a little space in the rafters for the ill, *up sick* was how it was usually phrased.

"Mine's not contagious. It's from the dragon. Me and a mate had to bring his ale-draft. Auguriscious always wants a whole hogshead when he comes in from a flight. Most dragons take a little wine now and then, but he's the only one I've ever met that likes beer. He burped it back right into my face. What a reek. I've been here two years and I'm still not used to it."

Ileth gave him an encouraging nod and smile.

"They rag me about it. Call me Tosser."

He had an interesting face. The two halves didn't quite match.

"That bad?" she managed to say, before a cough caught up with her.

"Like fish guts and rotten eggs. They burn this sort of gunk in the Beehive, but that just adds a sweet overlay to the smell."

"Oliban," she said, the word popping out easily. She was proud she knew it. "It's . . . boiled down tree sap."

"You been around it?"

"No, just heard about it some-somewhere," she said. "Never

sm-smelled it. I just know its origin . . . it comes from certain coasts. Deserts. Something—about fog a lot of the time and dry air the rest." All the talk brought on another coughing fit.

"Are you all right?"

"I stutter. Or the . . . the w-word won't . . . come."

"Oh, of course. My father does that a bit too. Especially when he's nervous, or when he's tired."

She nodded.

The youth smiled. "You are a student of dragons? Is your father a learned man? We get visitors, men of the sciences, here sometimes."

She shook her head. "Here as an applicant." She showed him the placard.

"Haven't they . . . They're—oh. I see now. Came too late?"

She nodded in reply.

"I heard at dinner there was an applicant girl who came late, all by herself. That's you, I take it?"

She just smiled and shrugged in reply.

"Long trip?"

"Twelve d-days, about. Got lost m-more than once."

"What, all on your own?"

She nodded.

"A girl your age? You're a credit to your father's name. From the north? You sound northern."

"The coast, north of Stavanzer. The Freesand."

"Ah. I'm from the other end. Practically under the Antonine Falls."

"What do you do here?"

"I'm trying to become a dragoneer, same as you. Applied. Noviced. Made apprentice last year. Who are your people? Uthrons?"

"Never met one. I'm of . . . of no name."

"Oh. Didn't mean to offend. Thought you weren't offering your name since no one introduced us, so I just assumed—I'm Yael Duskirk." He bowed, looking uncomfortable.

"Ileth," she said, bobbing in the quick manner she'd been taught from childhood.

"My people aren't much of a Name either. My father was in the

Auxiliaries and had been about dragons a bit there. Until he got a septic wound and they had to take his leg off above the knee. So he was out, but losing that leg more or less got me in here with a letter. Now Mother's hoping I can distinguish the family in such a way that we'll be the Heem Duskirks, or even the Dun Duskirks. Though really, titles don't count for much inside the Serpentine. People think they're all aristocratic throwbacks, but they're not. I've given orders to men with a *Vor* in their name. There are exceptions, but they prove the rule."

"What do you do when you're not bringing the dragons a drink or sicking up?"

He took the jibe well, tilting his head and scrunching up his face in a way Ileth found appealing, like a dog hearing a new whistle-call for the first time. "I'm apprenticed in the kitchens. The Serpentine—in the yarns it's all taking off into stormy skies and dueling and burning and triple-sealed message pouches, but it's not. Not in real life day-to-day. It's shoveling food at one end of the dragons and still more shoveling at the other end and keeping the middle trimmed and polished. Speaking of which, I should get back to it. I enjoyed talking to you. Ileth. Have I got it right?"

She nodded and started to speak, but her stutter and her cough joined forces and she had to discreetly bring up phlegm. She held up her hand so he wouldn't leave without her being able to say good-bye.

"Same for me. Busy—out here. Maybe they'll give me a job as an apprentice doorstop."

He joined his two fists, knuckles at her, as though holding a line. Or perhaps reins. "That's the angle, Ileth."

She'd never seen the gesture, but a smile spread across both halves of his mismatched face.

He turned for the door, giving her a chance to discreetly spit out the mucus she'd been keeping in her mouth. Then she coughed again, leaning on her thighs as she did so. The spasm exhausted her.

On the sixth day after her arrival the main gate opened. On the positive side, she was rarely hungry now and her cough had faded into a few morning hacks to clear out her lungs. She'd never developed a fever or other signs of serious illness. But the absence of hunger made her wonder if she was starving to death, and though she'd lost that discomfort there were others. She hardly slept, and the lack of sleep meant she could hardly think—though that may have been a blessing, as her thoughts as the days passed were a tumult of anxieties that fought and yowled like a barrel full of cats rolled down a hill.

She felt colder than someone camping outside should be, even in a mountain summer. She kept dreaming that she was back in the Lodge at night, and she whiled away the days trying to catch crayfish and snails.

So when the doorkeeper who'd refused her entry told her they were letting the rejects go and that there were drummers out front looking for workers, even girls, she forced herself to rise and act. She found the energy to even run briefly in her scramble to the corner of the tower, practically swinging on the hand ropes as she rounded the corner.

The selection had been made and announced, it seemed, and the rejects from the Academy filed out. A few had black eyes and bruises; all had nicks and cuts visible on their hands, knees, and elbows. What had passed within the walls? It almost made her glad she was starving next to the red door.

Some of the dismissed looked miserable, some relieved, some blankly unreadable. They all shuffled tiredly across the ditch before the walls, clutching musical instruments, cold-weather gear, tied-up stacks of books, or bundles and travel cases. A gathering of family members, servants, and not a few priests awaited them.

"The Auxiliaries need men *and* women!" a drummer, standing up in a wheelbarrow, bellowed as a broad-shouldered, older woman next to him rang a handbell for attention. "If you can push me a hundred paces in the road in this uphill"—he struck the metal tub with his booted heel hard so it made a *thump* like a drum—"you'll be enrolled as a first-rate and get meat-ration twice a day. No other qualifications required."

"Chartered Captain Thornstand Heem Trallsoap seeks brave hearts and nimble feet fit for sea duty taking seal and sharkskin. Shares on profit, three seated mealtimes, and supplied ordinary and shore clothes!" a man in a nautical coat balanced on the saddle of his horse called through a speaking-trumpet. "Seventy silver diadems to each boy on his last cruise, one hundred fifty to ordinary seamen."

Though the sum sounded fantastic, Ileth had heard enough sailor stories to know that such a "cruise" could potentially last years—not so fabulous a sum if it took four years off you.

"Servants needed!" an aged but hale man said, passing out placards. "Yearly or household! Earn your keep, all feast days recognized, and gifts of coin, tools, and clothing!"

"You want to meet dragoneers, girl?" An artfully turned-out woman in a rich overdress with a servant standing behind fell into step with her. "I can arrange it. Consort work. Not whoring. None of my girls ever get called whores. Fatten you up a bit and put you in a nice dress and you'd be called a beauty."

She ignored the drummers and shrugged off the insult of being paid to rut about with rich men, walking past them to stand in line for a drink at the cistern. It was crowded this morning, with people filling up their bottles and watering their horses before departing. The noise grew as some of the families celebrated.

"You're young, you'll be fine," a woman next to Ileth who was probably one of the waiting mothers said as they stood in line, gripping Ileth's forearm in a reassuring squeeze. She had only a little girl whose head came up to Ileth's waist with her, so her other child must have been accepted. "How'd you get that cut on your chin, one of those beasts? I've heard of men being crushed to death when one of them rolls over in its sleep while they're working on the scale. I say you're better off. Most of those getting in are fools; they work them half to death for a couple years, only to never ride a dragon before they shove them out the gate and no skills fit for any trade except shoveling up after horses. It's ten to one against my boy getting on with one and becoming a dragoneer. Probably hundred or more to one for the girls. As I was saying, you're better off."

Ileth shrugged.

Another woman, sunburned and tired-looking in a dress with a nice collar that suggested some wealth, added: "I know he's going to neglect his math, after good money spent on tutors and practice books. Raking up droppings when he should be figuring percentages!" Ileth marked her as an indoor type who kept a shop or sewed clothes for those even better off than her. "If you can figure percentages, well, doors will open for you, won't they? Better places than mucking about with dragons. But he will have his way. How are you on percentages, girl?"

Ileth just smiled vacantly in reply.

The woman seemed about to reprimand her for not replying to an adult's question, but a place opened at the cistern before she could add anything else to the conversation and Ileth escaped into the press.

By the time she'd drunk and washed, the throng sorted itself out as locals brought their carts and baskets in to deliver orders and exhibit their wares to the new novices. Family members of those remaining within the Serpentine rushed through the gate to congratulate their offspring, passing purses of money and rolls of writing paper. Ileth saw that the marketplace just inside the gate was roped off. Parents and siblings had to reach across a line to embrace the chosen and give their farewells.

One celebratory family was going around with a flower-haired daughter proffering a gathering-bowl of nuts. The father ladled out scoopfuls to anyone who held out a hand. Ileth hurried and just made it to the edge of the group accepting nuts when a hulking lad shouldered his way by her and struck the bowl on the bottom, sending nuts flying up into the faces of those around. A fistfight promptly broke out and she retreated from the fray. She didn't have the energy for it, and she'd sooner take a curse than be seen eating nuts off the ground like a squirrel.

Ileth considered going through the gate herself, but seeing the embraces between beaming parents and their embarrassed children, some obviously well-to-do, only a few common as wild onions, kept her from stepping forward. She had no money to spend in the market, and there were already smells of food from some of the carts being brought in. Some vendors had set up little charcoal braziers with skewers of meat already smoking. The mouthwatering smell of hot food would be torture.

Also, there were a couple of strong young watchmen in Serpentine uniform with those fore-and-aft-rigged hats flanking the gate watching her intently. They must have been warned against the girl with the cut on her face and the patched, ill-fitting riding cloak.

Somehow it seemed easier to just return to the doorstep. Maybe after she rested she'd have the energy to pick her way down and find more snails or, if she was quick, a few crayfish.

The faint hubbub of the market faded and vanished. She settled down in her usual spot. She noted, humorlessly, that her butt had scraped the lichen away in all her shifts in the long nighttime vigils. This life as a kind of doorstep decoration felt strangely normal now. The only question was how it would end. She wondered how long she'd last, and what they'd do with her body once she died. She wasn't truly starving yet. In the Lodge she'd heard stories of shipwrecked mariners lasting weeks on nothing but rainwater caught in their shirts and sun-dried seaweed. But those were hardened men. She'd collapse before then. Some said the dragons were allowed to feast on enemy corpses after a battle or pluck drowned sailors out of the water: "Secure your hatch or you'll be pickled drakemeat!" the Captain used to say. It made her think there was some truth to the tales.

She shuddered.

Falth's three blank letters could have the addresses covered and be sold, she supposed. It would certainly be enough to get her a good dinner and a loaf of bread for tomorrow. They were fine paper and paid up. Maybe she'd send him one, confessing that she didn't get in and had to sell the other two.

She stepped to the cliff. She marked where the birds were feeding when the bolt in the door made its familiar scrape. She turned. A man in velvets with a day cape watched her from the doorway. A face mostly hidden by a black party mask with gold linework covering the eyes and cheeks—a bad burn, it looked like—gleamed pale in the sun.

"I told you the applicants were all inside," he said. She recognized the voice as the first gruff one to turn her away from the door. "Yet here you are. Still."

A tempting cooking smell came out the door with him. Ileth's stomach growled in reply. She could hear music, as well as horns and whistles being sounded in celebration.

More to mask the noises in her stomach than to impress the man, she spoke: "I've b-been w-waiting seven years to touch a dra-dragon again. If I . . . if I need to wait one more, that's what I'll do."

"I'm beginning to think you would." She saw he had a rich red sash wrapped around his waist, with a gold tassel dangling where the sword-frog would be on a dragoneer. His fore-and-aft-rigged cap had some nice fringe, and there was a white cockade on the side where the two halves of the hat folded up and buttoned together. He had a strange lean and dragged a foot as he stepped out, reminding her of one of the locals back home who'd suffered a terrible rupture at the docks and cleaned the streets on the Governor's pension.

He was obviously someone of importance. The splendid uniform dazzled; it had a dash about it, so different from the grim plainclothes of most officials in the Republic. She was trapped between shrugging his question off and bobbing a greeting. Her body decided to try to do both and erupted in a spasm that must have been a curious sight.

He tilted his head and a ghastly smile opened. "You handle your stutter well. I like that you just talk your way across it. I've met some who just confine themselves to a word or two. Were you injured?"

"N-Not that I remember. I can . . . I can control it better when I'm . . . when I'm rested. Just tired now."

He removed his hat and dabbed the sweat at his scalp. A single patch of hair remained at the back, grown long and braided into a tail, but the few surviving growths elsewhere, black and spiky and looking like trees desperately clinging to a patch of soil on a cliff, were cut into stubble. He was clean-shaven on the parts of his visible face still able to grow hair. It was hard to guess his age.

Their gazes met. It wasn't that sort of look, the kind she had seen so often at the Captain's. More of a test, a search to see if some lie hid within her. She met it as defiantly as she could but broke and looked down, ashamed for some reason, and then angry because she was ashamed, and then ashamed again because she let a single stare from a scarred man anger her.

"You don't have to look away. I wear my injuries with pride. Doesn't hurt the younger generation to know that dragons aren't all parades and waving at the fishermen and farmers below. Some people get by on fixing on my nose. It was my best feature even before Ramshill."

She knew Ramshill was a great victory for the Republic, but not much more than that. He was also having trouble with his lower lip— *Ramshill* came out more like *wamshill*, but he also ignored it and just spoke as best as he could.

"I'm sorry," she said.

"No, I'm lucky. Ramshill was a disaster for us, though not for war. Two dead dragons and another crippled; fifteen of the Serpentine lost one way or another." When she didn't question him further, he continued: "The strange chance was, my portrait was sketched before my little scrape. The artist was just doing the color when I was struck off the flying list. I had him redo it once I'd healed up a little. But I'm vain enough to have kept the half-finished one. Not for display, just memories."

"I'm still sorry," she said. "I'd like to see that portrait. From before."

"You know how to flatter an old man," he said. "Where are you from, girl?"

"The North Coast," she said, heart pounding. This strange conversation was allowing her to hope again. "The-The Freesand, near St-Stavanzer."

"Who are your people?"

That inevitable question.

"I'm not from any kind of name. Grew up in an orphans' lodge. My name is Ileth, sir." She bobbed, a little more slowly and deeply this time. She'd settled on that story, even before her escape from the Lodge. She'd grown up there, that was true, and as soon as you say "orphan" she'd noticed people stopped asking questions. So far no one had asked her if *she* was an orphan, so she hadn't had to lie yet.

"That's a Galantine name. You look like you might have Galantine in your line. Perhaps around the eyes."

"I don't know, sir. I'm told my mother wasn't from the Freesand."

"Your father?"

There it was.

"A . . . a sailor."

"You ever do any work, Ileth of the Freesand?"

"Domestic, keeping house for the gen-gentleman who owned the Lodge. Some of us helped the shepherds who didn't have families yet. From seven to eleven I had . . . sheep and goats in summer pasture. I started ou-out with a pair of goats and took care of the sheep when I got old enough."

"That's lonely work. What about wolves and such?"

"None around our bit of the coast. There were wild dogs, but I had a sling."

"A slinger, eh? You northerners are supposed to be good with slings. Ever hit anything?"

"We had . . . had our own d-dogs. I fed them on rabbit."

"Do you have your sling?"

"No," she said. She'd not used her sling in two years and had given it away to a shepherd boy, as she didn't enjoy hunting and dressing rabbits. "If you could l-lend me one, I could show you."

"Oh, I don't have time for an exhibition of skill. I'm just curious. If you know how to use a weapon you get to prove it at the trials. Too bad you missed them."

"I didn't so much m-miss them as I was . . . was barred from them."

"Don't sauce me, girl."

"I'm sorry, sir."

He paused and folded his arms and rubbed his elbows. Ileth thought it was a strange gesture. On a man without a burned face it might be off-putting, but on him it could be called endearing.

"Well, I shouldn't talk your ear off; stars know I miss mine. Come in and I'll get you a pudding. Maybe we'll find you a sling and you can take shots at seagulls fouling our rain catchers or drive away those filthy pigeons in the upper dome of the Rotunda."

He went back to the red door and opened it for her.

"Welcome to the Academy at the Serpentine, novice. My name is Caseen—like you I'm of no name, no name at all—but even so, it would be best for you to refer to me as the Master of Novices."

2

ould it be true? she thought, gathering up her cloak and blanket-roll. The sad little pile of crushed reed basket and a patch of lichen-free doorstep was all that marked her long, hungry vigil.

"You're letting me in?" she asked, slowly and carefully.

"Asking you to join the Serpentine Academy," the Master of Novices corrected. "Provisionally. As a novice, like the others we just admitted. There'll be a few formalities, like your oath. But you impressed us."

She silently thanked Falth. As far as she was concerned, the Name Dun Troot had already rewarded her for keeping them informed about their daughter. She hadn't been intentionally reenacting the story of Sabian, but maybe her sitting out there day after day had struck a familiar chord with those inside.

She fought the temptation to bolt inside, forced herself to savor the feeling as it sank in. They were *asking* her. Ileth, the stuttering girl from the Captain's Lodge who caused housewives to whisper to each other when she walked past them, was being asked to join the Republic's Dragoneers. Provisionally. As a novice.

He let her take it all in. She warmed to him; he hurried her in neither speech nor action.

"Just a mo-moment," she said. She picked up the crushed basket. The dry old reeds crackled wearily. It had done her good service, and she couldn't just leave garbage lying about the doorstep.

Besides, something needed to mark the occasion of leaving behind the Captain, the pitying looks, everyone's talk of her "prospects," the Lodge and its cabbage smells, no one thinking she was or ever could be much of anything. She held up the broken reeds to the burning gas-pipe, let them catch well on fire, and went to the cliff and cast them out to the immense lake. They spun burning into the water.

Caseen watched her, his face neutral, but his good eye was alight with interest. "Whenever you are ready, young woman."

She straightened up her attire and, best as she could, arranged the stray hairs across her face and walked up to the door. She took a deep, bracing breath and stepped inside.

You've done it.

She was no longer one of the Captain's lodge-girls who had to press up against a wall or dodge into the street to make way for the quality. Who had to keep her eyes downcast when speaking to any official in black plainclothes. Who had to suffer the pitying or, worse, ap-praising looks from men who knew what the Captain was and what he allowed under his roof. She looked around, wanting to remember the moment, have the details ready to recall should her frost years ever come.

The flimsy door led out into a little landing below the rest of this part of the Serpentine. Some benches were set against the thick outer wall and a long, ill-lit tunnel went off on her right. It took her a moment to realize it was both wall and hall; a corridor ran the entire interior of the fortification, with windows and portals facing the inside of the Ser-pentine. She could see steps leading down to it and heavy beams lining the ceiling. Rain gear for the watchmen hung like giant bats near the opening to the Serpentine grounds. There was a little charcoal stove squatting on splayed legs over a mortared floor and a pot of what smelled like day-broth bubbled there. Some utensils, bowls, and cups hung by a rain-fed water cistern.

"Take our water, if you like," Caseen said. "We hardly ever have to draw from the well, there is so much rain. Good thing too, the dragon privies take a lot of flushing out."

She wasn't particularly thirsty, but she refreshed herself, not wanting to insult the Master of Novices himself by refusing the first water of the Serpentine offered to her.

The Master himself ladled her a little broth into a cup. There was no bread, but he found a tub of some mashed fruit that he scooped onto a tin plate. The fruit might have had a bit of brandy in it as a preservative, she decided from the taste.

He let her eat and watched her wipe her mouth and then collected the dishes himself and put them in a wooden tray with a carrying strap. They did things so differently here! She'd never seen the Captain or any of his gang so much as hand over a mug when there were girls around to do the work.

The tiny amount of food left her wonderfully restored. She felt like singing.

"Now, girl, you're inside. We'll give you a better meal in a little bit, but I didn't want you to go to the trouble of eating only to have it all come up again. You have to be careful about breaking such a long fast. Are you feeling all right?"

Ileth nodded. "P-Perfectly w-well, sir."

"I need to ask you a few questions. Usually this process is more formal, but I haven't the time to interview you properly in my chamber. You've made the first cut, so you've no reason to tip things one way or another or try to impress me. One of the reasons I have these tassels on my sash is I'm not much impressed by anything from outside the walls of the Serpentine. It won't hurt you in the slightest to be honest. It will be bad if I find out you've lied."

She wondered if he meant hurt as in "getting kicked out" or hurt as in the way the Captain ran his Lodge. In any case, she nodded.

"How old are you?"

"Fourteen. Spring born . . . almost at the equinox."

To his credit, he didn't look dubious when she announced her age.

"What sort of education have you had?"

"We had teachers at our lodge. Sometimes. St-Starting at nine I helped teach the smaller ones."

"The lodge, civic or private?"

"Private, sir. Does it matter?"

"The civic ones give a certain amount of education. I find the private ones are either very good or very bad."

Ileth certainly agreed with that, but she didn't say so. "I can tally, read, and write. I know my times tables. I can figure percentages."

"Any geometry?"

"I know the difference between a triangle, rectangle, square, and circle."

"No navigation, then?"

"I can . . . can r-read the stars to determine latitude. I played with an old plumb-gauge as a girl. The sun's harder, but . . . but I've done it."

"That's better than most. How are you with maps?"

"I love them. I c-couldn't have found my way here without studying them. I can read naval charts as well," she continued, anticipating the follow-up question. "We had lots hanging on the walls of the Lodge. Orphans from sea work, you see."

"Languages?"

"Hypatian, a little, just some of the high scripture. Prayers, mostly. Galantine—I can read it much better than I can speak it. What books we had were mostly in Galantine. I can say *hello, good-bye,* and *thank you* in Daphine and Poss."

"That's a fair list for a fourteen-year-old girl. *Va luse tendi dran?*"

"*Apt. Nasis apt, lal relisan.* But I . . . but I told you I c-could read it better than I c-could speak it."

"I've had novices with Galantine tutors who allegedly also gave them lessons along with manners, dance, and deportment, who bowed flat-footed and couldn't get beyond *Va vere?* when I questioned them. But then it's considered bad form in society to take after the Galantines these days, with the war—well, with the war and then the armistice. Some even find it suspicious."

"My—the patron of the Lodge, he was in shipping. Galantine family, but he was born under the Republic. They were Directist, though, so his family fled to the Vales to escape the p-p-purges. He had friends from both coasts and the Inland Ocean, so that's where I picked up Poss. He had a friend who liked music. I know a few Daphine songs. I'm not much of a singer."

"Did they raise the children in your lodge Directist?"

"Commonist. Our patron wanted everyone placed out of his lodge to mix easily in society. We had a Directist shrine in the Lodge and he taught us to use it. He wasn't strict about his faith."

"How would you describe the civic organization of the Vales?"

Ileth thought that was an odd question, but she did her best to answer it. She struggled more with the words than the ideas, explaining that they lived in a classical republic: juries at the local level, then the district or provincial governor, whose duty it is to obey the national laws of the Assembly and decisions of the Grand Appeal. She skipped the differences between a district and a province. The real strength of the system was the juries. Wrongdoers weren't hauled off to some faraway court and left to rot until the judges got around to hearing their case, a jury was assembled, and a decision made. The Governor could only lessen the severity of the sentence or issue a pardon; he could not overturn an innocent verdict.

"That's a good enough schoolroom answer," he said, with his jagged smile. "Do you feel up to a little walk now?" Caseen asked.

She nodded.

"Then follow me. We'll walk around the Serpentine. You haven't been here these six days, so it will help if everyone sees you with me. Saves questions. You're a young woman, so they'll notice you. I hope you're comfortable mixing with boys and men; you'll find yourself in a minority here."

He beckoned her into the sunlight. She nodded and followed.

"I take it you left no one behind? We had a girl a year older than you come through the gate to escape a bad marriage, once."

"No, nothing like that, ma-ma—"

"*Sir* is an ample honorific for the Serpentine, just like outside the walls. Use it on anyone in uniform or with a colored sash—that should be good enough to begin. There are a few special circumstances, like facing a jury, where you'll be expected to use *Your Honor*, but we don't hold many exams or inquiries here. If you do your job well, we'll know about it and give you a better job when there's a need. The dragons expect to be called by name. If you get a chance to learn any Drakine, take it. But as a novice you won't see overmuch of the dragons, so until you learn their names you can say *sir* to them as well.

"Remember," he continued, "in the Republic dragons have the same rights as a man. That's what the Troth was all about, long before the Republic. If you need one to accommodate you in some manner, say, shift so you can get by in a passage, *beg favor* is expected, even if it's a bit old-fashioned for these modern times. Some of these dragons were alive when the Hypatian Empire was all over this side of the Inland Ocean."

"Yes, sir."

"You are a little sheath of a thing, but that may be to your advantage. Even a new-fledged dragon could carry you. You'd be surprised how often a dragon passes over a great, broad-shouldered sculptor's model of a man and picks the scrawniest teen. Dragons get tired bearing a load, same as any man or animal."

They walked out into the sun, along a gravel path that led up to a wide road running the spine of the peninsula. Ileth felt lighter in her worn old boots, as though she were floating next to this scarred old specimen of dragoneer. Gods and Fates bless Falth for giving her hope when she had none. She would be a silent watcher of that Dun Troot girl.

"Don't take the 'Academy' part of the Serpentine too seriously. You won't sit on a stool memorizing Hypatian declensions. The name's for the gloves-and-laces set. We run on an apprenticeship system here. The Names wouldn't like it—their heirs being trained the same as a brick-layer. During your novice year, we'll find out what sort of person you are; then you'll move on to one or more apprenticeships under contract to the Academy. It's a distinction for the law and clerks of accounts you needn't worry about.

"Now the geography of the Serpentine," he began, taking her out onto the great field enclosed by the walls. Off by the gate she heard music, faintly. Caseen ignored it, pointing out landmarks.

She knew the names of some of the features from tales and ballads of the dragoneers. She counted them off under the brassy mountain sun. The Master of Novices added his own bits and bobs of apocrypha to her knowledge from tales:

The Serpentine, on its long, rocky neck, had three sections. Up by the main gate the jumble of principal buildings could be found. From there the peninsula fell away into more uneven land in the middle section, often compared to a dish like a long platter, complete with a lip of the walls to keep the juices from running off onto the table. At the center of the platter was a garden, both functional and decorative, built around the fortress's reservoir—not that much of one was needed in the rainy mountains. On the other side of the gardens it became rocky. An amphitheater, with columns in the center for tenting, filled a hillside where the ground started to rise again toward the rock piles about the Pillar Rocks. A road—the Bridge Lane—ran the whole length of the Serpentine in three great bends, which gave the peninsula fortress its name and threaded through the Pillar Rocks, over the long bridge, and to the third and greatest portion of the fortress: the Beehive with its famous lighthouse. The dragons lived within the Beehive.

The Beehive, from a distance, looked like an unusually symmetrical mountain of uniform rock, but it was actually a blend of natural stone and man-made masonry, plated in places with gray granite façades of the muted papery color of an ordinary beehive.

Ileth burned everything Caseen said into her brain. She felt lost in her personal exaltation (perhaps brought on by her first real food in eight days), an exaltation so profound she wobbled at the knees as she walked alongside him with a head threatening to give up into a swoon. The geography of the peninsula, the little huddles of buildings, the quarrylike amphitheater in the distance, and the unimaginable size of the caverns under its lighthouse with its dragons and legends and secrets beneath were more than a view.

It made her head swim. Her thoughts kept circling back to the realization that she wouldn't have to beg for work as a housemaid or work in a wharfside tavern, or chafe in some laundry with the lye eating away at her like age. Or worse, return defeated to the Captain to beg forgiveness.

A pair of spotty-cheeked youths trotted along a gravel path running at the base of the wall, panting with effort, their faces red with more than just blemishes. They gave her, or rather the Master, a wide berth. "Only two more times, boys," he said. One managed a bleak smile, and both stepped up their pace.

Ileth was forming and discarding questions when the Master of Novices began pointing. "Oh, and if you ask directions, it's important to know the Serpentine's informal compass. That's Bayside," he said, gesturing north toward a wide bay with a few farms on the slope leading up from it and old boats in the grass above the waterline. "You were waiting at the door Harborside, above the town of Vyenn. No harm comes to Vyenn, we see to that, and it's done well out of its association with the Serpentine. Here, at the gate and the halls, is *up. Down* is at the other end with the Beehive and the lighthouse. There are some older ruins farther out on the point, including the old lighthouse, but they're half flooded and full of rusty grates. Keep out of them. Understand?"

"Bayside, Harborside, up, down," she said, pointing out the directions with a minimum of tongue-trip.

"Now you're ready for that meal. We're heading for Joai's house. Everyone here needs to know Joai. She's solved more crises than the dragoneers and dragons combined."

He spoke a little bit about the peninsula generations ago as they walked. "There's an entirely different geography you'll have to learn within the Beehive. For now, it's enough to know there's a cave with a wharf at the bottom that leads into the lower sections. We call it the Catch Basin because it's mostly fish that get unloaded. The Skylake is rich in fish. Most places feed scrap food to pigs and dogs; all our waste goes to the fishermen and trap-keepers. I trust you've no objection to fish."

"My l-lodge was in a fishing town," Ileth said.

"We would have an impossible task feeding all these dragons without the Skylake and its river traffic down to the Gulf."

He talked about how the foundations of the Serpentine were laid by an old conqueror who fancied that he'd set up a kingdom on the Skylake. The whole peninsula had been his estate. A few of the old buildings were still in use. But that was long ago, before the Vales were even mapped out or the western coastline properly settled, long before the founding of the Republic.

"Kess in the Archive could correct me, I suppose, and argue that some old cottage or fire pit or who knows what used by trappers or miners is the oldest human structure. There are a few even older points of interest in the Beehive that are supposed to be the work of dwarves, who'd begun turning the place into a warehouse or something, if you're interested in where ancient history and myth start being knitted together."

They passed under the loom of Mushroom Rock—from up close it appeared to spread out at the top and lean over the viewer—to a wooden building about the size of a Freesand house. It stood on stilts with chickens running about underneath, leaning tiredly on both the rock and the end of the Bayside wall where it joined the Mushroom. While they walked toward the little house, activity caught her eye. On the other side of the bridge she could see a sort of cobbled plaza bordered by white-painted, rounded stones where a small green dragon was attended by a throng of humans. They appeared to be working it over with brushes and what she supposed was soapy water.

Her guide noticed her interest. "Scale nits, I'm guessing. We never quite manage to eradicate them. They're most active in summer. Get some sun on them, they don't care for sun, and they can be washed off easily enough." A gust of wind banked off the rock as they approached the little house, and she smelled food cooking.

"Joai always has a little soup on for those doing heavy labor, and takes care of any cuts and bruises that happen in the course of the workday here at the Academy. We have a physiker for more serious injuries, but he's often calling in Vyenn or asked for at some of the outlying farms and such, so most of the time the bandaging falls to Joai."

He led her up some weather- and weight-warped stairs to a door. The chickens objected to the disturbance. Caseen opened and held the door for her with a brief sort of turn of palm and wrist that reminded her of Falth. The Master of Novices had courtly manners.

She stammered out thanks as she stepped inside, following the smell of cooking. Drool threatened to wash out her mouth, and she wiped at it with the back of her hand. She suddenly felt a terrible yokel. She found the discarded red scarf and wiped her hand and the corner of her mouth.

The building was warm, with a low, sloping ceiling made lower by various foodstuffs held in nets up away from whatever vermin troubled the Serpentine. A woman shaped like a prize turnip was peeling potatoes by a vast hearth that looked more like it belonged to a smithy than a kitchen. Half of the room was taken up by the cooking hearth and implements for food; the other half held chairs, benches, and an assortment of medical devices, bandages, and crutches. Ileth stepped over to get a look at the wound dressings and smelled strong vinegar.

"Joai," Caseen called across the room, "this is the girl who's been hanging about the door taking in the view of Vyenn's lakefront. Since she has no other commission, she agreed to give life as a novice a try. If I left her out any longer I think she'd perish, and a corpse on the doorstep is terrible luck when we're about to oath in the draft of sixty-six. Give her a pudding, would you?"

"We must do better than that," Joai said, looking her over like a farmer being offered a pricey three-legged horse. "Her skin is as loose as a boiled chicken's."

Everything in the room smelled so good! Rich broth, a roasting-potato smell, pig fats on the grill, toasted herbs . . .

"I'll send someone over to the Manor to have them find her a room and such," Caseen said.

"She'll be washed and fed," Joai said. She sniffed. "We'll want to boil those clothes before giving her a bed to lie down in. Where's that lice comb now?"

"Must jump, Joai. I enjoyed speaking to you, Ileth," the Master Caseen said, working what was left of his face into a smile. "I hope you'll sprout wings someday." He turned to Joai. "How's that boy, oh, what's his name. The one with the injured foot?"

She lifted a tub half-full of water with an ease that bespoke great strength and set it down by Ileth. "Gralm. Broken toes, poor dear. I bound them up. He'll be fine. Just don't run him up and down the walls, sir."

"Joai!" he said, mocking a hurt tone. He moved to the door, brought his fists together, knuckles toward her in the same gesture she'd seen the Duskirk boy use, and left.

Joai turned to her and ground her teeth in thought.

"'A pudding,' His Honor says. No, you need a good chowder, flower," the woman said, wiping her hands and tightening the wrap around her hair. "With a sausage roll. But first, out of that stuff. Strip right down to your goose pimples. Throw everything but those shoes into that metal tub there. If you're shy, the sooner you get over it the better. Have a wash up while I cook." She indicated a poor man's bath next to the stove.

Joai advised her on how to mix hot and room water for the tub. Ileth wasn't at all used to hot baths; the Captain sent his charges down to a secluded cove not so much to bathe but to immerse themselves in the chilly waters of the bay to improve their health. *Strengthens the mind, body, and soul.* The attitude was generally shared in the Freesand, where a hot bath was considered a decadent indulgence.

But she was in the mood for a little decadence.

Ileth shed her filthy clothes, sheath as well, and climbed into the warm water of the bath. When she finished removing the last dirt of her journey from her scalp, Joai handed her a bundle. It consisted of a long men's work shirt, an overdress that buttoned inconveniently behind the shoulders, and a belt and thick wool socks. She sorted through a trunk and extracted a couple of worn but clean sheaths.

The new attire had seen better days. The shirt was more patches and stitch than shirt, and the belt looked as though every hole had been used at one time or another, but they were clean and the leather on the belt had been oiled. The overdress had been dyed to cover stains at least once but was of some good channeled material, thick like moleskin. The socks looked tired but willing to do whatever might be required of them. They had a cleverly concealed lace at the top where she could cinch them above her skinny calves. She suspected even with the laces they'd fall down; Ileth didn't have much in the way of either muscle or shape to her legs to hold them up.

The door banged open. A boy-man who was much more boy than man and mostly made of eyes and ears shuffled in. "Madam Joai—" he began, but the round eyes in a conking great head widened when he saw Ileth.

Ileth found the boy's wide-eyed astonishment a little funny, but then she'd grown up in a crowded lodge. He looked as though he wasn't entirely sure of what he was looking at, but he knew he liked it for some reason. Boys like this didn't bother her the way the Captain's leers and shambolic jests burned on exposed skin.

She held up the overdress like a curtain to ease the boy's discomfort.

"What have you been doing, skint?" Joai asked, looking at the thick layer of dirt on the boy.

"They put me on gravel-making, madam," he said, trying to look as though he were addressing Joai while still stealing glances at Ileth. "I'm flagging near to perishing, madam. I'm to have something to eat to put muscle on, sir says."

Joai wiped her hands again—Ileth wondered how many times she wiped her hands—and extracted a few eggs from a tinted jar. They glistened. "Pickled eggs and some good bread is what you need, boy." She tore a loaf in half, scooped out a handful of bread, and placed the eggs in the hollow of the half loaf so the boy could carry it like a basket. "Ask for milk tonight and don't mind the comments, nothing wrong with a working man drinking milk, especially if he's been busting stone. What's your name again?"

"Apenite Sifler Heem Streeth," the boy said.

"That mouthful will never do," Joai objected. "Sifler is better."

"If you say so, madam."

"We use *sira* here, Sifler," Joai said.

"Yes, sira," the boy said, and moved toward a stool by the fire. Ileth rotated to keep the housecoat between herself and the boy.

"Be off with you. We're busy," Joai said.

"Sorry to walk in on your dressing, sira, should have knocked," the boy said to Ileth, backing out the door, leaving chalky dust and foot-prints behind.

And that was the first time in her life Ileth, from the Captain's Lodge in the Freesand, was called *sira*.

While she dressed again Joai turned a tap that ran out of the stove. Steaming hot water ran into the washing tub, and she added lye and flaked soap to the hot water.

"You won't see this stuff again unless you go to the rag room, so if any of it has sentimental value, get it and hang it now," Joai advised. "You'll keep your boots. Is that how they do the lacing up north? All around the calf top? I have musk oil if you want to give them a cleaning."

"Are you a . . . a dra—"

"Oh, skies, no. Tried it, flower. Tried. Made it through novice, initiate—they don't use that term much anymore, it was dying out when I did it and we just use *apprentice* now—became a sojourner—that's what they used to call a wingman. I was good at most everything back in my day. The dragons seemed to like me around them. Got a few compliments on my cooking. But every time I took one up, well, it turns out I'm fearful when it comes to heights. Paralyzed, my flower. Paralyzed with terror." She stiffened and the whites of her eyes showed as she remembered. "I covered my face with my scarf until the dragon landed again every try; so much for that. They said I'd get over it, but I never did. But I was a good worker, so I kept on here. I like working with you young people, and there's often excitement, as you'll see. We get news first here, good and bad."

"Did you know a dragoneer named Annis?"

"Why yes, Annis, terrible, died just before the armistice. The armistice might have even been signed when she died; they just didn't hear about it in time. She came in as a novice, oh, I'd given up flying then but I was still working in the flight cave. Liked her right off. Are you two related? I don't remember her as northern."

"No. I-I met her and her . . . dragon once, when I was little. She put me in her own saddle. Wanted to come here ever since."

"Sounds like her. She was like me, wanted to see the girls like you get a chance, and the fancy ones here to snag a husband and get their curls singed. I'm no leveler, mind, but just because you popped out of a chute with a fancy name attached, you don't get to lord it over the rest of us. That's my angle on the Republic and why I shouted for it when I was your size."

Joai set her on a chair by the fire. It had little cushioned horsehide pads on the arms and an upholstered back. Ileth took a moment to think about what a wonderful thing chairs were as her feet basked in the warmth.

Faster than she would have thought possible, Joai appeared with a tray. Even so, Ileth was sliding into sleep.

"Do you take wine?" Joai asked.

She nodded. Wine was scarce on the North Coast, save for a few locals who did their own from berries or dandelions, but they left her with a thundering headache. Ales made her gassy. She'd had real grape wine a few times, though, out of the dregs of glasses from the Captain's parties, and enjoyed its flavor and warmth, even if it was in tiny doses. The Captain himself drank brandied wine but never left a full swallow in the glass even when in his cups.

The wine appeared in a little sort of shell-design bowl with two handles. "Not an everyday practice, mind, but after what you've been through it'll do you good."

Joai continued talking and working as her charge ate.

"Remember, my flower: it's sand and broken shell for girls here. They'll ride you from the time you wake, hard, and ride you right out the gate, if they can, before they let you near a dragon saddle. Testing you, like. Watch that you don't favor any single boy. It makes for trouble, though it seems to me that's more the fault of them than the girls. Not that half of them are worth keeping, unless money's all you're after. Here hunting husbands? No? For the honor and glory of it, then? Some of these toppy nameseys, they saw a dragon in a parade with someone like your Annis on top of her in formal velvets and wanted to be her, covered in flower chains and laurel."

"I never saw a parade. Dragoneers don't come to the North Coast much. Wish they did. We wouldn't lose so many sailors to the Rar-Rari."

"Rari? Those pirate fellows?"

Ileth nodded. "They take our fishermen and sailors. Make slaves of them. Not many get away."

"Well, what's your governor about? Can't afford the sheep it takes to garrison a couple dragons? Scared the riders will deflower his daughters?"

"I wouldn't know. I w-wish I did."

"Well then, maybe someday you can sort them out."

Her belly was full now, or as full as her shrunken stomach could handle. The wine, warmth, and food teamed up with her exhaustion. She watched the fire and drowsed.

Joai took her shawl off the hook by the door and draped it over the snoozing girl. "Well, if you can sit out night after night with nothing to eat but rain, you should last at least through the first year. The rest is up to your wits—and the dragons."

When she awoke, her first business was the introduction to her lodging. Joai walked her over after fortifying her with more soup, as she had slept right through the dinner bell.

Most of the female novices and apprentices of the Serpentine lived together in what could charitably be called a great house. They called it the Manor, at least to the girls' faces, but Ileth soon found out it had other, coarser names. The Manor was a long rectangular building with narrow windows and a steeply pointed roofline and a decorative bell tower with no bell. It was old, dating to the aristocratic families who'd once claimed the peninsula. It had a high-ceilinged ground floor, a cramped second floor that was a warren of hallways and subdivided rooms, and an even more cramped attic arranged as a dormitory. Most of the new novices slept in the dormitory. A few sheets had been hung up to improvise dividers for dressing and toiletry. They were all under the watchful eye of a sort of human whiskbroom called the Matron. No one called her *madam*, or *sira*; she was the Matron and you'd better say it clearly and in a respectful tone that implied the capitalization.

The Matron sniffed out that she was of a lower quality compared to the other novice girls and set her up in a hammock with two other no-names right at the top where the stairs met the attic. There was noise anytime someone entered or left. The others had beds, but when she saw the lumpy state of some of the sleeping mats and her fellow novices itching their tender flesh because of bedbugs, she was grateful for the easy-to-wash hammock.

"Always crowded after a call-up," the Matron said, pointing Ileth to some hooks where she could tie up her hammock. "It'll thin out by midwinter."

The attic was fireless, warmed only by the heat rising from below and the four chimneys of the house. It was stuffy but warm enough in the summer weather. Ileth wondered what the winters were like, and if cold had anything to do with novices giving up. She had an advantage on the others there; she was inured to cold thanks to her years at the Lodge. The roof was sound; if a fault appeared they'd know about it, as their noses were practically pressed up against its beams.

Below on the second floor the female apprentices and a few of the well-bred novices like Santeel Dun Troot slept anywhere from two to six to a room. Santeel was in a crowded room and often appeared at the morning meal sleepy with tufts of rag stuck in her ears. One of her roommates snored. Ileth found herself admiring Santeel despite herself; she seemed to know a great deal and did everything well, whether it was washing spoons or reading aloud. But there wasn't much to report to Falth yet, except that Santeel had lost or someone had stolen a tiny pair of scissors Santeel used to trim her toenails. Santeel believed it the latter. She complained to the Matron, who refused to turn the entire Manor upside down to find scissors.

A part of her wanted to dislike Santeel, a girl her age given seconds and dessert when they handed out beauty and voice and everything else not just on a platter, but on individual doilies resting on the platter, each item polished, arranged, and engraved with her renowned initials. But the circumstances of Santeel's birth were no more under her control than Ileth's, and Ileth was thoroughly sick about hearing how her mother's conduct brought her no shining platter, but a stutter that made everyone think she was slow. Ileth resolved that she'd like or dislike Santeel Dun Troot only if her words and actions merited it.

Santeel didn't seem to mind Ileth hanging about her. She liked, and expected, to be the center of attention.

There was only one female of wingman rank living in the Manor, and she had a room to herself, even more spacious than the Matron's. She was hardly ever in the Manor, though. Every time she had more than a few hours of rest she'd go down to rooms she rented in Vyenn where there were servants to cook for her. All Ileth knew about her in those early days was that she was small and flew many errands for the Charge of the Serpentine.

The Matron slept on the first floor just off the kitchen, where her bedroom also served as the pantry. Much of the first floor was taken up by a dining temple. Everyone ate their breakfast on narrow benches, all facing the same way, from a small shelf that folded down from the bench in front, forming a ready-made audience for one of the Matron's lectures or an inspirational reading. Those seated in the front row ate with their plates in their laps. The women and girls were expected to prepare and eat breakfast together, then join the men and boys in the dining hall for the evening meal.

Everyone wore basically the same attire, a men's work shirt and a knee-length overdress of that durable, channeled weave Ileth admired when it was first handed to her. The overdress brushed clean easily. You weren't to decorate or enhance either garment in any way, though if it became hopelessly stained you were allowed to dye it.

Novices wore a small brooch of white dragon scale. Her group didn't have theirs yet; it would be issued once they were oathed in, and their oathing ceremony had been delayed for some days because of a lack of a sufficient number of dragoneers present to attend the oath.

Apprentices wore a plain white sash tied about the waist but out of practicality took it off for work. You had to buy or make your own sash, and the sammarind* fabric preferred as fitting for future dragoneers was as dear as it was delicate. Two of last year's novices had only just

---

* A luxury-grade fabric with a metallic shine to it.

recently been promoted and had bought the last ones at a ruinous price for a used length of white silk.

The Matron's discourse rarely wandered from her obsessions: the cleanliness of Academy linens and furniture, and that the Academy's novices and apprentices must eat moderately so that a healthy bowel could be maintained. She treated their outsides with bristle brushes and hard, gritty soap that scoured their skin and had them fill up on practically raw oats, bran mashes, and summer vegetables that did the same to their insides. Such was the Matron's belief in the power of substantial and regular evacuations that she grew nonplussed at the continuance of Ileth's stutter after a week on the goat's feed. Ileth wondered if she'd cured a stutter with the feed or her victims were too busy chewing and squatting to talk. In any case, the subjects of hygiene, mealtime denial, and a purpose-filled bowel mentally combined, like three cow paths joining together to become a road, when it came to their chastity. They could look at boys, talk about them in a respectable manner, but you could no more think of kissing one than you would a barnyard animal. Her standards of purity were such that had she found out about the boy who had barged in while Ileth stood undressed in Joai's kitchen, Ileth would be considered tainted.

The hour before bed was devoted to sewing and polishing. Groups of novices and apprentices worked while a few others took turns reading from the short list of works the Matron considered appropriate for young female ears. They had regular servings of the Old Rite's Temple Maxims, or On Virtue by Tonerone, or short "plays" that were just catechisms of manners on the perils of dancing with the wrong sort of suitor.

Ileth often amused herself by imagining the Matron presenting her series of moral and uplifting entertainments at the Lodge to the Captain's friends.

As the evening hour wound down, the Matron would post everyone's assignments by their room number on the first stair landing where you couldn't help but see it as you went to bed. Old engraved and painted wooden signs were hung up on little hooks next to each of the thirty lettered or numbered rooms—Ileth's stairway hammock-eyrie with the other two was *D* and they had a private joke that it stood for the desperate, or the despaired of, or (in whispers) the damned.

Behind all the discipline was a threat to the novices, rarely spoken, that if they indulged their youthful follies their names would be put down in the Blue Book in the chamber of the Master of Novices. You went into the book and shortly afterward, you went out the gate and into the gutter.

But the routine of chores, roughage, lectures, and duty finally had a most welcome break when the newest novices were invited to join their male counterparts and finally take their oath the next day.

The news caused an excited rush to the washtubs and basins and there was great borrowing and sharing of brushes, pins, and ribbons and *oh, I know I shall break down reciting.*

Ileth went to bed nervous and had difficulty sleeping.

3

On the morning of the oathing ceremony, Ileth studied the long string of words the Matron placed in front of her. The others had already seen copies their first day in the Serpentine Academy, and again after the failed applicants were dismissed. This was Ileth's first encounter with the words she was to speak. The dread of the ceremony unfolded from the paper and enveloped her like a burial shroud.

"M-M-Must I say it aloud?" she asked the Matron. "I could . . . sign it, with witnesses."

The Matron thrust out her lips in disapproval. The expression looked oddly like one of her "sisters" at the Lodge when she imitated a kiss from her latest swain.

"Everyone here has spoken it, from the dragoneers on down, when they enrolled. If you're going to be here, you're going to speak it. Even the dragons swear in on the winds or the elements or their fire and water. But by the judgment they swear on something when they join."

"Could I do it in private?"

"The rules here are the rules." The Matron thrust the paper into Ileth's hand and sent her out the door to join the others with something like a shove. "Be grateful the gods gave you a lovely morning for it."

The Manor had a tall female apprentice whose duty it was to supervise the younger girls. Her name was Galia. She was watchful and confident and still in the dangerously poised manner of a perching hawk. Galia did not talk or flitter about much, which Ileth found refreshing.

Galia put them in line and walked them to the amphitheater. Ileth decided Galia was probably city-bred, as she nipped in and around others as though she'd been doing it since learning to walk. She cut her hair into bangs, an urban fashion that Ileth had been told dated back to Ancient Hypat. She also presented well in her brown uniform dress, since she'd had the time to properly alter it and remove the pilling.

The morning sun was already hot and the air unusually still. Ileth heard bells echoing up from Vyenn.

On she marched them, down into the quarrylike stone amphitheater. She paused them at a little canopy, where a Commonist priestess and her assistant dabbed them with mud under each eye and shook a wet, leafy birch branch over them, reciting some prayers in Hypatian as they were presented to her three at a time.

"Half of you will be gone by next year," said a man holding a pair of painted mules, probably the priestess's conveyance. He smiled, happy in his knowledge that so many of them would fail. They shuffled past, hands clasped to suppress the instinct to wipe the mud off their cheeks. "It's only one in four for the boys," he added.

Whatever ritual the boys had gone through, they had it worse. Their heads had been so closely cropped that almost nothing remained but a dusting of their original hair color, and their faces were streaked with mud and soot. The boys wore a sort of stablehand uniform of the same soap-faded oat color that might charitably be called "white." They stood barefoot in patchy trousers that ended somewhat randomly. Some were practically wearing a child's short pants; others had to roll up the cuffs to keep from stepping on them.

Her chambermates, one of whom was a moon-faced, friendly girl named Quith, said the boys underwent all sorts of humiliations in the first week before they were oathed in. In any case the boys, being the larger contingent, had several apprentices supervising them. They set about arranging them into ranks of ten according to their enrollment order, finally mixing the sexes.

Out on the stage, with an assembly of faces already in the audience and more showing up every minute, Ileth stood, acutely aware that she looked like a bad, last-place finisher in her thick, shapeless overdress at the end of the line of one hundred and nine novices. Their place in the lineup, the Master of Novices took pains to explain, had nothing to do with any kind of grading, it just happened to reflect the order in which their names had been entered on the official roll.

The Master of Novices, Galia, and a few male apprentices counted heads and faces. The new novices silently recited the oath, or double-checked against a printed paper copy. Many had been practicing since the first night they'd slept in the Serpentine.

The audience was formally attired, for the most part. Even Ileth, a newcomer, knew the rankings, from both common tales and her intro-duction to the Serpentine. The dragoneers were splendid in their velvet dress uniforms of gray and wine-red, high riding boots polished to a gleam, each with a sash for their sword-belt that matched their dragon's color. Reds and golds predominated, but there were also greens, silvers, blacks, and a white. They were seated closest to the stage but mostly ignored the novices, calling out to comrades they hadn't seen recently and talking as they waited. Above them, in little groups, were the wing-men, not full dragoneers but wearing the sash of one in black or red or gray, it seemed. Almost all wore swords; carrying arms marked one as a wingman, and some of the swords showed a good deal of pearl and gold at the hilt in defiance of republican simplicity. The wingmen acted as seconds to their dragoneers, flying in their place at need, acting as a pool of fliers for dragons who had not chosen to have a dragoneer, but otherwise supervising the conditioning and feeding of their dragoneer or their dragon. Then there were the apprentices in brown or blue or gray work clothes, rotating through the various specializations as ser-vants who took care of meals, clothing, and tools, flying with them and learning their skills on all but the most dangerous of commissions. Most wore white sashes but there was a smattering of brilliant green, though whether this was some mark of achievement or just an indica-tion that they could afford sammarind Ileth didn't know. She searched out and marked Yael Duskirk up there in a plain shirt and brown coat. She tried to catch his eye, but he appeared to be watching Galia as she paced about behind the group of novices. Those few from the previous year's group who were still novices lurked at the back, standing or sitting on the top stairs of the amphitheater, their white dragon-scale pins holding their work jackets closed at the neck.

On the "stage" to either side of them, in high-backed wooden chairs, were the Masters of the Serpentine, senior dragoneers who were no longer tasked to ride dragonback and now saw to the internal workings of the complex machine maintaining dragon and rider that was the Serpentine. Caseen, Master of Novices, sat right at the edge of the stage. As soon as Galia reported to him that all novices of the '66 draft were present, he stood.

"Welcome, novices. I congratulate you on your achievements so far. But before your service to the Serpentine can begin, we must go through a formality. Perhaps you've heard that expression before, *go through the formalities*, probably as something that must be hurried through to get to a pleasure. For all of us fortunate enough to be a part of the Serpentine, this formality deserves respect, for it is a matter of life and death. You are about to be sworn in to the service of the Republic as protectors of the Vales, and through it our citizens, and to the company of the Serpentine, present or attending to their duties elsewhere. You were taught the oath but have not yet said it aloud to an audience. I hope you have committed the words to a place deeper than memory and considered their consequence."

With that, they brought out the young dragon.

Ileth thought the dragon looked about as uncomfortable as she felt. It was a male, its scale the color of a brass mirror reflecting a roaring fire. The dragon's back still had scar tissue visible under new scale where it had uncased its wings sometime in the last year. Perhaps the others had been told the significance of the young dragon to the ceremony while she was on her vigil outside the gate, but Ileth supposed the dragons wished to show that they took the formalities as seriously as the humans and sent a representative, young and new as the novices.

The first rank of ten was instructed to stand and place their right palm on their breast, their left set like a horizontal bar across the small of their back, head dead level and heels together. Some in the ranks behind surreptitiously tested the pose.

At a word from Caseen, the line of ten novices spoke their oath in unison, speaking toward the dragon and the audience. The lines of the oath broke up and came together as this or that novice stumbled over the words or forgot them until prompted. Ileth felt the sweat running down her back go cold and clammy as she agonized over the coming ordeal.

"I, _____, *affirm that I am free, understanding of the consequences, and fit in mind and body to take the following Oath: I, at the Serpentine, on the Midsummer of this, the two thousand nine hundred and sixty-sixth year of the Resolved Hypatian Calendar, promise to serve the Republic, its laws, its citizens, and its possessions. Every oathed dragoneer is my kin, irrespective of family, birth, or altar. I will treat each one and act at all times as though we are of the same Name. I swear I will respect the Serpentine's best traditions and honor my superiors.*

"*I will exemplify our discipline and comradeship, proud of the trust those of this company have in me. I will display this pride in appearance, behavior, and speech, keeping myself and my quarters neat; continue my education, taking as example those who came before me; and pass my skills and knowledge on to those who follow behind, leaving the Serpentine better and stronger through my attention to duty. As one of the Republic's assigns I will attend always to duty; keep well and respect those people, places, and tools necessary to carry out my commissions; and see to it that the dragons of the Serpentine are healthy, content, and certain of my dedication to their needs. Any commission or order lawfully given shall be my sacred duty to fulfill. I will adapt to any circumstance, obtain or improvise and use whatever resource required, and overcome any obstacle to accomplish the same, in the expectation of risk to everything but my honor. In fulfillment of those duties, I will respect the vanquished enemy and will never abandon the wounded or the dead, nor will I under any circumstances break the ancient troth between dragon and dragoneer.*

"*All this I swear on my honor without reservation or secret intent.*"

The first rank, upon completion of the oath, was ordered to turn around, sit, and face the next row, looking up at them from a cross-legged position. Again, they fought through the words, sometimes together, sometimes a bit apart, and then turning, sitting, and listening to the next line.

Finally, the last rank came.

"I . . . Ileth, affirm-affirm that . . . I . . ." she began.

It was just as awful as she imagined.

The rest of her line finished before she was a third of the way through it, and on and on it went. She tried half reading from the Matron's note and it didn't help. She tried fixing on the undersized boy with the oversized name she'd met in Joai's day kitchen. She sensed a restlessness in the audience; they were vague, out of focus, as though her eyes had willed themselves halfway blind. Her blood roared in her ears. Stinging sweat ran into her eyes, turning the audience into even more of a blur. She feared for a moment she'd faint out of sheer embarrassment.

"Of all the curses, we have an idiot," Santeel Dun Troot, the third from last, muttered to the girl next to her as Ileth lurched through it.

". . . w-without res-s-res-sa-reservation or s-s-s-se-se-secret intent," she finished.

And with that, she broke, bending over and crying into her hands.

"Ffft, girl," the boy next to her said. "It's done. Straighten up."

She took her mind off her embarrassment by considering the youth. His head was shaved clean. He must have arrived between Santeel's and her admittance at the end of the testing. She didn't remember seeing him arrive; perhaps he came in through the main gate.

She tried to blink away her tears. Cheeks glowing with shame, she wiped her eyes.

Galia and the male apprentices brought the novices to their feet and faced everyone toward the audience again. Ileth shuffled sideways, hiding behind a tall male novice as applause and a few cheers broke out.

The audience in the amphitheater rose and filed out, except for those who stayed to chat with friends, or because they had an interest in one of those onstage.

With that, they had to step forward, one by one, and give their name, year of birth, and place of birth for entry into the rolls. She was glad of the time to collect herself.

"Chest out, chin out," the boy next to her said quietly, out of the side of his mouth. He had refined features and a restless manner, nervous and quick. He reminded her of a dog bred for running down rabbits. "You're through it. Look happy."

"Seal it, you two, the Master is watching," Santeel Dun Troot, next to him and the third-to-last to have her name enrolled, whispered. Ileth's *Seal it* must have been preemptive in nature, as she hadn't said a word since she finished her oath. The Name flicked her delicate little chin toward the Master of Novices, who was looking at Ileth.

His countenance was unreadable. He was probably just as relieved as she was that the ceremony was over.

She looked up at the fine summer sky. It was a beautiful day. She was in the Serpentine. She was formally enrolled and oathed. She'd sworn herself to the Serpentine, and in a way the Serpentine had sworn itself to her. The Captain couldn't touch her now, even if he had guessed her destination and attempted to retrieve her. She wondered how much bother he'd gone to over her desertion.

Each novice waited to sign their name on the enrollment. You were to write your name, then beneath it the exact date and place of your birth. By the time the quill came to her it didn't take the ink well at all; it had been hastily recut at least twice. Santeel Dun Troot made a frustrated yip half-way through her signature and walked away with ink-smeared fingers.

The eastern boy before her was named Zante, born in Vallas, the same birth year as hers, she read.

It was her turn. Writing she could do easily enough.

As she bent and wrote, she felt a prod. Santeel had tried to clean the ink from her finger by discreetly wiping it on Ileth as she asked Zante polite questions about what his father did. Ileth didn't have to bite her lip; staying silent at an insult came naturally to her. She did, however, make something of a show of turning the roster to Master Caseen when she finished. He scattered a little drying-powder on the fresh ink.

Well, everyone would blame the worn-down pen for her terrible script. Her signature and origin didn't look much worse than that of Santeel Dun Troot, who'd left an awkward fingerprint on her famous Name. Though Santeel had done a better job with the width of her lines, thicker on the up and down and the curves and thinner right to left and at the inclines and declines, each letter elegantly drawn. She probably had had a tutor in penmanship.

With that, Caseen handed them their first badge of recognition, a little pin brooch fashioned out of a single white dragon scale. "From the Republic," he said as he passed them out, but by the time Ileth received hers he was shortening it to *the Republic*. A tall dragoneer with a purple sash and pauldron, very good looking and clean-shaven, handed him the pins from a rich-looking jewelry case.

The brooch wasn't nearly the size of an actual scale, more of a broken chip filed and shaped. Being organic, no two were quite alike, but all vaguely resembled an arrowhead, with an organic ridge running up from the point. The pin looked exceptionally sturdy. She examined the pin closely. It was a bit scratched up. Maybe novices who departed the Serpentine were forced to give theirs up and they were reused.

Their apprentices instructed them to wear it on the left breast where you could feel your heart beat. Ileth managed to pin hers on using just her left hand, keeping her right casually against her side.

And it was done. Galia quickly walked up and down the line and helped anyone having difficulty with their novice brooch, then led the girls up one of the sets of steps out of the amphitheater. One girl asked if she could wash her face and Galia said, "Not until sunset."

"I'd no idea we were that desperate," one of the dragoneers commented to his wingmen as Ileth stepped past him. He wore a bright red sash and an intimidating pauldron of bright, blood-red leather and brass on his sword arm's shoulder.

The purplish-sashed dragoneer who'd helped hand out the brooches, who'd been following several paces behind Ileth, quickly stepped up and tapped the dragoneer across the back of his neck with the end of a heavy gauntlet. The purple-sashed man had obviously shaved in a hurry before the ceremony. There were three half-healed cuts on his face and neck.

The dragoneer whirled around at the tap, bristling. His wingmen squared up behind him.

"Set an example for a change, Roben," the purple-sashed dragoneer said, in a low, musical voice, as calmly as if he'd been discussing the day's sunshine.

"You'll push me too far, one day," the one he called Roben said. Roben had several gold teeth. "We'll see which of us is sharper."

Ileth felt the loom of someone near her. It was the apprentice, Galia. "What now, Ileth," she said, exasperation hard in her voice, but fell silent when the purple-sash dragoneer motioned her to be still.

Galia moved to stand just behind the purple-sash dragoneer, putting her body between Roben and Ileth.

The dragoneer who had intervened for Ileth hooked his left thumb in his sword-belt and made a show of stroking his chin, smiling. "A threat? At a swearing-in? Roben, Roben, you forget yourself. Not that I blame you. The rest of us forget about you whenever we can."

One of Roben's wingmen made a step to move forward, but Roben stilled him with a gesture. "He's right." He turned to Ileth. "I am sorry, novice. It was wrong of me to think that, and saying it aloud requires me to beg the forgiveness of you and those who heard." He quickly swept the surrounding faces with a glance. He raised his voice slightly, so all could hear: "Congratulations on your entry into the Serpentine. Know you're of the company and welcome. Satisfied?"

The last was aimed at the purple-sashed dragoneer.

"At your service, sir," the dragoneer said.

Roben and his companions moved on. The dragoneer watched them go, particularly the way they held their heads together, talking. Galia started to say something, but the dragoneer addressed Ileth.

"Congratulations, novice. I was silently calling for a grace on you the whole way. You reminded me of a sprained runner determined to cross the finish line. You must be the one who sat outside the door for five days, as you were the last on the rolls."

Ileth nodded. "Th-Tha-Thank you, sir," she said, instinctively making a girl's obeisance.

"I'm Hael Dun Huss, dragoneer to Mnasmanus."

He seemed to expect something in return. "Ileth, sir, applicant f-f-from the F-Freesand."

"You're a novice now. Your badge proves it, Ileth. Glad to see a northerner sworn in. There's often too much of Sammerdam and Asposis in these walls."

"Thank you, sir," she said in a voice just above a whisper.

He finally turned to Galia. "Galia, good of you to come to the aid of your novice. Ileth, if no one else has told you, I will; Galia's one of our finest apprentices. Watch her. Now it's my turn to ask your forgiveness. Mnasmanus just had a long flight yesterday and I want to tend him."

He hurried off, holding his sword so its sheath didn't strike the legs of the others filing out.

Ileth assumed the dragoneer had shared that long and hard flight yesterday, but he didn't mention it, or even look all that tired. An ideal dragoneer, right out of the poems and songs and tales. As she turned, she saw Galia watching the back of the dragoneer, with amazement, or something like it, in her eyes. Her lips silently formed words that might have been *one of our finest*.

Hael Dun Huss paid no more attention to the pair but continued on through the press, picking out other novices with a word or two about their homeland as he moved off to the bridge. She watched how well he maneuvered his sword, so the sheath didn't strike anyone as he navigated the crowd. Odd how much easier she felt from just a few encouraging words. She wondered if there would be trouble between this Dun Huss and the gold-toothed Roben. What if they fought a duel? She knew men fought duels sometimes but knew nothing of the traditions and particulars—there must be questions, accusations, and agreements. Just what she needed in a strange new place. Suppose one of them was killed over her? They'd brought her in without trial; would they throw her out the same way?

No, her imagination was getting the better of her. She'd heard too many romantic tales. It was time to put away these little-girl fantasies.

Galia lined up her novices again. Ileth stepped lively to get behind the Dun Troot girl. "Next stop, the workshops," the tall apprentice said. "You'll all get your first work assignments and be issued whatever tools you need. Look after them. You'll need to have your work clothes cinched and fitted by then, so we have a busy night of sewing ahead of us."

She moved them off. Santeel Dun Troot decided to reposition her pin and Ileth plowed into her. "Sorry," she said.

"Don't your eyes work either?" Santeel asked. She turned away in a huff, her hair flying so that it lashed Ileth's face.

They walked, the inky quill Ileth had been concealing in her right sleeve now firmly stuck at the back of Santeel's overdress, just at the buttocks where it waved like a rooster's tail as she walked.

4

Her first duty, as it turned out, was gutting fish. And no matter how many fine sentiments you wrapped around the word *duty* in an oath, her duty was a slippery, smelly business.

She reported, so early in the morning that dawn was just a fringe of light behind the Sisters across the lake, to her new station, taking her first trip across the Long Bridge. She wondered how many heroes she'd heard about in stories and songs had walked that bridge under the eyes of sculpted dragon heads and heroic human figures.

She was told to meet the apprentice Gorgantern at the far end of the long bridge yawningly early, and that he was big, easy to pick out in the murky dawn. He was tall and vastly wide, and something about the way the bottom of his canvas pants hung low about his thighs made Ileth think of a trained bear she'd once seen rearing up on its hind legs.

Gorgantern introduced himself at the other end of the bridge by saying, "I'm in charge here, understand?" as he issued her a thin-bladed, sharp filleting knife and an oilskin apron. The knife's handle had cracked at some point or other and whoever had used it previously decided to just remove the broken part. There was a whetstone and oil she could use to keep the blade in working condition, but fixing the handle would be up to her. Three other new novices, all boys, started with her. Gorgantern led them to the outer stair down to the Catch Basin.

"Much faster, if you don't mind walking in weather," Gorgantern said, taking them down a narrow track that followed a break like a crack in the massive side of the mountainlike Beehive. A hand rope helped them along and gave them confidence. There wasn't any sort of lip between the stairs and a steep plunge to the rocks and water at the bottom of the Beehive. "The stairs can be slippery, especially if you've fish guts smeared all over your feet."

As they picked their way down the treacherous, uneven stairs, Gorgantern explained that they had the honor of having to travel the farthest to their work of anyone in the Serpentine. The Catch Basin was at the bottom of the Beehive, on the other side where it met the deeper waters of the Skylake. Only the Guard patrols and some of the cargo helpers went out beyond the Catch Basin onto the old point at the end of the Serpentine's peninsula, the bit with the old half-flooded battlements and defunct lighthouse.

Gorgantern had a meaty face and red arms and hands. He had to cut the sleeves off his shirt to be able to fit in it. He was a fully grown adult, about the age of most of the dragoneers, around his third or fourth decade of life, she suspected.

One of the city-bred boys asked for a pause at a widening of the path. Gorgantern sighed heavily. It gave Ileth a chance to rest her legs from the endless steps and survey the Vyenn waterfront. She wondered about the climb back up at the end of the day.

They started down again. The stairs at this length were steep, irregular, and, worst of all, narrow. Ileth tested the condition of the hand rope. It should be tarred. She hated to think about what would happen in the winter if the stairs were icy and you started to fall. You'd go right out over the edge and into the lake. Or worse, the rocks. There were landings only every hundred steps or so.

They passed through a short tunnel and she caught a sulfurous dragon-smell coming from a passage going deeper into the Beehive, then passed it and went down on the outside again, with the lake just beneath this time, washing up against a pile of great boulders. They came to the bottom of the Beehive and turned left into a tunnel at the base of the peninsula. You could smell water coming in off the lake and fish.

"This is the Catch Basin," Gorgantern said.

It was a watery cavern carved out of a natural rock overhang that had been improved so barges could be warped in and tied up. There was a yardarm-like device to make lifting loads out of the hatches an easy task, and wheeled carts for moving barrels and other heavy burdens. A pair of draft oxen waited with the patience of their kind in a small pen with feed and water. She later learned they pulled cargo up the ramp and into the Beehive's warehouse in the lower floors, which connected to the dragon kitchens. For humans, there were also ladders and stairs going up into tunnels leading to storage alcoves and various kinds of workshops.

A few fat lamps lit the ramp and worktables. They reeked of fish.

One of the novice boys also tasked to the Catch Basin had a small tattoo on his hand of a knotted rope. Ileth knew enough of tattoos to know that it meant he'd completed a deep-water voyage, navigating out of sight of land. He just wrinkled his nose at the smell. The other was a farm boy with wind-chafed skin who knew a lot about wheat and barley, and strangely enough had a great head for maps and directions. The farm lad looked pained, as if he were fighting nausea. "This is like pigs, only worse."

"Just let it fly. Into the water, if you please," Gorgantern said. "You'll feel better, after."

The third, the city-bred boy who'd asked for the rest, wondered aloud how you'd obtain a new work assignment.

Ileth didn't say anything. You had to start somewhere.

Every morning they had to help unload the fishing boats. They weren't allowed on the vessels (whether that had something to do with the prohibition on novices leaving the Serpentine unaccompanied, Ileth didn't know). The catch was mostly a long fish that reminded her a bit of an oar. She didn't know much about freshwater fish—the only ones she immediately recognized were perch, but she never saw river fish such as trout here. All she knew was that they were big and had mundane, descriptive names like crescent-gills and bluebacks. Some were nearly as big as the saltwater fish the boats of the Freesand used to catch. There were also great cages of things like crayfish that were bigger than any lobster Ileth had ever seen and mollusks that lived in tubelike shells. The fishermen took their catch from the fishing boats and piled them onto big wooden trays that they would weigh and then the novices would carry them to the gutting table. The trays had sides cut and notched so they could be easily stacked.

Gorgantern spent his first days with them watching from the other side of a long wooden table as they gutted the fish and stripped the catch into fillets. Some days they'd leave the fish more or less whole, bones in, as the dragons preferred them that way, once dried and smoked or pickled in brine. White-fleshed fish went outside the sea cave to dry in the sun. Those ended up at the human tables. Fattier red fish, like the long oar-things they were working on in their first morning, generally went to the dragons. The fish's gutted entrails were either dried for use as chicken feed or put into buckets. The full buckets were hauled down to a skiff for dumping in the slop pools around Vyenn. The slop pools fed the giant crayfish (one sailor called them *pigbacks* and though the coloring was a little off, they did have spots like older pigs often bore), fish farms, or bait fish, which were used on lines to draw in the larger lake specimens.

She soon learned that Gorgantern disliked having a girl on "his team," as he styled it. "Every year, I tell them not to give me any girls, and every year, I get one," he said, shaking his head at the unfairness of it.

"I can't . . . I can't help it that I'm—a girl," Ileth said. "But-But-But maybe . . . but maybe if you tell me how the others gave you—trouble, I can do better."

She thought it was a "good angle," as they liked to say on the Serpentine, showing the right attitude, but Gorgantern just snorted.

"Don't complain about being cold, then. Never met a girl who didn't complain about the cold in the Catch Basin. It gets blasted cold in winter. If you don't complain to me about being cold, all will go well, no matter how slow you are at the work."

Ileth couldn't fight back openly, but she could still stick a pin in him where he might feel it. "Sir, how long h-have you been apprenticed here?"

"Think my age bothers me? Well, I'm just to turn thirty-three this fall. I've been here seventeen years. Never rose above apprentice, true, but I do good work. There's never a complaint about the Catch Basin. Never. I make sure it stays that way," he said, hooking his thumb in his belt. The green apprentice's sash underneath had so many rends it might be mistaken for lace, poorly wound up.

She wondered if the fact that he hooked his thumb so close to his knife sheath was significant.

The fishermen either ignored her or offered their opinions on what she should eat at mealtimes to put some flesh on her hips and breasts. Ileth preferred to be ignored. But there was one, an older red-faced fisherman who acted as sort of a go-between and tallied the catch, who was kindly. His name was Bragg.

"The Catch Basin job's a terrible one. Were I still a skint your age I'd beg to hose dragon scat. But nothing is forever at the Serpentine. That's the blessing and the curse all rolled into one bundle. Just do your job well, and you'll move up. Gorgantern will ride you. If you survive him, you're tough enough for most anything." He smiled and brought his fists together, knuckles toward her.

He also told stories of life on the lake. All the dragon waste dumped into the Skylake made the fish grow huge and sometimes strangly mis-shapen, though Ileth knew from experience to allow for exaggeration in sailor stories. Anyway, he liked to talk, spoke to her as though she were a relation, and didn't mind that she kept silent.

The work was smelly and tiring and the broken knife handle would grow dangerously slick. Both she and the city boy cut their hands deep enough to call for a bandage almost daily. When she complained about the knife's handle, Gorgantern called her "Fishbreath" and said that she'd be more careful with a slick knife and less likely to damage the catch or herself. Lake fish were a good deal smellier than the saltwater specimens she'd sometimes had to work with on the coast, especially the ones they brought up from the bottom mud. In her first week she learned that certain kinds of breakfast, anything greasy or oily, didn't mix well with cleaning fish. She never brought up her meal, but it threatened her a few times. She learned that her stomach passed the mornings a good deal happier if she filled up with yesterday's rolls and nibbled at a bit of cheese before setting off on the long walk down to the Catch Basin.

Gorgantern sometimes ate her lunch that the Matron, and the girls helping her, had wrapped up in a clean rag, if it appealed to him. He advised her to snack on salted raw fish to build up her muscles and tendons and drink from the brining barrels. The salt would help keep her going.

She thanked him and ate the raw fish and drank the brine. He was big as an ox; maybe there was something to his method.

The afternoon was usually better. With the catch gutted, the novices went to work salting and brining and bringing in the sun-dried fish, laying them in copper carriers to go up to the kitchens. Some of the fish were to be hung in the smokehouse, and Ileth always volunteered to do that, though Gorgantern quit selecting her as soon as he sniffed out that she found the labor a relief. Gorgantern and the boys loaded the heavy and even smellier hoppers that would go in the boats to take the piscine offal back to Vyenn while she scrubbed down the tables. With that done, Gorgantern seated himself on a barrel and took out a tiny clay pipe and had one of the boys fetch him a light, as Ileth couldn't be trusted not to trip and set fire to the Catch Basin: *That would be my fate, some clumsy buttonback sets me afire trying to light my pipe.* He'd watch them clean and scrub and, when he was in a particularly good mood, sometimes get them fresh water or spread a little sand on the floor after they washed it so they wouldn't slip the next day.

She was always exhausted and sore when Gorgantern released them and waved them away as he sat with his pipe, rendered comically small by his huge hands. The long climb up the outside stairs was hard and she usually made it no farther than the Manor, so she missed dinner in the Great Hall most nights. The Matron approved of exhausted young women who stayed safely behind locked doors at night and allowed her a certain amount of freedom in making herself dinner. She was usually dozing over a book when the others returned from dinner, lively from the chance to socialize, even sing and dance, and given the balance between male and female in the Serpentine, no girl who wished to dance sat without a partner.

Ileth was usually too tired to share much in the talk about the after-dinner mingling.

As the days marched on, her roommates in the attic complained about her "reek"—water only washed off bits of fish guts from her skin, and the smell clung to her clothes and hair. She tried changing in the Manor's cellar laundry as soon as she returned from the long climb, even washing her hair in the laundry vats, but nothing could quite remove the fishy smell. And so she became "Fishbreath" at the Manor as well. Someone must have told the story of Gorgantern's name for her over dinner.

Santeel Dun Troot wasn't one of those who used it. She rolled her eyes at juvenile silliness like name-calling. As far as the Name was concerned, Ileth wasn't worth noticing enough to joke about. The moon-faced girl, Quith, was another one who refrained from either names or complaint about work odor and became the closest thing she had to a friend in the Manor. Quith loved to gossip about the little cliques and coteries that had already formed among the novices in the Manor, and especially which male apprentices were taking an interest in the new arrivals. Ileth, who did not have anything like Quith's memory for names and social connections and delicate class and geographic strata, just nodded dumbly when Quith spoke with unusual excitement of an apprentice with a *Heem* or a *Vor* in their name retrieving a dropped spoon for one of their dormitory mates or refilling their table's pitcher of water.

Three girls left in those early days. One slipped in dragon waste and ended up facedown in it and got into an altercation with a wingman who ordered her to finish cleaning the dragon before washing herself. "Honor of it!" she exclaimed, packing. "Honor, my grandfather's wrinkled prong for your honor." That night the Matron spent the evening lecturing on ladylike language being required no matter one's emotional state. Another, a sixteen-year-old who'd come in to escape a loveless arranged marriage with a wealthy gentleman, decided a loveless marriage wasn't such a bad fate after all after scrubbing the floors and washing grease off the stained glass of the Great Hall for a few weeks. A third left in tears, hurrying to her dying mother's bedside. Ileth was happy to miss that scene.

The city boy who complained of wanting a new job didn't show up one morning. After three mornings, Gorgantern announced that he'd "quitted" another one, as he phrased it, as though proud of the fact. "And I know who'll be next," he said, looking at Ileth with a sly smile.

While her senses revolted at the messy work and her spirit chafed under Gorgantern's dissatisfaction with all things Ileth, her body made up for it by adapting to the constant, repetitive labor. Her back, shoulders, legs, and feet quit hurting so badly each night and her strength improved, especially in her grip. She found herself able to haul whole loads of wet bedding out of the laundry cauldron with a wooden hook one-handed. The Captain always told the Lodge's boys that strength started in the fingers and toes and worked its way in.

She even found the energy to do something about her balky knife. After work one night she hunted around in the workshops above the Catch Basin for some good thin line. With no small amount of difficulty she removed the rest of the knife's handle and, by clamping it in a workshop vise (it was a clever thing; she'd never seen the like but figured it out on her own), tied and wrapped the line tightly around the haft of the blade to make a corded handle. Then she anchored the other end of the line with wire and soaked the hilt in some resin. No one would mistake it for the work of a craftsman, but the knife gave her no more trouble after that.

On her twentieth weary day at the Catch Basin, she learned that service there was a punishment of sorts. They gained a pair of apprentices a year older than she was who'd brawled over an insult. Or two insults, one a word and the other a gesture, as they later told it. They were from provinces at opposite ends of the Vales, and both word and gesture were only known as insults from the context of their use, but it was enough to start a fight. Two weeks' work in the Catch Basin was their punishment, with the added instruction that they were to work each task shoulder to shoulder.

The exiles almost came to blows again describing their brawl. Each wanted to claim victory.

As the boys spoke of their banishment, Ileth wondered if her being placed under Gorgantern was yet another test. Surely the Masters must know what sort of man he was after all these years. He tortured her relentlessly, criticizing and complaining about her efforts even when she worked as hard as both of the new boys put together. Yes, he kept the place clean and the day's catch was efficiently divided and dressed, but why hadn't they thrown him out? His chances of ever being matched up with a dragon or even being a wingman must have been vanishingly small. But what were they looking for in this test? The ability to endure nasty comments? Or did they expect her to stand up to him, get the better of him somehow? Perhaps they just wanted to see how badly Ileth wanted to be a dragoneer.

After seeing how they glared at each other, Ileth quietly suggested to Gorgantern that maybe they be given work that didn't involve knives.

"If they're dumb enough to try to stab each other, I want to watch," Gorgantern replied. "I've been yearning for a fight all summer; the heat isn't doing its job this year. If they start to stabbing, holler right away and for once don't stutter!"

5

My Dear Falth,

Forgive me for not writing you sooner. In truth, there was little to report these past weeks. There is still little to report, but I did not wish you to think your trust in me misplaced.

You will be pleased to know that your late charge Santeel of the Name Dun Troot is doing well in the Serpentine. Her health is excellent and she eats with appetite. I was practically next to her when she swore her oath. I'm sure you understand that she did much better than I at that ritual, and you can tell your family that the white pin she now wears flatters both her complexion and her family name. They do not let her powder her hair here save for when we dress for dinner on the duty day of the week-over, and that bothered her (and the rest of us who were asked to commiserate at the deprivation) at first. Though her collection of friends does not, perhaps, reflect the number she deserves, she gives direction as one of the leading novices in our residence. We can always rely on her to become involved in our labors, and she freely draws on her wealth of knowledge to offer suggestions for improvements.

At first, she was put to work in the smithy, but the work didn't suit her talents, so she moved on to the chicken runs. The Serpentine has several substantial sets of chicken coops to supply us with eggs and meat. Chickens, as you know, are not the cleanest of birds, and she does a good deal of scrubbing after her work there and must sometimes bandage small wounds received in the daily retrieval of eggs. I hope she's not giving off some kind of odor that makes the chickens think her hands are their fish-meal! Perhaps you can send her some strongly scented soap. Address it to me if you wish to avoid giving her embarrassment by implying that she needs a vigorous application of pine or lavender. I will pass it to her discreetly.

But she is far from discouraged! I often return later than she does as I have a long walk that is half climb, but I believe she is continuing her studies in her free time before the dinner hour. The study volumes she had in her baggage are all in a neat row, dust-free, and so well taken care of they appear new from the press. She did have a mishap with her correspondence, though, when she confused her ink-jar with her tea-cup. At least I think that is what happened. The stains in her teeth eventually came out.

As for me, I am grateful for your advice and showing as much patience as I can. I did look at that statue whose story you relayed. It is near the Long Bridge out to the dragon delvings and is small, that is to life, but extremely fine work.

I do not have Santeel's advantages in enjoying society. Other than a dead rat that ended up in my bedding the other night, I've hardly touched hands with a friend. My appearance is altered so that you might not recognize me; my hair was cut radically short one night when I returned to the Manor late (I often miss dinner, as the apprentice who supervises me gives me extra cleaning duties at the end of the day) and so tired that I spent the evening in a half-awake daze. I must have been sick of caring for it and cropped it off, because I was shocked the next morning to find it almost entirely gone. The boyish cut does have advantages. It is easy to clean, at least.

The paper runs out. If anything goes seriously amiss with the honorable young Dun Troot, I will make haste to acquaint you with the facts. I am certain they will make an apprentice of her in time.

Faithfully yours in this commission,
Ileth

There were rules to living at the Serpentine, strictly enforced on all the novices by the many layers superior to them. You had to keep yourself and your berth tidy. Everyone had their principal job, their common work, and a few "furthers," as they were called—the Serpentine expected its novices to be educated enough to converse and trade with anyone in the Republic, and ideally be able to supply their dragon outside it. Random fighting would be punished, but formal duels were allowed under the usual rules for those in the Republic's service. You always had to show respect to the Masters of the Serpentine, dragoneers, and those who supervised you. Outside the Serpentine, you were expected to be an exemplary citizen.

But Ileth never had a chance to get outside the Serpentine. She had no money for the few marketing trips and wasn't of an illustrious enough name that she'd be invited to dine in town.

The punishment system was expedience itself. You would be removed from the Serpentine for any crimes that could have you bound over to trial. Repeated rule breaking, such as not cleaning and maintaining your footwear and dress, eating when you were supposed to be on duty, or trading and dealing outside of market days or trips into town, would also get you put outside the walls in whatever rags were handy. One of the previous draft's novices who hadn't yet made apprentice was discharged for buying smuggled wine and tobacco "over the wall," as they styled it.

There was next to nothing in the way of instruction, as Caseen had explained her first day, and if such a thing as a lecture hall existed anywhere in the fortress, she'd not yet seen it. She attended one lecture about crossbows almost by accident; the Duskirk boy ran into her and Galia on the Long Bridge on an afternoon off and they joined him for the session, held in the amphitheater. Ileth found it more interesting than she thought; her mind was so starved for a break in the routine that the lecture enthralled her. The military expert told them about the tactics the Galantines had used with mixed success to take down dragons (dragon scale would often deflect a bolt fired from head on; crossbow men on the ground had to have the nerve to wait until they could get a side shot or, even better, a rear shot at a dragon) and showed them the latest in notched sights.

The Santeel Dun Troots of the world had tutors admitted to give them lessons in the Great Hall or the Visitor's House near the gate. Ileth had no tutors, or lesson books, or allowance to spend. All she had was her old travel boots, her issue of clothing, the knife with an improvised handle, and some socks that kept slouching.

She was also the last of the year's novices to speak to a dragon, and that by accident, as she'd been sitting on the doorstep when the full tour of the Beehive was given to the others and they were introduced to a few of the friendlier dragons who spoke Montangyan well.

Her first meeting came by chance, in the kitchens above the Catch Basin. The kitchens, as might be expected, joined the rest of the Beehive from several directions. Sort of a sub-warren all their own, the kitchens contained storage areas for fresh and preserved food, washing and laundry space, and two big portals up to the dragon levels, all branching off from the cooking galley itself where the fish and other provisions met fire and water. Once the workers in the Catch Basin had loaded a cartload full of fish for the dragons, it was pulled by an ox up the winding path to the galley. From there it would be emptied onto a cast-iron grating that could be maneuvered on a sort of ceiling rail into the central cooking fire. Ordinary cooking utensils, even for masses of humans such as ate at the dining hall, were inadequate for the dragons, so they'd created ways to char or roast entire cartloads of meat.

The cavern kitchens were painted in a durable red, lit by the charcoal fires, and smelled of dragons, a greasy-metallic smell that reminded her of scorched oil. She always returned from the kitchen smelling of it. But after fish guts, she welcomed a strange scent, even if the heat of the cooking fire was intense enough to singe her nostril hair.

The cooks were kindly men. Some were former dragoneers, injured in such a way that they no longer could fly, or no longer wanted to. They told fascinating stories she rarely had time to hear in their entirety, like the time Jeroth's dragon couldn't be roused to wakefulness after a long flight and big meal. Ileth got through Jeroth shouting in its ear, pulling at its lip, and pouring water on its head, and he was just about to lift its head using a shovel as a lever when Gorgantern shouted for her from the Catch Basin to bring "primed water." They often had a crock of cider or water with berries and mint leaves to cool it and shared it with her.

Because the cooks were looking so she couldn't spit in the tankard she filled for him, she idled for another moment watching them work.

She caught a reflection of an eye in the darkness of the passage up to the dragon caves. An angular, horned head appeared. The head was smaller, she thought, than Agrath's had been when she met him in her youth, even allowing for her change in size. It had a long snout like a horse but was feline in the set of its eyes and mouth. It was a unique color—gray as ash, though the skin sometimes rippled with color changes. Its nostrils opened as it sniffed at the worktable. A forked tongue flicked out and gently explored the brown-crackled skin of a turkey fresh from the roasting oven, sitting in a row with five others of varying size.

Something struck Ileth as odd about the dragon and it took her a moment to realize it. It had no scale.

"Wait, it's almost ready," the cook nearest the turkey said.

Ileth knew it must be a youngish dragon to be able to make it through the human passageways to the kitchens. She also knew he was male; female dragons were green-scaled, or rarely, white, and didn't have horns growing out from the bony ridge behind the eyes.

She could smell it, too. The oily odor, strong and fresh off the dragon, hit her nostrils hard enough for her to squeak in shock. Though it was a tiny sound, and she would have sworn no one who was not next to her could hear it, the dragon turned its head and gave her a look. The cook used the distraction to push the turkey out of reach of even the dragon's long neck.

The dragon's gaze reminded her of the evaluative glance a shepherd might give to a stray dog who'd wandered into his flock's pasture. She'd never been looked at this way by an animal before. The dumbly friendly stares of sheep and goats, the eager-to-please or wary looks from dogs, even the contempt of a cat didn't quite match it. Childhood fables of people being mesmerized by a dragon's stare turned from vague legends to certainties—she could see how the power of the creatures overwhelmed you into an instinctive stillness.

"This is Aurue, girl," the cook by the turkey said. "Wings uncased, but hasn't decided on a rider yet."

"Nor do I need to," the dragon said, in heavily accented Montang-yan. His color went briefly darker as he watched the cook work.

"You're just lazy, drake," the cook said, letting the dragon sniff the spoon he'd been using to drip juices over the roast bird. "Only like to work when it suits you."

"Dragon," Aurue said. "I've breathed my fire. I have my wings. I've flown. I am a dragon."

"Oh, of course, of course," the offending cook said. "No harm meant. I've just always known you as a drake since I've been here. It falls off the tongue, like."

"No harm done," Aurue said. He moved and his skin took on the color of the kitchen's red walls, or the black of a great stove near it.

"Your s-skin is . . . beautiful," Ileth said.

The dragon stared at her and sniffed the air about her again. "No, it's a curse. Born without scale. No good in battle."

"Ahh," the senior cook said, "don't talk like that, Aurue. You're quick as thinking in the air, being light. Faster even than Vithleen. Speed's got a power all its own."

"Still not faster than a crossbow bolt," the dragon said. "They'll never give me anything important. I was warned off coming here and mixing with humans. Said I'd end up dead or bored. So far I'm just bored."

Ileth felt a flash of sympathy. So dragons had their own doubters too.

"Then why'd you bother?" the cook who'd called him a drake asked.

"I like being around humans," Aurue said. "There's always something underfoot. And I don't care for hunting up my own food." He flicked his tongue out to taste the turkey again.

Ileth, keenly attentive to any and all dragonly matters since the age of seven, spent the rest of her day and some time before bed wondering at that. The dragon hadn't been born here but had come before uncasing his wings. Where had he been bred, and why a long, inconvenient, and potentially dangerous journey before his wings emerged?

The next night Ileth met someone even more important than the dragon Aurue. The Manor accepted, with gratitude and respect, a visit and address from Roguss Heem Deklamp, Charge of the Serpentine, First Master and Dragoneer Laudii. He was a man who would have no doubt had other titles in one of the aristocratic lands, but those were ample for the Republic.

He didn't look anything like a dragoneer from romantic fancies, except perhaps in uniform, which was simple and immaculate. A small gold pauldron, hardly more than a curved nameplate, hung from the shoulder of his gray tunic, which had a high black-and-gold collar and matching belt.

As a man he was short and potbellied, with droopy, staring eyes. While a few of the other novices seemed disappointed that he wasn't much larger than a teenage girl, Ileth's heart warmed to him immediately. Perhaps size and reach and fencing ability and your aim with a crossbow wasn't all there was to being a dragoneer.

There was, however, something vaguely alien about him. His gaze roved across his audience as the Matron introduced him, sad eyes watery and staring, and then when he fixed on something his face would turn quick on his neck like an owl's and stare for a moment, before the eyes began their survey again. There were stories of dragoneers drinking dragon blood and being changed by the drafts, and after watching him hunt about his audience and room in that raptor fashion, she was willing to believe it.

After the Matron (all bobbing and giggling in a coquettish manner that was even more unsettling than the Charge's stare) finished emphasizing how fortunate they were in his visit, he stepped to the center of the little hall and spoke in a deep, ringing voice that seemed to come directly from that potbelly.

"Thank you for having me, novices and apprentices of the Manor. It always lifts my spirits, whatever news comes in from outside the walls, good or bad, to see our latest novices. It restores my belief in the durability of our Republic when I see such healthy, spirited young people. I like to come and speak to our newcomers after they've had a chance to settle in and the new jobs are no longer quite so new, and you are used to the routine. You're probably grappling with your first disappointments and difficulties here. Well, that's the ideal time to meet you, in the hope that now that you've found your feet, your heads will be ready to absorb what I was told when I came into the Serpentine . . ."

He did not speak long, or perhaps he did, but it didn't seem like it. Afterward, Ileth could remember only a specific line or two, one being "your job is not your duty." He went on some time about duty. To him, your job was just your task, a way to earn your bread and fish. Duty was something you owed both to the past and to the future. In his tradition, the most important duty the novices had was to learn all they could about dragons and how the different parts of the Serpentine kept them healthy, happy, and ready to support and defend the Republic and its citizens. How the Serpentine's dragoneers and dragons worked as a team, or even better than a team, as a single organism capable of achieving feats neither humans nor dragons alone could accomplish. If they absorbed some idea of what it took to keep the dragons and dragoneers aloft, and took pride in their being part of the Serpentine, however humble, and agreed, one day, to pass on what they learned to a generation not yet born, well, he would know that he'd done his duty to the dragons and dragoneers of the past and the Republic's future.

Ileth found her eyes full of happy tears. She'd never been so proud to be in a room. She glanced around. Santeel, bright and shining as always, took in every word with a trembling lip as well. Quith looked like she was studying the collar of his uniform.

By the end of his talk, if he'd asked his novices to charge a Galantine pike-and-crossbow line with nothing but fireplace pokers and rotten apples, they would have gone in shrieking the Republic's barking battle cry. Ileth didn't know what to make of it. In a less enlightened time, she supposed she would have thought him some kind of sorcerer who put girls under his spell. But she was full of resolve to learn all she could about the Serpentine, up and down, Bayside to Harborside, until every face and stair step and task was known to her.

After his speech, the Charge asked for music. Galia and a few of the other apprentices, less overawed than the others but equally proud to be in his company, started things off with a song and a tune played on a smallhorn and bow-loom.

The Charge delighted in it from his seat in the front row, lightly tapping his palms against his thighs in time to the music and smiling. The apprentices' example gave the others courage to step forward, and they heard songs from all over the Vales. From time to time he'd lean over and speak to the Matron, asking a question or making a comment. The Matron usually spoke back. Ileth caught a few names and hometowns or districts in the Matron's answers. It seemed music was a way for their Charge to get a peek at the personality behind the face.

The songs Ileth knew, sung by the Captain and his gang in the Lodge, would not have been well received by the audience at the Manor, at least under the Matron's eye. Ileth and Quith did find the heart to get up and dance in couple when an informal band struck up, along with some other paired girls. Even the Matron briefly joined in for a reel. In the end, the Charge gave another brief speech, thanking them all for a delightful evening before bowing his way out, his swivel-mounted head turning this way and that.

"That is what I call a man," Quith said to her after the door shut, panting from the dancing and the heat that had built up in the hall. "I wonder if he's married?"

Ileth thought it strange that her status-and-connection collector friend didn't have a complete biography of their Charge.

"Good luck with that, Quith," Galia said, chuckling as she passed. "He had an unfortunate landing with a wounded dragon years ago. Very unfortunate."

The novices went to bed that night without a single argument over a rinsing bowl or arrangement of socks and washcloths on the drying line. Perhaps Charge Heem Deklamp was a sorcerer after all.

Newly inspired by Charge Deklamp's speech, Ileth tried, tried her best, to see Gorgantern with some amount of sympathy and learn from him. See the good side, perhaps hidden because he kept others from getting too close, because they might rise to full dragoneer while he remained in the Catch Basin. He'd hardly been on dragonback at all, and rumor had it the dragons didn't much like him, perhaps because of his size. He'd failed a key test called a "survival," whatever that was, so an apprentice he remained and would be until they found some excuse to be rid of him. He was an excellent worker, always taking on extra duties and tasks, helping with the barge and fishing boat lines, keeping up the pace at unloading, and made sure that the barge-men didn't wander off into the caverns in search of scales. He volunteered for dirty jobs Bragg didn't care for and was educated enough to keep and help with the tally sheets while Bragg did work more to his liking, like dickering with the barge captains over the price of their fish and celebrating a particularly rich catch by passing around a bottle.

He also frequently stayed late at the Catch Basin. Certain fishermen seemed to like him, and he liked to go on their boats and help with minor repairs or just swap stories. Ileth suspected he might have a souvenir or two from the dragons concealed in his clothing—she'd heard whispers from the girls at night that there was good coin in even a few dragon scales or better yet a claw—but Gorgantern was clever enough to do that sort of thing, if it was happening, out of sight of anyone else.

She also worked late, thinking the harder she worked in the Catch Basin the sooner she'd get away from gutting fish with her wretched old knife with its improvised twine handle. She missed dinner often enough that she sometimes snuck upstairs and begged a little dragon feed from the cooks. It wasn't cooked fancy at all—most of the dragons wanted nothing but salt on their meat or fish—but it was plentiful if you didn't mind it frequently being underdone. The dragons liked their meals juicy. When she finally returned and started up the long outer stair, Gorgantern sometimes walked her up and "steadied" her on the trickier steps in a pawing manner that reminded her of the Captain's drunken friends. She always said, "Thanks, I'll manage," and hurried away up the long flights until she was gasping for air and he was far behind.

Gorgantern held his own lessons at night after dinner. He'd picked up a good deal of seamanship and taught his novices about knots, lines, how to splice together a break, and the best way to store ropes and work a block and tackle to advantage. He could light a fire in a blizzard.

Ileth put up with him as best as she could and begged off his seamanship tutorials. She knew her knots from working with both small watercraft and livestock. She would rather hear dragon stories from the cooks or hurry up to the human side of the bridge where there were geography and mapmaking lessons for the students who'd shown aptitude for it as furthers. She crept in and joined one of those circles to better acquaint herself with those subjects and the use of the tools for drawing maps to proper scale. Most of the novices were from moneyed families who had been educated with something better than a shelf of old reference books in Galantine, books of humorous letters that the Captain found amusing on the rare occasions he read, and Hypatian philosophies that had, at one time or another, held up an uneven table.

Gorgantern used her absence to complain to Master Caseen that she wasn't attending to her studies. They called her and Gorgantern into the dining hall as the clearers were washing down tables, and, bathed in stained light from his windows and surrounded by trophies collected from battlefields and bits of dragoneer equipment, Caseen heard them both out. She demonstrated her knowledge of knots and quoted the weight of dry and wet line of the two most common types the Serpentine used. She explained instead that she'd been learning geography, map reading, and the art of sketching landscapes, which Galia was teaching as she was so good at it and allowed the odiferous novice to sit in, provided she kept out of her air. Caseen was satisfied and suggested that perhaps she should take over Gorgantern's tutorship, before he released her of any further need to study lines and splicing. Gorgantern's expression remained calm on the outside, but his inner boil erupted on his face with a choleric red. She heard him huffing out his anger behind her as they passed out of the dining hall.

"Girls! Always finding a reason to beg off," Gorgantern said.

Ileth had to bite her tongue to keep from replying with an insult she'd picked up from one of the Captain's friends.

From that day on Gorgantern "rode her" as Joai had predicted, with an aim of getting her kicked out of the Serpentine. He ordered her to remove the wrist bracer she wore (a gift from the cooks above—they wore them to help shift the huge dragon-meal-sized frying pans they worked with) for long hours of knife work because it was not part of a novice's uniform for Catch Basin work. He made her ask his permission to attend to her bodily needs (generally you just slipped away; it was obvious to everyone that you were headed to the little outhouse built out over the lake, and he liked to recite as loudly as he could for all to hear the number of trips to the privy she'd made that day), and if she did not keep her gutting-board spotlessly clean he made her run all the way up the outer stairs and back down again with a fish eyeball in her mouth. The sooner she came back, the sooner she could spit it out.

One thing he couldn't do was beat her. He could (and did) beat the male novices, provided those in the Catch Basin gathered to hear the offense and witness the punishment. The Matron could discipline her charges physically—she struck one novice across the palm with a dried reed for sneaking out after the door was locked—but ignored the note Gorgantern had scrawled demanding that she be beaten for disrespect (he'd said that with her close-cropped hair she could be mistaken for a boy, and she replied that with his fleshy breasts and belly he could be mistaken for a mother in expectation of her third child). She relayed the entire story to the Matron. One of the Matron's oddities was that what her girls did or said to her within the Manor and its grounds was suspect and assumed to be an evasion even if it wasn't an outright lie— if you told her you'd cleaned the windows in the second-floor bed-rooms, she'd check each one—but whatever happened outside the Manor door, her "young charges" (as she styled them) became unimpeachable in word and stainless in deed. The Matron didn't even give Ileth her usual sharp look when she recounted the conversation; she just folded up Gorgantern's note, said, "We can't have disrespect shown to an apprentice," and made her walk back and forth across the dining room with a platter balanced on her head (along the shorter wall of the rectangular room beneath where *LET YOUR PRESENCE IMPROVE ANY ROOM* was painted in neat block letters) three times.

On the Matron's discipline scale, this was the equivalent of most girls her age getting a sharp look from their mother. The Matron made you scrub out the privy by hand if you left a sock on the floor.

The Matron had her return the note with *Ileth was punished according to her fault* written on the back. When Gorgantern demanded to see the marks left by the beating he'd demanded, Ileth told him she'd plunge her arm into a hornet's nest before she'd let him see her backside.

Things came to a head during the next week-over pass day at the Serpentine. The summer lingered on into fall, waves of heat alternating with storms, making their rooms stuffy even in the mountains next to the chilly lake. Food went bad quickly, and all the Serpentine sweated, chafed, and quarreled.

On pass day no real work was done, save for a switch where the kitchen staff had a day off from preparing meals and other groups took their place at the stoves and ovens in rotation. All but the novices and a few members left to supervise them were allowed to leave the Serpentine if they wished, to go down to the lakeshore to bathe and refresh themselves, walk in the cool of the nearby wood (called the Scalewood because every year they held a dragon-scale hunt for the children of Vyenn at the conclusion of a lesson year), or visit the town.

Gorgantern, showing his usual enthusiasm, had volunteered his team for kitchen work that pass day. They worked in the Great Hall, the newest and finest building in the Serpentine. The hall was partially circular in a style Santeel Dun Troot described as an "auditorium." It was built around one of the great natural rocks of the landscape, which had been shaped and used as a kind of great tent pole for the dragon-scale roof (outside the Serpentine, a dragon-scale roof would be an expense only the richest of the great Names could afford). Captured flags and banners decorated the columns and the rafters above. All around the walls stood trophy weapons and armor, and glass cases containing tattered old pieces of uniform, art, and equipment, colorful relics of the Serpentine's history.

The diners ate either seated at long tables or at the counters at the walls if they wished solitude at their meal. A pulpit was carved into the central rock so that someone might observe or address, if necessary, most of the room, but the Great Hall had never been filled to capacity

in Ileth's time there (though she missed most of her dinner meals because of extra tasks in the Catch Basin and the long trip to the up end
of the Serpentine). Everyone was served across a broad, waist-high
counter in a wall that divided kitchen from dining hall, one gap for
food, a second for pitchers of water—or beer and wine, on feast days
and celebrations. The wall also held a wide double door leading into the
kitchens that stood open at mealtimes, allowing plenty of room for
wheeled pushcarts that could bring out clean crockery and utensils and
return them for the washing-up staff.

To Ileth, it was a marvel of efficiency, a well-ventilated kitchen as
up-to-date as it could possibly be. Even the charcoal stoves were easy
to rake out. You could feed hundreds with not much more effort than
it took to feed twenty at the Captain's Lodge.

It being Gorgantern's team's job that pass day to prepare food, Ileth
was working in the kitchens at the soup, an easy enough dish she'd
made, following instructions to fill a vessel that could only be described
as a cauldron. Someone else had started it; all she had to do was keep
the broth up and the fire coaled and stir now and then when she wasn't
serving the soup. She ladled it out into wooden bowls passed to her by
Gorgantern, who shuttled them to the food counter as the diners asked
for it.

Gorgantern's work did not engage him, so he livened up the steaming kitchen with what passed for jokes. "Another s-s-s-soup," he called,
mimicking her stammer. "A-A-Another s-s-soup."

She'd been stirring the cauldron with a wooden stirrer the size of a
small oar. The steam tingled on her face and arms, and she kept
changing hands so the arm with the ladle would not be cooked along
with the soup.

Santeel Dun Troot stood a few steps away at the water pump and
drink station. Ileth thought it strange that she'd volunteered to work
the kitchens on such a hot day. The Master of Stores had purchased
barrels of cider from the northwest as the fall apple crop had come in
and been pressed. Santeel had nothing to do but fill pitcher after pitcher
of the cool cider and hand it to an apprentice named Rapoto who was
shuttling drinks to the tables. He was exceptionally handsome. He

took good care of his hair and brushed it out in the style of a Name, but she'd never spoken a word to him, just overheard the Dun Troot girl brag him up as a favorite of hers to her coterie.

"Have you tested the cider, Rapoto?" Santeel asked, for the third time since they'd started serving. This time she added: "You're from Jotun—I expect an expert opinion."

Rapoto just gave her a sour smile and took another pitcher through the window.

Ah, he was from Jotun. It was to the west of the Freesand, on the other side of the mountains from her chilly bay. And it was famous for its apple orchards and honey. Pigs, too. *Fat as a Jotun pig* was an expression. Though it was considered an insult to say it of anyone but babies and livestock.

Santeel watched Rapoto through the window, then sniffed another pitcher of cider as though suspicious. She glanced over at Ileth, who just shrugged. Maybe he didn't like cider.

"C'mon, you titted calamity, your arm's as slow as your tongue today," Gorgantern said.

She left the stir-stick sitting in the cauldron and retrieved the ladle. She filled it brimfull and slopped it into the bowl with such force that it cascaded back out of the bowl to land hot on Gorgantern's forearm.

"Stones!" he bellowed, dropping the bowl. It struck the tiled floor and spun on its rim like a dancer in a hooped skirt. "You northern sow! I'm burned!"

What came next happened so fast she had to mentally sort it out later; it was just a series of shocks as it happened. Before she knew it he'd slapped her, cuffing her hard enough on the ear to bring a sharp bolt of stabbing pain and fill her ear with a ringing sound. The pain, some of the worst she'd ever experienced in her life up to then, left her insensible, but later she worked out that the force of the slap knocked her off her feet and against the cauldron. She remembered that the sweat on her arm—she'd rolled up the sleeves on her too-large man's shirt so that they wouldn't dip in the soup—hissed on contact and the smell of burning hair filled her nostrils.

She bounced off the cauldron in a move that was half ricochet and half fall. She was on the floor when she could think again, feeling weirdly embarrassed for some reason. She rose to her feet, off balance and mazy with pain.

Ileth, who'd been aiming to have most of the soup remain in the bowl and just splatter him, tried to form words but her tongue found itself more reluctant than ever. She held up her arm to guard her face, using the long wooden spoon like a swordsman parrying a swing.

He shouted something that might have been "Oh, will you" and grabbed the spoon and wrenched her sideways. Arms that felt like heavy chains bent her over the steaming soup.

"Say you're sorry!" Gorgantern shouted into her ringing ears. "I'll dunk you, by the gods I will!"

The steam rising out of the soup burned. She felt the heat of the cauldron through her apron and smock. The heat on her face turned to agony. Words weren't coming and wouldn't have been an apology if they had. She shut her eyes tight, anticipating a burning plunge into the soup.

He forced her head lower. Her forehead and nose touched the hot liquid and she yelped.

"Off her, oaf!" Santeel Dun Troot shouted from a faraway place. She heard a curse.

The pressure released.

Ileth reeled away from the steam, blinked her eyes open, and saw the comic-opera vision of Santeel striking Gorgantern about the back with a long wooden candle lighter and extinguisher. And by strike, the effort Santeel put into it would have done a Stavanzer lumber-cutter proud. She struck him, then whirled the long wooden stick in a great circle, putting her back and waist muscles into it like a man splitting cordwood, briging it down on Gorgantern's fleshy torso.

Gorgantern managed to get his arms on her and threw her like a bag of oats against the wall. She bounced hard and fell, but for a rich girl she was made of some quality steel. Santeel rolled, her usually pallid complexion flushed as she looked up at him, and her lips were pulled back, baring her teeth like a wolf.

Ileth, her mind throwing off sparks like lightning, each thought bright and clear in the heat of the confrontation, thought that while she had never wished to call much of anyone sister, at that moment, with her face burning from the heat of the cauldron, she'd have been happy to have Santeel as hers.

Shouts from some of the other novices working the kitchen registered in Ileth's ringing head. Footsteps and a sudden presence of others around turned the struggle into a brawl. She found herself free, away from the heat, able to breathe, picking up the dropped candle-snuffer and holding it like a spear aimed at Gorgantern's stomach.

A swirl of novices had formed around them; she saw two other boys, each holding one of Gorgantern's arms. Someone else wiped at her face with a rag. She saw blood dabbed from her ear.

"Witches, the both of you," Gorgantern said. "I get burned and you use me being hurt to gang up on me! Conspirators! You combined against me!"

"You-You-You swipe!" Ileth managed to say. "I'd have . . . apologized if you had-hadn-hadn't hit m-me."

"Why don't you just call it even," Rapoto said, a hand soft on Gorgantern's arm, not that he could have restrained the lumbering apprentice any more than a lace kerchief. He must have come into the kitchens during the ruckus.

Gorgantern ignored him. "Worthless slut," he said, looking at Ileth. "Who did you spread it for to get in here? A dragoneer let you in on your back?" Ileth threw herself in his direction, screaming every profanity she'd ever learned on the fishing docks in the Freesand. For once she didn't stutter. Santeel helped another novice hold her back.

"If you're going to give us entertainments with our meal, you should perform where we can see you," someone said through the food window. All those not physically in the kitchen already seemed to be crowding between the serving counters and the kitchen wall.

"What? A fight? Is this going to turn into a duel?" another voice said from the crowd at the drinks window.

Ileth's brain latched onto the word. "I'll have y-you . . . outside," she said. But it fell flat; the challenge must not have been in use in that part of the Vales.

"Have me," Gorgantern chuckled. "You can't have a conversation."

"You've stru-struck m-m-me and insulted m-me," Ileth said, slowly and carefully, perhaps overloudly because she needed to speak above her own pounding heart. She kept her hands clasped so Gorgantern wouldn't see them shaking. "I have the right to ask for a fair duel in return."

The word *duel* spread through the dining room like dragonfire.

"No. That's not how it works at all, girl," Rapoto said. "You don't fight. I heard the insult. I'll stand against him for you."

"What? You don't even know her!" Santeel said.

"He fought with you too, Santeel. I'll stand up for both of you."

"I don't—I don't need anyone to s-s-stand up for me," Ileth said. "I'll fight—I'll duel him myself."

"She *is* unbalanced," Santeel said. "She received a blow to the head. She's not in her senses. Rapoto—stand up for me—us, I mean! Fishbr—Ileth and me, that is."

Ileth shook her head at Rapoto. Her face still burned from the heat of the soup. "I know wh-what I'm-I'm—doing. I'm quite c-c-clear of mind."

Gorgantern nodded. "Huh. She's clever. Thinks she can humiliate me by making me apologize because I won't duel a girl. Your little plan has no bottom, and it'll sink you. Suppose I accept."

"Pl-Please do," Ileth said.

"Women don't fight duels," Santeel said, stepping between her and Gorgantern and unleashing a glare hot enough to melt snow into Ileth's face. She jerked her delicate chin at Rapoto.

"Oh, they do," a new person put in. It was Galia, the apprentice who helped oversee the female novices. She stepped forward, the heels of her tall riding boots making distinctive clicks on the floor as she walked. The buckles on her riding-coat added their own chimelike notes. She must have been spending the day among the dragons. She glanced from Ileth to Gorgantern and back again. "Even against men. Garella did—years ago. She told me the story."

"I'd still rather you let me stand up against him," Rapoto said.

Galia cocked her head. "You, Rapoto? I didn't know you could fight."

"Don't know the first thing about it, Galia. But if I'm going to have one, I'd like it to be against someone who knocks down a girl half his age and a third his size."

"I'll fight fancy-boy and the girl both," Gorgantern laughed.

"Stop . . . s-stop swanning into this," Ileth said. "It's my challenge, it's my fight."

Gorgantern sensed the crowd's feeling. "You want an apology, mushmouth? So be it. I'm sorry you are such a useless whelk that you spilled soup on me and burned my hand."

"Everyone dislikes you, you know," Santeel said to him, though as far as Ileth knew today was the first time they'd spoken. "You could do the right thing and beg her forgiveness. I do mean *beg*."

"He made her bleed from the ear," Rapoto said. "In the law that could be maiming. An apology isn't enough. We should bring this to a jury."

The crowd, excited by the prospect of a duel, loosed a few groans at the idea of the drama sputtering out into questions and answers in front of a jury.

"I've a mind to give her that duel," Gorgantern said.

"I d-d-doubt that," Ileth said.

Gorgantern scowled. "You *d-d-d*-don't think I could be master of the Catch Basin if I didn't have brains? That takes hard work and a mind both. You have your duel. Since you demanded it, I'll set conditions. Uh—dueling swords."

"Dueling swords?" Galia growled.

"Dull. Rounds on tip," Gorgantern temporized, as though he was beginning to have doubts.

"I'm n-not afraid of a . . . of a—of a point," Ileth said, slowly and carefully. "Let's have-have points. The sight of blood doesn't bother me."

"Enough," Rapoto said. "You shouldn't set conditions with blood still wet. If they're going to do this, it needs to be carried out properly so there's no question of law. Let's give it until tomorrow, to let tempers cool. Who will be intermediary for, uhh . . . ?"

"Ileth," Ileth said.

"I will," Santeel volunteered.

Rapoto put his finger on his chin. "As you were part of—"

"All the more reason to speak for her," Santeel said.

"You'll have to take her place at the Catch Basin until the duel, you know," Galia said.

Santeel grimaced. "If I must."

"And for Gorgantern of the Catch Basin?" Galia said. Gorgantern crossed his meaty arms and frowned at the women. "Nobody? Very well, I'll be intermediary for you, old lad."

The watchers at the windows had a job of it passing the news about sides back and forth to the crowd behind.

"Too many women involved in this," Gorgantern said. "Seems unfair to me. You're ganging up."

"Oh, for wind's sake," Rapoto said. "This is turning farce. Let's finish our meal. Ileth, you should go see if Joai is about and have a dressing for your ear. Gorgantern, you ladle the soup for me. Watch that you don't douse me, or you'll be fighting a second duel if you're still alive after this one."

By tradition of the Serpentine the parties were not bound by Rapoto's need to meet again, in daylight, after one full day had passed in order to try to reconcile. The duel would go forward as challenged and accepted, with the only questions left those of time, place, and weapons.

Also by tradition of the Serpentine, the place had to be outside its walls and out of view of the gate.

The long-established rules, which Galia explained to Ileth the evening of the brawl in the kitchen, revolved around ending the contest. The duel would last until one party accepted defeat or shed enough blood to become unsteady of arms, legs, hands, or balance; a physiker intervened in the name of humanity; a duelist's weapon was dropped, lost, or thrown away; the seconds both agreed that one combatant had suffered a defeat; or the insensibility or death of one party. The Serpentine had a further tradition outside formal dueling: both parties could, at any time after the first exchange of blows or shots (in the case of pistoled crossbows), agree to shake hands and call the matter settled. In any case the aggrieved party would have honor restored and the challenged party would consider the matter settled.

The final twist the Serpentine put on dueling was that seconds were not to become involved in the combat in any way. If, for whatever reason, the aggrieved or challenged party could not participate in the duel, it defaulted to the credit of the duelist who did enter the dueling ground. Seconds attended only to see to their party's interests and could intervene only in the case of foul play.

Back at the Manor, Ileth bore up under pitying stares of the sort she would have had if she were in her eighth or ninth month of carrying a socially unrecognized child. Santeel Dun Troot's alternating bouts of contempt and indifference had curdled into something like hostility, but she still displayed the same partisanship as the Matron when it came to affairs outside the Manor. They might be contemptuous of each other within, but in the rest of the Serpentine they stood as sisters.

Gorgantern and Ileth agreed, through their respective intermediaries, to duel on the beach Bayside. Ileth's demand that they use pointed dueling swords—which she was entirely a stranger to; she'd never even held one—was settled. When she was a child still able to run around in summer shirtless she'd played with an old curved naval falchion the Captain had hung up on the wall of the Lodge and held mock-scabbard duels with some of the weathered sailor-folk calling for dinner, but the only fighting advice she'd ever had from the Captain with swordplay was *Yell so's they hear you in hell and swing short*. He also told her that getting wounded wasn't so bad in the moment. You were too excited from the fight to feel pain; you just felt the impact, more like getting unexpectedly shoved.

Which might be useful advice now, if she'd asked him what *swing short* meant.

"Why do you want a real edge?" Galia asked when they met in the garden behind the Manor where Ileth had been put to work gathering summer herbs for drying to keep her out of the Catch Basin. "You could die on those points. This isn't mock and muck, you know," she said, using slang for the Serpentine's weapons drills.

"I have a . . . chance of drawing blood with a p-point," Ileth said. She went on to explain that with blunt weapons it was a contest of strength. She doubted she could either wear him down or do him more than enough damage to enrage him with a blunt weapon, whereas more likely than not he'd just hammer her into the ground. With a point she might score a lucky hit and satisfy the conditions of the duel.

They chatted for a bit about the interest in the duel across the Serpentine.

"How is my opponent handling it all?" Ileth asked.

"He hardly spoke in the Catch Basin. Santeel is, well, you know Santeel. She can make anyone feel small, even that mountain of a man. Some of the fishermen jibed him for fighting with a girl half his age. I get the sense that the jokes were much cruder before I walked in. Gorgantern blushed. I reminded him that even a dueling sword could be deadly and told him how quickly he'd bleed to death if one of the big vessels in his leg was pierced. *Dead before a dropped piece of paper would waft to the ground*, I put it. That put a thoughtful look on his face, for a change."

"Can I ask you another question?"

"Certainly," Galia said. Her self-assurance was like a balm.

"What does *swing short* mean?"

"In swordplay? Hmmm. I don't think I've heard that exact expression. I believe it means keep the blade in front of you. You don't want to hack away with all your might, or you wind up off balance, gives your opponent an opportunity to strike. Do you want a quick practice? We could use rug-beaters; they're about the right size."

"Please," Ileth said.

Galia went to find two appropriate instruments and they were soon knocking them against each other. Neither laughed when a blow was struck or one of them tripped.

The morning of the duel, the Master of Novices called her in for an interview. She'd pretended to sleep until the Serpentine's cocks were crowing at each other but fell asleep just at dawn. She had to be shaken awake as it was her morning to help in the Manor kitchen for breakfast. The Manor would keep its routines, duel or no.

"Today's the day," the apprentice charged with supervising the breakfasts said. As if she'd forgotten, blinking out the few minutes of sleep she'd managed. What a morning to wake up exhausted. "The, uhh, fall of Gorgantern. We hope."

Caseen's note summoning her arrived in time to save her from the washing-up. It did specify *at once* in the summons.

The Serpentine lay under a blanket of fog and there was a fall chill in the air. The hot summer weather had vanished quickly, as though fall wanted to crowd in and see the duel. It suited her mood as she walked. She might be dead and cold tonight. What would they do with her body? She hadn't seen a funeral at the Serpentine.

The Masters' Hall was one of the newer constructions on the Serpentine. It had been built next to an old family graveyard, shaded by some now-impressive oaks growing in filled soil. An old archway was all that was left of a wall that had surrounded the burying-ground. The archway now projected out of the front wall over the threshold of the Masters' Hall. It was built in the new Republic style, gray stone from top to bottom, a colonnade of deep arches on the first floor, triple windows above that, and then double windows on the top floor capped by a fan design. It suggested order, hierarchy, simplicity, and a good deal of labor for whoever had to keep all those windows clean.

She entered, gave her name to the page, and went up the squared-off stairs that branched out after the first grand landing to the first floor.

The place smelled like lamps and oil soap. The hallway was wide, with a black-and-white checkerboard pattern tipped so you walked down rows of diamonds.

Master Caseen's door was open. He was sorting papers on a side table beneath a shelf of books. She entered, and he invited her to sit. He did not sit but put down his papers and paced back and forth a few times, scratching his elbows in thought. She suspected that meant trouble.

He finally settled down into the red leather button-back chair at his desk.

"I don't care for dueling," he said, frowning at her as best as he could manage with the scarring. A wandering calico cat entered, glanced at the two of them, thought better of it, and returned to the hall. "Duels set the whole Serpentine at the bubble until the matter is decided. The whole Academy's talking instead of attending to their duties."

She felt there was more, so she waited to reply.

"It's a throwback to the Counties and the Law of Kings and affairs of state being tangled up in affairs of blood and all the petty brutalities that people fled to the Vales to escape, even if it's dressed up in romantic stage costume."

"Order me to m-m-miss the duel, then."

"Remember that line in your oath where you are expected to risk all but your honor in carrying out orders? It's just as well that line is in the oath; it keeps a tyrant from using the dragoneers for his own ends rather than the Republic's. It also makes me powerless in an affair of honor."

"Then why am I here?"

"You are a—young woman. No one expects you to fight a duel. Even more, no one expects you to fight a duel against a man, and even more than that, no one would think the worse of you for refusing to fight a man the size of Gorgantern. He's twice your age and more still in physical power. You had a blow to your head. You were disoriented, spoke in pain and anger."

She remained silent.

"I'll compliment you by being completely frank. You're obviously not from a part of society where blood spilled requires more blood to be spilled in return."

"Where's that republican ideal, sir? Law of Kings when it suits you?"

"There's ideals and there's not wanting to lose a promising young woman. Gorgantern has a mean streak. I was still a dragoneer when he was oathed in. I saw him in Vyenn as a youth. I don't think he's had much success with women. You're old enough to at least know in an academic manner some cruel facts. Natural desires that can't flow through the channels dug for them by society will build up. Dreadful things can happen when the blockage gives way. He won't be thrusting his sword at you, I fear, as he'll be hacking at his own private torments and failures with women. He has had some training with a sword and I know he has been the victor in fistfights."

"How do you know I've none?"

"Not many fourteen-year-old ladies have dueling experience. But if swordplay was part of your upbringing in your lodge, I'll wait out this day in hope that you do know what you're doing," Caseen said, pushing back some errant hair on his irregular scalp. "Should you embarrass him, it could solve a problem or two. I know the Master of Apprentices would like to see him gone. Most who approach anywhere near his age leave to pursue another line, once they realize they're not destined for anything much here. The Master of Apprentices is something of a believer in destiny, as you'll one day learn, I hope. But Gorgantern is like a limpet down in the Catch Basin. He clings and there's not much we can do about it. He's a good worker and obeys the rules. Still, I hope you teach him a lesson."

Ha! Well, if she was going to go down, she'd go down defiant. "We'll know in a few hours, won't we?"

Caseen stood and walked around behind her, leaning in to breathe in her ear: "If you're trying to make your name dueling, there are better places than here. Nobody wants a duelist on their staff issuing a challenge at the first slight. And every duel is a chance. Even the best of them slip up." He paused. She remained immobile, hands clasped in her lap to keep them from giving away her utter lack of nerve. "So be it. I've tried to reason with you. We're bound to lose at least one of you, and the Serpentine will be worse off for the whole mess stirring things up and setting us against each other. I don't like factions within these walls. If you're nothing but pride and brag, most likely you'll be cold and dead tonight. Apparently you aren't as smart as I gave you credit for, Ileth."

That stung deep, intended or no.

He turned away, pushing an errant book in his library back into alignment. "Think about that, Ileth. You can back out. Even at the last moment. It's just not worth the risk, and it will be to your credit with me if you show that kind of sense."

The rest of the morning rushed by, as quickly as the night had dragged. They were to fight at noon.

She'd been wondering about funerals at the Serpentine and she had an answer, of sorts. The parade down to the beach felt funereal. Santeel walked just ahead of her, wearing an outfit more appropriate for horse riding, with her hair bound up tight under a reinforced hat that could do as a helmet in a pinch. Did she expect a brawl to break out? Perhaps she didn't know seconds were never expected to fight by Serpentine tradition.

Five of the dragoneers walked behind them, including the one, Hael Dun Huss, who had spoken kindly to her after the oath. They were probably curious to attend the event that had generated so much chatter. He walked with two other dragoneers near his age that she'd glimpsed him speaking to here and there, perhaps friends from his younger days as an apprentice. Joai and some other officials from the Serpentine brought up the rear of the column.

Down on the beach the fog thinned, though it obscured the Serpentine, to the disappointment of those who'd planned to pass around telescopes so they could watch from the wall. On the shore of the bay, sheltered by rocky arms, there was little wind. The fog muffled sounds. When Gorgantern arrived, shuffling and looking about as if expecting an ambush, he had only Galia with him. Out in the open he didn't look quite as vast as he did in the confines of the Catch Basin.

Not long now. But she still worried she'd vomit up her breakfast. She'd forced herself to eat as if it were just another morning with nothing more ahead of it but a day of salting and hanging and smoking fish.

Ileth ignored the others working out the ground for the duel. Out in the bay there were river otters running up and down stones sticking out of the water like tiny islands. One of them was bashing a shelled creature against an edge.

Joai set down a basket with wound-vinegar and dressings. She sidled up to Ileth. "I have some brandy. You want a sip to steady your nerves?"

She shook her head. She might be dead in five minutes, and those otters would still be playing. The one with the mussel, or whatever it was, managed to get it open and had its meal. She'd be one of millions of deaths that day.

The Serpentine's physiker-in-charge, an older man with what was left of his white hair swept back and cut at exactly shoulder length, supervised Joai. *He must put something in his hair to keep it so neatly arrayed,* Ileth decided, wondering at the strange things her brain was forcing her to attend to. The physiker stood by, close to the demarked zone (they used two old, holed, and overturned boats as the north-south borders, the shoreline as the east, and the seconds standing as two points on an imaginary line to the west, making something that approximated the traditional dueling alley. The physiker's own apprentice carried the dueling swords, and together they checked and cleaned the blades before handing them to the seconds. It was terribly close now.

"*Please* let me stand for you," Rapoto said, appearing next to her out of nowhere and startling her with his words. She hadn't even noticed him in the procession. He was dressed to fight. Loose trousers, tight leather shoes, no coat, just a loose shirt allowing plenty of freedom of movement. Perhaps he'd nipped out early and waited by himself at the dueling ground. She wondered how he had worked it, as the Masters had piled extra duties on everyone, from the new novices to the wingmen, to forestall the entire Serpentine decamping to view the duel.

"No," she said.

And now Santeel stood before her, holding the sword point down. "You have to step to your side, now," she told Ileth, casting an apologetic look at Rapoto.

The dragoneers performed some sort of ritual among themselves involving putting their hands inside their clothing between bracing vests and outer coat, then opening their coats in a flash to reveal some kind of countersign. One, a sandy fellow with staring eyes that seemed to protrude so the whites showed, accepted the approval of his fellows and stepped to the edge of the dueling ground. He wore a greenish-gold short cape with a rich Hypatian-curtain-style fringe, and instead of a sword on his belt, he carried a brass-headed walking stick with a snarling, ogrelike face engraved on it.

"Gorgantern, you great toad, you got me, lucky fellow," he said, planting his walking stick and leaning on it insouciantly. He turned to Ileth. "Have we met? I ride Etiennersea. When she lets me. I don't think we've been introduced."

"Dath Amrits," Galia said from her position next to Gorgantern, "this is Ileth of the Freesand."

Amrits gave a short bow. "Now that the introductions are out of the way—ahem! I've been selected to supervise the duel, with our good physiker Threadneedle."

The physiker sighed. "Amrits, this is no occasion—"

"—for you to open your mouth until the blood starts flying," Amrits finished. "As if we dragoneers need a physiker around to tell us someone's dead. Have cheer, now. It'll be over for one of you soon. But don't take it too hard; the other will have a big bill to pay, so the dead one will have escaped that bother. What, you think anyone will want to use a sword that's shed one of our company's blood? And dueling swords go in pairs. You'll have to buy both. Last chance to back out. No? Not a brain or scruple between you, then. My kind of reprobates. Choose up your weapons and retreat to opposite ends of the ground, my honorables. Go on! I'll have you know I have a whole basket of undergarments still to pick up at the laundry and sort through today, so I want one of you stretched out for burial double-quick. Show some leg!"

Ileth suddenly couldn't remember who was supposed to take a blade first. Gorgantern didn't move, so she took the one nearest her. Galia was right, they were about the length of a rug-beater, only heavier. The blades were one-edged, straight as a plumb line, and had a heavy shield hilt, ornately engraved. It would cost the victor a good deal to pay for it. More money than she'd ever seen in her life.

She "retreated" to the northern end of the dueling ground. She swung the sword experimentally, trying to look as though she knew what she was doing.

On the other side, Gorgantern removed his coat and stood there in his shirtsleeves. He had a pained, faraway look on his face.

She realized she was still in her overdress. It was hard to move in it, and almost impossible to run or jump about without pulling material up, an impossibility while holding a sword. She stuck her sword in the sand, worked the buttons at the back, and shrugged it off.

Santeel gasped. "What are you doing?"

"Getting . . . ready to fight," she said, kicking the overdress up onto the boat behind her and retrieving the sword.

"You're in your shirt!"

"You think I should ta-take that off too? I have a sheath beneath it."

"Don't joke. Have you no shame?" Santeel asked.

"Grew up poor. Couldn't afford it!" She felt clairvoyant. *Mad as a day owl*, Santeel Dun Troot was clearly thinking. She felt alive, *focused*, like she could count grains of sand on the beach just by looking at them. Gorgantern's face was the color of a frog's belly and the hair on his forehead stuck there.

Santeel picked up the cast-away dress and folded it, then folded it again and draped it over her arm. "At least you don't have to tie up your hair. Which reminds me. I need to tell you something. I want to tell you . . . no, *need* to tell you . . . this is hard. I need to tell you"—she gulped—"good luck. Slice off something embarrassing. From him, I mean to say."

Over at the edge of the dueling ground Dath Amrits was speaking low enough that she couldn't make out a word and probably wouldn't have noticed his moving lips save for her current heightened sensitivity. He faced stolidly forward, ignoring both duelists, gazing levelly out into the lake. The physiker leaned closer to hear what he was saying.

Amrits waved the physiker off and paced to the center of the dueling ground. "Will the opposing parties please step forward?"

They paced toward each other. Gorgantern kept glancing at her pale, fleshy thighs. The air tingled cool against her skin and she felt scandalous. At the very least she'd make for a titillating story. *Might as well be remembered as the girl who fought in just a shirt rather than the starving stutterer who botched her oath.* Maybe they'd tell it in the men's smoke-and-liquor dens in Vyenn. She'd never been inside a tap-house but she'd looked through smeared windows. Paintings of underdressed females, even nudes, were popular in those sorts of places, depicting bawdy jokes or old stories. Maybe she'd be decorating a tavern wall, in time. The Vales were mad for paintings, and anyone who could afford it filled their walls with art. She could just picture the painting: the sea in back; the otters; her bare legs; her sweaty, pale opponent. *It was right funny up until she was stretched out cold . . .*

Why wasn't she imagining any ending that didn't involve her dead?

"I have here," Amrits said, pulling a silver cylinder about the size of his thumb from a pocket in his bracing vest, "a dragon whistle. When it blows, the duel is over." He tested it softly to let them hear the tone and it gave a *tweee!* loud enough to make Gorgantern jump. It would be louder than any shout or cry. "Now don't go claiming you didn't hear it. When I blow this, they'll turn around on the far wall of the Serpentine. The instant you hear it, lower your weapons and take three steps back. Not another blow struck."

Gorgantern looked like a mountain this close. He smiled at her like a cat contemplating a bird with a broken wing.

Galia, behind Gorgantern and marking the edge of the dueling ground, gave Ileth an encouraging nod and did that knuckle-wall gesture toward her. Ileth realized she could die not knowing its significance. She supposed it was meant to steady her. She didn't feel steady right now.

Amrits backed away from them, raising his voice to say: "Ready your weapons."

They held up their blades, pointing at each other, the deadly tips one long step apart.

"Steady your feet!" Amrits said, more loudly still.

Gorgantern shifted on his feet so his forward leg held his weight and dragged the other one back behind his body.

Ileth had no idea what to do with her own feet, so she just brought the front heel up near her rear toes, toes pointed out, the way she'd been taught at the commencement of a social dance with a partner. She liked to dance. And it did allow you to shift quickly, forward or back, right or left, or bob.

"Begin!"

Gorgantern lowered his blade so that it pointed to the ground just in front of him to his right. He forced out a bleak smile.

He's surrendering, she thought wildly, before he brought up his free hand and beckoned her forward. He was offering her a chance to strike. The contempt in the gesture made her angry.

The smile turned into a sneer. It made her angrier still.

"Who's the dumb one now?" Gorgantern said. "You're not even holding your sword right."

That made it easier.

She lunged at him, clumsily. His sword came up in a flash. It must have felt light as a reed at the end of that huge, fleshy arm, she thought, before it rang against her own blade, knocking its point away to her right.

She danced back—literally; her change of feet was that of a dance partner, not a duelist—expecting another strike. She'd mostly worked on parrying with Galia.

Galia had stressed that when parrying, you should take the blow as close to the hilt of your own sword and near to your body as possible; you were stronger there and then your muscles were bunched for a fast and powerful counterstrike. Gorgantern raised his blade again, giving away the coming blow—the Captain had never taught him to keep his blade in between himself and his opponent's blade—and brought it down with all the power in his huge body. It gave her a chance to try the one attack they'd rehearsed over and over and over and over again until she could hardly cross rug-beaters without using it.

Ileth danced in close, well inside his reach, sword at her side and held back so that the point only projected a few hand widths in front of her. At this point he was a wall of flesh; it would be impossible to miss with her stab—

But her move came just a lightning flash too late.

Though he missed her with the blade as she was inside his reach, his arm still struck her between head and shoulder. Her vision went white. She only knew she'd fallen when she struck the beach on her side. She wondered if she'd been cleaved in twain by the sword blade—

Her sword hand was empty.

Tweeeeeeeeeeeeeeeeeeeeeeeee! The whistle blew so loudly Ileth felt like her body had, just for a moment, been magically transformed into sound. She felt like an extension of the whistle.

Now that she could see again, Gorgantern loomed over her big as the Beehive.

Gorgantern ignored the signal. He raised the sword again, this time holding it in both hands with the straight blade pointed directly down at her belly. She shut her eyes as she tried to twist out of the way—

Youdon'tfeelthepainyoudon'tfeelthepainyoudon'tfeelthepain . . .

A footstep thumped by her head and she sensed motion above.

Galia, a fair-haired blur, struck the giant in a flying tackle. She hit him low, she hit him fast, she hit him hard, and he hadn't braced for it and folded around her as though his massive body would swallow hers. He was off his feet and on his backside with Galia atop him.

His sword had struck after all, plunging into the sand not quite harmlessly, for the point cut Ileth on the buttock as it went down. She felt the cold steel against her muscle, then the warmth of blood.

Gorgantern screamed painfully and Ileth saw her savior with teeth dug into his ear, biting into him and clenching on like a fighting dog. Blood dribbled on her face and Gorgantern's shirt.

The whistle blew again, even louder. So loud it hurt. She sat up, covering her ears.

Galia rolled off him and came to her feet with an athletic ease, her face smeared with blood, bright-eyed and ready for more. Ileth got up with more difficulty. Her leg muscles had turned to bags of water hardly able to straighten her knees.

"I stood up for you, you pile," Galia said, getting her hair out of her eyes. The blood on her mouth made her look savage, like a stable cat who'd finished off a rat.

"Worst mistake I ever made," Gorgantern said, still seated and inspecting the blood at his torn ear. "You betrayed me from the start. Can't stand that I won?"

Ileth picked up Gorgantern's dueling sword and stepped over to stand next to Galia. Ileth pointed the sword about a hand's breadth from his throat. Gorgantern's eyes widened in fear and he jerked back.

"Ileth!" Galia said. "It's over!"

The blade wavered a little. Ileth found herself shaking uncontrollably as her nerves started to release in the realization that she was still alive. Gorgantern leaned away from the point as though it were a poisonous snake.

"It's over," Gorgantern said. "The whistle blew."

Ileth added a second hand to the sword's handle and it steadied somewhat. "Not much fun, is it?"

"None of that!" Amrits shouted, hurrying forward with Rapoto just behind. "You kill him now, it's murder!" She noticed he'd shifted the grip on his walking stick. The ogre-faced end was held down, but toward her.

"He'd have done the same to me," Ileth said.

"He's disarmed now," Amrits said. "Put it down."

Rapoto retrieved the weapon from her hand and Santeel hurried to pick up its mate and bring it to him. "You're bleeding," he said, leaning to glance at her wounded flank.

Santeel moved to stand between her and the watching men. "Cover up, Ileth."

The physiker—was his name really Threadneedle?—joined the party around the former duelists. "The bandages and vinegar, if you please, Joai. Our novice here needs stitching up."

"Get them off the dueling ground before you stanch the blood," Joai called. "Bad luck if you don't. An ill taint will enter the wounds and they'll go septic."

The dueling party turned and moved toward the spectators.

Galia passed her her overdress. "Can't have you walking back through the gate in nothing but your shirt."

With the duel over, the insults and blows and challenges exchanged in the kitchen would all be treated as if they'd never happened, but Ileth suspected life in the Catch Basin would be even more unpleasant. She wondered what new tortures Gorgantern would invent now, with injury piled on insult.

The physiker pronounced Ileth's wound a "mere scratch" that a plain dressing would be sufficient to seal and set Joai to work cleaning it out with the vinegar before she pressed a dressing to it and bound it in bandage. He sat Gorgantern on one of the overturned boats and cleaned the bite with something from a brown bottle that made the aged apprentice howl, then put his assistant to work with needle and thread while he observed and gave advice.

Galia knelt and washed away Gorgantern's blood in the lake.

Dath Amrits took Gorgantern's mind off the stitching by standing before him. "Well, old sponge, you've landed in the camp soup this time."

"Huh?" Gorgantern said, turning his uninjured ear to Amrits.

"I blew the whistle and you struck another blow. Not the mortal one you intended, fellow-me-lad, but it drew blood that a jury can see. You made it *so* easy for us. Me, two other dragoneer witnesses, old Thread-needle there who's a strict Formist and wouldn't lie if you hung him over coals. I'm calling a jury of Masters this afternoon and you'll be out the gate in whatever clothing from the pauper's bin will fit you at the stroke of midnight. Good luck to you. If you bear me any ill will, re-member, you have only yourself to blame. I'm the owner of the loudest whistle in the Serpentine."

"But-But I run the Catch Basin."

"No fear," Amrits said. "I'll break the news to the fish gently. Head up, now. You can always try explaining to the jury how a disarmed wisp of a girl flat on her back in the mud presented a mortal threat that re-quired you to stab her through the stomach. I wouldn't advise it, though; they might refer you to the magistrate in Vyenn. I wouldn't mind telling my story again to a jury with the power to have your head and your body buried separately. That'd be worth funking my laundry day entirely."

I'll never have to see Gorgantern again. She felt a dull relief wash over her, and her body seemed to be trembling. She willed it to stop, but her nerves ignored her. She wondered if Joai would give her brandy to steady her nerves even though the duel was over.

Amrits walked over to Ileth, whom Joai had put well clear of the dueling ground before setting to work on her cut.

"I told you to show a leg, but there's such a thing as overstepping your orders," Amrits said, holding her overdress so she might step into it, careful to keep the hem out of the dirt.

"She doesn't need your patter now, sir," Joai said.

"Sir, did I win or lose?" Ileth said.

"On the dueling ground you lost, quickly and decisively. Yes, you definitely botched it. A tactical loss, though, can turn into a strategic win, so let's see how time and tide treat it. Bravely done, anyway. Here. Just in case the fact that you're still breathing our salubrious mountain air isn't enough of a reward."

He extracted the dragon whistle from his bracing vest and, passing the cord lanyard over his head, handed it to her with a little bow. "With my compliments for standing against the Beast Gorgantern, Terror of the Catch Basin. Let's hope you find a use for it someday."

"Sir, I—can't—I . . ."

"Don't act like I'm trying to foist polished nickel off on you. It's solid silver. Take it to the jeweler in town, he'll tell you. Girls these days. Spoiled rotten. Good day to you, Joai. Why don't you seal that wound up with some of your biscuit dough? It's impervious to gravy—I doubt blood would do any better."

With that, he turned on his heel so that the golden fringe on his cape flayed the air and walked back to the other dragoneers. Hael Dun Huss met her gaze and gave her a friendly nod before he turned for the path up to the shrouded Serpentine.

"That Amrits," Joai said, watching the dragoneers depart. "I bet they pulled him out of his mother wearing a clown hat. Still, the Serpentine's well rid of Gorgantern. No good having a wrinkled apprentice hanging about like an old hide. Some other novice can move up. Want that mouthful of brandy now?"

Ileth held the silver whistle in both hands, as though she were afraid birds would come and snatch it away. She wanted it, but some clear chunk at the back of her brain reminded her that the Masters were watching, one way or another, and she didn't want to be thought the kind of person who needs a drink to get them through a crisis. "No, I-I'm . . . calm enough."

"Rig yourself." Joai sampled a swig. Her cheeks grew a little redder and she offered Ileth a conspiratorial wink. "I need calming down after all that."

Ileth took a deep cleansing breath, looked out at the otters (who'd been frightened by the whistle blasts and were nothing but eyes and curious noses sticking out of the water), and shrugged. "I could be a lot calmer, if you understand m-my m-meaning."

6

By dinner, the tale of the duel had reached all the Serpentine. The wildest rumors passed up and down the creaky stairways of the Manor, like a nursery game of touchback that grew wilder at each contact.

"You didn't *really* fight him naked?" Quith asked.

Ileth shook her head, adding an emphatic "No!" once she recovered enough to get the word out.

Quith leaned in close. "SDT just said you were in your sheath, but then later I heard that you were naked and she'd heard it from SDT and I thought maybe SDT didn't tell me the whole story because the Matron was listening, but then—"

"Not naked," Ileth said. "Santeel Dun Troot doesn't even have it right; I had my shirt on."

"Well, whatever, brilliant tactic. He must have been so distracted. No wonder you beat him."

Ileth doubted her knobby knees would distract anything but a wading bird. "I didn't beat him, he . . . he beat me. He struck me after the whistle. That's why he's up before the Masters."

The Matron found extra duties for Ileth around the Manor, saying that as she'd indulged herself all day with the duel nonsense, well, she'd have to make it up at night. The other novices crowded around, saying it was deeply unfair that she could not enjoy a night of glory in the dining hall. Santeel told and retold the story. She'd stuck to the truth as far as Ileth could tell, except for the sheath business. For once, she wasn't the trip-tongued girl who smelled of fish, but something like a Name.

She didn't hate it.

In truth, she was relieved to be given extra duties. She wouldn't have cared if the Matron had ordered her to clean the privy with her only remaining sheath (the one she'd worn to the fight mysteriously disappeared from where it was soaking away the bloodstain in the washtub). She worked with such mind-numbing diligence that she had to return to the Matron and ask for more.

After dinner, Galia returned with news. A jury of Masters heard the evidence against Gorgantern. The physiker and Joai verified that she had been purposefully wounded after the whistle had blown. Galia and two others testified that he struck intending to kill. It was enough to burn Gorgantern's career as thoroughly as if a dragon had spat fire upon him. Stripped of his tattered sash and put out the gate with rags tied around his feet because no footwear in the beggar's bin would fit him, he left with a curse against a conspiracy to ruin him. The gate-watch said he took the road down to Vyenn.

That settled her mind.

While the others were bent over their night-work she made herself an infusion of tea and herbs and took it out into the garden. There was a bench against the back wall, well away from the privy, where you could just see the bay over the fortress wall—if it hadn't been dark and overcast. Still, even without the view it was peaceful. She'd run a terrible risk and had Galia been a trifle slower she could be dead, instead of enjoying a quiet bench and her infusion.

The cup was hot in her hands and the chilly air felt delicious. It was a miracle to be alive. If the Captain himself had stomped up to the Manor door with dirty teeth glinting, she'd have bobbed and smiled and told him she missed running to refill his tankard and get a light for his pipe.

"How is your wound?" a voice called from the darkness.

Rapoto stood on the other side of an apology of a gate, askew on rusty hinges. Ileth was sure the Matron wanted it that way to better sound the alarm against male intruders.

"It's nothing."

"What are you doing now?"

"I live here. I should ask y-you, lurking in the-the dark outside a house full of . . . full of girls."

He didn't mind her trip-tongued sauce; in fact, he smiled. "Want to come away? I can offer you better than warm milk."

"Against the rules."

"Official business with the Master of Novices. Then a victor's cup of something stimulating."

"Stimulating?" She'd been amply stimulated for one day, coming within a missed stab of death. But Rapoto had the sort of face that put her in an agreeable mood.

"Oh, yes. Well, I hope. Interested in a pile-in?"

"A . . . a what?"

"A pile-in. Sort of an after-hours party. We apprentices still aren't allowed out of the Serpentine without a gate pass at night. Since we can't all get passes to town, we're celebrating Gorgantern's fall inside the walls. Complete the night if I could get you to join in to receive a toast."

Ileth thought it odd that they'd celebrate one of their own being kicked out.

"*She'd* never let m-me attend."

Rapoto waggled one of the tails of his knotted sash. "That's where the official business comes in: I have a signed note calling for you from Caseen."

Curiosity roused her. It must be important for Caseen to ask for her at night.

She sighed. "I suppose I must go with you."

He turned up one corner of his mouth. "To the pile-in, as well?"

"I want to hear what he . . . what Master Caseen has to say, first."

He found that amusing, though she didn't see the humor. She found she liked it when he looked at her. Some men were easy to read. Venality often was. Rapoto looked at her attentively, like he was listening to a five-string well played. Appreciative, not appraising.

"C'mon. I was a novice for two years, or close to it, the last of my draft but one to make apprentice. Never had any fun at night the whole time."

"Why ask me now instead of on the way?"

"Maybe you want to dress."

"You're looking at my-my-my best overdress. Also my w-worst." She laughed, a little tiredly, and instantly regretted it. She disliked people who laughed at their own jests.

"No one is going to care. You are going to be talked about anyway. You might as well be there. I don't think anyone believes me when I try to tell the truth of it. Galia will be there."

Meeting some of the other apprentices could be advantageous. It couldn't be that much of a violation if Galia was about; she was a stickler for rules and shifts and how things looked to the Masters. She'd like to hear some stories about what inspired an offer of apprenticeship. She'd learned the value of specific intelligence from Falth.

"I reserve the right to leave if I don't like it," she said, after a moment's thought.

"You're a strange one. I have to be seeing to the Masters' Hall door lamps at the midnight bell anyway. Then I have to be back in that filthy hovel under the parapets. My family wouldn't think it fit for their dogs. Signal me and I'll make my excuses and walk you back."

"They'll . . . gossip," she predicted.

"I don't mind. Honestly, it'd feel safer with someone as fierce as you alongside after dark. Keep the gargoyles away."

Ileth was washing her face when Rapoto showed up at the door.

She returned to the common room to see Santeel Dun Troot introducing Rapoto to the household. She looked pleased to be able to show him off.

There weren't many visitors to the Manor with a Vor in their name, even among the moneyed and influential scions who were sent off to the Serpentine by their families.

"The Vor Claymasses are from Jotun, I understand," the Matron said, taking charge of the guest as soon as she heard his full name.

"Most of them, sira," Rapoto said.

"Do you have orchards?" Quith asked. "We would get barrels of these lovely Jotun apples yearly. Golden, stamped with a beautiful sort of two-tree insignia that formed a shield between."

Rapoto's face went blank. "Yes, that would be my family. My grand-father invented that type of apple."

"How clever!" another novice said. "I didn't know you could invent an apple. I thought they just grew."

"It's just as exciting as it sounds," Rapoto said evenly. "We grow three different kinds. Each strain does best in different sorts of soil and weather."

"Imagine that," the Matron said.

"Which is your favorite?" Santeel asked.

"Depends. The Golden are flavorful and just a little sweet; that's my favorite for eating. Quite reliable. The Green Crested make a good cider—or you can cook with them. The Huskies, they have a reddish-streaked patina and the quality varies depending on how dry a summer we had. Too wet or too dry and they end up going to the pigs. But if we get a fair summer, well, they're like apple-flavored cake, then."

Some of his audience made hungry noises. *Oh, how I want to try one! I wonder if they have them in Vyenn? Would you tell us how to get them?*

"I'm—ready," Ileth said, having retrieved her old, reliable boots, suitable for walking in the dark.

"Excuse me, ladies. Thank you for your attention, sira," he said to the Matron. Then he turned to his audience. "I regret leaving. I could talk apples all night. Apples apples apples."

The assembly laughed with him.

"But I must get Novice Ileth to the Master." He bowed and most of the audience bobbed back.

"Your attention to duty does you credit, sir," Santeel said.

"I hope it's nothing serious. I don't know what we'd do without our Ileth," the Matron said, in a tone that suggested life would go on were she removed.

He stepped ahead and opened the heavy Manor door for Ileth. Not a few rapt looks—and one jealous one—followed them out. The babble began even before the Matron closed the door behind.

"Glad that's done," Rapoto said. "I always feel like a bull at auction when people ask about the family holdings."

For him, it was done. She would have to return. She couldn't get it right. Either none of the other girls her age paid attention to her and she felt invisible, or too much attention was paid and she felt despised. Quith liked her only because she was someone to pass gossip. But she couldn't expect Rapoto to understand that.

"It's been an odd day," Ileth said, when they were out of earshot of the house and going up to the graveside Masters' Hall. "If you'd . . . told me this morning that I'd be-be-be hearing a discourse on apples tonight . . . I'd have laughed."

"Laugh away," he said. "I can't stand the things."

"No?"

"I've had to pick them and taste them and judge them and talk about them my whole life. My father is a great believer in getting us out to our trees and hives and working alongside our people. Of course, it's not just fruit. It's who we are, how the family rose; well, that and mining. Mining money allowed my great-grandfather to buy a lot of land in Jotun. The apples were just something to do with the land at first. I'm here to get away from them."

"Let's not go-go on about apples or our families, th-then," Ileth said, hoping he wouldn't notice she'd added to the list of forbidden subjects.

"You talk, then."

A rarity, that. Someone asking her to talk. "You d-don't mind my . . . stutter?"

"No. You can't help it, after all." He walked in silence for a moment. "When the words come, they're interesting enough. I don't mind waiting."

She quickened her pace. They walked together in silence. Now that someone wanted to listen to her talk, her wits failed her. What did men like Rapoto talk about? Mining profits? Business of the Assembly? Would the negotiators ever make peace with the Galantines?

"You said . . . you said you were two years a n-novice."

"Yes," he agreed. "Kept flubbing jobs. Somehow things always go wrong for me. In the bakery I killed all the yeast. Thought it was some bad water in a dirty bowl. In the garden I thought the young carrots were weeds—they'd not put them in nice rows, you see, it was more like a patch. I shot wingman Dun Leckert in the foot with a crossbow. He was cheery enough about it, though, said he was grateful I remembered to notch my bolt with the bow pointed down."

The few lights in the Masters' Hall resolved out of the fog.

At the Master's, in the now-familiar office, her interview was friendlier than the one that morning. Had it been just that morning? It felt like weeks ago. Caseen carefully set down the pencil he was using to make a margin note in a volume he had open on his desk and inquired about her wound. She assured him she'd bled more at the fish-gutting table thanks to her slippery knife.

The subject changed to the expulsion. He reassured her that Gorgantern had left the service of the Serpentine and said he hoped she was a little wiser for the experiences of the morning and potential consequences to threats spoken in anger. He relayed that Gorgantern had been defiant in front of the jury (not that a different attitude would have changed the outcome). He'd used some bitter words about a conspiracy against him but hadn't threatened anything.

"A grudge is an unpredictable thing. I've already warned Galia. We on the jury thanked him for his years and offered our help in obtaining him a fresh start elsewhere. He refused. We will put a wingman or two in Vyenn to keep an eye on him while he remains within an easy walk of the walls and try to discreetly find him a situation on the other side of the Vales, perhaps Jotun. That apprentice Rapoto offered his family's aid, do you—oh, yes, he brought you here, didn't he? My, I shouldn't work so late. As I was saying, the Master of Apprentices is just down the hall writing letters to do just that now. Gorgantern has friends among the fishermen, and they bring their boats right into the Beehive, as you well know. The Serpentine is far from impenetrable, especially to one who has lived within our walls as long as that one. It's hard to know what a mix of wounded pride and resentment might bring out of a man like Gorgantern. Keep around at least two or three others for the next few days. The Manor will be watched at night. I don't expect anything to happen; he knows he would be flogged for just set-ting his oversized foot inside the walls, but I want you alert."

Ileth gulped. She imagined those massive hands on her throat. She knew the strength in Gorgantern's fleshy arms. But she wanted to seem worthy of her present company. "Sir, it's . . . it's hard to imagine Gorgan-tern sneaking about."

"Would you like me to ask for a volunteer from the wingmen to walk with you for a few days? We have a few who've been at swordplay since they could walk."

"May I give you an answer to-tomorrow?"

"Certainly. In happier news, I'm hoping to move you up in the Bee-hive. You've worked the bottom of it, so we'll switch you to the top. There's always work for you nimble young things in the lighthouse. Fascinating contraption. It uses dragon-crystals, quite rare and valuable. They need a lot of polishing and turning on sunny days. It's a good view from up there and you'll find the air stimulating. You can help the lookout log weather. I used to keep myself fit by climbing up to it every day, but I hardly go now-adays. Introducing you up there would give me an excuse to make the climb again. How does that sound?"

"Fine, sir."

"Well, get along. Seems Rapoto is anxious to escort you home. I see him hanging about outside the door."

"Thank you, sir."

"Oh, and Ileth," Caseen called after her.

"Sir?" she said, turning around to face him.

"No more duels. Get some sleep."

She bobbed out her obeisance in acknowledgment.

"That took a while," Rapoto said, when they were safely away.

She laughed. "He warned me against Gor-Gorgantern. Thinks Gor-gantern is capable of doing something desperate." She passed on the warning against dueling too. "I don't want to be thought combative."

"Interesting thing for someone who trains to saddle up a dragon to say. Perhaps now they'll be afraid to tease you about fish."

"How d-do you know I'm teased?"

"A would-be dragoneer should be skilled at acquiring valuable intelligence."

She laughed. It was good to laugh.

"In the north they'll put one of your . . . your eyes out for g-gathering intelligence by peeking through windows."

"Why are you here, Ileth? I can't make it out. Not hunting a husband, no family pressure, and as jobs go it doesn't even pay. Do you have a father to avenge or something?"

She wondered if he was mocking her. It was hard to tell with these Names just how much was pose and how much was purpose. "I'm determined to make a new start here."

"You've only just arrived. How much newer could you be?"

She took a deep breath of the night air. It turned into an exasperated sigh.

"Ileth, you're not a fire-breather, obviously. Your manners aren't what most here are used to. I find it difficult to avoid issuing a challenge to you to a duel myself with the way you cut precedence when we go through a door—that's an insult in my social strata—but you are not a fire-breather, any more than I am."

"'Interesting thing for someone who trains to saddle up a dragon to say,'" she repeated.

He smiled at her and she smiled back. Nice to have someone who gives and takes jokes. Perhaps he was lost in similar thoughts, because he grew quiet and thoughtful.

"So family life not for you, children and such."

"Never . . . never met anyone who made me want to, want to have his babies."

"I'd like them, someday. Give them an ordinary name. No responsibilities attached. Freedom to pick their own path."

It was the sort of thing that someone who'd never had to share one pot of oat porridge out among ten said, and it didn't much impress her. But he meant well. Meaning well went far with her, a lot farther than a pot of oat porridge did at the Lodge.

They crossed the open plaza under the loom of the gate. "Where are we going?"

"The stables."

"Your pile-in." Ileth had seen enough carousing in the Captain's Lodge to last her a lifetime, but perhaps the well-bred apprentices with their triple-bar names were different.

In the pre-dragoneer days of the fortress, there'd been a stable and a hippodrome for exercising the horses in the wet weather. Now there were just a few veteran mounts inured to the constant arrival of dragon smells. She knew in a vague sort of way that there was still a Master of Horse who taught the apprentices to ride—horse riding was good training for being on a dragon, and a horse was still the best way to send messages over a short distance, saving the dragons work. She hadn't been introduced to him yet.

"The Master of Horse is a good sort of fellow. The harder you work, the harder he lets you play. But I should warn you, it gets a bit charry in there. Most of the girls tie up and cover their hair. The stable's dusty and people will be smoking."

"I-I don't have a—"

"Here, have mine." He handed her a handkerchief. It was a little hard to tell what color it was in the dark, but at least it was clean.

"I meant, I don't have any hair to tie up."

"Oh, yes, well, I thought you might object to what's left stinking. No, keep it, I have others."

Secretly, she was a little worried that they'd demand a retelling of the duel. She dreaded the idea of speaking, answering questions, watching her audience exchange looks and fidget. She'd have to admit that if Galia hadn't intervened, she'd be either dead or dying, run through the stomach or liver or womb. Worse, they could ask about her upbringing, the Lodge, who her parents were and what had happened to them. If they suspected she was attempting to hide something, the hard questions would start. She'd been around the Manor apprentices enough to know that they could sniff out weakness and lies better than a jury.

She decided she'd just decline to talk about it. Nervous exhaustion. She thought she could rely on Rapoto's name and kindness to spare her any long speeches.

Best start laying the groundwork now.

"Rapoto," she said, as they cut through the crowd of old buildings about the up end of the Serpentine, "I hope I don't have to talk about the duel."

"Why not? If I knocked a bear like Gorgantern out of his cave, you couldn't get me to shut up about it."

But he let the subject alone, and soon they were at the stables.

The wide, horse-height main doors of the hippodrome were shut, so Rapoto knocked at the smaller, human-sized one on the side of the stable next to the storeroom. They were admitted by one of the wing-men, acting as both a lookout and a filter to make sure only approved personages would get in.

Ileth saw a few curious, big-eyed horse heads glance at them from the mostly empty stalls as she followed Rapoto.

The pile-in appeared to be much as Rapoto had described it, something just for the apprentices and a couple of the younger and more social wingmen. They'd taken over a low-beamed storeroom with hay-loft and workshops and arranged a snug retreat.

The storeroom's sacks of grain had been removed from the heavy wooden racks that kept the feed up off the floor and turned into floor cushions or approximations of lounges and chairs. You could climb into the hayloft above through a rough ladder nailed onto one of the vertical supports. Two lamps and a few candles were the only illumination, unless you counted a small stove. It sat in one corner of the storeroom that had used to be a blacksmithing workshop, she supposed, as it jutted out from the stable and had a skylight and a masonry floor. A few old tools that were still of use maintaining the place and shoeing the horses hung from the walls. A black soup pot bubbled with something that smelled like licorice on the stove.

"Is that gripe?" Ileth asked. She'd had grog, a mix of tea and molasses-spirits, at the Lodge, and she knew gripe was mountain-style grog, heavy on the licorice. Same tea, different spirits and flavorings, and both an all-purpose remedy for ailments of the nose, throat, and chest. Grog pots reminded her of the Captain. He mostly drank brandied wine, but he used to make a pot for friends and old shipmates. She'd smelled gripe only once or twice before in shepherd campsites.

"I believe so." He watched one of the apprentice girls who had somehow also escaped the Manor tonight pour a little in a wooden soup bowl with a handle, taste it, make a face, and add some syrup from a glass jar and then what was probably liquor from a big earthenware jug. Ileth recognized it as the sort of vessel that country folk use to make their farmhouse wine out of dandelions or blackberries.

She heard laughter from above. A pair of dainty but callused bare feet dangled, a little silver chain on one ankle. She recognized the bauble; it belonged to Galia. Galia had told her that ankle bracelets were popular in Sammerdam, the city where she grew up. Ileth was relieved. She had one ally here, if matters became truly desperate.

"Way-hey, we have our heroine," somebody called, as Rapoto took her up to the grog pot. Or gripe pot. The libation.

"Well, do you dare?" Rapoto asked.

"A . . . a little." She'd had spirits forced on her when she was ill. It might be interesting to try some just for fun.

Rapoto had the girl pour him a cup (everyone was drinking out of a different type of cup, and a few were just using kitchen ladles or small saucepots) and split the measure out into a small soup bowl, after checking to make sure it was clean. He gave her the smaller of the two portions.

The girl at the grog pot did something with her tongue and lips that Ileth suspected was obscene.

"Quit it, Evire," Rapoto said, scowling at the pot-stirrer. "We're celebrating. It's not like that at all."

"If you say so. She may have other designs," Evire said.

Rapoto raised his voice: "A toast, to Ileth, banisher of Gorgantern."

It wasn't received in the same spirit. After a few curious glances and a smile or two, the membership of the pile-in returned to their former conversations. So much for Rapoto and his belief that she would be the celebrity of the pile-in.

The gripe was sharp but sweet and awfully strong. She suspected they were using the licorice and what tasted like cloves to cover up the amount of spirits inside.

"It's my own recipe," Evire said.

She counted heads. A good thirty apprentices were here. She didn't know how many apprentices worked in the Serpentine entire, but guessed it was in the hundreds.

"Bend an elbow for our savior," Yael Duskirk, the apprentice feeder she'd met outside the red door and one of her friends from the kitchen, said from the loft next to Galia's feet, raising a wooden bowl. Galia's foot rubbed against his suggestively. "Brims up to love and havoc!"

The crowd liked Duskirk's toast a little better, there was a stir toward her. "To love and havoc!" most repeated, drinking, smiling at her through gripe-washed teeth. Even the wingmen bridged the social gap with the apprentices—and one out-of-her-home-waters novice—in the salute.

She accepted the toast, then tried to look around and acknowledge all the faces. That was what you were supposed to do, anyway, but it was hard in a dimly lit sort of hay barn full of shadows and motion.

"Where are your *laudii*, Ileth?" joked a young woman who had a waterfall of thick dark hair falling out of her scarf. Ileth had an idea that she was one of the girls who lived in the Beehive practically under the dragons' snouts. What they did was still a subject of much conjecture and not a few wild stories in the Manor, but they were generally called *the dancers*. "Well done. Well done, indeed. I did six months gutting and salting under that towering prong. He used to stick fish tails down my back."

"I'll drift behind that," said another young man with the long, thick sideburns Quith had told her were favored by the stylish youths in artist free-cities like Zland and Tyrenna. He extracted a white pipe and began to fill it from a leather pouch that had a name crest embroidered on it. She'd passed the young man on the bridge a few times and knew in a vague sort of way that he was a new-fledged wingman. Sleng, something. Pasfa Sleng. That was it. Quith had a terrible crush on him. She'd described him, in detail, several times and the thing that had stuck in Ileth's head was his sideburns, so whenever she'd seen him she'd mentally called him that. On closer examination, they were as thick and well-tended as a rich house's border hedge. She'd keep the way he was nestled up next to the dark-haired dancer from Quith, when she'd inevitably beg for details later.

The pair who'd spoken to her shifted closer to each other and made room on a pile of grain sacks. They shifted about until they formed a rough sort of horseshoe. Ileth sat on the end of the horseshoe, giving Rapoto ample room to sit between her and the others. Galia and Yael were laughing and chatting above.

Stripped to her sheath, as sure as I've hay in my hair!

Ileth tried to ignore the half-heard conversation above. The first thing they did was ask to see the whistle. Word had passed around that the dragoneer Amrits had given her his silver whistle as a token of his esteem. Ileth had shortened the lanyard and wore it around her neck beneath her work shirt.

With that out of the way, the party settled in.

Sideburns tamped down the tobacco in his pipe, extracted a thin stick of wood, and stood to set it aflame at the gripe pot. He put the flaming end of his kindling to his tobacco, and his cheeks worked until smoke blossomed from the pipe's pot. He passed it to the thick-haired girl, who took a few puffs and handed it back.

"How about you, uhh, Ileth, you game?" asked Sideburns.

"Thank you," she said. She'd tried a pipe several times before; tobacco was almost as popular as tea and potato-crust lamb pies with the people on the North Coast. She took the pipe, made of the white clay favored by society but small and simple in size, and tried to check the mouthpiece without making a show of it. She stuck it in her mouth and took a pull of the smoke. It was sweet and a little spicy, softer in the mouth with a good deal less bite to the tongue than the rough square-cut tobacco cubes she knew from the provinces.

"Thank you, s-sir," she said, passing it back. She exhaled slowly, letting it out in a thin column.

"Dragon style! Wings out, girl," Sideburns said. He put his fists together with knuckles toward her.

"Good tobacco there," Ileth said. She meant to ask him about the fists-together gesture, but he started speaking and her natural reticence left him to his discourse.

"It's called Blue Mood, from Sammerdam. I'd send you a bag as a mark of my esteem for putting Gorgantern on his vent, but I've none to spare. My family seems to think this place supplies everything I need. If I'd known tobacco would be so dear up on the lakeshore, I'd have filled up another couple pouches from my father's crock. They shave it close here, don't they? No spare money for anything."

"Be lucky you get meat twice a day," Galia called from the loft above. "Dragons eat a lot of coin."

"Fa! Fish isn't meat where I come from," Sideburns said, taking his pipe back. "Fates, I should have gone to the art academy in Zland. Sketched milkmaids instead of picking scale nits. This isn't an academy, it's a labor camp with statues. Smells besides."

Ileth didn't mind the smell as much as some. It was an oily stink and clung to you, but it wasn't that unpleasant to her nose.

"The dragons only take coin on holidays and feast days," the dark-haired girl said. "Mostly they eat ores and scrap metal for their scale."

"I always heard it was coin," Ileth said. "Up north they talk about taxes going down a dragon's hatch."

"Novices," Sideburns said. "You'll learn soon enough. It's not like the ballads and paintings here."

The dark-haired girl shrugged. "This whole Academy is a swindle, I'm starting to think. They work a couple hundred boys and girls like slaves, promote six or seven now and then, let the quality ride a dragon a few times just so they can say they done it, and when the poor kids wise up and quit, just bring in a new batch."

Sideburns took the pipe out of his mouth and passed it to the dark-haired girl. "Apprenticeship's almost as bad. Six years is a long time when you're pulling nits out of scale and raking dragon waste checking for worms."

"Beats the Auxiliary or the Sea Lines Warrants," Evire said from the pot. "I lost a sister to the Auxiliaries and a brother in a whaler in the North Bay."

"If the armistice with the Galantines breaks down again, they'll have us all flying quick enough," Rapoto said. "Blood and fire all over the Scab."

Ileth just listened. She knew the Scab was a sort of fortress on the great river that ran the Republic's border, some point of long contention, and that the Galantine flag now flew above it.

Sideburns shrugged. "My family wants one son a dragoneer."

"Lucky you ended up here," Rapoto said. He picked up Sideburns's pipe and studied it. "I'd rather be on dragonback than clerking at the Assembly."

"My father always spreads his bets," Sideburns answered. "We're wealthy enough, but not a Name. It's on me now to get a *Heem* into the family name, or better yet a *Dun*."

"I wouldn't mind walking out with a Name, one way or another," the dark-haired girl said, and the others laughed.

"That's the spirit, Peak," Galia said from above. "Marry for place. As long as it's first place."

The talk moved on to smaller doings among the apprentices.

"I'm . . . feeling that drink," Ileth said quietly to Rapoto. In truth, she was just tired.

"You're looking it," Sideburns said. "It's been quite a day for you. Rapoto, you need to get this girl to bed."

Rapoto looked up from Sideburns's pipe. He started to say something but thought better of it, and he looked over at Ileth with that appreciative stare of his. She'd never held a man's gaze for so long—at least a young man's gaze. The Old Croakers in the village street would stare at her, but they stared at any woman. Here, now, in this stuffy storeroom that smelled like mold and tobacco and oil lamps, with six other girls her age to look at, he chose her.

She felt both unsteady and thrilled. She didn't know what to do, how any of this worked with people with great names. Even her knowledge of coquetry among her own class was rumor and quick glimpses stitched together with guesswork. She reclined on her chair of feed sacks and smiled at him, then shifted her gaze to Galia's feet above. Her toes were curling and straightening; whatever was going on up there, she seemed to be enjoying it. She suspected the dragoneer Dun Huss would not like her to follow Galia's example in this instance. The rough sacking she sat upon tugged at her overdress and she sensed the sack was tearing. When she rose, she'd have to be careful about it or she'd end up with a mosaic of dried grain stuck to her backside.

Rapoto let out a great hacking cough. She glanced over and saw him struggling with the pipe, holding it as if it were a piece of chalk.

"Keep the smoke in your mouth," Sideburns suggested. Rapoto nodded dumbly and inhaled again, making a face.

"Never smoked a pipe?" Peak asked.

Rapoto shook his head. "Yellows the teeth."

Sideburns smiled. "I care about the soothing, contemplative frame of mind it offers. My teeth are subordinate to my brain."

"I don't feel soothed. Nauseous, if anything," Rapoto said, and the youth next to him laughed.

Evire continued tending the grog pot, making a show of stirring it with a long wooden ladle.

"Rapoto, another dip?" she called, plunging the ladle in.

Rapoto ignored her, gave the pipe back to Sideburns (*I need to tell Quith about his brand of tobacco*, Ileth thought), and turned his attention back to Ileth. Evire took it in with one quick, contemptuous glance and concentrated on filling up the mugs being passed to her.

Several of the couples were kissing or caressing each other. Some of the apprentices were leaving. Peak caught Ileth looking at one of the uniformed wingmen, old enough for a thick mustache, half whispering, half kissing at an apprentice's ear and neck. She'd loosed her hair and her hand gripped the wingman's forearm that she was resting upon, hard enough for her knuckles to go white. She and Peak shared a knowing smile.

The pile-in was turning into one of the Captain's outdoor bonfire nights when his gang brought their "wives."

"I should go," Ileth said.

"I need to get back too," Rapoto said. "Want another toss of gripe before you climb into the saddle?"

She shook her head and stifled a yawn. All the gripe had done was make her sleepy. The pile-in felt stuffy and the exhaustion of the day had finally caught up to her excitement. Night air would do her good, the chillier the better. She stood up and felt dizzy. What in all the locks and falls of the Republic had Evire put in that gripe?

They moved through the reduced crowd. Rapoto took her hand to assist in threading around the remaining apprentices and to keep from being pulled into a congratulation or conversation. Perhaps it was the gripe, but she decided he was as far above the run of the other apprentices as the snowcaps on the Sisters across the lake were above sea level. It was like every nerve in her body had been pulled into her hand and set aquiver.

They left the pile-in and walked out toward the door, passing the scattered horses. Long, thoughtful faces watched them from their stalls with the empty stables open between like knocked-out teeth.

"I have to take my chance," Rapoto said. He pulled her into one of the dark berths and pressed her against the stable wall, kissing her full and hard on the lips.

The intimacy shocked her, but it was the best kind of shock.

Maybe it was the gripe, but time slowed as his hands traveled around her waist. His touch was a little hesitant, as if he feared what he might find. She liked that. It was like being explored. She was used to being grabbed fast and hard by rough hands that didn't linger anywhere but their objective. Rapoto had thin fingers and a delicate touch. She pressed herself into him; he was tall and she slight, and her chin just fit against the bottom of his breastbone. He had to bend to kiss her and she had to tilt her close-cropped head far, far back.

She felt him take her overdress in his hands and start to lift it. She stiffened, pressing back against the stable wall to keep it in place. She hadn't expected Rapoto to go to *that* so quickly, like a pig pawing up a truffle.

Something white loomed behind Rapoto. For a moment she imagined it was Gorgantern, blade raised to stab—

Ileth squeaked in alarm.

"Rapoto!" Santeel Dun Troot screamed.

Ileth shielded her eyes from the lantern. The light hurt.

"Santeel, what the hounds . . ." Rapoto gasped, struggling to tuck his shirt into his pants. Ileth's overdress hem fell to its usual place as though it too were acting as if nothing out of the ordinary had been in progress. She felt a flush of embarrassment rush to her face.

"I went out after Ileth. The Matron was worried about her. She is wounded and should be in bed. In a *real* bed."

I'm sure you did! thought Ileth.

"I inquired at the Masters' Hall, then the Guards' halls, and they said there was a sort of gathering at the stables. You were seen walking toward it. I asked for admittance at the door, not suspecting I'd discover this sort of depravity . . ." Santeel stared at the kerchief tying up Ileth's cropped hair, at Rapoto, and back again in increasing fury.

Depravity? For all her name and education, Ileth thought, Santeel hadn't lived much; Ileth's hem hadn't even made it halfway up to her thighs.

"I don't know what you think you saw, Santeel, but it was only a kiss."

Santeel grew larger in her anger the way sparring birds fluff themselves up. "A kiss, he says. With, with this . . . You forget my Name! And while I'm on the subject of names, you forget yours! Rutting with this northern trash."

"Don't speak of her that way," Rapoto said. "She's a novice drag-oneer, same as you."

"You called her that yourself," Santeel said. "Don't deny it!"

"Trash?" Ileth asked.

Rapoto's attention bounced from one to the other. "I did not say *trash*. I absolutely did not say *trash*, Ileth."

"Your exact words when I told you where she was from were: 'A lot of trash washes up on that coast.' What else could it mean?"

Rapoto put himself between Santeel and Ileth. "Ileth, I did not mean you! Not specifically you!"

Others from the stable were gathering. Ileth, no longer tired but feeling strangely bodiless, saw Galia in the audience. And that feeder, what was his name, the one who'd vomited her first night outside the door—Duskirk, that was it. The dancer Peak was whispering something in Galia's ear. Galia would be in attendance. She appeared at so many of Ileth's imbroglios she could pass a hat around and collect coins in exchange for the show. The thought made her giggle. Then she fainted.

Galia and Santeel took her back to the Manor, Galia helping Ileth and Santeel casting about ahead, swinging the lantern like some sort of suspended doom.

"What are you doing, Santeel?" Galia asked.

"Checking the corners. The wingman keeping an eye on the house said they're worried about Gorgantern coming back."

Ileth felt as though they were a procession marching a condemned man to the block, and it turned out to be not far from the truth. Upon hearing Santeel and Galia explain things, that Ileth had been discovered up against a stable wall with a man pressing between her legs, the Matron rose to her feet at a speed that would do a scalded cat credit and ordered her to report to the Master of Novices. Even if she had to sit on the doorstep all night. Which was where she should have been left to begin with.

"I haven't had, don't have, and will not have slatterns in *my* rooms! Go, and do not return," the Matron said, white-lipped with anger.

Quith looked as though she would explode in a burst of gory scandal. Santeel hurried to her bed, too upset to enjoy the drama and talk that immediately broke out among the novices in their nightdress. Galia, looking a little drawn and unfocused—how many drafts of gripe was she concealing?—seemed to be fighting some kind of internal struggle. Ileth wondered what had been going on in the loft above her with Yael Duskirk. She had suspiciously puffy lips.

"I'm not sure much of anything happened," Galia said thickly. "It was but a moment between her leaving the pile-in and Santeel's shout."

"A moment is ample with a boy that age," the Matron replied. "Remember your place, Galia. You're still just an apprentice yourself, flight experience or no."

In the end, Galia took her out. Hurried her out, even. Which was just as well, as they were still in the yard of the Manor when Galia burped loudly.

"I knew I shouldn't have had gripe after that pepper stew," she muttered, wiping her mouth. "But I think it'll stay down. Fates, why does Evire put in so much peated water?"

"I don't . . . don't see that I did anything all that wr-wrong. He kissed me is all."

"Don't play so innocent; I got a good look at his trousers. Ileth, what *are* we going to do with you? You should have either run away or tried to accommodate him in another fashion. I suppose you don't know any of those tricks, though."

She was too tired and cold to blush. "My wits fled as soon as he kissed me. Happened so fast."

"He does have a reputation as a bit of a rabbit. His is a name worth pursuing. You might have yelled 'Rape!' when Dun Troot charged in. He might have offered betrothal right there and that Dun Troot pinch would've dropped dead of shock. Triple laurels for you, if you add in Gorgantern."

"Are you mad? I don't see how I'm any worse than-than-than you, beyond getting caught. What were you doing when you heard Santeel scream?"

Galia took her hand and gave her a friendly but intimidatingly strong squeeze. "I'm not a liar either. So I'll pretend I didn't hear that question so I don't have to answer it."

Rapoto was already in the Masters' Hall. Caseen, bare-legged in a coat and night scarf that concealed what looked like bedclothes, shook his head wearily as she approached.

It was the first time Ileth had seen the Master of Novices without his mask. His face was a furrowed horror of scar and twitching muscle and tendon. It reminded Ileth of a body she'd seen once, brought down from the hills after being frozen in a mountain shelter for goat-shepherds. Scavengers had been nibbling at the frozen skin.

"Ileth, do you have some love of my rooms that you cannot bear to be away from them for a few hours?" Caseen asked. "I can't seem to get rid of you."

"I'm for bed," Galia said, turning away. She quietly burped once her back was to Caseen.

"Just a moment, apprentice," Caseen said. "Rapoto here—quiet now, boy—has given me an explanation of the night's doings. You could help me by telling what you observed."

Ileth tightened her jaw to keep from speaking. *She was in enough trouble.*

Galia turned and took a deep breath. "I didn't see anything. Ileth was at the pile-in with Rapoto. There was a pot of gripe, but I didn't see her have any. They left, and I'd only just started conversing again when I heard Santeel Dun Troot's shout. I hopped up and came as fast as I could. Both of them were fully dressed and upright in an empty stable stall. No mystery. Ileth said they'd been kissing and I not only believe her, I can't see how it could have been anything but a kiss."

"There were . . . intimacies, sir," Rapoto said. "As I said. I am entirely responsible for them. But it did not go so far as Santeel or that woman at the Manor believes." Galia glared at him as if angry with him that he didn't simply deny anything but a kiss in the dark.

"Thank you, Galia. You may go to bed. Careful with the gripe, you reek of it." Galia bobbed, much in the same manner Ileth had been taught, and departed. Caseen collapsed into an armchair among the bookshelves with a groan.

"This often happens with a new batch of novices," Caseen said, looking from one to the other. Ileth feared that when his gaze finally alighted on one of them, it would be her. "Behavior of this sort—it makes for problems. We make an example of the first offense."

"Will we be—expelled?" Rapoto asked.

"Expelled? People are discharged from the dragoneers, not expelled." Caseen chuckled. He let that hang there for a moment, then added, "Novices are released from their oath and dismissed, since they're not subject to the apprentice law or any of the military regulations. However, I'm not Master of Apprentices. I don't think Master Selgernon is about to discharge a Vor Claymass for a dalliance with a jade."

Ileth startled at that. "Sir, I'm no jade."

"Then don't buck about like one, young woman," Caseen said. He turned back to Rapoto. "Exhibit the manners worthy of your name, or we'll send you home, great name or no. I'm afraid I'm behind on my Assembly gossip. I was under the impression there were hopes between the families with our own Santeel Dun Troot."

"This is the first I've heard of it, sir," Rapoto said, face as shocked as if the Master of Novices had kicked his shin. "I don't follow politics. I'm here to get away from that."

"That's admirable. If your skills matched your attitude you would have been apprenticed quicker. Don't you have lamps to fill?"

Rapoto glanced uncertainly at Caseen, then Ileth, and started for the door.

"Now, as to your punishment, young woman," Caseen began.

The boy stopped and turned neatly on the ball of his boot. "Wait, sir, you're going to punish Ileth?"

"That's none of your concern," Caseen said. "It is, on the other hand, my office and commission here."

"I persuaded her to go off with me. I gave her drink. I lifted her dress. She didn't seek seduction. If anyone should be walking out of this room with just a stern warning, it's her."

"As I said, that's not your concern. I dismissed you," Caseen said. "I'd rather someone more appropriate acquainted you with the facts of life, young man. But you must realize that a woman risks much more with this sort of debasement."

"Debasement? Sir, well—I'll marry her before sundown tomorrow, if that's what her reputation here requires."

Ileth felt his words, a shocking yet warm stab to her gut.

"Rapoto," Caseen said, "I think you've had your quota of impulsive decisions for one day."

She looked at Rapoto. In her surprise she hardly stuttered. "From my—from my soul itself, th-thank you. I think you're already regretting making me such an offer. But I can't accept. Your family wouldn't accept. I'm not even sixteen yet. We'd have to wait."

"Hear me out," Rapoto said. There was such an air of command to his voice that Ileth fell silent; Caseen merely listened with new interest. "A marriage offer from my Name, if accepted, would rearrange the pieces on the table. I would be no longer a scoundrel, just a foolish boy in love. She's not a slut; she's my intended. Instead of being vindictive, my family will spend a few frantic weeks making increasingly tempting offers to Ileth that she release me from a bad match. Eventually my family will use its influence to do the Serpentine some great favor at the Assembly in exchange for you pressuring Ileth, and then we will break it off. All concerned breathe a sigh of relief and are happy."

Ileth, whose mind could at least follow his words, even if it wasn't up to conceiving of such a plan and its myriad of angles and dangles, was about to say that she'd be willing to go along with a lie to retrieve her place in the Serpentine when the Master of Novices spoke.

"For a young man with no interest in politics, you have a sense of it." Caseen leaned back, scratching his elbows. "Suppose she's playing her own game of hazard and demands that you follow through on your pledge."

Rapoto stiffened. "That's my concern."

Caseen smiled. "So you're not the self-satisfied spawn of a great name I first took you for. We may be able to do something with you after all." He set to scratching at his elbows in thought.

"A family is an accident of birth, sir," Rapoto said. "I'm here to be something other than a famous name."

"Good for you. Make your own name. But don't do anything drastic. Matters may look very different when you're on the other side of your early years. It's late, and I can't keep up with such dramatics of youth. Let me finish with Ileth. Don't worry, young man, I'm not sending her out into the cold and dark."

Ileth straightened her shoulders, lifted her chin, and turned to Rapoto. "Vor Claymass, I'll face the . . . the rest of this on my own. I appreciate you standing f-for me. Trying to. But please go."

Rapoto sighed. "I'm sorry, Ileth. Don't do anything desperate. My family can easily set you up for life."

"I'm here to set my own life, sir," she said.

The *sir* stung, she could see it in Rapoto's face. Well, he did go fumbling about with her body.

"Half as much consideration an hour ago would have saved you both a good deal of trouble," Caseen observed, echoing her thoughts.

His elbows were soothed and he pointed an index finger at Rapoto. "Now out. Please close the door when you leave."

Ileth kept her face to the Master, waiting until she heard Rapoto's boot heels on the stonework and the door shut.

"Well?" she said. "Am I out?" If she was, she might as well throw herself from that cliff the girls sometimes mentioned. To be oathed in, then lose it in the space of a single season. Better to never have a place in the world than to lose the Serpentine.

"You are the victim of an injustice. It's my sad duty to see that injustice carried out. I'm not happy to do this."

"Say it, sir, whatever it is. Please."

Caseen took a deep breath, as though readying himself for some decision. Then scratching at the door interrupted him.

"That infernal cat," he muttered. Then he blinked several times, rapidly. Ileth wondered what that meant. A slight smile worked its way across the undamaged part of his mouth.

"I believe the first time we talked, I told you the less you saw of me, the better you were probably doing."

She nodded.

"Things have gone wrong for you here."

"A b-bad start is still . . . a start."

The muscles in Caseen's face that still worked registered surprise. "Where did you get that?"

"I thought it was just a saying. I must have heard it up north."

"Ah. Still, it's true. I first read that phrase when I wasn't much older than you. It's one of the maxims of an old dragon of history, one of the Tyrs from across the Inland Ocean. He briefly ruled Hypatia, you know."

Ileth had no idea what he was talking about, but she thought it best to keep quiet and listen.

"Back to the matter at hand. A certain amount of foolishness we can overlook. But if you don't know, I'll be explicit. Women with child can't continue here. There's a home in town for young women who gain a more permanent legacy from an act like this. Don't look as though I'm going to chase you off with dogs; we can wait until the winter solstice and have a look at you then."

"There's no chance, sir. I understand the mechanics of all that."

"I hope you understand motherhood better than dueling, then. Ileth, I must show official disapproval in some manner. The people who send their famously named children don't expect us to allow their sons and daughters to rut about in haylofts."

"Stable. It was a stable stall." She could have added that Galia was the one rutting about in a hayloft, but getting someone else in trouble wouldn't help her predicament.

"It doesn't matter if it was the king's old bedchamber in Asposis. We can't have it."

She couldn't look at him, and not just because of the burns. Miserable, she hung her head. In the Lodge, she'd seen so many girls get moonstruck over a boy, and she'd sworn to herself to be different, to follow her star to a dragon's back and on that to horizons she couldn't imagine—and yet it happened to her as easily as a strong wind could blow a dry leaf across a yard. *Stupid, Ileth! So stupid!* Stars in their courses, she'd be sniveling next. She dug her nails into her palm, hard. That stalled it.

"But on to your case. I get the impression I won't have to write any kind of explanatory letter to your mother and father, no matter what happens a few months from now?"

She shook her head. The chopped hair was too short to hide her face.

"There will be talk; there's no avoiding it. I will have to put your name down in the Blue Book." He gestured to a blue-dyed leather ledger book on his desk. "Before I was Master of Novices, when your name went down in this book, you were out the gate and never allowed to return. I believe that even the best of us can make a serious mistake, especially at your age, so I've improved on the tradition, I like to think. Now you are given a second chance when your name goes into the book. Another serious problem, and you are thrown out and I draw a line through your name, so that you are never readmitted. Some who go down in the Blue Book choose to leave voluntarily and reapply the next year with the slate wiped clean. Would you like to do that?"

Ileth had no friends, no resource to fall back on to support her for a year. This was her one chance with the dragoneers. "No, sir."

"I understand. Nothing to go back to."

She nodded.

"We'll remove you from the Manor. I must reinforce the Matron's discipline, and a swift banishment will make an impression on your sisters there."

Sisters! Yes, well, that's one way to think about them. If only Santeel hadn't started shouting her head off!

"We have two apprentice girls living and working in the dragoneer hall, but that's a distinction, even if you're just wiping windows and sweeping floors and fetching morning tea. It would be counted as a reward. I can't send that impression. Since you've proved yourself hardy and have shown a certain amount of physical courage in that dueling business, and are, well, worldly, I could put you in with the dancers."

"Dancers, sir?" There'd been a dancer at the pile-in, that Peak girl.

"Yes. Don't get the wrong idea, it's for the dragons. It's not Sammer-dam's face powder grotto here. Not at all. You don't know we use them? I forget how new you are. The Catch Basin isn't exactly in the center of the Beehive. Yes, we have a troupe of dancers. They have a curious history here. At one time they were Auxiliaries, not even part of the drag-oneers, more like experts on retainer. Eventually they had to be put under Serpentine discipline. Too much trouble among the dragoneers over them."

"Why do the dragons need dancers?" Ileth asked.

"Surely you've heard stories and legends about dragons and human women."

She nodded. Almost every girl had heard stories, if not from parents and relatives then from other girls, or books for those with access to them and the ability to read that male dragons found the presence of human women pleasing, pleasing enough to risk the wrath of entire populations by carrying them off. Since Ileth had been quietly collecting dragon apocrypha since meeting Agrath and Annis Heem Strath, she'd heard different versions. They said in folk tales that it had something to do with smell, but no two legends quite agreed on the nature of the smell or ways to increase or decrease its potency. Folk tales of maidens bewitching dragons with songs or dances to distract them, then retrieving some treasure or extracting a promise, were common enough that she'd grown up with childhood rhymes about them and even seen an example in a copybook: a girl hiding behind a fan, revealing half a smile to a serpentlike creature with almost human eyes and stubby legs and wings: *CHARM conquers even a DRAGON.* The picture had annoyed Ileth, as a real dragon looked nothing like that.

"Ottavia, she's in charge of the troupe, can tell you more. There's ancient tradition to it. Goes back a thousand years and more to Ancient Hypatia and the time of that old Tyr you quoted. It's not dull work. It'll put you in contact with the dragons in a more important way than trimming and polishing scales while they snooze."

"I do—I do like a dance, sir." And it was better than gutting fish.

"That's the angle. You could even look at it as a promotion. You'll be around the dragons. If you design to build a life in the Serpentine, that's always helpful."

"I have my personals at the Manor. Might I say a few goodbyes, too?"

"Not at this hour, I'm afraid. I'll send a note to the Matron with my judgment and some instructions. She'll think it just; to her the dancers are a coven of—well, you know her as well as I. Your things will be bundled and delivered to the Dancers' Quarter."

"Thank you, sir. I'm sorry . . . sorry for tonight."

"I understand. And don't drink any rubbish to flush yourself out, no matter who gives it to you or what they say about it. A girl died that way when I was young." He looked pained at the thought. He cleared his throat and stood up, using his good leg.

"I won't," she said.

"Follow Ottavia's direction and this night will soon be forgotten. The Serpentine changes with the moon. New excitement every time a dragon lands. If you haven't figured that out yet, you soon will."

She nodded.

The smile vanished. He leaned across his map table. The light from the little two-flame oil lamp threw deep shadows into his eye sockets from this angle, and she found herself fascinated in a way by the scarred horror that was his face. "One more thing about the dancers. Some of the dragoneers here fancy themselves rakes—these men will consider your favors easily had in that role, as though you were dancing on a table in the most libertine pipe-den in Tyrenna. Don't let anyone tell you your job is anything other than working up a good sweat for the dragons. Ottavia is *exceptionally* deft at handling those sort of situations. Bring it to her and hold nothing back. I hope the lesson you learned tonight sticks. I want everyone to forget it, except you."

Ileth briefly wished she'd had a man like Caseen as a father, or just visiting now and then as an uncle. Stern but kindly. Interested but neutral. But as Rapoto said, her family was an accident of birth and there was no helping that.

"I've lost track of the time," Caseen said. "Have you heard a bell?"

"The midnight bell rang while I was walking here with Galia," Ileth said.

"Well, we can't wake Ottavia up at this hour, at least not for this."

"I don't mind sleeping in the hall," she said. "Discomfort right before a turn in fortune is my style."

"The chair by the fire is comfortable. It's stuffed with horsehair. It would only take a few minutes to build the fire back up again. You'd be warm. I sleep in a little room on the other side of the fireplace. Once upon a time this was a clerk's and manservant's office and my bedroom the master office, but we live more to a republican ideal now. I much prefer this. I'm a lazy old man. I like a comfortable bed nearby and am reluctant to leave it once warmed, so you'll be able to sleep later than you are used to at the Manor."

Ileth asked if she could leave the door to the hallway open. "We don't want to start another rumor."

Caseen chuckled at that. "No. I might have to offer to marry you as well and then we might end up with another duel to win your favors. I'm not sure the Serpentine could handle the excitement."

The Master departed. She heard a groan or two from his inner room as he settled down for what was left of the night. She added a little charcoal to the fire before pulling the chair close and settling in. The chair had a rich, masculine scent to it, some kind of barber oil most likely, and she found it comforting, especially warmed as it was by the fire. Scent can be a powerful signal. She wondered what sort of message her own body sent to the dragons.

At one point in the morning today—no, yesterday—she was sure she'd be dead and cold by nightfall, and here she was, warm and alone and considering her sense of smell and the potential of her own effect on dragons. She'd tempted and dodged two dooms today. And no more hygiene lectures from the Matron! That was almost worth having your name set down in this Blue Book of Doom or whatever it was called. She decided she had much to be grateful for and resolved that it would be a long time before she tempted fate a third time.

Relaxed and with a relieved feeling that could pass for happy, she swiftly slipped into sleep.

PART TWO

FIRST STEPS

Life calls the tune.
You decide how you dance to it.

—*A DRAGON DANCER'S DIARY* (MEMOIR, 3114)

7

As promised, Caseen stayed in his sleeping room long after the rest of the Masters' Hall was busy with activity. She woke, and with nothing else to do she cleaned out the ash from the small hearth and warmed the fire again. She used a bit of the ash and the corner of her skirt to polish the dragon whistle Dath Amrits had given her. Then she retreated to the chair. Novices and apprentices were passing in the hall, tidying and bringing the day's business. She heard the cat yowl at some outrage.

One apprentice in a kitchen smock came by with tea and toast and peppered fish and left when he saw that Caseen was not out of his sleeping room yet; another boy entered with coal, removed the ash, and refilled the bin with a nod of recognition, and then one of the novice girls from the Manor swept the hall and exchanged a wary nod with her.

"Not kicked out? Herself said you'd be kicked out."

"He wrote me up in that . . . in that book. In the book and out of the Manor," Ileth said. "The Master is finding new duties for me."

"Hardly a one of us slept last night, what with all the whispering back and forth. You wouldn't believe what's—"

"I would. Could you ask Quith to roll up my things for me?"

The girl nodded and moved on down the hall with her broom.

Ileth thought about what a sorry figure she must have cut, being thrown out of the Manor in the middle of the night. No wonder they'd talked. The cat peeped in, sniffed at what must have been the scents coming off the tea and toast, and looked at Ileth expectantly. She just looked back and the cat turned away, as if indifferent to the smell of butter, and set about washing its face with its back toward her.

Caseen rose about the time his letters appeared. He had his mask back on. He wished her a good morning, scribbled a note, and went and found a page to bring note and notable to Ottavia Imperene.

"She's not spent much time in the Beehive," Caseen said to the page. "Make sure she can find her way out again."

"Heard you got blued," the page said as they walked out the hall door and into the morning. Ileth shrugged.

So back in her traveling boots, Ileth walked down the familiar, curving gravel road toward the Long Bridge. The overcast looked to be breaking up and giving way to some sunshine. She wasn't superstitious, but the glimpses of the sun that turned the lake from its usual dull gray to gemstone-quality blue, reminding her of her first daylight look at the Serpentine and its surroundings, put her in a hopeful mood.

At the familiar turn to the Manor, she took it. Not by accident.

"Uh, what are you doing?" the page asked.

Ileth ignored him. She approached the Manor. An armed wingman she didn't know exhibiting a shaped beard and mustache that must have required a great deal of attention in front of a good mirror raised an eyebrow.

The novices and apprentices had long since gone to work.

Ileth rapped on the door, a polite sort of knock.

"Ileth!" insisted the page, though she wasn't certain what he was insisting on.

The Matron opened it, eyes hostile, mouth set. The page shifted around behind Ileth to avoid the withering stare.

Ileth sensed the novices who helped her keep house behind the Matron, keeping a distance to avoid potential contamination.

"You," the Matron said, with the tone that suggested *you* stood for other, despicable words.

"Madam," Ileth said, slowly to minimize her stuttering. "I was passing and wanted to thank you."

"*Thank* me?"

"Yes. Yes, I grew up in a lodge, you see. I know how difficult it is to keep a crowded house clean and fed."

The Matron didn't respond for a moment; perhaps she had to parse the words in search of insult or ambush. "Yes. It can be difficult."

"You have . . . you have been kind to me. I am sorry for last night. I am grateful for your hard work keeping house."

Perhaps she'd overdone it a bit. The Matron gave a practiced but not friendly smile. "Well, that's good of you to say, Ileth."

There. She used her name, and the *you* no longer contained an accusation. It wasn't so hard.

"That's . . . that's all, madam. Good morning and good-bye," Ileth said, giving a little bob. She backed away and looked expectantly at the page. He bowed at the Matron, and once off the threshold they turned and moved down the path toward the guardian wingman.

Ileth listened. There was a long moment before the door was shut behind them.

"What in the underworld was that all about?" the page asked once they were on the main road again.

"Honor," Ileth replied. That shut him up.

Even the bridge was deserted, except for some chatting wingmen passing around a pipe. She heard some talk of updrafts, but the wingmen ignored an insignificant novice and a page bearing a note.

She entered the Beehive proper from the main entrance for the first time that morning.

A geometric pattern in a blue-and-white mosaic decorated the border of the finely finished cavern entrance. Air moved inward with a faint snuffle, as if the Beehive were sniffing its visitors.

As though he were placed there to give the entrance a to-scale perspective, a dragoneer lounged just outside the cave entrance, occupying two simple wooden chairs set so they faced each other, his booted feet up on the seat of one. He smoked long, thin rolled tobacco, a curious indulgence because she thought only wealthy men could afford rolled and sealed tobacco. Even seated, Ileth recognized him. She'd seen him before hanging around with the kindly Hael Dun Huss. He was a tall scarecrow of a man, needed a shave on his plain, long face (many of the dragoneers wore fashionable mustaches), and was a little unkempt about the hair, as though he never bothered much with it. A battered brown planting hat, the epitome of republican simplicity without hatband, cockade, or feathers, sat on his bony knee as though keeping him company.

Her escort page nodded as they passed the dragoneer. The dragoneer watched her the way you'd watch a horse and rider approaching on an empty road, not having anything more interesting to look at. He didn't turn his head as they went by, but he did take the tobacco out of his mouth and held it away from her so she didn't have to walk through smoke to enter the Beehive.

"That's the Borderlander. He's a northerner. You're a northerner, right?" the page said.

"The Freesand coast." She'd never been to the Borderlands, a high, cold plateau between the North Bay and Jotun. She'd only heard that life there was hard, with bandits, gargoyles in the mountains, bear-people, and other kinds of unpleasantness. The Borderlands people had a reputation for feuding and lawbreaking, and some said they belonged to the Republic only because nobody else wanted to bother with them.

The page led her into the Beehive. The walls in the entryway to the Beehive were painted in a subdued green. She heard a banging echoing from far off and sensed that something vast crossed the tunnel far ahead.

The passageway sloped up a little and Ileth got the sense of light ahead, which must have been from the vast round chamber crowning the Beehive where the dragons met, the Rotunda. She knew of it and had seen it in paintings. The page cut short her anticipation of finally seeing it and ducked down a narrow (even for human size) side passage and they descended through a mix of natural, tunneled, and improved alleys, lit by lamps or the cheapest and smelliest of candles. Other small tunnels led off at the lights, some emitting noises and smells. The page rattled off names: some almost poetic, like *Granthan's Bloody End*, some strictly utilitarian, like *Coal Shaft*. They came to another wide dragon passage. The air was oily and smelled of dragons and the oliban braziers.

"This is the Under Ring at last. Ottavia's troupe is here. You haven't been in here?"

"Just the Catch Basin and the kitchens."

"At the top you have the big hall above where the dragons meet, the Rotunda. The Rotunda is where the Dragon Horn is too; you may have heard it when they opened the gate to let you applicants in, if you were there that morning. The Over Ring is beneath that and connected to it. Most of the dragons live in the Over Ring. That's where we entered. The Under Ring, that's mostly for the younger dragons. Then there's the Kitchens; it's also a ring, but we just call it the Kitchens. At the bottom there's the Cellars; the tunnels there branch out like a big starfish. There's a dragon living in the Cellars, I'm told. Dunno if he guards the stores down there or what, but he practically never leaves. If we get a female who wants to lay her eggs, she goes down there a lot too, just because it's quiet and she can be at ease without noise all the time. We just came down what's called the West Twist. There's the East Stair too; there are some rooms off the landings there. The Dancers' Quarter is off the East Stair."

"Rotunda, Over Ring, Under Ring . . . Kitchens, Cellars. West Twist . . . East Stairs." By reciting the words syllable by syllable she hardly stuttered. He'd left out some parts she'd already heard about, like the flight cave, where dragons and dragoneers met and readied themselves for a flight, and the lighthouse, and the Chimney, a sort of air-circulation shaft the dragons used to climb between levels quickly.

"Lots more, but that will get you started," the page said. "Busy as a beehive here, sure enough. When I was first apprenticed, I helped the physikers, stitching dragon wings and pulling broken scale. We saw a lot of the dancers. People say that the troupe's just an excuse to give the dragoneers some—well, it's venting. They do help keep the dragons calm, even if their outfits would be a scandal in Vyenn. The dragoneers leave 'em alone. Mostly. They earn their tuck and kip, by my oath. I wouldn't want to extract a highpoon point without a dancer or two around to keep the beast's mind off the pain. Some of the females like the dancers too, but for the art and music of it being soothing, more than sucking in scent."

He took her to an entrance that wasn't much more than a shaped crack in the wall. The crack was surrounded by its own decorative painted border in lively reds and whites. The doorway had been painted with cryptic signs by a succession of artists, or perhaps one gifted painter trying to look like several. She recognized an icon or two of religious symbolism, and one was a mark that a hunter would sometimes carve into trees up north to commemorate the spot where he brought down a beast, but the rest were a mystery to her.

A velvet curtain blocked the short passageway at the inside.

"Master's page, with Novice Ileth and a message for the Charge," the page said into the curtain.

"Come in and be welcome."

He opened the curtain. The rings made a good deal of noise as they moved along the bar, clattering like a basket full of dropped finger cymbals. Maybe they were designed that way.

The voice turned out to be Peak, whom Ileth had met at the pile-in last night. She was massaging her feet with something medicinal-smelling, and the hair about her face was matted with sweat.

"Didn't expect to see you again so soon," Peak said. The page looked confused but Ileth gave a tentative wave.

"May I land her with you? She needs to speak to the Charge," the page said. Peak didn't stop working her feet.

The chamber within wasn't cavelike at all. It was more like a great tent from a story of an exotic land. It was heated by a little stove with a teakettle on and a pipe to carry away the smoke. Three matching stools sat around the stove. Curtains and rugs and tenting and netting covered it from floor to ceiling. Oil lamps, each of a different design and none native to the Vales, lit the area, either hanging from loops driven into the ceiling or in small alcoves in the wall. There were trunks and cases scattered about, and a folding desk with writing things atop it.

"Ottavia is in Vyenn and not expected back until late."

"Ileth here has asked to be a dancer." Which wasn't exactly how events had unfolded, but perhaps this was some ritual. "I have a note from the Master of Novices."

"That is news she'll want to hear. She was hoping for someone from this batch. Does this have anything to do with the pile-in?"

"I've been turned out of the Manor," Ileth said. The news would pass through the Beehive anyway; she might as well own up to it.

"Mmmmm," Peak said, as though she were the third disgraced girl dropped off that morning.

The page dropped his note on a metal tray by the writing things. "He said the note was important."

"The Serpentine doesn't run on fish and dragon wings, but paper," Peak said. "I'll see that it's brought to her attention."

The page thanked her, said good luck to Ileth, and bowed out. He closed the noisy curtain behind him.

Peak slipped into a quilted robe and put on wood and leather clogs. "I shall dash down and tell Ottavia now. She's not in Vyenn; she's arguing with the laundry. I just didn't want Muggins there to think every time a Master's page shows up, we jump about like trained monkeys. Now whether Ottavia rearranges her day to sort you out, I can't know. If not, just wait here. Lie down on the cushions and put your feet up if you like. We all do. You'll soon learn to be off your feet whenever you get a chance."

Ileth did not have to wait long. Though she didn't find the nerve to just lie down on one of the cushions with her feet up, after testing the ointment Peak had been using on her feet by rubbing it between her finger and thumb, she went over to one of the cases that had one of those eye-catching boxes atop it and examined it.

It was at the very least painted with gold, with pearls on the lid and luxuriously heavy. Ileth gulped. She supposed it was safe enough here, in the heart of a fortress filled with dragons, but from the weight of the thing she guessed it would buy a new tin roof and windows entire for the Captain's Lodge with enough left over to replace every stick of furniture and add a plush carpet or two.

Daring, she opened it. The interior had a small mirror and a perfectly oval seashell with a reclining nude figure painted in it, her long hair artfully maintaining her modesty. It also played a delicate tune. A music box!

She'd seen a few before, though nothing like this one. It sounded as though two sets of different chimes were playing. The tune seemed content to play forever. She closed it again.

She was sniffing at the tea—it was exotically spiced and vaguely smoky—when her new Master (perhaps!) arrived. She swept the curtain aside with a metallic crash that startled Ileth.

Ottavia Imperene, Charge to the Dragon Dancers, was one of those women who combined maiden, mother, and crone all in one person. Her hair was thin and drawn up into a simple bun, with a great deal of gray showing among the brown, which accounted for the crone, and she clasped a light walking stick in one fleshless hand. Lines about her eyes and the firm set of her mouth and a certain air of authority suggested mother. Ileth couldn't help but be drawn to her eyes, bright with vivacity, and her smooth carriage as she crossed the tented chamber to greet her new novice. Ottavia Imperene was all maiden when in motion.

Peak worked the curtain and retreated behind a wall of fabric to some other, unknown chamber.

They exchanged names. Ileth mentioned the note, but Ottavia ignored it for now.

"Novice, tell me: what brings you to us here?" she asked. Ileth suspected she already knew the story beginning to end—Peak was at the pile-in and she remembered her excited witness of the affair in the stable stall—and just wanted to see what sort of explanation she'd get.

"The Master of Novices suggested I might . . . f-fit in better here, sira. Until . . . until . . . until yesterday I was working down below the kitchens gutting fish."

"I heard something about a girl who got into a duel with a man. What's-his-name, the aging apprentice, stuck there like a rotting tooth? You were the duelist?"

"His name was—is Gorgantern."

She tapped her walking stick, once, hard on the floor. "If I wanted trivia like his name I would have asked you. Answer the question."

"Yes, sira, I fought the duel—the duel you heard about."

The Charge to the Dancers walked around her, evaluating her. "You've never danced before."

She wasn't sure if she should turn and face her when she talked—that would be the polite thing to do—but the Charge seemed engrossed in her calves. "Certainly I've danced, sira. Up on—"

"I don't mean gathering-room parties. I meant as a trained entertainer."

"No. Not . . . Nothing like that."

"Your arms are too long."

"I'm sorry?"

"Proportionally. Were you not fed properly as a child? Big feet, too, but that can be good, if they're strong. Well, if Caseen will send me no one else, a girl built like a blighter will do. At least you're pretty. You may grow into a beauty, which makes those arms all the more a shame."

Ileth thought it best to remain silent, as she hadn't been asked anything.

"Health good? Apart from the stutter? Are you a fainter? Get out of breath? Are you much used to running?"

"I've run all the way up the outer stairs, and back down again." Maybe she had something to be grateful to Gorgantern for, after all.

"Do you read music?"

"No."

"You know what we do here?" the Charge asked.

"You dance for the dragons."

"I said 'we,' so you should use it too, if you're to join us."

"We dance for the dragons, sira."

"Why did you come to the Serpentine?"

She'd never heard it put so directly. "To be around dragons."

Ottavia twitched her nose. "When you did dance, at parties and so on, how did it make you feel?"

"Feel? I . . . loved it. When I've had an opportunity." There weren't many gatherings in the Freesand to begin with, and even fewer invitations to parties to a girl from the Captain's Lodge. The Captain didn't care for music.

"Do you have reservations about joining us? Think you've fallen into a den of whores?"

She gasped at that. "No!"

"Then you don't know much about the world. In Asposis or Sammerdam, court dancers not all that different from our method are often involved with the scions of great names. They like to take them as lovers and show them off, like a hunting falcon or the latest in racing horses."

The Charge said all that with a matter-of-factness, as if she'd been discussing nothing more controversial than the weather. She went on: "'Tis quite the cockade for the bucks to have a dancer on your arm at certain gatherings. Much better than an actress, I mean, any jade can put on a wig, some face powder, smudge her eyes, and call herself an actress. Being a dancer takes training and work. I can watch someone walk through a crowded room once and I'll tell you whether they're a dancer or no. You're not a trophy here, you're a skilled dragontender. We're here for the dragons, not the men. At least not under me, or the woman who instructed me, or the woman before her. Even if you wish to be more like the dancers in Asposis. No social climbing on your back."

"Understood, sira." Her Charge seemed to demand precision when you answered her. Ileth was more than a little frightened by her demanding manner.

"Relax, girl. I believe most any girl can dragon dance well enough to soothe a dragon if she works hard at it." Ottavia wasn't just formidable, she was a mind-reader. "It's just a matter of practice, sweat, and being able to keep to the music."

Mentally, Ileth added that at least you didn't have to speak much when you danced, unless it was far different than she imagined. "I should like to try," she said.

"Excellent! Don't worry about never having danced before. It would have gone worse for you if it turned out you were a professional. I won't have to break any bad habits."

The Charge summoned a dancer named Zusya. She was curvier than Ottavia or Peak but moved with restrained energy, like a held-back horse eager for a gallop. "Zusya, I'm sorry to steal your day off. Find Ileth here a berth, do a pass-round for some training clothes, teach her to stand for drill, and then feed her. Add her to both drill lists indefinitely. That should be ample for today. You can be excused all of tomorrow, Zusya. There's nothing on. Go into Vyenn if you like. I'll manage myself if there's an emergency."

Like Ileth, Zusya was dressed in a ratty men's work shirt that was even more of a bad fit for her than Ileth's, but she'd tied her apprentice sash at the waist and turned the bottom into a slanted fringe.

"With certainty, sira." Zusya spoke rapidly and well, but her phrasings didn't sound quite right and she accented her words as one who'd learned Montangyan as a second tongue. Her eyes had an intriguing shape to them.

"First, your berth . . ."

As in the Manor, the dancers lived in tight quarters, dividing their bed-space with curtains. Ileth and the other dancers, with the exception of their Charge, lived in a dim, triangular tunnel called the Notch. It reminded Ileth of a cramped part of a ship she'd once visited with the Captain (who had once commanded her), a deck where the sailors slept in piggy warmth called the in-between. A man of ordinary height could just stand outside the curtains, and the cavern roof sloped down to anchored woodwork holding rope-net beds with mattresses and bedding. The Notch opened up on a cistern room that had Sammerdam-style taps for drinking and washing, and a wood-walled toilet cabinet and drain in the corner for elimination and disposing of wash water. A nice wooden lattice in the cabinet built around the drain saved your feet from soil.

In the center of the Notch, where it was widest, an iron stove warmed the place and had a few pots hanging over it for cooking. "The big red-painted one is for boiling laundry, so don't be a clever-clog like Vii and try and win our favor by making a big bowl of Mother's famous soup in it," Zusya said. "Don't go off and leave your monthly dressings in it to boil clean either or you'll be up at the midnight bell doing drills and fatigues with Peak birch-thrashing you to tempo-count."

Zusya turned around and continued speaking while walking

backward through the sleeping quarters. It made Ileth nervous, but whenever she looked about to plow into something—like the steaming stove—she executed a brisk hop and navigated around it. "This was once quarters for an order of monks. Supposedly they watched the dragons sleep on astrologically important days, and how the dragon slept foretold the future. Something like that. They're long gone.

"Here's yours." She pulled aside a curtain and Ileth examined the lightless corner. A bed with rope supports and a linenless, sweat-stained mattress were all the room held, unless you counted some circles of guttered wax candles atop a little shelf carved into the wall.

"Some put their religious statues or icons in that. I have a spare caduceus you can hang on the wall, if you do your devotions," Zusya said. "Don't despair, there are usually linens on market days and you can paint if you want. Has your family money for a good mirror? It would be so nice to get another good mirror in here. I am aware that there is no window. Sunlight is hard to come by in the Beehive, I'm afraid. To make up for this we do our reading and sewing outside in almost any weather. Or study. Do you have tutors come?"

"No."

"Ah, well, more time for drills or attending the dragons, then."

"It's fine. It's actually roomier than my Manor space."

"You're next to Vii. The next spot after Vii's, the one with the yellow curtain, is Preen's. She has a wonderful tea-kit with a huge well that she puts guttered candles under. Has tea on it all day. We've had as many as nine taking tea with her. Her father is in the tea trade. Or maybe it's he owns ships that bring the tea. I forget. He sends her the stuff by the tenweight."

Ileth was used to old leaves livened up with flower petals or a bit of dried fruit. *Real, first-steep tea!*

"Sorry, you're newest here so we've put you on the end farthest from the stove and next to the washroom. As the newest your job is cleaning the sinks and sluice. But have a cheer, we've room for one or two more, so if someone else joins you'll be senior to them! Vii will be happy you've arrived. She won't have to be the scour anymore. You'll see her at drills tomorrow morning; she went into Vyenn.

"We eat out of the dragon kitchen. Pure laziness. Such a walk to the dining hall. Occasionally we'll all go as a troupe, but it's hard to get everyone together off the music. The fish in the kitchens is all right. It's almost always fresh, but the other stuff that comes in barrels . . . just watch yourself and trust your nose. Pickled eggs are safe. I eat them instead of meat, and so do the cooks, to get them through the day. The cooks haven't an idea between them. It's not worth your life to touch the beef and mutton!"

Zusya, she was learning, was a bit of a chatterbox.

She showed off the taps in the washroom: "We wash often, usually at night to keep the bedding cleaner. Our costumes, well, that's another story. We earn our keep by sweating, and some of us—I'm one of them—use herbed skin oils too. The dragons are fond of spice. No florals, never florals, they don't like sweet at all. Best ask if you're in doubt. You don't use perfumes, do you?"

Ileth shook her head *no*. She was already fond of Zusya. You didn't have to say a word. Ever.

She chattered her way through the laundry procedures, where to get a clean towel or a canvas slipper, and who had the best headache powder.

"Don't let anyone tell you anything about bathing. Shatha, she's second oldest after Ottavia, she says a dragon dancer should hardly ever bathe. Nasty thing. Do whatever you like. Hair doesn't matter much; again, Peak's advice on long hair is just that, advice. I don't think the dragons care. Keep your soldier chop if you want. What you do with the hair on your head and body is your own business. Ottavia will tell you. Peak and Vii will play the old wise woman and say that you mustn't pluck a hair, as it captures and keeps smell. Nonsense! Shatha grew up in the old court city of Asposis. She shaves her head like a boy being deloused. Just wears wigs. She's quite popular with the dragons, and not a hair on her head. Just don't wash with turpentine or use flowery oils and you will be fine."

"Turpentine?"

"That's a story for another time," Zusya said. "Peak played a nasty joke on Vii when she first came."

"How long have you been a dancer?"

"Five years. I started right from novice, just like you. What are you, thirteen, special admittance?"

"Fourteen. Last spring."

"Oh, you look a bit younger. I was thirteen when I came through the gate. I lied about my age—shhh. Nineteen in the spring."

"Did you dance before?"

Zusya laughed. "Tears, no! My parents would have locked me in the attic. My dad kept a tavern, but it wasn't like some. Dairy men soothing their muscles with beer and swapping stories about cheese. A dancer would have been tossed out on her ear, same as a pimp."

"So how did you end up here?"

"Master Caseen, he knows people. I don't know what made him decide I would be happy as a dancer. I guess I'm a bit wild; maybe being sat on all the time by my elders and parents in a cow patch made me a bit flash once I found my feet here. But he sent me to the Charge and I've loved the life, once I limbered up my feet. Who else is around the dragons so much, and having fun besides? We are the luckiest of the Serpentine, I think."

Ileth smiled at that.

"By the way, is that boy Rapoto a good kisser? I'd hate to think that face wasted on someone who couldn't kiss."

Gossip spread fast in the Serpentine. Probably that Peak. "It happened so fast. I suppose. Yes."

"Not much to compare it to? I was the same way when I got here. Don't delve too much into that. Ottavia's correct, we're not bed warmers. Though there's a dragoneer or two whose bed I wouldn't mind making warm, given time and tide.

"Now. Attire, the Charge said. I'll pass a bag around tonight. One thing you'll learn about dancers: we have clothes and odds-and-ends enough for a year-away school. You won't be getting rags, either. We've all been the scour. It's good for the soul to put something nice in when a scour's bag gets brought around. Just remember that when your feet are half callus."

"Ottavia said something about 'teach her to stand for drill.'"

"Oh, yes, we're coming to that. I'll show you where we drill. Have you been to the Rotunda yet?"

"No, I don't think so."

"Then let's go. You'd remember it if you'd seen. It's just above the flight cave on the bay side of the Beehive. There's a passage out in the center of the floor where the dragons can jump down if they need to get at the flight cave fast from the Rotunda. Ever seen a full-sized dragon leap, by the way? They're just like cats; they fold themselves up into a crouch and then explode. It's like a house falling down around you. Down there's a good place to collect scales; sometimes they miss and knock a few loose."

"I thought we weren't supposed to do that."

"Oh, we're not. We gather them up and turn them in. Though we will often keep a scale of a favorite dragon as a souvenir. Peak made the prettiest hair clip out of one. Souvenir's one thing. They just don't want anyone smuggling them out for coin."

Zusya, walking backward as she talked, led her up through progressively larger passages until they reached companionways large enough for a dragon to pass through. The human-mined tunnels, though, struck Ileth as irregular, almost organic, like a huge tree had sent its roots through the stone and then was later drilled out and removed.

They passed others now. From somewhere Ileth heard a booming dragon voice say, "Ouch! Careful now."

Ileth felt the Rotunda before they reached it. Her senses were alive to the light and air and space ahead. Now the floor was elaborately tiled and the walls showed mosaics with writhing knotted shapes twining in and out of each other like vines. She tried not to gape.

The walls curved away and they entered the Rotunda.

Everyone was right about it. The space made you go all still and quiet, like a mouse fallen into the middle of a ballroom.

It felt unnatural to have so much space indoors. She felt the weight of time and historic events; it made her want to walk with slow, gentle steps and keep silent. She supposed the dragons would need a great deal of space to meet. If it also overawed intruders, that was all the better.

"It rains in here sometimes, if they have a crowd in here and the weather is just right," Zusya said. "They say it was built by dwarves. I find it easy to believe the legends about dwarves when I stand here."

"Are those—perches?" Ileth asked, walking over to one of the spurs jutting out of the wall.

"The dragons lie on those when they have meetings," Zusya said. "Someone told me it was modeled after another dragon hall."

Ileth counted eight perches. But the room would probably hold two or three times that in fully grown dragons if some didn't mind curling up on the floor. Just above the perches, writing in an unknown, slashing script appeared in a regular ring around the walls. At the pinnacle of the Rotunda was a dark, metallic cavern of shadow. "That's the mouth of the Dragon Horn. Only a dragon has enough lung to work it. The mouthpiece is down by the flight cave; it runs through the floor, and you can see some of the tube there, see how it gets bigger?" Zusya said, pointing to a greenish tube of metal that gradually widened as it moved from floor to ceiling, engraved with more of those slashing icons. "Loud enough to wake the dead. Turns the whole Rotunda into sort of an echo chamber. But they only blow it a couple times a year. Troth Day, during the exchange of cups. Or if there's an emergency.

"The dragons don't always have meetings here. They're fond of discussing things below, too, in the rain room when they bathe, when there's just two or three of them. The most favorite grooms work them over down there. Hard duty but they're rich as anything; it's the one job in the whole Serpentine where you get to keep all the odds and ends you pry off the dragons and sell. Some tradition going back to before the Republic. They earn it; it's hot as a kitchen in summer. I've had to perform there, too, and then you just sit quietly and let the sweat pour off you while they talk. Drink a lot of water and bring a hunk of salt to lick if you have to dance in the rain room."

She took Ileth over to the well-like hole, if *hole* was the right word for such a drop. It was as big around as a castle tower.

"Down there is where we drill. Used to be the main grooming room, before they built the new one with the skylights, and it's still used for that, sometimes. There's an easier route to it, but I thought it would be nice if you had a good look at the Rotunda first. There are big mirrors in there. Wall of Mirrors, it's called. Dragons like to look at themselves too, and they're the biggest mirrors in the Vales. Bigger than at the Silver Palace in Asposis, Shatha says. They had to manufacture them right here, I'm told. It's a miracle they're intact, the way the dragons whip about with their tails when they're in a hurry. Maybe they figured that when they worked out the size of the well."

"Do they jump down on you—us when we're doing drills?"

"I've never had that happen. Not even close. Often there's a dragon or two watching us drill. They tell us to get out of the way when they climb down. That floor is thick hardwood beams covered with planking, like a ship's deck. It's springy, easier on the feet. I forget, you're from a nautical family or something?"

A flash of movement caught Ileth's eye. A green dragon scrambled out of an entrance to the Rotunda opposite, hopped down into the well, and disappeared into a wide, sloping passage. A leather case bounced at its position where it was slung at the base of her neck. She was smallish, and skin covered with scale-stubbles showed where her wings had uncased and scar tissue was slowly being covered with scale. Her wing-assisted leap allowed her to land with surprisingly little noise for a creature so large. Ileth noticed that the female kept her claws semiretracted (unlike a cat's claws, they couldn't disappear completely, but they did retreat like a turtle's head pulling back into its shell).

A young man with his long hair tied tightly back emerged from the same entrance and put his hands on his knees, half collapsing from what looked to be an exhausting run keeping up with a four-legged dragon.

When he could finally draw breath he shouted: "Jizara! You forgot your salve!"

Zusya dismissed the scene with a wave. "There's always excitement around the flight cave. I wouldn't care to keep track of all the comings and goings."

"How often do we perform?"

"We're ready all the time, more so than the Guards, I'd say, in case there's an emergency. The dragons are polite about it; they'll ask if it's convenient to perform. The answer is yes. Always yes. Understand? We sweat for our supper."

Zusya took her down a carved set of steps going down to the Wall of Mirrors.

The floor in here had an inlaid wood design that made her think of a compass, but the mirrors were the real attraction. Never mind their size, she'd never seen mirrors that could compare to these in their lack of flaws. Each mirror was perhaps three times as tall as she was. Ileth regarded herself in the faultless reflection, tried a few smiles and poses on for size.

Her guide pulled up a little thing that was like a chair without a seat or a miniature small drying rack that could easily be moved in front of a fireplace. It came up to about her bottom rib. On someone as tall as Ottavia, it was probably hip-high.

"This is your support. You'll need it, and not just at first. Even the most experienced dancer spends a long time at her support."

With that, Zusya taught her how to stand. They stripped down to their sheaths and overshirts. Zusya had the well-defined leg muscles of a draft ox.

They spent Ileth's whole first afternoon just working on how to stand before a dance, going up piece by piece on her body and back down it again. Dancing was all in the feet. Except the part that wasn't all in the feet and was in fact all in your central muscles around your spine, it was all in that. And then there was the part that said dancing was all in how you held your head and the way it kept steady no matter what your body was doing . . .

She accepted this sort of musicless instruction until the dinner bell sounded. When she was sweating and exhausted from learning how to stand, Zusya showed her some stretches on the support: raising her leg, bending her back across it, even sitting beneath it with her arms up in the way she'd once seen a prisoner tied to a boat's mast when they brought him in.

That night Vii, the previous scour at the bottom of the dancing chain, presented her with what would become her favorite piece of dance attire. Vii was a plain sort of girl not much older than Ileth with a sculptor's model of a body. She'd fallen in love with dragon dancing and defied her family's wishes to continue the art. They'd even publicly disowned her (though they supported her privately with a generous allowance). Vii gave her a sheath of a lovely flexible weave and material that made up for the fit, a color like lilacs, with little sewn-in bits of hairlike baleen at the bust to offer extra support that Ileth didn't yet have the breasts to truly require. Other dancers donated delicate dance skirts that were no thicker than a fog, canvas slippers, and hose, and Ottavia gave her a good set of washcloths and towels. One of the towels was so vast and thick Ileth slept under it on her rope bed.

The drills started the next day. Ottavia led them. There were two distinct activities, drills of dance moves and *fatigues*—exercises of one kind or another. Ileth found the drills more fatiguing and the fatigues more like drills because they went on and on and on until your muscles quivered and your body turned to porridge. Ottavia paid constant attention to Ileth, often coming over to nudge her this way and that with her walking stick. At a break, gulping water from the nearby cistern that had been installed for grooming the dragons, one of her fellow dancers said she was lucky. More experienced dancers got a rap on the shin or the forearm with it for being inattentive or slacking. She showed a thumb-sized bruise just above her ankle as proof.

After the drills and fatigues they did dance a little, as the others rested while each exhibited the progress they'd made on routines. Ileth didn't understand why there had to be so many leaps and spins and falls to the floor and rises and arm gestures if the only point was to work up a soothing sweat for the dragons, but then she remembered Heem Deklamp's visit to the Manor and his speech about her duty being to just learn how things worked in the Serpentine.

The other dancers were deeply respectful and attentive to Ottavia. For the whole group of them to be collectively mad seemed improbable, so Ileth just accepted that it was vitally important for the well-being of the dragons that your toes pointed in unnatural directions and that you kept your shoulders relaxed and open even with your arms reaching above your head.

For music on the exhibitions Ottavia brought out a music box, which played a simple tune they called "The Maiden's Serenade." Ottavia taught Ileth a simple dance she could do with it; you only faced one direction, toward the mirrors, and took but three steps from side to side and back again, with some simple arm movements, raising them to shoulder height and then bringing them down again as if cradling a baby. At the end you bowed in four directions. After she practiced it, first placing her weight on one leg and then the other, back and forth, back and forth, always trying to stand correctly as she'd been taught the day before, all the other drillers, starting with Ottavia herself, hugged her.

"See, you can be a dragon dancer. Welcome to the troupe," Ottavia said.

Then the real work began.

8

Zusya was right. The drills made parts of her body ache that she didn't know existed.

The movements all had names, and the names were a mix of the movement itself and the body part, or direction, involved. But it was all built around the idea of your earth leg, the one you stood on, and your air leg, the one performing its evolution. In an actual dance, they switched constantly, even rapidly in some of the leaps and turns.

The more senior dancers taught Ileth her own anatomy along with leg raises and arm positions. She wondered if the odd poses and demands on the muscles had a reason other than to make you as sore as possible and sweat out your earlobes. Though you could say this for the relentless discipline of dragon dancing: all of her fellow dancers were sleek and bright-eyed, with seemingly boundless energy and an even, graceful carriage that would be the envy of even someone as mirror-polished as Santeel Dun Troot. Ottavia barked out corrections to the other dancers for what seemed like minutiae, and if you failed to attend to the correction she'd tap you on the offending limb with her cane. Well, you got a tap at first. Later, it seemed like something between the gentle prod of a shepherd on a wayward lamb and the corrective whack of a mother on a disobedient child.

Ileth found the drills calculated to be just hard enough to bring out the sweat but not so hard that you collapsed exhausted after your tune. They kept at it through entire mornings sometimes. Ottavia would sort the dancers into little groups; the more senior ones would exhibit some movement, and the rest of them, including Ileth, would do their best to copy it.

But on the other hand, she did get to hear music every day, even if it was just from one of Ottavia's many music boxes. There'd been very little music in the Lodge, as the Captain couldn't stand it. Thinking about the various dances they'd worked through at night in her rope bed, she decided she was hearing more music daily than all but the wealthy families who might have their children constantly at practice with instruments and keyboards.

For all the fresh joy of daily music, the art itself could be intensely frustrating. She mixed up her feet, turning to the right when she should go left, continuing with one evolution while the other dancers, in unison, had switched to the next leg lift or bend. On their breaks she often broke down and cried in the little break room. The most she got out of the other dancers was a gentle pat when they saw her with her face in her hands, sobbing.

"Don't take it so. You're new. Catch your breath," Zusya said, putting a warming blanket about her.

"You have to eat more," Peak advised her one evening when they were all having tea. "Eat all the time, every chance you get, especially at the beginning. Have pickled eggs and drink the juice. You feel like you're wasting away. You're not; you're rebuilding."

Ileth took the advice about eating to heart and trotted across the Long Bridge to Joai's little hole-and-corner kitchen, where she'd bathed and eaten on the day she'd been admitted to the Serpentine. Joai said most of the food in the Beehive wasn't fit for cat meat (true enough, though the dragons chucked it down) and she was too desperate to wait for the dinner bell. Joai, who seemed to sense that a dragon dancer's life needed an extra plate here and there, shoveled out soup that she called "Odds and Ends" with fat sausages floating in it like geese on a lake.

"You like being a dancer?" Joai asked.

"It's b-better than the Catch Basin. I hear music all the time. I like that. I didn't have much as a child."

"I thought you wanted to ride dragons someday."

She paused, a spoonful of soup in one hand and a sausage on a fancy three-tine fork in the other.

"Why wouldn't I?"

"Well, being a dancer is nice, if you like dragons. You're around them all the time. But I never heard of one going on to become a dragoneer. I'd just like to see you use that whistle someday, is all."

Joai's comment took some of the glow off her growing strength as a dancer.

"Your technique is not yet there, but you move well," Ottavia said, at the conclusion of her first ten days. They sat together at her little writing desk, having tea and nuts. Ottavia seemed to exist on nothing but tea and bags of nuts and a single glass of wine every night. "Your joy in this lets one overlook your mistakes. I even forget those arms of yours now and then."

Dax, their jack-of-all-trades musician, accompanied her first real performance. He was of Vyenn and not the Serpentine, Sammerdam-bred, and he had a quick way of speaking, as though his throat were on fire and the words keen to escape. He couldn't always work with the dancers, as he was frequently in demand in Vyenn. Even more curiously, he seemed to be able to come and go from the fortress at will, something only the wingmen and dragoneers were allowed. Zusya told her he'd been brought in to help out with the All-Comers Feast a decade or so back and made himself so useful to the Masters that he stayed on as kind of a specialist, like the engineers sometimes brought in to say whether it was safe to take an old wall down or fix the Beehive's drains.

That first true dragon dance they taught her to perform on her own was a simple one, called the Invocation. It was a tribute to an old priestly rite going back before the Republic, before the Catastrophes, perhaps even before Old Hypatian civilization where a priest called on the spirits of earth, air, fire, and water. You simply did a skip run forward on the balls of your feet, then did a slide into a bow where you folded yourself over your right outstretched leg, the other leg tucked under you, hands reaching ahead and head down against your knee in supplication. Roll over, rise up on both arms as the feet slide out, launch yourself to your feet, go to another compass point, and repeat. The jump-up became progressively harder as you tired, but Ottavia demanded that each be performed identically. Repeat until the music stopped.

They showed Ileth off late one evening in the hall in front of Shrentine, a female dragon who had encouraged Ottavia's attempts to perfect the art since her early days at the Serpentine and now was something of a patroness to the dancers. Shrentine had a musical ear and swayed about herself when music was playing. Shrentine had a dream of putting together a musical complement of dozens of musicians playing to accompany a stage full of dancers.

"Is art universal, the music and dance, for no words needed," she said in her heavily accented, almost unintelligible Montangyan.

Ottavia had Dax play her an appropriate tune on his impeller, his preferred instrument—though he seemed able to play anything, whether it was keyed, plucked, bowed, or blown—a fascinating contraption worked by a hand crank that combined a keyboard that worked the strings and the ability to somehow produce a mournful, vibrating bass note. If you turned your back and had him play you a tune on his impeller, you'd swear before a jury that there were three musicians playing (he slapped the curvy wooden case to make a drumming sound with it as well).

She danced through the evolutions, trying to ignore everything but the music.

When the music ended, she bent with legs and waist in the stance she'd been taught, first to Shrentine, then to Ottavia and the troupe, and finally, lingeringly, to Dax. They all applauded. The dragon opened her wings a little and shivered them, making a sound like someone flapping leather curtains with a whip-crack, and folded them up again.

"Ottavia, this one too many times," the dragon-dame rumbled. Ileth actually only made out Ottavia's name and the word *one*; Zusya had to explain to her what she said. It took some time to get an ear for Shrentine's pronunciation. But at least she tried. Ileth had heard that some of the dragons talked to humans only in Hypatian, figuring they'd learned one human tongue eight hundred years ago and it was too much bother to learn another.

"Your hands still need work," Shatha said from beneath an elaborate wig. "Your fingers were all over the place when you stepped. Your costume—"

Peak nudged her aside with something that might have been a pinch.

"Four rounds, all prettily done, before you started to give out," Peak said. "Vii, you could learn something from her. You're still thinking too much and getting behind the music. Shows in your face. Ileth gets it wrong, but she moves with the beat."

Ileth nodded through the criticism, bobbing out thank-yous with body language. That was the lovely thing about dance: you didn't have to speak.

"Delightful! You live through the music!" Dax said, coming forward. He had a funny way of standing when talking informally with "his girls," as he called the dancers, with his hips askew and facing a different direction than his shoulders, and his head somewhere in between. Ileth still didn't know quite what to make of him; she'd been taught from an early age to square off your body so it aligned with the person you were addressing. But he meant no insult; he never addressed her, or anyone, in anything but a kindly tone. He kissed her somewhere in the neighborhood of each ear, swinging the impeller on its strap neatly behind him. His beard smelled of sandalwood oil and he had sweat streaking the powder under his traditional musician's wig, which he'd donned for the occasion. Wigs, especially on men, were old-fashioned and frowned on by the more opinionated of the Republic's assigns, but Dax, she was learning, did things his own way.

"Promising," Ottavia said, bringing up the rear of congratulations.

That night Ileth found her bedding wetted. Someone had dumped a bucket of water onto her sleeping pad. It would take days to properly dry. She didn't say anything, wondering if it was some welcoming ritual. She rolled up the pad and dragged it down to the kitchens and spent an hour toasting the worst of the wetness out of it while the cooks, cleaning up after sending up the dragons' dinner, invented obvious jokes about her no longer being a virgin dancer until they became bored and left her alone. Once it was dry enough that hanging would do the rest, she upended her crude wooden bed, hung the mattress on it, and slept on the floor.

Ottavia roused her early the next morning, chopping off the other end of her shortened sleeping time. Only Preen was up, at the little stove boiling a big pot of water for her tea-well, but then she was always the first to rise. She liked to read in the quiet before the day began. Her trunk had a layer of books at the bottom beneath all the sheaths, wraps, scarves, and hose of a dragon dancer.

Ottavia waited to speak until she was fully awake. She had that lamp-oil smell of the dragons on her—she must have been around them either very late or very early. She supposed, living in the Beehive, that they all had a slight airborne dragon-taint, though after a few days your overwhelmed nose simply gave up and you ceased noticing it so much unless you thought about it.

"I have a job for you, Ileth. Kind of an odd one, but it's within your abilities and I'm caught between frying pan and fire. It will take you away from us for a while—no, not like that, still in the Beehive. You can bring a support down and do your drills and stretches."

"Yes, sira," Ileth said, wiping the sleep out of her eyes.

"I'm always short dancers, but it's worse than usual. I committed to a performance in Zland and Peak is taking a couple with her for that, so my dancers will be overworked keeping up here. Good thing for us some of the males and dragoneers are out for the hunts. But to your case: the job is basically companionship for an old dragon. So old he'll never leave here again, I expect, until he breathes his last. All you have to do is sit with him between your drills, and sleep down there to keep your smell about. You impressed the Masters sitting on the doorstep, I hear. I should think you could sit next to a dragon for a good long while."

Ileth had picked up enough of the currents in traveling up and down the Serpentine that she knew that anytime you were assigned a dragon it was a matter of importance. She was wide awake now. "Yes, sira."

"We call him the Lodger. If he has another name nobody's told me. He sleeps most of the time, only eats now and then. That's the problem, I understand. He hasn't eaten for weeks now. A few days with a dancer might rouse his appetite. It's worked before. Then again, it might not, so whatever happens, don't worry—it's not your fault. As I said, he's very old. The physiker says he's older than any tree, even redwoods."

Ileth nodded.

"You don't have to do anything fancy except move about at his nose end where he can smell you. He's down in the Cellars, so it'll be quiet for you."

"May I . . . ask a question? Not to do with this Lodger."

"Feel free."

"Why is Peak . . . going to Zland? Are there dragons there?"

"Oh, no, this is a bit of a couple things. People like entertainments, and dragon dancers are curiosities. Peak and two others will perform in a music hall. It's been a nightmare working out the music, and Fates know what she'll do for scenery. But there's a great deal of interest. I had a letter saying they've added another week of performances and begging my forgiveness. That's Zland for you. Never know what those people will go mad about.

"Our costumes would be considered obscene in Asposis or the rural districts. Zland is artsy and freer about such things. It's because this famous painter, Risso Heem Tyr, have you heard of him? No? Well, he lives there now. You could say he's the center point of the Republic's art culture; it all revolves around him. About two years back he showed up here to paint a dragon on commission, and as sort of a side project he did a series of studies of the dragon dancers—I was one of his models, I'm not too modest to say. I'd like to see the actual painting of me sometime; all I saw was sketching on canvas. They caught on for some reason, maybe the costumes again. One way and another he's made enough money to build the finest house in Zland. He's paying for the trip, with a generous allowance for the dancers besides, going to do his sketches when they practice and so on. I thought Peak would be ideal for him. She has the most beautiful head of hair in the Serpentine, Heem Tyr is famous for the detail he puts into hair, and she knows how to use it when she dances. If any of us should be in a painting, it should be she."

Ottavia was about to accompany her to the Cellars when Shatha woke up with a leg cramp that made her cry out and Ottavia knelt down to work the muscle loose.

Ileth, curious about this dragon, wanted to be off on her task. And she was fiercely hungry now that she was fully awake.

"I can find my way. I'll ask in the kitchens and pick up some breakfast while I'm there."

She gathered up her little basin of hygiene tools, took one of the extra supports kept in the Notch for morning stretches, stuffed a spare drill-sheath into her sleeve, and set off for the Cellars.

Outside the kitchens she ran into the Duskirk youth, pushing a huge sort of wheeled bin filled with smoked fish.

She fell into step beside him. He didn't object to her company and the fish were beyond caring. After a few stuttering pleasantries, she asked him for directions to this "Lodger."

Duskirk moved his bin to the side. "I'll show you. It's a slow morning, lots of dragons out for the hunts."

He led her to the lift, in a vertical tunnel. The lift was a kind of platform on wheels, save that the wheels ran on rails going vertically. Four other carts of fish and one fellow apprentice already stood there.

"Picked up a stray dancer," Duskirk said.

"Aren't you having a morning, Tosser."

"Down first, Rael," Duskirk told the young man at the device that reminded Ileth of a handbrake on a beer wagon. The man at the device put a speaking-trumpet to his lips and shouted an order up.

"This lodger-dragon. I am to keep him company," Ileth explained.

"Don't know much about him," Duskirk said. "He's not a pensioner. They generally go out to big landholders who can afford the glamor of a dragon about the place. I don't think he ever flew for us, but I know he had something to do with the foundation of the Vale alliance in the early days. He was here for the Troth, I know that. Way before the

Republic. Something about the whole arrangement here was his doing. You'd have to ask one of the Masters."

"So they have him stay out of gratitude?"

"Oh, nothing to do with the Masters, or even the Charge. It's the beasts. Dragons are touchy about their elders. They're imaginative enough to see themselves old and weak and vulnerable. I think if we tried to get rid of him there'd be a . . . well, I don't know what there'd be, but I wouldn't care to see it. In fine summer weather, the year after I arrived, a couple of the younger dragons helped him climb out and spend a few days in the sun. He didn't feel up to it this year, I guess. In decline, seems like."

The lift started down. She felt the air move and grow colder. They had to be below lake level. She wondered how they'd dug this level so it stayed dry, or was it carved out of solid rock? She didn't know why such things interested her; engineering wasn't considered a feminine pursuit, but she liked to know what ship had the highest mast or where the deepest mine was. When she was first learning her letters and asking questions, the Captain used to joke that she should travel around and find out all those things and put it in a "Book of Useless Facts."

They arrived at the bottom. It was damp and dirty at the bottom of the shaft.

"Cellars," Duskirk said, pointing to a tunnel. "You can always climb back up. There's a drilled-in ladder right next to the track on either side of it. There's also a ramped tunnel off the main junction in the center. It's the only one that leads up. It's a bit roundabout, but you'll get to the kitchens eventually."

"You can show her the way," his workmate said. "I'll get these offloaded. Just don't spew all over her when you get a whiff of the Lodger. He's ranker than rank."

Duskirk wrapped an armful of smoked fish in his apron. "Maybe you'll give him an appetite."

"I believe that's the idea."

Duskirk led her down the hall. This one was practically lightless. No magic crystals or even smelly candles were wasted on the Cellars. A lamp glowed somewhere ahead and their eyes soon adjusted to the darkness. Their passageway was narrow, not because of the tunnel but because the sides were crowded with crates and mysterious tools and pieces of equipment beneath tarry canvas.

"Repair gear for the lift, I think," Duskirk said, tapping a metal-rimmed wheel.

They reached the junction of the passages (yes, there were five, like a starfish, if you didn't count the one leading up toward the kitchen level) where the lamplight was, then passed an apprentice and novice who had no occupation beyond having moved a few barrels so they could kneel and throw dice against the wall. They were using a few coins, bits of broken dragon scale, and buttons as wagers.

Ileth had seen both of them before. They had often come up to the Catch Basin and spoken to the fishermen, and one of them was the novice who'd been oathed in next to her. Quith had solved the mystery of his arrival without her noticing it: he'd been flown in by his father, a dragoneer. They had one or two favorite fishermen and sometimes went into the shelter on their boats. She'd assumed they were drinking or enjoying tobacco.

"Uh, Yael, you're supposed to warn—" the older of the two said.

"Got a coin for a throw at Boone?" the other asked.

"She's to stay with the Lodger for a while. Ileth, these two fine young gentlemen are Griff and Zante."

"Zan to my friends," Zante, the one who'd invited her to "throw," said, rubbing his close-cropped head. "You're the new dancer. Heard about you. Put down in blue, right?"

The one called Griff looked her up and down and licked his lips, quickly, like a lizard. "Leave off, Zan. Griff's a nickname too. Actually it's—"

"She's not impressed by great names," Duskirk said. "And I think Vor Claymass has his eye on her. Having a *Heem* in front of your surname's nothing to that."

"You need anything, girl, you just tell me," Griff said. "I'm the man to see down here. How about that, heh? Charge to a whole level of the hive at my age."

"Starting at the bottom means there's nowhere to go but up,"

Duskirk said. "But don't credit him overmuch. They just thought he'd do less damage down here. Ileth is here to cheer the Lodger up."

"Oh, him. He's in the southeast chamber; it's the only one with water. Yes, we've had no luck feeding him. Just sleeps. I'd say he's a goner," Griff said, picking up the dice. Ileth's growing dislike of the youth crystallized. *Imagine speaking of a creature that could be over a thousand years old as though he were a dying mutt.*

Duskirk motioned her out of the room and toward a wider, emptier passage, just as dark as the others. She could see faint light at the other end. Ileth imagined Griff licking his lips again as he watched her leave. Her skin tightened and prickled.

She was glad to reach the other end, and gladder for Duskirk's company. The passage opened up on a cavern. It was about the size of a cozy inn, she decided. You had to step across a gutter to enter the cavern. The gutter was fouled with still water and dragon waste.

A dragon slept within. Most of him was in shadow, but she sensed he was enormous, one of the longer-necked types with a matching tail that never seemed to end.

A portable twin lamp—two oil lights hanging from a cross arm on a stand—was the room's only light. And one of the lamps was unlit, probably to save oil, because it was full. There was a wall box full of candles, however, so she lit another, set the second lamp alight, and carried her candle in a holder so she could get a better look.

He looked old. Scale faded and not looked after. He had a fleshless, sunken-in look to him everywhere except the eyes, which were half closed but still showed bright golden color. His skin was folded and wrinkled, oddly reminding her of an unmade bed. He had a curious sort of coloring to the scale, dark stripes running vertically all along his body against a rust color. The stripes added to the sunken effect of the skin that had collapsed between his ribs. She wondered if they were some kind of draconic heraldry or tattooing. Dragons of the Serpentine had their deeds dyed onto their wings in decorations she'd heard called *laudii*. Maybe those stripes were a testament to a more ancient accomplishment. But they looked natural enough.

The Lodger showed no sign of even seeing that she'd come in. He breathed in his sleep with a gentle wheeze. There was a dirty, sour smell about him.

She placed her support, her spare sheath, and the little lidded dish that contained her tooth scrubber, skin scraper, and hairbrush out of the way to one side of the entrance.

Duskirk looked through his meal cart and found the most tempting morsel he could: a flat but tasty specimen Ileth now knew was called a spearfish. Stepping forward, he waved the smoked fish under the dragon's nose. The dragon's nostrils twitched, then an eyelid flicked, but the Lodger did nothing more. Duskirk shrugged and turned.

"Leave the fish," Ileth said. "I haven't had my breakfast."

"Please yourself. There's a big barrel over there with shovels and brushes for . . . uh, his waste and such. Those two woodheads out at the join are supposed to attend to it, but if he goes and you're stuck here alone at night and can't stand the smell, you should know about it. If you need help with anything, just send Zante or Griff. I'm pretty sure as a dancer in charge of a dragon you can order them about—same goes for me, for what it's worth, if the beast needs anything. That's how it works up there. You dancers outrank everyone but physikers, dragoneers, and wingmen, if nobody's told you." He gave her a friendly salute and left.

Too bad she didn't keep a diary. *Received my first subordinate-to-superior salute today, from a feeder who empties out his stomach whenever a dragon belches.* Maybe she should ask Falth for a notebook in her next letter, even though her news of Santeel had been reduced to Quith's gossip when she had the energy to walk to the dining hall for dinner.

Alone (if you didn't count the dragon!) again, Ileth sat and breakfasted on smoked spearfish and considered that she had the (maybe so, maybe not) ability to order some boys about. As she chewed, she tried to remember some of the Captain's stories about command. According to his roustabout gang, at one time he'd been considered one of the best masters on the North Coast. She finished, having barely begun on the big fish, and cautiously took a walk around the dragon. He slept close to the wall, on an elevation that made brushing waste into the gutter easier. Suppose he shifted in his sleep? He could easily crush her if she was in the wrong spot between him and the wall with no path to back up. Someone on her trip to the Serpentine had told her that he wouldn't mix with dragons for love or coin: they could take a man's head clean off with an accidental flick of a wing. She didn't know if that was true, but their wings must be strong as thunder to get such a body off the ground. Stories of hollow bones filled with magic gases or bladders in their body that created some kind of buoyancy were probably just that, stories. Even the reduced specimen in front of her looked solid enough.

He wasn't clean at the back end. Did the groomers not even come down to this level? Perhaps without a dragoneer to check their work, he was rarely tended. She left the cavern again and cast about futilely until she gave up and asked the roustabouts at the barrel for grooming tools.

After a couple of boorish jests about what she could do in exchange for the information, Ileth said she was willing to walk all the way up to Ottavia if need be. They told her to calm down and showed her.

The tools were in a case under the Lodger's neck, as it turned out, and with their help she rolled his head off it, eliciting a soft snort and a grumble that might have been words. The boys retreated, saying something about it being bad luck to wake a dragon. She found a slime-filled cistern and managed to acquire a bucket with soapy water, another for rinsing, and some rags.

She disturbed a vast array of bugs with her activity. They should inspect the Cellars more often. Ileth considered taking notes and building a case to toss that Griff out on his idle ear. What good was bragging about responsibility if you didn't carry out the most basic of your duties?

She returned to the Lodger's chamber and went to work on what she could reach. Well, they wanted her to work up a sweat, and this was as good a way as any.

There wasn't a functional drain as such down here. The end of the gutter was a hole, but it hardly drained. She poked at it with a hand brush and it began to drain a little faster. She went back for a refill of clean water and to try to work up a lather again with the soap that was apparently indifferent to its effects and found that the Lodger had shifted to expose his other side.

The one facing the wall.

This would be trickier. If he rolled back she'd have to climb atop him sharp as a squirrel with a dog after it or she'd be crushed. She'd never watched the grooms at work and had no idea how they handled such situations. She'd seen stout stepladders and such on the upstairs levels; maybe they used them as braces between a wall and body. She stripped off her overdress so she could climb about more easily. Just in case.

"Hello!" she said loudly.

The dragon's batlike ear flicked toward her, then drooped again.

"Hello!" she said as loudly as she could without shouting.

One eye opened a little more. The nostrils opened and pulled air hard enough to cause her work shirt to flutter.

"Beg pardon: I need to wash your other side. Could you not squash me, please?"

The dragon gave a tired sigh.

Nothing to do but try. She took her short brush and pole brush and tossed them behind the dragon, then clambered over its neck (weren't dragons chary about men being about their necks?) with Dath Amrits's whistle clamped between her teeth and went to work. If he threatened to roll on her she'd blow and climb for all she was worth.

This side was much, much worse. A good deal of scale had fallen out and there were sores of some kind, ugly, with some blood. There didn't seem to be any pus, she was glad to see, if dragons indeed produced such a thing when they were wounded.

She gently cleaned the sores with the hard soap and water and her newer rags. She struck a nerve or sore spot just behind his rear leg, and the leg kicked out. Luckily the leg lashed out toward the opposite direction of the room from her and she threw herself out of the way as the creature rolled back toward the wall, blowing the whistle for all she was worth.

The dragon's head came up and shook so that its *griff* rattled loosely. She was reminded of a dog emerging from a pond.

His eyes blinked a few times and he sniffed.

"Hello . . . hello there," she said.

"You are not known to me," the Lodger said, slowly, tiredly, but in decent enough Montangyan.

He explored the air above her, close enough so she could feel the heat (and moisture) of his exhalations.

"You smell like pain. Have they been treating you badly, girl?"

"Not at all. I'm with the d-dancers. I think that might be your blood you are smelling on me." Strange, how easily words came when she was talking to a dragon. Then again, she'd just had a scare; her heart was pounding.

She sensed a presence behind. The dragon shifted his gaze.

Griff peered around the edge of the chamber, Zante behind him. "We heard . . ."

"The pair of you I know," the dragon said. "Both of you: be off." The dragon gave his body an experimental stretch. Again, it reminded her of a dog. A great lanky dog rising from a nap. She'd always thought dragons were like cats in their movements. Maybe they grew more dog-like when they aged.

"Right," Griff said, pulling Zante away.

"She's not wearing a dress! Those legs, man," Zante said as they went.

"Useless, those two," the Lodger said, yawning. "The older one trained as a groom, I think, but they know not the brush or file."

His forming of human sounds was excellent, and his Montangyan good, but he spoke it in a slow, archaic manner. It reminded her of a very old nursery song about cats and mice, or the hoary phrasings of isolated shepherds she'd run into with her sheep and goats on remote mountainsides high above the Freesand.

"They couldn't even be bothered to . . . that's just wicked," Ileth said.

"Be you my new groom?"

"I'm a dancer."

"That's a fine thing, the dancers," the dragon said. "I think they brought me up on the lift, oh, years back. To see them play. Lots of leaping about and I couldn't even tell how to keep score. But it does hold one's attention."

Ileth gathered up her tools. "They told us it was s-something to do with the . . . smell of our sweat."

"I know the scent of a human female. I've enjoyed it. In moderation. You don't make it to my state of decrepitude sniffing around human females overmuch. The need grows in you. Greater and always greater. Soon, you are living inside the need. Always leads to trouble. Always."

"I will only dance as much as you ask," Ileth said, dumping out her water. The flow was stopped again. Something must be blocking it.

"I never intended to wash up here, you know," the dragon said.

"You didn't?" She liked the dragon. He was the first, well, conversationalist who didn't ask her about her stutter.

"I felt my years growing on me and I decided to visit some places where I thought I'd made a difference, see how things were getting on. I saw Hypatia, or what was left of her. They were a great people. If you ever get a chance, go and see the ruins. There's still some lovely art that's endured. Some of the old families are still around. Or is it crawling with gargoyles now? Somebody told me that. Too much dragon blood. I came here as well. I helped design these caverns, after all. I thought a touch of the Sadda-Vale would impress, even if they couldn't build quite on that scale—and even the Sadda-Vale is a poor imitation of an older palace. I'm particularly proud of the Dragon Horn. Got the idea from a blighter fortress ruin over on the other side of the Inland Ocean. Theirs was circular, winding round a tower like a snake. Took five years to build the one in the Rotunda." His eyes closed and she thought for a moment that he was going back to sleep. Then he opened them again quickly. "I'm sorry, young human, I'm sure none of this interests you. You have a blockage in your drain."

"Bugger the drain," she said. "I like stories."

"You do? Well, I can supply you for the rest of your life, if I'm granted that many more years. I do believe I'm almost the last living link to those times. I did put some of it down. There might be a volume of mine here. Some humans did write it all down in one of your tongues. I think it was yours. You can read? Only accept humans who could read. That was my urge to the first dragoneers."

Her spotty education had mostly been through curiosity. The

Captain and the wretches who tried to pass themselves off as tutors didn't think any of the girls needed to do more than read, do enough math to buy flour, and mark a calendar.

"Was this the ... the end of the ... tour of places you'd lived?" Ileth asked.

The Lodger winked slowly at her. "You think I've lost the trail? As I was saying, I meant to visit here one last time, see how things were getting on. Well, a storm blew up, and instead of going to ground right away, I wanted warmth, a bed, and a hot meal. So I fought my way through the storm. But the wind howled at this height and something in my left shoulder gave way. A hard landing. I made the rest of the trip afoot dragging a wing. I'll never fly again. I meant to die in the Sadda-Vale, but I'll have to wait for death to see it again, it seems."

"Dragons travel after death?"

"We all do. I'll complete my journey when I've shrugged off this wreck of a body, if I'm allowed."

Ileth wasn't comfortable with these sorts of conversations. She'd had them once or twice with the Captain's drunken friends who considered themselves learned. "How is that?"

"In the life beyond life. You know this yourself."

She'd never much cared for the priests and their depictions of existence outside life. She wanted to hear this dragon's. "How do I know it?"

"Tell me about your first memory of seeing something beautiful."

Beauty was in short supply in her childhood, but she did what she could to think back. "I remember ... I remember there was a teapot. Supposedly it belonged to my mother. My real mother. It was white, and there was sort of a raised depiction of flowers on it. The color was part of the workmanship; it wasn't paint. There was fluting at the top; you removed the lid to pour the water in on the tea leaves. But we hardly ever had tea in the house. I just remember thinking it was beautiful."

"You were a child then, yes?"

"Yes. I'm not sure how old I was. Not seven. Before seven. It's when they started making fun of me for my stutter."

"Your human languages are challenging to imitate. My tongue

gives me difficulty. But back to this teapot—when you thought it was beautiful, what made it beautiful?"

"Maybe—maybe how the white was so pure. The brightness of the colored flowers against the white. The delicate fluting on the lid: I remember wondering how they made it so exact."

"Those certainly sound beautiful. But you were a child. You'd had no training in what made a good teapot or a bad one. You knew nothing of art."

"No, how could I?" Ileth said.

"Yet you knew."

"I suppose I did."

"So how did that knowledge that it was beautiful come to you?"

"Maybe . . . maybe s-someone told me? Or because it was on a shelf where I couldn't reach it."

"That might be because it was valuable. Beautiful and valuable don't always go together."

"True."

"You are starting to understand. *Valuable* is not a fixed constant. Valuable to a dragon, a human, and a dog might be the same, might be different. Certainly in the case of a dog. Beautiful, on the other hand, humans and dragons usually find common ground, which suggests it is a value external to experience. I know these days elves and dwarves have fallen into legend, but they did exist, maybe still do, and they had similar ideas on the subject. So 'beautiful' is value we probably have when we come out of the egg, or when you emerge from your mother in that messy mammalian fashion. I'd suggest that a millennium in the past or a millennium in the future that teapot you remembered would probably still be considered beautiful."

"How does that mean there's an afterlife?"

"Nothing comes from nothing. Ever heard that expression? A terse dwarf might be the one who first said it, but others have translated and quoted him. There are constants that we, those with the right facilities, humans and dragons and dwarves and so on, know from our earliest years. That means either we learned them in previous lives or certain kinds of knowledge exist outside our organic life and are able to move back and forth between a plane of ideas and truths and into our existence."

This was a bit thick for Ileth. She had a mental picture of ideas fluttering into the world like birds returning to shore. She wondered if the Lodger was typical of dragons and they all talked this way. Perhaps having such long lives made them philosophers.

"Never underestimate your native powers to reason a matter out," he continued. "I know humans use writing and tutors and so on to gather and pass on knowledge. That's useful. I am fond of books myself. Yet learning doesn't stick until you've tried to work things out according to your own lights."

Ileth had to follow some of this speech from context; the Lodger was using words she wasn't accustomed to. She wished she had something to write with so she could find out more about the words at another time. "You're a philosopher, sir," Ileth said.

The Lodger gave sort of a rumble that struck her like thunder trying to purr like a cat. "When you get to my age, the choice to become a philosopher is made for you. Nothing's left but your mind and the memories it holds. Places. This rock. I helped design it, you know. Searched all these mountains for the right sort of elements." He fell silent and she decided not to speak until spoken to. He seemed to be breathing deeply and regularly. She decided to turn back to the drain. She poked about in the hole with the brush handle and didn't accomplish much except make the handle filthy.

"It needs pumping out," the Lodger said.

More investigating was required about what pumping out meant. The Lodger did his best to explain, fighting sleep. It turned out there was a two-man mechanism that "cleared the sump" (whatever that meant) and got rid of wastewater or rainwater that somehow made it down to the Cellars. She and Griff searched until they found the mechanism the Lodger described. Because Griff and his novice didn't want anything more to do with wash water than they did the Matron's chastity lectures, they rarely had need of the pump. After some bickering back and forth, they agreed to take turns, two pumping and the third resting. It proved to be hard work, pulling down on a chain handle that was attached to something projecting out of the lift tunnel out on the kitchen level. They were at it for hours, but the sluice cleared with a blast of odor that was worse than all the horrible smells she'd experienced in her life combined. Exhausted, she dozed on a sleeping mat Griff offered her—the Cellars boys seemed to have napping nooks everywhere—as near to the Lodger's nose as she dared.

She was awoken by Zusya. Ottavia had a request that she visit Ileth and have her report if possible. The Charge wanted an update on how she was getting on with the Lodger, as it had already been a day. It was hard to tell time in the Cellars, unlike the rest of the Serpentine. There did not seem to be any kind of routine; Griff and Zante obeyed their own schedule, it seemed; and every now and then apprentices came down to check and refill the oil lamps and the Guards who strolled through it now and then, seemingly as an excuse to join in a game of Boone with Griff and Zante.

The Lodger was still asleep. She drank from the dragon's trickle and warmed herself by doing the morning stretches and exercises Ottavia demanded of her dancers. Zusya corrected her form and chirped like a bird about Peak's departure for the performance and painting studies. She was expected back in time for the Feast of Follies, though if winter came early, she might have to take a series of boats home the long way by river and lake. They went up to drill, filching some pickled eggs out of the dragon kitchen.

Ottavia asked her if the dragon had spoken or eaten. She was pleased that he'd spoken, thrilled that he had questioned Ileth, but disappointed that he still hadn't eaten. Ileth promised Ottavia that she'd do what she could. Ottavia suggested she get him talking about food and find out his favorite dish.

Someone said the sun was out, so after drill she sat in the air and sun for the time it took to drink a growler of water. She took her old route by outer stair down, unwilling to give up fall sunshine so quickly, and halfway down remembered she hadn't peeked around corners for Gorgantern. She threaded her way back through the Catch Basin and the kitchens to the Cellars. The Lodger was still asleep when she returned.

She took a candle and went around to check the sores on his other side. They didn't look any better. Four scales had fallen off. She took them away and examined them closely. They were sort of an orange-red and had a lot of deep fissures. They felt like the bottom of an old cast-iron frying pan. She could scratch them deeply with her fingernail. She doubted that was a sign of good scale health. Maybe she should take them to the physiker.

It occurred to her that with so many scales dropping off, you'd think there would be more about. He hadn't moved about that much.

She decided to stretch and think about it. Maybe she could beg her Charge for the use of one of those music boxes—a less valuable one— to help when she practiced. It wasn't nearly as much fun without music, just dull exercise.

Her leg raises were coming along; it was surprisingly fun to tax her tendons and joints in this way. She could hear Ottavia with her endless *lengthen and open . . . lengthen and open* as she went through the evolutions. She was trying to get her forehead against her knee when she heard the Lodger's familiar rumble:

"You still. What is your name, human?"

"Ileth."

The Lodger tried saying her name a few times. It improved each time.

"What are you doing here?" the Lodger asked.

"They told me to keep you company for a few days—"

"No, I understand that you're here to evoke me or however they phrase it in the Dragonsforge these days."

She guessed he meant the Serpentine. Was that an old name for it?

She lowered her left leg and turned around. "I came here . . . to the Serpentine . . . to fly."

"Fly? I understand. I've always felt bad that humans don't know flight. Some try. The devices they come up with! Someday one of you will get it right, that is my firm belief. But you don't need a dragon to fly. The rocs, oh, perhaps none are over on this side of the Inland Ocean. I forget where I am."

She shrugged. The biggest bird she'd ever seen wouldn't support a human. "Not just fly—make a name for myself. Be respected. For doing something admirable."

The dragon looked her up and down. "A hero?"

"The fables about orphans growing up to be heroes, sir—it doesn't seem to work in real life. I was told the most I could hope for was being a maid somewhere, or marrying a fisherman with more than one boat. I'll settle for some flying. Visiting lands where they don't know anything about me or care about how many names I have."

The dragon went away for a while, staring off at something only he could see. Ileth wondered how many hundreds of years back the journey took him. Then he came back.

"Have you flown yet, Ileth?"

She shook her head, then, realizing that the dragon might not understand human gestures, said, "No. It's not for novices. Or dancers, I'm told. Anyway, flight training doesn't start until you're an apprentice."

"Nov—novice? I'm not familiar with the term. It doesn't matter. You're small; any dragon would rather carry you than one of those blighters."

"Fates allow," Ileth agreed.

"Keep your eye on that young female, Jizara. I know her line. They'll surprise you. In the best kind of way. With your sort I'd watch the males. Don't jump at the first offer, unless you have worked with them. They might just want to live as a pet. I've seen it many times. Not much of a life."

"I've seen Jizara. Always in a hurry."

"That sounds like her line."

"Would you answer a question?"

"I'm an old dragon who's good for little else, provided I know the answer."

"Why are you dragons helping us? You used to prey on humans. Or whatever you call it."

"Why do men join the Dra—your Serpentine? Is everyone here following a dream to fly?"

"Oh, I understand. The reason depends on the person. So it's the same with dragons?"

"Yes."

"I wouldn't think it mattered to dragons if the Republic fell or not."

"Dragons—I will let you in on a secret. Most of them might be called lazy."

"Lazy?"

"Easier to have a tasty meal well prepared by others than to hunt. The food here is ample, some of it good. When I have an appetite, I enjoy it. A lone dragon could never hope to eat like this. There are many dangers for a lone dragon, especially one that is tempted by the livestock of hominids."

"Would you like some food now?"

"No, perhaps later. My appetite isn't much these days. There are other advantages to living here. I'm fond of reading. I can get books here. Histories, geographies, even stories. Do you read Drakine?"

"Not at all. Oh, *gknuss*, I know that: *stop!* Could I read one of your histories? I'd like to know more about dragons."

"Dragon histories aren't that different from human histories. Maybe they see more of it. Like humans, they're resourceful in a pinch, but that's nothing to how adept we are at making ourselves comfortable. Having humans care for our more mundane needs is a habit in place since before your grandsires' time. You're familiar with the idea of a habit?"

"I know you can pick up bad ones more easily than good." Secretly, she felt crushed. The Lodger wasn't at all what she expected, and she'd enjoyed this time (when he was awake, anyway) more than anything she'd done since coming here. But he had to bring up habits. The Captain was a great exemplar and expounder on habits. He demanded good ones from his charges and ignored all the bad ones he'd picked up himself.

The Lodger yawned. "I enjoy this sort of talk. But it tires me these days. I think I will sleep for a while."

He settled down with his head between his forelegs, again reminding her of a lanky old hound.

Ileth saw a scale nit making for the dragon and smashed it with her foot.

"My appetite has come back a little thanks to your conversation. Maybe you can order me a light meal. Nothing that'll pry another tooth loose, perhaps some warm broth and cow liver, sliced thin."

She couldn't suppress a spin. The dragon had asked to eat! Interestingly, she cared for the dragon's sake, not that she'd carried out her first commission on her own successfully.

The dragon set his head down and took a few deep breaths. She sat cross-legged opposite his nostrils, watching. She rose as she'd been taught in the dance classes, using just the muscles in her legs and trying to keep her spine upright, and faked a loud cough. The Lodger didn't stir. She stepped forward and touched him on the bridge of his nose between his nostrils. The skin felt like river-smoothed stones, but warm and slightly yielding like the tissue of her own nose.

One golden eye popped open and she startled.

"You have to be careful with older dragons, human, especially in the transitions between sleeping and wakefulness. We have violent dreams. That may persist into waking."

"I'm sorry."

"If you want to touch, just ask first. I take it as a compliment. Other dragons don't."

"They warned us about that. I thought you were asleep."

"Everything takes a long time with my years riding one's back. Even going properly to sleep."

Ileth nodded.

"I'll give you a tip: a dragon's *griff* relax ever so slightly in sleep."

"The *griff*, they are—?"

"These," he said, extending two projections like armor-plated fans from behind his jaw. He rattled them against his neck scales. "They protect the upper neck in battle. Well, that's the original purpose, I suppose. You can read a dragon's mood by studying his *griff*. But when I am asleep, you should go stretch your legs and get something to drink and eat."

He closed his eye again and wiggled his shoulders down. When his *griff* dropped again, Ileth sidled out and hurried up to the kitchens.

She'd lost track of time underground again. The kitchens were nearly deserted. She smelled baking bread and her own appetite roused. Interesting that they were making bread. Perhaps there was to be a feast with humans and dragons. She didn't think the dragons ever requested bread.

The kitchen worker was an older man. He had a curious artificial leg. It looked like it was made out of the same sort of clay as the pipe she'd smoked at the party.

The Lodger's words came back to her. Why a leg made out of, or coated with, pipe clay? She could reason it out, right? Something to do with impact? No, she didn't see how clay would be better than wood. Of course! He was a baker. He'd be standing by hot stoves all the time. Wood would dry out and rot unless it was constantly cared for, and metal would heat up and conduct to his stump. Pipe clay was built to handle heat and remain comfortable. She supposed it would show dirt and be easy to clean as well, both important matters for a baker. One hoped.

The baker had shaggy eyebrows and raised one as she changed her walking lantern for a larger one that threw more light.

"You hungry, dear? I have a warm loaf and I'll share a bit of cheese with you. I remember how hungry I got when I was your age, and I wasn't even leaping about all day. A swallow of brine wouldn't go amiss either. Eases the sweat cramps."

"I'm looking for some . . . for some liver for the Lodger. He says he has an appetite and there's nobody about. Thin sliced, the liver."

"Back on his feed, is he? Good. Terrible when a dragon gets old and starts to go."

Since the Lodger was the first dragon she'd ever known, she didn't know whether to agree, so she just gave what she hoped was a sympathetic nod and moved to the cool storage. She hoped she could find a liver. Did they throw all the organ meats together for sausages or something?

She heard a dripping sound and followed it to the cool room. A pipe ran up the wall of a carved access shaft and branched out like a three-limbed tree here, part of the feed system that used a tank somewhere high in the delvings to keep ready water at the cisterns and the mouths where the cleaners stuck canvas hoses for washing out the gutters and flushing out the lavatories.

She wondered at the intricacy of it all. Light. Air. Water. Dragons. People. Food. Sewage. All following their paths.

A cat, disturbed in its prowling, shot into the dark mass of hanging meat and sausages. After a few attempts, she found a brine barrel with livers, right next to one with brains. No kidneys. Perhaps they were turned into pies or sausage right away.

She wrapped the liver in a leather apron and carried it like a swaddled baby back up through the bakery. The night baker resumed his discourse as if she'd been standing there the whole time:

"When I was an apprentice we lost one—he just went to sleep. And kept sleeping. The filth piled up and it took a lot of doing to shift him and clean him. Being fulsome of energy at that age and strong besides, I was on that detail. I keep my fingernails cleaner now." He held up his hands with palms held so she could see his nails.

He covered a series of trays filled with long loaves of ration-bread with flour-dusted cloth and placed them into a slotted cabinet as he spoke.

"Went on sleeping and breathing for a year or more. Nothing could rouse him. We dribbled water and honey and broth on his tongue, calf's blood even, kept him going as we could, and one day—I was there—his last breath came out like a wind. Better they go outside, you know? There's a village on the lake-belt road where one died not far from here. Arzenine. He was holed in a battle, a highpoon head got stuck deep where they couldn't get at it, and Arzenine didn't want to die in a cave. No reason for the village but for it growing up around his little shrine from the pyre. Nowadays them mendicants hanging about the spot sell pine ash with a bit of rust scraped into it claiming it's from the dragon. You passed it on your way here, probably."

"I came up from the south."

"Truly? You got that barky accent of a northern girl, though. If you're from south of the Pass I'll eat my apron."

"It was a roundabout trip."

"Ah. We need more northern types here. Sooner starve than steal food." Ileth inwardly winced at that. She'd stolen food more than once. And there was plenty of dishonesty in the Freesand. "Some of this bunch, from the best homes, the best, but they'll steal scale right off the dragons and sell it out the Catch Basin before you can say dinner's-in-the-trolley."

Ileth returned, quietly and thoughtfully, to the Cellars. She passed the digs of Griff and Zante, the little corner they'd made out of barrels where they idled, ate, drank, and diced.

They must be in their beds, asleep.

Bottles and tobacco were tucked away. She examined the bottles. The labels were printed beautifully, with ornate lettering. One even had a wax seal. They weren't drinking cheap village wine. She found a pipe, wood with a fine finish and hard as a piece of stone, beautifully fitted to its clay mouthpiece. Good tobacco, of the quality Sideburns at the pile-in had been so precious about. Even their dice and playing cards were new. She'd never seen a deck so fresh in her life. Perhaps the others, used to little luxuries and comforts, didn't notice that this apprentice and novice were living at a standard no Freesand family of her acquaintance could match. Perhaps the apprentice had a generous allowance.

Then again, maybe not. Hadn't he said something about his family wanting to make a man of him?

The Lodger still slumbered. She set his meal down where he could smell it, careful not to disturb him, and settled down herself just outside his chamber. She should see about getting some kind of rope frame for her mat if she would be many weeks down here.

Tired now on her sleeping mat, she reclined and examined the scales she'd gathered from the Lodger. Using her small scissors that she used for everything from sewing to her toenails, she etched two bars near the tip of the reverse side of each scale, then tucked them under her pillow.

The next morning the Lodger was still sleeping. Disappointed to see that the food hadn't been touched—at least it wasn't crawling with bugs; flushing out his drain had helped that—she heard the noise of metal being moved about. Empty barrels were being moved back upstairs by a team of apprentices, with Griff watching his novice help roll the last one to the ramp.

Ileth tugged on Griff's sleeve. "I know we're supposed to pick up these when they drop, but I've no idea what to do with them."

The apprentice's eyes widened at the scales she held. "Well done, novice," Griff said. "The Serpentine gets a good price for these. It's important that they be counted and collected. You have four there, looks like?"

Zante trotted up to look at the scales. Ileth ignored him.

"For n-now. There may be more to come."

Zante cackled, "Good luck for us, Leith's boat is—"

Griff frowned at him. "Not our concern. I wouldn't laugh if I were you, Zan. One of your jobs is to check the Lodger daily for loose scale. Here we have a dragon under our care and you're missing these."

Zante shrugged. "He's moving around more now. I'll just bet these were behind—"

"Don't bother me with excuses," Griff said.

Zante looked Ileth up and down. Mostly down. "We know now what makes the old goat wake up."

Ileth handed over the scale.

"Quite good, dancer. Quite good indeed. I'll see that you are rewarded." He wetted his lips again. "We, uhh, sometimes get premiums for turning in scale, you know. Don't listen to that fool Zan. By the way, down here, we never get to see you girls dance; as long as you're here—do you think we might—"

His tongue had business to take care of again.

Ileth's stomach convulsed. "I must run. Late for drill."

She hurried up to the Dancers' Quarter off the East Stair. She was lucky; Ottavia was at her desk, eating. It wasn't nuts for a change. Or perhaps not, she thought as she sniffed, smelling the paste of nuts and honey smeared on fresh bread.

"Charge . . . I—"

"How are matters with the Lodger, Ileth?"

"Improved, sira. Hungry-Hungry at last."

Ottavia straightened. "That's good news. I had a feeling a healthy, active girl was all he needed."

She didn't know quite how to form the rest, so she fell back on the sort of talk she heard from the Captain and his friends. "I must report that I suspect theft and neglect of duty, or per-perhaps suspicion of it. I'm not . . . not quite sure what to do, or how to phrase it."

Ottavia put down her knife and bread. "Tell me what's troubling you. Never mind proper form."

Ileth told her suspicions in her halting fashion. She believed Griff and Zante had intentionally neglected the Lodger so he'd sicken and drop scale. They'd gather it and sneak it out on fishing boats. She described the meetings she'd witnessed in the Catch Basin.

Ottavia thought for a moment. "So much for my day. We must take this to the Mistress of Chambers. I'm surprised they were stupid enough to speak in front of you. Did they offer you something for scale you brought them?"

Ileth hadn't met the Mistress of Chambers, though Ottavia had pointed her out once as she passed. A former dragoneer, the Mistress supervised housing, feeding, and sometimes healing the dragons.

"I just suspect them, sira. There's a way to tell. I marked all the undersides of the scales with a pair of small scratches near the tip. I'd check the fishing boats when they go out again this afternoon. The scales will be on board one of them."

"Aren't you the detective! What, you thought that up all on your own?"

People often mistook the stutter for stupidity. Too bad Ottavia was one of them. No, that was harsh.

"It's quiet d-down there. Plenty of time to think."

The Mistress of Chambers had her rooms in the tunnel between the Wall of Mirrors and the flight cave. There Ottavia and Ileth were told by her wingman that she was touring with some assigns of the

Republic, who had arrived to confer with the dragons on finally ending the war with the Galantines. Ileth wondered at that. What did the dragons have to do with a human war? Did the dragons act as diplomats? But Ottavia kept them to the matter at hand.

"We can't tear her away from that," Ottavia said. The two of them cast about the Upper Ring and found Hael Dun Huss supervising a claw-and-tooth polishing on his dragon, Mnasmanus. She'd heard that he was the only purple dragon anyone had ever seen, but she had never seen him in the flesh. He was magnificent and not just because of his unusual coloration; the dragon seemed a perfect specimen physically. From the crown of his head and down his spine, Mnasmanus's coloring verged more on red, but the red purpled as it descended his body, with the usual grays and creams at the belly. The grooms had propped his jaws open with a wood-and-leather rest, and Mnasmanus was submitting to the scrubbing and scraping of teeth as if bored by the whole thing.

The dragon's fangs were as big as Ileth's forearm. She resisted the urge to touch, but it was interesting to watch. A rotten smell wafted toward her whenever they extracted a bit of old dinner from his gums.

Ottavia begged his help. Dun Huss didn't have to think it over, or he was bored since the grooms were doing all the work and spoiling for something to do. He ordered one of the grooms to carry on. Ottavia led them away from the others so they could speak privately and explained Ileth's suspicions.

"Getting them out through the Basin, you say," Dun Huss said, looking at Ileth. "Well, nothing like catching villains in the act. You did right to say something, Ileth. Do they believe you suspect them?"

The dragoneer remembering her name pleased her. A warm thrill ran up her body. "I . . . I can't say, sir. They took the scale."

"More than that," Ottavia said. "Ileth marked them before turning them in to—" Here she whispered names in Dun Huss's ear.

"So much for oaths and sacred trusts. The Zante boy, he's from this year's batch, if I remember? I can't say that I know him, but I've heard he's of good family. Stupid of him to get involved in this. Griff's people have a distinguished name but a bad reputation."

As they traveled down the West Twist to the kitchens, Dun Huss gathered together anyone he saw who wasn't involved in more pressing business, so they had quite a procession of feeders, grooms, and a couple of wingmen who were only too eager to close their map-reading workbooks and put away the navigation tools. Ileth felt lost in the procession of tall men and stuck close to Ottavia.

In the kitchen Dun Huss paused the party, told the cooks that no one was to leave, and selected one of the older wingmen. He told him to go down and find a fisherman named Leith and inquire about purchasing big whiskerfish. When the rest of the group entered the Catch Basin, he didn't want the fisherman to throw anything overboard: he was to be wrestled to the deck of his boat if necessary. Another wingman and a couple of muscular grooms were tasked with forming a ring around Griff and his novice to prevent them from hiding, dropping, or disposing of evidence.

He gave his wingman a few moments to go on board and distract the fisherman, then brought the rest of his party into the Catch Basin and wharf with a rush. They caught Griff and Zante on board, sharing something out of a rag-wrapped bottle with the fisherman Leith and his crew. Dun Huss had the apprentice and novice hustled off to the other end of the Catch Basin, under guard of his preorganized team. The Catch Basin workers stood by, knives in hand, ready for anything.

One of the surprised young fish-gutters nodded in recognition of Ileth.

Ileth watched the rest from a collection of onlookers. The ship was searched, and a box with some scale wrapped up in old sacking to stop it from rattling was found. The fisherman denied knowing what the scale was doing in his chart box. He went on to deny ever opening his chart box at all, denied knowing what dragon scale was or that it was valuable, and probably would have gotten around to denying any knowledge that dragons even lived in the Serpentine if Hael Dun Huss had let him go on long enough. Dun Huss told him to be quiet and examined the recovered scale closely, then lifted his head and looked at Ottavia and nodded.

All Ileth could think about, watching her old workmates at the gutting table, was how relieved she'd be to be able to put down her knife and be distracted by the drama of the raid.

As they walked away with the scale, Dun Huss leaned close to Ottavia. "We got lucky there. Leith there's committed no crime, but I don't think he knows it. He could have said those were his scale, made up whatever lie he liked. He's not breaking the law by owning scale."

"I thought he seemed nervous," Ottavia said.

"I might have said something about our having capsizing and boat-burning training later, and that sometimes our new riders get confused and set the dragon on the wrong target."

"That would account for the nervousness." Ottavia smiled.

"Indeed."

With that, they moved on to Griff and Zante. They'd been sat on the floor and both looked miserable. Zante was wiping his nose and blinking back tears. Ileth was tempted to tell him to straighten up, as he'd suggested to her after the oathing, but kept quiet.

Dun Huss stood there for a minute, tapping a pair of recovered scale together with a metallic click. He walked around them, *click click click click*, a circling vulture waiting for one of them to crack.

"Are we in trouble?" Zante asked. "He told me everyone does it."

"Shut up," Griff said. His gaze fell on Ileth in the group confronting him, and he did the lip-licking thing again. It must have been subconscious.

"The game's up, you two. You're through here," Dun Huss said. "Zante, your esteemed father will be disappointed. I would think he'd have cautioned you. Do we have to go to the trouble of assembling a jury of Masters, or will you spare us the trouble and just quit in front of witnesses?"

Griff tried denial. "We didn't sell him scale. Must have been someone else. One of the fish-gutters or—"

"Denial is useless. These scales are as distinctive as Mnasmanus's. They're from the Lodger. What's more, they were marked," Dun Huss said. "Two little parallel marks on the ones Ileth gathered off the Lodger."

"You can't mean it, sir. My family won't allow it. Sponsorship from the Heem Grifforn to the Serpentine goes back to before the Repub—" Griff started to stand up, but a groom shoved him back down.

Dun Huss's wingman laughed. "I wouldn't brag up that family of yours. Half of them left for their Galantine properties when the Republic was declared. They fought with the Alliance of Kings against us."

Griff flushed. "Yes, and my grandfather fought for the Republic, just as my father did. Did yours?"

Dun Huss held up his hand. "Enough! We will have to decide what to tell your family about your leaving. What do you wish them to hear, that you were caught stealing or that you decided it wasn't for you and resigned?"

He let that sink in and then continued: "If you were doping him with gambane to make him sleepy so you could pull scale, I'll see you locked up and starved to death as a poisoner. I know what a dragon's eyes look like with a gullet full of gambane."

Griff's false bravado evaporated like water spilled on a hot griddle. "No, sir. He truly is mazy. I'd never poison a dragon! We tried to feed him, we did, and he wouldn't have it. We helped the girl as we could, pumped until our backs broke, got him up again and properly clean. Give me another chance—I'll sleep next to him with a sponge in my hand!"

Dun Huss stepped intimidatingly close to Griff. "Your family is going to be embarrassed by a scandal if they make anything out of this. The more quietly you leave, the sooner it will all be forgotten. If even a whisper of the Lodger being mistreated gets out to the Rotunda upstairs, they'll want vengeance. Dragons don't leave the punishment of those who've offended them to others. They'll see justice done with their own eyes and taste some blood. Shall I assemble a jury of dragons?"

"Dragons?" Griff said. "They can't form a jury. Can they?"

"If you knew your country's history as you ought," an apprentice groom said, "you'd know that dragons can serve on juries. Just like any other citizen. Just doesn't come up is all, courts being built for humans."

Ottavia gave an evil-sounding chuckle. "It's not unknown. They do. When that young drake—forget his name—was attacked in Vyenn in sixty-two, the dragons formed a jury and questioned witnesses and came to a verdict."

The boy slumped. "All right, I'll leave. Let Zan stay, though. He's just a kid. His old man'll hang him upside down until his eyes pop."

Zante found his voice. "Griff already had the scheme all set up when he took me on! All I did was collect dropped scale. He didn't give me a penny; just said he'd make sure I made apprentice. I'll make it right somehow."

"'Price is irrelevant when it comes to a dragoneer's honor,'" Dun Huss quoted. Or at least Ileth thought she'd heard the phrase in some maxim or other. "But, Zante, if you are truly remorseful, you may reenter next summer. We've seen that before and it's worked out surprisingly well for all concerned, provided the novice in question has truly improved himself in the meantime. Your father can tell you Preece was discharged and reapplied. He's one of the best young dragoneers here, and my wingman. You could do worse."

The novice wiped his nose on his sleeve, looking hopeful.

"By the way, how much were you paid for these?" Dun Huss asked.

"Eight silver each," Griff said. He was blinking back tears now as well.

"Even there you funked it. While the quality isn't the best, being off a sick old dragon, the coloring is quite unique. Polished up and readied for the jeweler, you'd see fifty or more easily. Leith there was making a four- or five-hundred-percent profit off you for a little grease polishing these."

"The wretch!" Griff said. "He told me black were the valuable ones."

"Anyone other than you a part of this? If there's someone else getting you scale to smuggle out, I'll make it easier for you two. I have friends outside the Serpentine who will assist you getting back up."

"No, just us," Griff said. "But if you think I'm the only one sneaking scale out, you're a fool."

"All the more reason to make an example of you," Dun Huss said. "Zante, make this a lesson for you. The only people who can promote you to apprentice are the Masters. If anyone's going to make apprentice now, it'll be Ileth."

"Maybe that's the idea," Griff said. "She could have set us up! How hard would it be to mark some scale, sell it to the fishermen, and then blame us?"

Ileth stiffened at that but triple-sealed her mouth. The last thing she needed was another duel.

"For what purpose?" Ottavia asked, putting a restraining hand on Ileth.

"This is useless. You already confessed," Dun Huss said.

"Make her look good to you. She's looking to redeem herself after being caught selling her favors at the pile-in in the stables."

"Selling!" Ileth gasped. "Is th-th-that the story now? I was selling—"

Dun Huss cut her off. "Leave the insult before it turns into another injury. You two, follow me," Dun Huss said.

Ileth once again followed the procession back to the fishing boat. She fought the urge to shove Griff off the cave wharf. Imagining the startled scream and the splash would have to do.

Dun Huss marched the two exiles up to the boat captain. "You've broken no law, so we can't punish you. I suppose we could ban you from the Catch Basin, but I assume you and your men have families to feed. We'll still buy your catch, but we'll buy from other boats first, and if we still have need, then we'll take yours."

So Dun Huss also used *we* when speaking to those outside the Serpentine. She suspected if she were to start throwing *wes* around in Vyenn, she'd get in trouble. It reminded her a little of Ottavia's emphasis that she think of the dance troupe in *we* terms as well.

There was no small satisfaction in the thought that she was part of the *we*.

"One more condition," Dun Huss continued, breaking in on her fantasies. "When you leave this afternoon, take these two with you."

"What am I supposed to do with them?" Leith asked.

"Dump them in the bay for all I care. I suspect you made enough off them to put them up for a while until they sort things out with their families, but that depends on how much of a sense of honor you have when it comes to people who've risked—and, as it turns out, lost—a great deal to fill your purse."

"Well, boys, you heard the dragoneer," Ottavia said. "Get on board, or we'll toss you through the catch hatch."

"I'll help toss," Ileth said.

"What about my—" Griff started to say.

"It'll be donated to the poor lodge," Dun Huss said. "Next market day. Dig around then."

Griff looked Ileth levelly in the eye, then called her a vile name. Then he marched on board and sat down in the cabin with his back to the audience. Zante stood on the gangway, looking at them as if in expectation of a *Hey, it was all a put-on to frighten you into better behavior; return to the bosom of the Serpentine!*, but nothing like that was forthcoming. Finally he crossed over the ship's side, sat on a pile of netting, and wept.

Ileth now felt more than a little sorry for him. Small against the boat's side, suddenly he seemed too young for such a hard lesson. She'd seen, hundreds of times in the Lodge, how a younger person modeled on an older one, for good or ill. Oddly, she felt an impulse to go get him some of Joai's stew and put an arm around his shoulder while he ate it. Or tell him to straighten up.

The party broke up. Dun Huss sent the wingman named Preece to report on the event to Heem Deklamp and dismissed the rest to their duties, except for the two biggest grooms, whom he told to make sure that when the fishing boat left, Griff and Zante remained on it.

Dun Huss pulled her aside, and the wingman with him halted exactly one pace behind. "You're observant, aren't you, girl? You notice and remember. That stutter of yours may be a blessing; you use your eyes and ears more than your mouth. I suspect several people saw what you did, but while seeing they weren't able to forget about the rest and just notice the vital detail."

"Thank you, sir. Griff had it right about one matter."

"What's that?"

"I was out to get him. I think I was. For neglecting the Lodger."

"Hmmm. Be careful with taking a dislike to someone. People live up or down to your expectations more often than not. We don't much care for feuds among the company. Human nature being what it is, factions can't be helped, but—well, there I go again. You've done well, and I'm lecturing you when I should be saying thanks."

Ileth bobbed.

"One more thing: if you ever set out to get me, do me the honor of letting me know. I'll retire and go off somewhere remote. Seems like it would save us both trouble."

Ileth laughed at that, and Dun Huss's eyes twinkled. With that he gestured to his wingman and strode up to the kitchen.

She almost skipped down to the Lodger's cave, where she found him nosing about in the meal she'd set out.

"These livers could be fresher," the Lodger grumbled.

"All they had," Ileth said. "Should I ask the cooks to get m-more?"

"Don't attend my grousing," the Lodger said, chewing slowly. "I should be grateful I still have a sense of smell and taste. All fades as you get older. You are bright. What passed?"

"They're putting new grooms in down here. Griff and Zante are gone."

"There's an old piece of lore that says you're often better sticking with a familiar bad than hazarding an unfamiliar worse, but I'm not sure how much worse we could do than those two."

Ileth, sensitive to the use of the word *we* today, swallowed. Then she did a brief stretch on her support and began to dance.

The Lodger blinked. "What are you doing?" he said.

"Dancing."

"Without music?"

"It's in my head."

"Well, it's not in mine. If you're going to hop about like that, you should at least have some music."

"Hopping about for-for-for you is my job. I must do it to the best of my ability. Whatever the challenge." She tried one of those movements she was so jealous of that Shatha could do where she touched her toe behind her knee with her standing leg while her flying leg pointed directly out from her hip at what seemed an impossible open angle, matching with her opposite arm.

It did not go well. But then she was discovering that it never went well, at first. The challenge was to keep at it until it did go well, and then keep at it ten thousand more times until it was impossible for it to turn out any other way.

9

Her days with the Lodger grew until her time in the Cellars could be marked by a calendar. The old dragon took food, sparingly at first, mostly of meat or fish stews, then began to chew up joints and hams. He never did eat with the ravenous enthusiasm Ileth expected—she'd always imagined dragons tore up their food like wolves—but whether it was because he had no great appetite or just had whatever a dragon's version of table manners were, she wasn't experienced enough to say.

The retired dragoneer who served as head groom came down for a personal inspection with a team and cleaned him up properly. He apologized to the Lodger for not coming down since the new group of novices joined and promised to make amends. For two days a parade of apprentices and novices worked his skin and scale and a physiker dressed his wounds and rubbed an ointment in, leaving a large pot of the stuff for Ileth or other grooms to use.

Though it wasn't her duty, Ileth listened as attentively as the other novices as the head groom showed them how to spot a weak scale, dress sores, and work about even a largish dragon like the Lodger safely.

"I've never much liked humans crawling over me and tweaking this and that," the Lodger said to her. He accepted his scale being checked and polished and having cracked and loose scales removed, but he drew the line at filing and shaping. "A dragon should let his scale stand as nature designed. All this making patterns and painting, my own sire and dam would call it decadent."

He showed an intelligent interest in her dancing, more because it was something he hadn't seen much of, rather than out of some inner fascination that her smell and movements evoked. That, or he was an accomplished dissembler. She arranged a performance for him, even, bringing down Preen and Zusya with music boxes to each show off their favorite routines. They were going to dance as pairs at the Feast of Follies, and it gave them a chance to rehearse before an audience. Ileth set floorlights all about and helped them with their costumes. The new Cellars apprentices, who were more diligent about the pump that kept the sluice clean, attended as well. After it was done the Lodger rustled his wings and waved the tip of his tail about a little as the limited space would allow. He apologized to them afterward that he had no sacrificial chickens or sheep to give them, which left the pair nonplussed, but they left with copious thanks from Ileth.

"What was all that about chickens?" Zusya whispered to Preen as they went out.

"They do say he's mazy."

Duskirk and his novices followed, Duskirk solicitously inquiring of Zusya if she was cold in her costume. He'd feel responsible, you see, if she became chilled in the Cellars and became ill . . . Ileth snuffed out the floorlights and picked them up.

"What was that about sacrifices?" Ileth asked.

"You know, I believe your art is derived from old ceremonial dances in Hypatia. All the emphasis on being up on the balls of your feet, or your toes, as that . . . oh, I've forgotten her name, the darker one, as she did: that's for invocation of air spirits and such that control the weather."

Ileth couldn't quite manage the toe-work yet; you needed to wrap your feet well and have special shoes with a hardened leather cup that had to be made to fit her.

"Some of the other movements," the Lodger continued, "are meant to evoke fauna. The Hypatians had a lot of mythology about the connections between humans and swans, swans being a beautiful soul that would remain on earth for a while with the power to bring peace, I think it went. Or was that doves? *Ha-harumm*, my memory isn't what it was. Oh, dragons bringing calamity, and later luck when it became more politic for the Hypatians to rechoreograph them as heroes and guardians, I believe holding the arms up above the head in a manner that is supposed to be wings or horns. Cats were always popular, snakes, oxen—but I didn't see those females imitating any oxen so maybe those parts have been lost. If I'd known that flourish of their culture would thrive all the way over here, I'd have paid more attention. I remember the male temple dancers being proud of the height of their leaps. The number, too. Audiences would count them off. I recall one dancer who could do sixteen, turning each time in a great circle. He must have had legs like a stag."

Ileth tried to imagine a great clumsy man dragon dancing but failed. "I don't know if I'll ever be really good at it. I can work up a sweat with the best of them. But it's a good job for-for me. There's n-no talking when you dance."

"Talking makes you uncomfortable?"

"Yes. I'd g-give anything to be rid of this . . . this stutter. But I can't beat it."

"Yes, you can."

"Easy for you to say."

"You can do anything," the Lodger said. "Standing before me, I see millennia of triumph."

Ileth made a choking noise. "Ha!"

"Girl. You had a mother and father."

Ileth fought to keep a grimace off her face. "Yes. Obviously."

"And so did they, and so on going back each in their turn. Sires and dams, generation after generation."

"I suppose. Don't know much about them." All she knew was that she looked nothing like the Captain or anyone related to him, in person or portraiture, for all the Freesand talk of him being her father.

"You don't? I do. I've seen it with my own eyes. You've no idea, no idea at all what your line has overcome. The challenges they lived through, and didn't just survive, slinking off grateful that breath was still in their bodies; they managed to bring the next generation into the world and keep them alive long enough for them to reproduce in turn.

Triumph after triumph after triumph! If there was a failure anywhere along that line reaching into the mists of prehistory, *fssssssht!* Finished. You wouldn't be here. One jaguar's leap not escaped, and you wouldn't be standing here, believing you can't overcome a stutter. Your blood got through famines, droughts, earthquakes, plagues, invasions of barbarians. Strength against strength, cunning against cunning, craft against craft and they won, won against other men, beasts, storms, even dragons. They fled the fall of civilizations and built them up again out of sweat and wreckage. They escaped dragon raids and slaves' shackles and the chariots and spears of—I don't know what you call them in your tongue, ogres maybe. You, Ileth, are a diamond, the product of millennia of immense pressure. Your line didn't shatter, it hardened and cleared and sharpened. Don't tell me a bit of difficulty like a stutter is going to stop you. Ha!"

She could just stand there, a little awestruck by the epochs he described.

The Lodger sighed. "You even conquered me. I'm tired now; I think I shall rest. Isn't it about time you went upstairs and had a good dinner? All that dancing must have given you an appetite. Join your kind."

She went to sleep thinking on what he had said and the next morning was the first in place for morning drill, her exercise sheath as clean as her freshly washed face, hands, and feet. She went through the drills losing herself in music and motion, her standing leg a piece of supportive iron, her flying leg reaching new heights and holding with foot perfectly arched.

"Ileth, you're on your toes this morning," Ottavia said, smiling as Ileth's arms fell gracefully back to the resting pose at the end of the second set. "I can't seem to tire you out."

"Then try harder, my Charge," Ileth said, smiling.

As her dance slowly—or rapidly, over the next few mornings— improved, the Lodger also acted as her tutor.

It started on an ordinary morning. They were talking about the different kinds of people who came into the Serpentine. He didn't ask about her origins, and she was grateful for that, and though the reason for it could have been that he just didn't care, now that she knew him a little better she decided he considered such questions bad manners. But she said her education only went as far as being able to read, write, and do basic arithmetic, no arts or formal training in other languages (what Galantine she knew, she knew out of the Captain's use in the Lodge). She told him she was a little envious of some of the girls who had private tutors visiting a few times a week. The Serpentine made allowances for the novices and apprentices to continue whatever studies their families were willing to pay for.

"I don't know that I possess an education of much use to a human here, beyond teaching you Drakine," the Lodger said. "You can't dance all the time, and it's something to keep me awake. You'd find it useful if you wish to build a life here."

She'd been told to learn Drakine if she could, and she eagerly accepted.

Learning Drakine often led to talks about other subjects. He recited, from memory, a list of books and compilations of old scrolls he wanted her to read, and she turned it in to the Mistress of Chambers, who was in overall charge of meeting the dragons' needs. Two or three volumes appeared almost immediately, available at the Serpentine's small library, and a bookshop in Vyenn supplied one other, though where the funds for its purchase came from Ileth didn't know. The rest would require some expertise in finding and the project had to be shelved (literally; the Master of Novices put her reading list on his bookshelf with a promise to write a friend of his in Asposis who knew some of the old libraries there). She had more than she had time to read in any case.

Ottavia alarmed her briefly just before the Feast of Follies by calling her in for an interview. Ileth went up, fearing that she'd be removed from duty with the Lodger now that he was on the mend. It turned out that Ottavia was equally relieved by their talk, because she had what she thought was the bad news that the Mistress of Chambers thought it would be best if the Lodger had company through the winter at least. The physiker hadn't liked the sound he heard when he put an ear to his chest and listened to him breathe. He worried about the old dragon's health and wanted to make sure he stayed active and engaged. Ottavia thought it was strange, the Cellars business; old or badly hurt dragons were generally sent off to one of several locations for "pensioners," as they were called, with plenty of fresh air and mountain sunshine. For some reason the Lodger stayed hidden in the Cellars and no one spoke his name. It was a mystery.

Ileth was only too happy to agree to continue attending the dragon she increasingly thought of as hers. He was the most unusual tutor one could imagine, but she wouldn't trade him for the most famous sage in the Vales.

Ottavia finished the interview with good news. "Oh, and a parcel arrived for you. If I read the posthouse legend it comes all the way from Sammerdam."

Ileth thought it would be a book from the Lodger's list, but Ottavia handed her a wooden box about the size of a loaf of bread. Someone had been in a hurry to get it to her—there were wings stamped on the labeling from the posthouse and the final destination of the Serpentine. It had gone by dragon courier.

That was most strange, and a very expensive way to send a gift, as she understood such things.

Ileth borrowed a knife from Ottavia and managed to work it open in the privacy of her own sleeping area. With mounting excitement, as it certainly didn't look as if there were books within, she extracted the object and removed the old, lightly oily rags protecting it.

The box contained a music box. It was carved out of something that reminded her of whalebone, with a design of moon and stars on the lid.

She showed it to Ottavia, who identified both the material—ivory—and the tune it played, "Dance of the Fireflies." Ottavia, something of an expert on music boxes, pronounced it exceptionally fine and pointed out that it had two wind-up keys, allowing the owner to play the tune at two different tempos, slow and solemn or fast and twinkling.

There was no note enclosed, no token that might give away who had sent it to her. She wanted to ask Ottavia how much she thought it was worth but sensed that crass subjects like the price of a gift were beyond discussion for Ottavia's class of person. So she had to speculate in silence. It drove her to distraction.

She thought about the timing. The most likely candidate was Rapoto; his family had money and perhaps he felt as though he owed her some kind of restitution for being turned out of the Manor. She wondered if she could let it drop that she'd received an expensive gift next time she saw Santeel or Quith at the Great Hall and gauge their reactions.

The music box played a lovely tune at either tempo, and she danced to both for the Lodger. She used the slower tempo for drills and fatigues—the Lodger showed an equal interest in those as he did in pure dancing—and the lighter, quicker tune for a variation on a dance they'd rehearsed for the Feast of Follies. It was still missing something, though.

In happier news, Peak and the others were due to return on the eve of the feast. They'd been much delayed by encore performances, social invitations, sketches by artists who wished to imitate Risso Heem Tyr, and the inevitable problems of travel as fall gave over to winter.

Outside the Cellars, preparations for the Feast of Follies were under way, and they chatted about the feast. It was the one feast day that did not have a regular and predictable spot on the calendar. It was reserved for a warm spell in late fall. North of the Notch in the Vales you didn't always get a final taste of summer after the equinox, but south of it there was almost always a reliable span of balmy warmth that gave the citizens one last chance to gather outside. For summer to come after fall seemed folly, thus the name.

This year in Vyenn and the Serpentine, the date had been settled on by the Masters and a quick in-town jury of the guild heads and an innkeeper's wife who had a sixteen-year run of predicting the weather and having it not rain on the feast day she selected.

On the Serpentine, it would take place on the Long Bridge, which would have every available lantern and candle strung between the existing lamp stations, oiled to burn all night. Tables would be spread out in the shelter of the Pillar Rocks just in case (the innkeeper's wife's run would have to end sooner or later) with food to be served by the

Masters and dragoneers instead of the usual workhorses of the Serpentine, the novices and apprentices.

It was one of the highlights of the year, especially for novices and apprentices, who for once had nothing to do in the feasting. Ottavia put her heart into it, especially as it would be a farewell performance for two of her veteran dancers.

Ileth had her own set of worries. By tradition you appeared at the Feast of Follies in a costume representing some bit of foolishness, ideally that you wished to be rid of, but she had no money for the purchase of odds and ends. She took her problem to Ottavia, as she was expected to perform with the others in costume.

"I'd be happy to help you if you wish to create a costume. As Charge I'm handling drinks. Small beer, courtesy of the Serpentine and the fishermen's guild."

"I've never attended a costume party," Ileth admitted.

"They're fun. This is the only one the Serpentine holds. But the tradition is a mote confusing," Ottavia said. "You're from the north and I don't think it's much celebrated up there. No? Well, you wear a costume that's supposed to evoke a folly. The problem is, some celebrants wear one they wish to indulge, and others wear one they'd like to be rid of. It can be confusing. Pride, for instance. Lust is always popular at both ends. Ignorance, profligacy, it seems like there's no end to them."

"Will there be dragons, as we're dancing?"

"They come out and watch, many of them. I believe they enjoy the color and noise. They perch up on the rocks or coil around the bridge supports. One year Mnasmanus managed to get his horns tangled in the lantern wire. Dun Huss was *so* embarrassed. Then he's easily embarrassed. I gave him my last veil once during a removal dance and he blushed about it for half a year."

Perhaps those imaginings of hers about Ottavia and Dun Huss had some foundation. She and Ottavia talked over sources for costuming.

Ileth returned to the Cellars deep in thought. There were plenty of venalities she'd like to be rid of, but she didn't see how wearing a costume would help. Or how to depict it. Still, it sounded like fun.

She'd just served the Lodger his dinner and started warming up to dance for him—a little ritual they enjoyed before they settled down to the lessons on Drakine imperatives—when Zusya burst in.

"Oh, hurry, by your guiding star!" she gasped. For Zusya to be too winded to talk there must be a crisis shaking the foundations of the Serpentine! "Peak is back. The trunks. The trunks, Ileth, you should see them! She says they're full of costume. It's like a caravan out of the *Great Green Book*! Hurry!"

The Lodger rumbled in what Ileth now knew was a draconic chuckle. She looked up at him. "By all means, go attend your bazaar. I would welcome an early night. Imperatives won't disappear from Drakine in your lifetime."

They hurried up to the dancers' rooms. Though she'd been named, several times, and was treated in every instance as a member of the troupe, for some reason this wild upstairs dash racing Zusya—who, despite being winded from her run down to the Cellars, was still nimble as a two-year-old deer—made her feel at last that she belonged to Ottavia's dancers. It seemed there would be no more "oh, and Ileth" when it came to rosters or rotations during the drills.

So they joined the throng. Peak was just opening the last two trunks. The outer chamber behind the curtain looked like a seamstress shop had sicked up through the curtain. There were shoes, sheaths, hose, headdresses, scarves, leg ties, hairnets, skirts, and other performance accoutrements spread across the floor, chairs, tables, and cushions as though they'd been sacked by raiding gargoyles. At the center of the floor a light rug had been put down and jewelry and stage paint was spread out before kneeling dancers, examining items. "I know you don't much go in for stage paint, Ottavia, but it's practically required in Zland," Peak said.

"It can be expensive," Ottavia said. "Far too much for day-in, day-out use. But it's timely. You can teach the rest of us how they apply it in the fashion of a Zland performer."

"Which gives me an opening for my real news," Peak said. "I'm moving to Zland. I'm to be married!"

Everyone except Ottavia and Ileth squeaked some variety of "*What?*" Ottavia looked stricken and Ileth curbed her expostulations.

"It's true," Peak said. "I am to be wife to Risso Heem Tyr. Can you believe it? It still seems impossible to me."

"It should be impossible," Ottavia said. "Isn't he on his third wife?"

"I'll be fourth! You can't blame him for the second: she died in childbed. He was only sixteen when he married the first. I was going to tell you all at the Feast of Follies. But I just can't keep it in."

"I have the opposite problem, once I get my hand around one," Zusya said.

"The Feast of Follies would have been an ideal time for this announcement," Ottavia said. "What about wife number three?"

"Dreadful woman. She wears bracing so her breasts shelf out. She's a schemer just after his money."

"His money," Preen said. Ileth had heard that Preen and Peak had joined the dance troupe together. "Which you don't care a raisin about, I'm sure."

"Spirits, no. It's art. I shall be art, evermore and forever! I'm his muse!"

"How amusing," Preen said.

"I thought we were going to announce together?" one of the older dancers, Tassa, said.

"What's this now?" Ottavia said, her hand going to her throat as though a thief were reaching for her necklace.

"I'm betrothed too. He's Heem Tyr's painting dealer; he sets the price and so on. He handles other artists too. It's the place to buy art, Zland. I didn't know so many paintings existed! He came backstage with a great mass of flowers after our debut performance. He was to deliver them to Peak, but he saw me and was overwhelmed. They went to *me* instead."

"He couldn't help but notice you," Fyth, the other dancer from the trip, said. "You were twirling around backstage stripped to your earrings and gushing about how many bows you took."

Ottavia collapsed onto a costume-covered cushion.

"Ottavia, are you well?" Zusya asked.

Ottavia groaned. "I feel like Mnasmanus himself has sat on me.

You're my two best dancers! Fyth, Fyth, please tell me you're not leaving as well."

"Fear not, my Charge," Fyth said, posing with hands on heart and chin nobly raised. "I kept my sheath on, and my legs only went in the air when I danced, so no offers at all."

Peak shot Fyth a dirty look. "Oh, Ottavia, I'd be heartbroken if you are unhappy about this. Press-gang a few novices, or beg one of the apprentices to join, appeal to the need of the Serpentine. You've done it before. The dragons don't care about extension, they just want sweaty women."

The Charge rolled forward and put her head in her hands, like a drunk suddenly doubtful about the last round.

"I care about the discipline. I'm trying to make something here, you know. Not just me, some of the motions and balances you all invent. You realize we're creating a new art form. It's universal. We could tell a story, just like actors, but it would have nothing to do with language. All the emotion comes through movement and music."

Ileth looked around. She liked Peak, but the only constant in life is change, as Caseen had told her.

"Oh, we forgot to reveal secrets!" Vii said.

"It's not a betrothal ceremony," Fyth said. Some argument back and forth broke out about the definition of a betrothal.

Peak scowled. "It's as close as I'll get to one. Why not? Ileth, won't it be fun? You have good secrets, I'm thinking."

"I'm—I'm n-not sure what . . . what you mean," Ileth said.

"Never been to a betrothal?" Shatha asked. "I went to my first when I was a little girl."

"Oh, it's simple," Zusya said. "The bride's friends take her aside and her guests each reveal a secret to her. Sometimes after you reveal the secret, you get to ask the bride a question. Well, that was the tradition around us."

"We just did secrets in Asposis," Shatha said.

Ottavia stood up. "I will let you girls share secrets. At my age, you don't have many secrets, but if you reveal them you'll end up facing a jury. I'm going to see what Joai has in the way of rotgut brandy. Perhaps I'll be lucky and die of poisoning."

None of the troupe let Ottavia's acidity spoil the party atmosphere.

"Let's start," Peak said. "Who's the youngest?"

"Ileth, I think," Vii said.

"Oh, but Ileth's never done secrets, Vii. You go first."

Vii took a breath. "I'm in love with a wingman. I just say that, Peak and Tassa, because I hope you love your future husbands as much as I love him."

There were a few excited gasps. Questions for her to elaborate flew from everyone but Ileth, who was still trying to work out the tradition.

"Oh, Vii, you can't leave it at that," Peak said. Ileth wondered if Vii was playing a spoiler and stealing some of her betrothal glamor. "As the betrothed I demand to know more!"

"I'm betrothed too," Tassa said. "I don't give an old sock who Vii's mooning about."

"More, Vii," Peak insisted.

Vii sat back. "No, said all I'm going to say. Ileth's turn."

Ileth cast about, wondering what sort of secrets she had. The Lodge was a poor place for secrets, and she'd been too busy since coming to the Serpentine. She could admit that she stole food on her journey there, but that didn't seem right for the occasion. No, it should be something about life, probably. Marriage . . . children.

Ileth looked at her hands. "I . . . I met a dragonrider when I was young. Annis Heem St-Strath. She st-stopped for water in our t-town. I gr-grew up . . . grew up in a lodge. Made up . . . made up this story in-in-in my head where Annis was actually my m-mother. Secretly. She'd-She'd had to give me up to be a dragonrider. Wanted to grow up like . . . like her. I'd imagine myself asking her things . . . just silly things like what she thought of a bracelet I braided out of twine, stuff like that. I . . . wanted to tell her that when I, when I came h-here, but I learned she'd died against the Gal-Galantines. I say that because if you have little girls and they show you a bracelet they m-made out of some old twine, make a big deal about it."

Ileth lifted up her gaze. The last time she'd seen so many vacant eyes staring at her was the gutting table.

"Oh, Ileth . . ." Peak said. She looked sad.

"That's not how this works, Ileth," Vii said.

"Oh, be quiet, Vii," Shatha said. "She's never done this before."

They moved on to Fyth, who put things back on track by saying she much preferred wearing men's clothes when going to Vyenn. Not because she thought she looked good in them, more because she could go about her business in peace and if she accidentally muddied herself in the streets no one thought twice about it. And she could have a nice big porter in one of the alehouses without anyone raising an eyebrow that a woman ordered herself a worker's tankard of beer. She encouraged the others to try it and everyone started describing what sort of man they'd dress as.

By the end Ileth was laughing with the rest of the troupe.

Talk shifted to the Feast of Follies and costumes, and the party broke up. Ileth waited her turn to congratulate the future brides. After she embraced Peak, she tried a question she'd been mentally rehearsing. "I've wanted to ask about your name. Now I'm worried I won't get another chance."

Peak smiled. "Oh. I thought everyone knew. My family is from the Medi Islands. There's more history than I like telling, but we had to flee, and the Vales had my grandfather's most remote trade-hold. Girls are traditionally named for landmarks—White Blossoms on the Stairway to Urun Temple is my mother's full name. I'm Peak of the Golden Road, which is where my father happened to be when I was born. So . . . Peak. In Montangyan."

"You ever see your mountain?"

"No. Thought I might, being with the dragons, but it looks like I never will now, unless my husband takes it in mind to paint it."

"What is your future husband like?"

"Not like what you'd think. I imagined he'd be quiet and artistic, but he's big and loud and messy. Droll sense of humor. Shouts a lot. Slightest thing sets him off."

"You don't m-mind being shouted at?"

"Oh, the house is so big; I shan't be able to hear him often. I will get him to heat his studio better, though, even if I must do a bit of shouting myself. Zland isn't that high up, but it still gets cold this time of year. He works in a long coat to keep the paint off, so he doesn't notice. It's a miracle I didn't catch the most dreadful cold. Chilly work, being a muse."

Ileth decided to go to the feast dressed as greed. Greed was easy; you just needed coins, or things that looked like coins. They had a lot of scarves with little imitation coins that tinkled away and complemented certain dances, thanks to Peak's trip where they were popular with tavern dancers, so it was just a matter of strategically wrapping herself up in a few of those. In the Serpentine, among the dancers, there was a certain relaxed sense of propriety. Her costume would never pass the Matron's inspection, but the Matron could ride off on a bristle brush.

She didn't think she was greedy in the traditional sense, but now she found herself constantly jealous of her fellow novices and apprentices, few of whom had ever wondered how they were to "clear the housekeeping," as the Lodge's cook used to put it when she counted out the coin the Captain had given her to feed them that month.

Ileth also wondered if she wasn't greedy for things other than coins. Status. A place in the world. Praise. She'd had plenty of examples lately of life going wrong when you became greedy, for coins or for . . . other tokens that indicated that she mattered. But it wouldn't hurt to publicly be done with greed.

There was to be a performance at the feast and she found herself anxious about it. They would be dancing for an audience of humans, not dragons. She couldn't help but feel nervous: a gut full of darters, as they put it in the Freesand. But it was a good kind of nervous. Mostly. Dancing. She wouldn't have to say a word. Flick out onstage, smile, make obeisance to the audience, smile, dance, smile, keep time, smile, make another obeisance to the audience, give one last smile, flick back offstage. Easy as cold roast breakfast.

She was to dance with Preen and Vii, and also do the initiate's solo they taught her, only three times through to keep the audience from being bored. Ottavia suggested a little flourish with her arms and head that she could add on the third run-through of the compass points, since she was comfortable with the rest of the routine. Her performance backing up Preen with Vii was even more simple, more of an exhibition of basic support and floor drills than anything taxing. Ottavia would stand off to the side and give a short introduction (Ottavia was dancing herself in both the first and last performances).

Their stage was a little platform flanking the main tunnel into the Beehive. Once upon a time, she'd been told while out with the troupe, a dragon had always sat guard there, day and night, but the tradition had been abandoned because the dragon never had anything to do and they tended to just get bored and go to sleep, and a snoring dragon on the doorstep made the fortress look undisciplined. Anyway, it made a perfect stage. When she wasn't onstage she'd be in the mouth of the tunnel, behind a temporary curtain helping with costumes and such.

The feast was already in progress when the dancers emerged from their quarters, all wearing long plain overcapes to hide their costumes until they were onstage. They danced in a short procession back and forth across the Long Bridge to the Pillar Rocks to help draw a crowd. The weather had held; the air was soft and warm, so the innkeeper's wife could buy another bracelet or whatever she did to mark her score at seventeen perfect predictions.

They passed the food tables under Mushroom Rock. Caseen was pouring out cold party soup and making a mess of himself and his table. But he smiled, splattered with soup as he was. For once his mask did not look out of place; instead of ominous it could pass for festive. The tempting smells made her mouth run. She and the other performers wouldn't be able to eat until after they danced.

There were town folk mixed in as well, faces of all ages. Ileth saw several groups of Vyenn girls, in fine gowns with just a mysterious hint of a folly they wanted to give up, under the eye of an elderly chaperone.

"Good hunting for the townies at the Feast of Follies," Vii said to Ileth, quietly.

"We're performing as soon as the musicians are ready," Ottavia said, over and over again. "We invite your attendance."

An artist from Vyenn hastily captured the scene on easels, sketching rough to be filled in with paint later. Ileth watched in astonishment as he made three different sketches of the bridge scene facing different directions from his carefully located stool, each in what had to have been but a minute or two.

The dance began as soon as they finished their procession and the musicians signaled that they were ready. Ileth was at the back with Vii, who kept falling out of line to greet friends. Ileth helped Preen light the footlights ringing their watchpost-stage. Dax and a few musically minded apprentices were warming up. There was another man with arms like a blacksmith, perhaps a local friend of Dax, who supported an awkwardly stringed instrument that must have been difficult to haul around. As he stood with his bow, ready to play it, he looked like he was dancing with a rich man's coffin. His only bit of costuming was a hat tied on upside down.

Dax had outdone himself. He displayed a bizarre outfit made to look like he was upside down, walking around on his hands. A mannequin head hung down from his backside, hair dangling almost to the ground. She wasn't sure where his head was hiding in the rigmarole (she finally decided he'd built a wire box around his head), but she saw hands tuning the impeller partly hidden by false footwear. Perhaps he could see a little through the stretched-tight fabric in front of his face.

Ottavia gathered them up and arranged them in performance order. Peak helped Vii with her costume. She'd managed to catch it on something and tear away a part during one of her embraces.

"Remember, it's no different from the dragons," Ottavia said. "Make eye contact. Pick someone out in the audience and look at them. If you engage with one, you engage with everyone. And smile!" She nodded at Dax and the music started.

She waited her turn, feeling she would be a bad follow-on to the other dancers.

Seemingly before she could draw breath, it was her turn. She made it through her solo, to some polite applause, nothing like what the opening number with five dancers had. She forgot to make eye contact. She wasn't even sure she smiled, but she did keep her head up and kept in time to the music, even if Dax sped tempo up on each run-through to give her an extra challenge and keep the audience interested. By the second slide of her third repeat, she was ready to turn him upside down for real. But she finished.

The drill demo with Preen went easier. Ottavia explained the routine as a set of exercises her dancers used to train their muscles and perfect their posing and then stood off to the side. She talked about the delicate balance the troupe tried to maintain, so the performers worked with muscles hot and loose, yet not exhausting themselves, by rotating them on and off the floor for rest and water that would keep the sweat flowing. Having her present, like a protective mother hen keeping watch while her chicks pecked about, gave Ileth the confidence to examine the audience.

The drill began. She recognized Dath Amrits (who had a tapped keg of something hanging at his gut like a mother in her ninth month of expectation) and Hael Dun Huss standing next to him. Amrits in particular seemed to be enjoying himself. Or perhaps he was a cheery drunk.

Dun Huss pointed straight at her and leaned over and said something to Amrits. He chuckled and waggled his eyebrows at her. As Dun Huss shifted to hear Amrits say something, she recognized Rapoto Vor Claymass behind him, standing next to Santeel Dun Troot, who was hardly visible in the crowd, just a bit of her face white like the moon behind mountains.

The sight of Rapoto caused her to flub a leg lift. She recovered and caught up.

Vii's hand tapped the side of Ileth's head as they flung themselves left and right, arms rising and falling in synchronization. Ileth glanced over at her and saw that Peak's repair on Vii's costume had come undone. Vii's daringly abbreviated top's shoulder strap had fallen down her arm and only sweat was keeping the material over her left breast.

"Tit," Ileth said to Vii out of the corner of her mouth.

"Cow," Vii whispered back.

"Your top will fall," Ileth managed through her smile-grimaced teeth.

Vii fixed it in a flash, showing more deftness and skill than Ileth would have believed. She seemed to make it part of the drill. She rewarded Ileth with a smile and a nod.

Rapoto must have seen the byplay, even if he didn't understand the words over the music. He smiled at her. Santeel leaned close to whisper something in his ear. Ileth picked a different audience member to watch.

It was over just as she was getting comfortable with the idea of performing in front of a crowd. This time there was more applause. "If you are interested in a challenge and working right under the noses of the dragons, we do have vacancies in the troupe," Ottavia said. "I hope a few of you will consider it. We don't wear elaborate costumes all the time. And it is an excellent way to get to know some of the dragons."

Ileth politely waited until the finale, smiling so widely she felt like her cheeks would split. The dancers in the finale took their bows; then Ottavia called the musicians and the rest of the troupe up onstage for a final bow and it was done.

Food, at last. She hurried across the Long Bridge and its festoons of lights.

Her first spot was Caseen's cold soup. Caseen was messier still; he seemed to be getting one serving in four on himself. The cold soup was tomatoes (how he got them this late in the year she couldn't imagine; perhaps someone in town jarred them, but they didn't taste stewed) and spices and mint and something crunchy that was probably dry crumbs, she wasn't sure, and most miraculously for the end of the year, ice, but the sharp acid chill was welcome to her thirst.

"I hear you're finding your feet with the dancers, Ileth," the Master of Novices said as he poured a bowl for Preen.

"I wish I could lose my feet again, sometimes," Ileth said. "They get very tired."

"How are things down with the Lodger?"

So he knew about that.

"Yes. He's much better . . . I-I think."

His tortured face relaxed and he stared off at something only he could see. "He's a great old dragon. I'm not sure we'd have our Republic if it wasn't for him. The first Alliance of Kings about did us in. My grandfather and all three of his brothers died then."

"Caseen, save some soup for the bowls, would you," Dath Amrits said, pushing through. He turned to Ileth, and she had to pull back to avoid being knocked flat by his barrel of a belly. "Hear you brought Old Stripes back to life. He talk your ear off about the Imperial Rock? Or has he only worked his way through ten thousand years of ancient dragon history up to now?"

"He's teaching me some Drakine."

"Costume's a daring one, Ileth," Dun Huss said. He gracefully drew another soup-eating apprentice out of the way before Amrits could bowl him over.

Ileth shrugged and tried to guess what Dun Huss had done as an example of folly. He looked much as he did other times she'd seen him. She realized he had the middle buttons undone on his tunic and his sword-frog was only hooked in two places on his belt, not all three. *The madman! What if the Master of Dragoneers saw him like that?*

"You two never change," Caseen said. "Where's the Borderlander?"

Amrits slapped the keg on his waist. It gave a sloshy, half-empty wet sound, making Ileth think he was sampling his own costuming. "He and Catherix are on watch in the flight cave. You know that worn hunk of old boot leather: only way to get him to attend a party would be to chain him in a box like the Great Efreent and haul him to it in a cart. He'd probably escape even quicker."

Dun Huss ignored him, especially once he started filling a cup on a chain from his obscenely placed keg tap. "Did Galia tell you, Ileth? She passed her survival, brilliantly. I've made her my wingman."

Ileth had heard something called a "survival" mentioned a few times, some sort of test with a dragon in the wilderness for senior apprentices, but the exact nature of it was still a mystery to her.

Caseen raised a drippy bowl of his soup in salute to Dun Huss. "I hadn't heard. Always was the best of her year, Galia. Is the eve of the Feast of Follies the best time to announce that?"

"Unofficial. I talked to her this morning and she accepted. Thought she deserved to have a bit of a spree tonight without anyone thinking the worse of her on the news. I'll officially present it to the Master in Charge in a day or two."

"I think it's wonderful," Ileth said.

"The way she flew in in that duel." Dun Huss smiled. "If I'm ever up against it, I want her coming in the same style."

"Legally it wasn't a duel anymore, Hael-me-lad," Amrits said. "I'd blown it over. She could have run him through, claimed she was defending our future Speaker of the Assembly here."

"As you mentioned flying in, sir, d-do you know anything about-about a music box?" Ileth haltingly relayed the mystery of her ivory music box from Sammerdam.

Dun Huss glanced at Dath Amrits.

"Don't look at me, I gave her my silver whistle, and she sniffed about it being just nickel, the ungrateful whelk. Well, must be off. See if there are any thirsty townies from Vyenn about trying to give up on lust. Convince her to reconsider."

"I am sorry, I don't know anything about a music box, novice," Dun Huss said.

Caseen shook his head at her as well.

"I see Galia," Ileth squeaked. "I must con-congratulate her. Master, dragoneer." She handed the soup cup to a man at the washtub.

"Just your humble servant tonight, Ileth," Caseen said.

Galia stood against the thick decorative railing of the Long Bridge, looking out at the lake and the lights of Vyenn. They were feasting down there as well; what she guessed to be the high street was all lit up.

Her costume was mostly made of feathers and lace. Like most of the things she did, it seemed expertly sewn, and if she was trying to look ridiculous, she had failed. She looked almost elegant. If a young woman wearing a bunch of chicken feathers couldn't actually look elegant, Galia came about as close as possible.

"I give up. It can't be cowardice," Ileth said. Galia turned.

"Ileth! I saw you dance. You can't have just been doing it since summer! You looked like you'd been practicing for years!" Galia squeezed her hand, then looked her up and down. "You're doing . . . poverty?"

"Greed," Ileth said.

"Oh, courses, I'm sorry. Greed! Don't know why I thought poverty. Good for you. It's—um, very daring, but you dragon dancers can get away with anything. You asked about mine, didn't you? I caught some of the novices clucking a little while after I told them off and put them on extra mending. They called me an old mother goose. I didn't have money for goose feathers so I made this with chicken feathers and a few stained doilies of the Matron's. But I've resolved not to peck at them all the time. If geese peck. Do they? I'm from the city."

"Will you be around to peck?"

"I saw Dragoneer Dun Huss speaking to you. Did he tell you?"
She nodded.

"I still think I'm dreaming. Me, a wingman, to Hael Dun Huss. Or wingwoman. I'll have to ask Kithiminee what she was called if she ever gets back. The language of the Serpentine isn't designed for us, is it?"

"I'd settle for toilets designed for us," Ileth said. "I get tired of-of-of squatting in cold pee."

Galia laughed. "You're so bad, Ileth. Or do northerners joke about such matters all the time?"

"As a wingman do you have a . . . have a dragon?"

"Sort of. Has no one told you how it works? Wingmen are always associated with a dragoneer. They are available to help him accomplish whatever commission has been handed to him. Sometimes they fly with one of the roster dragons, dragons who haven't paired up with a dragoneer; other times they care for their dragoneer's dragon. They might take his place if he's injured. Please let that never be the case with me!"

Ileth thought there was an unusual amount of emotion in the last for cheery, confident Galia. They talked a little, and Ileth learned that wingmen can be given commissions, take on an apprentice, and do practically all of what a dragoneer does.

"May I ask you something, Galia?"

"Oh, I've been running on. Yes, please do!"

"Is there some tradition about dancers? Not becoming dragoneers?"

Galia worked her lips in thought. "I don't know. I haven't heard of it happening, but I've only been here a few years. They're in their own world, like the physikers and tinkers. An important world: they keep the dragons happy. I know our men like them just as much as the dragons, for the most part. Ottavia's always losing them to marriage or—well, you know. The mothers' lodge in Vyenn," she finished in almost a whisper.

Galia brightened. "But you know, I've never heard of a woman fighting a man in a duel, and you did that, didn't you? So why not? That's what you joined for, right? You're not the marriage-market type, or a sage looking to write the definitive new dragon tome. I thought you might be a moonraker, but then that affair with Rapoto—speaking of whom, here he comes."

Ileth turned, and there was Rapoto with Santeel at his side, tight on the bride's arm. Rapoto had on a sleeping-jacket and a silk night-hat with such a long drape to it that it could also serve as a scarf while you wore it.

"Sloth!" Galia guessed.

"I'm not very original, I'm afraid," Rapoto said. "Right the first guess."

"Didn't you do that last year?"

"It didn't take." Rapoto smiled. "Ileth, your dancing was lovely. No sloth, you."

"Not onstage, sir. Thank you." Rapoto didn't seem to appreciate the honorific tacked on. He edged closer to her and she stepped over to replace a wayward feather on Galia to keep from being trapped between Rapoto and the bridge rail.

"Is no one going to guess mine?" Santeel Dun Troot said.

The assembly turned to Santeel. She wore something like a jester's outfit, well-fitted, with diamond-shaped cutouts showing off parts of the body a woman of her name could only reveal on a feast night like this. The weighted-tassel skirt she wore was stylish and expensive-looking and opened up in strips when she walked. Part of her face was obscured by black greasepaint.

"Oblivious!" Galia said.

"Ignorance?" Ileth asked.

Santeel glared. "I had it made especially for me. I'm incomplete!"

"I should think so," Galia said. "They left out half the material."

"You know, Galia, for someone from Sammerdam you're a bit of a prude. I'm serious. I wish to finish my journey to adulthood here, ready for a citizen's responsibilities to the Republic."

"Uh-huh. I thought your family came from old aristocracy," Galia said. "And your father was part of the Royalist gang in the Assembly."

"Their convictions are not mine. Don't we mix as equals here? Didn't I stand as second to Ileth, a nobody from north nowhere?"

Galia nodded. "And I had to jump in to keep her from being stabbed through the belly."

Santeel glared at Galia and turned to Ileth. "Is it true, what your Charge said about the dancers? You, uh, perspire all the time."

Ileth nodded.

"That's the idea," Rapoto said. "The dragons enjoy the sweaty smell. It's their job to stink. I don't mean stink. You know what I mean, Ileth."

"*Stink* is the word for it," Ileth said.

"Doesn't it make you feel uncomfortable?" Santeel asked. "Clammy? I would think you would faint. I have an aunt who faints just getting out of a carriage and walking across the courtyard on a hot day."

"We wrap up whenever we aren't dancing," Ileth said. "She m-makes us drink. She has this salty vinegar concoction she gets from the kitchens that they use for the pickled eggs. We drink it between drills."

"That girl with the thick black hair, Peak, can certainly spin," Rapoto said, shrugging off Santeel and stepping up to Ileth. "If I ever get a free morning, I'd like to watch you rehearse. Is that allowed? I mean, you're in the middle of the Wall of Mirrors and the dragons hang over you."

"We get the grooms up all the time. Cooks. Or dragoneers, even. We're used to it. Wh-Which reminds me. That roasting pig smells d-delicious. I must—"

"Allow me to get you a plate," Rapoto said. Santeel glared at Ileth.

"Thank you," Ileth said. "But—"

Rapoto hurried off before she could stammer out anything after *but.*

"I thought you dancers never ate," Santeel said.

"Not at all. They put us practically n-n-next to the kitchens because we're always eating."

"The dragon kitchens? I saw them on my first tour. You must have strong stomachs." Santeel looked up and down. "What are you, anyway, Ileth? Resolving not to accept charity anymore? It can't be putting a price on your virtue, that's too obvious. That would be like selling a swayback horse that's already been—"

"She's greed, Dun Troot," Galia said.

"Doing away with greed."

"Greed? What do you have to be greedy about? You haven't anything to your name but a secondhand silver whistle, if you haven't sold it, that is."

"Someone sent me a nice music box. Ivory. It p-p-plays at two tempos."

Santeel looked thoughtful. "It certainly wasn't me. No card with it?"

"No."

Santeel started to turn her head toward Rapoto but instead smiled at Ileth. "Well, tra-la-la, a music box. How nice. Your costume looks well sewn, anyway. Clever about using those coins, draw the eyes when you move. It's simple but well done, Ileth."

"This is my first Feast of Follies, so I thought I'd s-start with an easy one. Oh, still have the-the-the whistle." She pulled it out of her costume. "I promise to blow it if your Rapoto tries to kiss me again."

Ileth regretted the speech at once. Santeel looked authentically hurt. She'd been trying to be nice with the compliment on her costume. Unlike Galia, Ileth was inclined to believe her talk about duty to the Republic. There was no reason a rich girl couldn't be as patriotic as a poor one.

"We have a lot of people from town this time," Galia said.

Talk turned to the music and the size of the crowd. They looked up at the dragons—there were four up on the rocks and little natural ledges in the Beehive, watching the festivities—and tested themselves on their names; Ileth used her improving Drakine to help Santeel on the pronunciation by way of making amends. Santeel only got one right, Telemiron, Charge Deklamp's dragon, whom the applicants had met while Ileth was waiting out on the doorstep.

A mass of barbecued pig with Rapoto somewhere behind appeared.

"Left some for the rest of us, I trust," Galia said.

"You bid good-bye to the folly once your costume comes off, I hope?" Ileth said, setting down the platter on the wide railing of the Long Bridge.

"Rapoto, have you heard about Ileth's music box?" Santeel asked quickly. "I wonder who could have sent her such a wonderful gift."

He denied any knowledge but seemed impressed that someone had sent for it all the way from Sammerdam.

"Maybe it was the grateful staff of the Catch Basin," Galia said.

They sampled the roast.

This led to a short argument over whether greed covered food as well, or if that was solely gluttony's territory. Ileth said no, Galia yes. Santeel supported Ileth, as if to rub her republican convictions in Galia's face.

Ileth understood little about politics, but it evidently caused some sort of enmity between Santeel and Galia. She'd been out of the Manor for weeks and weeks now. They might have argued about the use of a hairbrush for all she knew. In the Freesand nobody talked politics; they mostly talked about fish, lobsters, and oyster beds, and the depredations of the Rari on the north side of the bay. Politics belonged to the rarefied air of the Governors and the Assembly, and no one Ileth had ever known spent any time talking about them.

Santeel moved Rapoto off to another group, this one containing a few apprentice friends of his.

"She's like a dragon on a bullock," Galia said, watching Santeel point out details of her costume to the other apprentices, still tight on Rapoto's arm.

"Santeel doesn't like losing," Ileth said. "Toenail clippers, boys . . ."

Which reminded Galia, who told the story of Santeel's nail clippers being found hidden in the bedding of the novice from her room who snored loudly. Santeel accused her of being a thief, the girl denied it, and Quith pointed out that it was odd that the snorer would steal toe-nail clippers and then not clip her nails with them, as both her hands and feet needed attention. The affair ended with the return of the small scissors and the snoring girl being removed to a corner of the attic where she wouldn't bother anyone.

"I can't believe she'd t-try to get someone dismissed."

Galia shook her head. "I can. I know her kind. She'll take a ride or two on a dragon, get a pretty sash she can trot out on the patriotic holidays, maybe ride dragonback down the Sammerdam Archway in the Declaration Day Review, and ride off on a pensioner dragon on her wedding day while people toss flowers. The Masters will run her through here like a twig washed down a drain spout. Entered, apprenticed, a few fun rides, and passed on to a husband. Her dragonriding stories will be the highlight of the high priestess's teas."

Ileth danced once more, an informal encore with the musicians, who'd continued playing all through the feast. She didn't drink anything but water. Not even the punches or ciders; she wasn't sure she could trust them. Many of the feasters were already feeling their drink.

A few of the girls from the Manor embraced her and congratulated her on the dancing. The Manor seemed so long ago. Increasingly, her life felt like it was divided between getting to know the Lodger and everything else. She'd come to the Serpentine with a girl's fantasies about riding dragons, swooping around temple towers and scattering herds of sheep or peering straight down onto a whale's back as it blew at the surface. What she found was something like a master who could tell her about ages no living human eyes had seen. About higher ideals. The ancient troth between dragon and dragoneer. The sorts of things that were the reason men like Hael Dun Huss served his people and land.

She couldn't wait to tell the Lodger about the evening, so she hurried down to the Cellars as soon as she was able. He'd be asleep, probably. Perhaps she'd curl up just outside his room so they could talk as soon as he woke.

For some reason the darkness of the Cellars bothered her. There was always a certain amount of mess and disarray, though it had improved a great deal since the new apprentices took over. She knew they'd been rolling out extra lamp oil for the party and breaking out spare torches and lanterns, and it showed. She couldn't put a finger on it, but she lingered under the lamp before setting off toward the Lodger's chamber.

When Ileth was about twelve, one of the old women of the Freesand, a bay widow who sold tobacco and nuts and oiled tie-pouches to put them in, told her that women especially needed to listen to their gut more than their head or their heart. The heart flew to all points of the compass, and the head was ready to rationalize away anything with *Oh, it's nothing to worry about, silly*. But the gut you could trust. The gut never steered you wrong.

Ileth's gut bothered her. Something was wrong up ahead. She had a horrible premonition of the Lodger, choked on a joint of meat, dying with no one there to run for help. She quickened her pace, afraid of what she would find at the end of the tunnel. It seemed a terrible distance to the light of the Lodger's chamber and things were still. But not quite still enough.

With increasing unease, she'd covered about a third of the distance when she struck something. Her first thought was that she'd walked into something in the dark.

But the beam she'd thought she'd blundered into turned out to be a thick arm reaching from the darkness. It held her hard. Something huge and strong and reeking of beer yanked her off her feet and pulled her among the jumble of crating and shelving and barrels lined up in the passageway.

Gorgantern couldn't resist a cackle of triumph. He slammed her against the wall and the world turned into fireworks and gongs.

"Got you, little piglet. You'll oink now."

He was wet, slippery. He'd greased his skin for a swim in the lake. She scrabbled for purchase with her feet and felt that he too was barefoot.

If his hands on her shoulders had closed around her throat, she would have died with a quiet crackle of cartilage and escaping breath. But he reached for her breasts. She'd been pawed there before. Her reflexes knew how to get away from *that* without much troubling her terrified brain. She slipped beneath his reach so fast it could have been mistaken for a magician's trick. He grabbed her cobbled-together costume as she went, and she brought her heel, every bit of her dancer's strength in leg and buttock behind it, down on his toes. She heard and—even better—felt an unmistakable crunch. The hand let go and she heard a howl through the blood roaring in her ears. Muscles strengthened and quickened by hours of exacting exploded and she was free of his reach.

She vaulted over a crate, caught her foot, rolled back to her feet in stride, and fled toward the Lodger's chamber, yelling for all she was worth. She heard Gorgantern shove a crate aside as he limped after her. Later she reprimanded herself for forgetting her whistle; it would have echoed in the Rotunda; but the strength and terror in those hands reduced her to bare instinct.

Gorgantern staggered after her, swinging a bent iron crate-cracker he'd found somewhere. "Wrong way, piglet. No exit back there."

"Murder!" she screamed as she ran. "I'm being murdered!"

She made it to the Lodger's cavern, shrieking as she ran, only to trip on the gutter. She heard Gorgantern hard behind, flipped onto her back as she scrambled away—

Then a yellow shaft of light, heat, and noise filled the passageway. It pulled air away from her face. It was as though a tendril of the living sun came down and ran a fiery finger up the tunnel. And Gorgantern simply vanished.

One second he was there, bathed in the approaching light, and the next vaporized clean out of existence. There wasn't even a body to fall or break into pieces. He was consumed.

She threw up her arm against the heat and the light. The next thing she knew, the Lodger had swept her up in his wing (she didn't even know dragons could carry things in their wings until later it was explained to her that they were sort of a long-fingered arm) and, relatively safe from the fire in the leathery cocoon, survived the flames as the Lodger dashed through them in the odd rocking stride of a dragon's leaping sprint.

Bounced around in the dark with an odd sensation of once again being a babe in arms, she felt dizzy and sick. When her head cleared, she was gasping, disoriented, out of a strange dream of the Captain knocking her down and standing wide-legged over her, roaring drunk. The dream dissolved and she was back in the Serpentine, drawing breath after gasping breath.

Sensible again, finding herself at the tunnel opening to the lift, she found herself looking into the alarmed eyes of the Lodger. His breath smelled like a hot lamp burning old grease.

"Ileth, can you talk?" the Lodger asked.

"That's a . . . f-foolish question," she coughed. Her lungs tingled. She broke into another series of racking coughs.

Figures dropped down from the ladders flanking the lift and she heard it clatter down to her level.

"There seems to be a fire in the—" The Lodger winced. "In the . . . passageway. I panicked. I must have some air."

He lurched onto the platform, tucking his neck and tail. "Up. I must go up," he growled tightly.

Ileth got to her feet, still coughing, and followed. She grabbed on to a trailing edge of wing and was pulled along as she used to be pulled when she'd grab sheep or dogs as a little girl. Yells of fire and a ringing alarm sounded from the junction. Others had discovered the fire. Finally she thought of her dragon whistle and blew it for all she was worth as she stumbled, clinging to the Lodger.

She smelled her own burned hair. There was some pain, especially on the arm she'd flung up to protect her face and on the exposed skin. The skin didn't look like it was otherwise damaged. She'd heard bad burns didn't hurt—at first.

The Lodger decided not to wait for the lift and climbed to the next level. Ileth hung on, listening to the dragon's labored panting in increasing alarm. *Oh no oh no oh no . . .*

"Need. Fresh. Air," the dragon said. He added something in Drakine she didn't understand.

After an eternity they reached the Upper Ring. The Lodger, who clearly knew his way about, made for the exit. He held his front leg tight against his breast, resulting in an awkward, three-legged limp aided by a wing. The image of the dragging wing, particularly, alarmed Ileth. Something was dreadfully wrong.

She blew on the dragon whistle. "Make way! Make way!"

They must have made some pair moving across the Long Bridge, both sooty, Ileth with her hair singed and costume awry, the dragon staggering across the bridge. Someone called for people to fight the fire in the Cellars. The party dissolved.

At the other end of the Long Bridge the Lodger's dragging wing knocked over the food tables. White-eyed and wheezing loudly, he didn't notice, but he made it through the tunnel-like loom of Mushroom Rock and, skirting the little house where Joai served up soup and bandages, stumbled for the wall. Ileth thought she spotted the physiker's white hair and ran to him, but it was just a portly man of Vyenn unknown to her. Ileth turned and watched in horror as the Lodger reared up, climbed over the battlements, and fell more than leaped over, his tail whipping up and over as loose as a cut line as he rolled down the precipitous slope to the bay.

Her injuries forgotten, Ileth ran after him. Heart pounding as though it sought exit from her chest, she found some stairs and made it to the wall. Disturbed rocks and dust were still heading down the precipitous slope to the bay where the Lodger was thrashing—no, swimming, snakelike, with limbs tight against his sides, for the shoreline.

She jumped down the two-man-high wall and bumped down the slope after him, at cruel cost to the skin on her legs and her feet. She hit the ankle-deep water at the lakeside and hurried along the shoreline just as the Lodger dragged himself up onto the beach, taking deep, strained breaths.

"For all the gods' sake, what is wrong?" she said.

"Air," he said around his tongue, which stuck stiffly from his mouth. He didn't seem to be speaking to her. He used the Drakine word. She sensed a dragon circling overhead and glanced up. There were several, turning tight circles. She could see part of the Long Bridge from here, with its festive lights, and the lighthouse atop the Beehive.

He panted for what felt like an eternity, ignoring her pleas to come to his aid. Where were the physikers?

Finally he blinked a few times. "Ileth?" he said in her own language, dry and breathy.

"Sir?" she said. "It's Ileth, I'm here."

"Did I make it?"

"You're on the beach. Your back legs are in the bay. Don't you feel the water?"

He gulped air around that horrid outthrust tongue, then managed to retract it. "I had the horrors of—being chopped up—and dragged out in hunks. Better here. Better now."

"No!"

"I'm dying, Ileth. Something broke inside. Heart, I believe, or a blood—oh, what's the word. Blood pipe."

He raised his head a little so he could gaze at her with both eyes. "So you are the last thing this life gave me to love. Fate could hardly have done better. A daughter of sorts."

Ileth tried to speak but choked on her words. "Love?" she finally managed.

"Read Lermonton's *On Planes of Love*. The only flaw is he does not speak of how . . . they sometimes blend."

"See! You're doing w-well. You wouldn't be quoting—"

"That's better. Warm," he said. "Warm," he repeated, this time in Drakine.

He gave a shudder. "See that I'm properly burned, Ileth. See to it! *Vhanesh luss.*"

The last was in Drakine.

"Don't talk. Breathe. The physikers are here. They say you need to rest and keep breathing. Keep breathing!"

They weren't. He didn't.

He took a deep breath and laid his head down at a more comfortable angle, as though settling in for a nap. One of his wings rattled and his *griff* relaxed.

"Sir," she prodded.

"SIR." She struck him, hard, where she thought the neck-heart was.

"*Vhanesh luss!* You're not going to t-tell me what that means, are you? You old fox! I'll have to—to figure it out for myself, won't I?"

He stirred, nuzzled her with his snout. She caressed the pebbled skin with her hand. His eye opened, twinkling merrily, as if he were looking forward to seeing what came next. Then the lid opened wide. The eye emptied.

His *griff* rattled and went limp.

"Gods!" Ileth threw herself down on his neck and cried. Sobbed as she had never sobbed before. Not for herself, not for anyone. *Vhanesh luss, vhanesh luss.* She repeated it over and over, committing it to memory.

Orphaned. Orphaned again, and she didn't even know his real name.

A presence loomed up behind, large, much bigger than a horse, but quiet.

"I am Aurue," the dragon said.

She couldn't answer him. The sobs wouldn't stop.

"This noble one is dead." His Montangyan was terrible, thick and utterly flat, but he could get his point across.

The gray nudged her with his snout.

"Be back on your way, Ileth," he said. "You are wet. You are cold. Go, take our gratitude. We will finish."

"I'll stay."

"Jizara and I, we are of his connected line, through my sire and sire-sire. Jizara is away. The vigil starts."

"Don't cut-cut him up," she managed. "He made me promise." She cast about at the boats and broke off an old tiller handle. It had an evil-looking pair of nails like fangs. "I'm not moving."

"When stop the vigil, we burn him. Until then, none will touch at him."

"Then," she said, feeling half-dead herself, "I sh-shall wait until he is bu-burned."

"Have your will," Aurue said.

So she sat by the body, with her improvised club across her lap. She dragged over one of the smaller overturned flat-bottomed boats that had once been the border of the dueling ground and set it by the Lodger's head and sat. The sun came up. She vaguely sensed that some dragoneers came down to the beach, milled about, spoke with Aurue or one of the other dragons, and left. Eventually, the sun went down. Galia came out with a blanket and some soup in a crock. She accepted the blanket and thanked her for the soup but didn't eat any. After two futile attempts at conversation, Galia gave up and returned to the Serpentine.

Three days she sat, not eating, taking a mouthful of lake water when the thirst became too awful, hurling rocks at scavenging birds who came to worry at the tender flesh reachable to their hooked beaks. Were the dragons not bothered by birds trying to eat their kin?

Two dragons were always with her, but they changed at dawn and dusk. They neither ate nor drank nor spoke when they were on duty. Now and then a few of the humans of the Serpentine visited. They threw braided brambles or green lake plants in place of flowers since it was not the season for them. Ottavia came, said she was sorry.

"You're only flesh, you know," Dath Amrits said, when he and his dragon visited. Dath left an old scroll-tube filled with some blank paper and a full ink bottle by the corpse. "Come up and have a meal and a night in a bed. They won't send him on until tomorrow night anyway. We have to fly out by sundown. Use my bed. Had the bedding washed for you. I know that drafty ruin that passes for the dragoneers' hall is like getting the warmest room in an icehouse, but it has to be better than the shoreline."

"No, sir. Thank you, sir," she said.

The third night turned cold, dreadfully cold, and she shivered under her blanket. She would fall asleep for a few minutes, but discomfort would soon wake her.

As the night wore on and snow began to fall, a dozen or more dragons gathered. Their scales seemed dull and colorless. She touched one of the larger dragons as it passed. Ash came off on her hand. They'd rolled in ashes. She wondered with torpid curiosity where one found a clearing full of ashes deep enough to roll in, but then realized they were dragons and could make one out of any pile or stand of timber.

An old dragon shoved Ileth's overturned skiff aside as the dragons stood in the center of a horseshoe shape around the corpse.

"Would it be . . . ap-appropriate for me to-to-to put on ash as well?"

"Normally, I'd say no," the dragon said. Emotion gave his dragon-tongued Montangyan an extra layer of difficulty. "But I—forgive me—I heard of his last words. In your case I believe it entirely appropriate. He called you his daughter. Feel free to take some off one of my *saa* for your own."

She did so.

It didn't last long. Several of the dragons spoke. It was all in Drakine. She picked up a few words; they seemed to be talking about wars and a dragon king and humans. She had come in at the end of a famous life, it seemed. They sang in their own tongue, some cawing out words, others sort of droning in a chorus, and the rest thumping their tails and cracking their wings and using their long throats as organic trumpets.

There were a few humans attending, discreetly, from a distance.

"Say something if you like, girl," the dragon at the center said, startling her.

She shook her head. "Good-bye, Lodger," she whispered. "I wish we'd had more . . . time."

One of the dragons must have given a signal she didn't perceive. In turns, running around the arc, they each spat fire on the corpse of the Lodger. Soon his flesh was alight. Horribly, the smell made her hungry.

He took a long time to burn. It seemed like hours. As soon as the flames began to go out, a couple of the dragons departed. Finally the rest nudged the blackened remains into the lake, sweeping fallen scale in with their tails.

"He is with his line now," the elder dragon said to her. "It is over."

"Is this how you always do it?"

"Sadly we can't always be this formal. Leave it to [something in

Drakine that began with a *Dhr*] to die at the joining of water, earth, and sky, good and proper traditionalist that he was. I imagine he planned it all out. There's always a proper wind off the mountains here."

Ileth's teeth chattered in agreement. Oddly, the knowledge that he died in a place of his choosing made her feel better. Almost happy. No, actually happy. *Happy?* Maybe she was going mad.

"Do you want to fly back to the caves with us, or walk?" the elder dragon said.

"I can't, I've never flown."

"As you like. But you came here to fly."

"Would it be appropriate?"

"I knew him. He had a generous soul. He'd like nothing better."

"Ausperex, you've no saddle. She'll be impaled on one of your horns," a female dragon said. She was mostly green but had white flecks blended into her scale. "Even after all these years, you land like a catapulted elephant." Ausperex did have a somewhat overgrown ridge of spikes running down his back, save where they were trimmed down somewhat for a saddle, though evidently one hadn't been on him in some time, so they'd grown back.

The dragonelle settled down next to Ileth. "My name is Taresscon. I don't fly as much as I once did. I'd be glad to carry you back."

She knew the female by sight, as she'd often seen her pace through the passages of the Beehive, speaking to all and sundry, but wasn't familiar with her role. She usually had a staff of humans with her, but she'd never seen Taresscon with a dragoneer.

Females had a webbed fringe running down their backs, much softer than that of the males, and Taresscon's fringe was neatly snipped off where a saddle would rest and much cut down elsewhere.

"I should carry you anyway," Taresscon added. "I have been meaning to thank you personally for what you did for some time now, but I've been so busy polishing diplomats and sealing assents. Your friend and I go back to, well, let me just be modest and say I don't go quite so far back as he did. I am happy he didn't die in a cave. There's a natural little well where my neck meets my shoulders, see, girl? Sit tight there.

Helps if you tip yourself a bit forward. If you want to set your teeth in my fringe, go right ahead; I can't feel a thing there."

She didn't see and even if she did she was busy summoning her courage. The Beehive suddenly seemed high up and far off. Now that she had a chance to fly, she was afraid to do it.

"I find if I sit around thinking about a fear it gets even worse," Taresscon said. "Climb up and let me worry about keeping you on. Not that different from a horse."

Somehow knowing that dragons had their own fears helped. Ileth hadn't had much more experience with horses than she did with dragons. There was just that time when she was six. She'd sat on farm horses a couple of times as a child. She'd never done anything that could be called riding on any kind of beast.

"I'll stick out my front leg so. This is my on side, you know on side and off, right? Good. Use the top of my front arm as a step. My, you're limber for being new, and up you go."

Ileth surveyed the world from atop a dragon's back for the second time. She was going up and taking whatever fears she had about it with her. With the energy that three days of hunger often brings, she shifted about until her hips felt comfortable.

"Just grab on to my fringe in front of you and lean way forward. Pull all you want, you can rip it out and it won't hurt. Go forward and grip with your legs like you're jumping a wall on your horse. Don't be afraid to dig your heels in. I hardly feel it these days. Hoo, I used to be tender about my throat."

What little she knew of flying on a dragon mostly suggested cold. The dragoneers wore layers of material and shields over their faces to keep the worst of it out. "We're not going up high, are w-we?"

"Stars, no. Just to the Long Bridge. I don't think either of us is ready for an attempt at a flight cave landing." The dragon jumped up and down in a quick hop, warming her wings. "Hold tight, we'll be there in a moment." Ileth gasped and tightened her grip. She felt the dragon jump in the air, but something bumped. When she opened her eyes again she found they were still on the ground.

"See, if you can hang on through that, you can make it to the bridge. I'll set down as soft as if I were carrying my own eggs."

Ileth nodded.

"Once we take off, I have to circle where we buried our relative. I won't do it like the others. You'll hardly know I'm turning."

Ileth, now that it had been pointed out to her, did see that the dragons above were swooping around the funeral site.

The dragon began to beat her wings, warming the muscles in earnest. "Once for your grip, twice for your legs, three times and we're off," Taresscon sang out, coiling her body along the spine and then springing into the air like a cat jumping for a ledge.

She felt the dragon's mighty blood vessels working through her skin and heard the wings behind her beating furiously. But she was in the air! Ileth, of the Captain's Lodge, with her stutter and her patched dresses, sat astride a dragon in flight!

She was so excited watching the tilt of her mount's head and the way the female's fringe rippled in the wind that she missed circling the funeral site entirely—guilt hammered her when she thought back on that fact in bed that night—they were approaching the Pillar Rocks before she knew it. It looked strange, and she realized the feast lights had been taken down and put away. Only the ordinary lamps glowed, with the reflected beams of the lighthouse above.

Taresscon was practically the last dragon to leave the funeral site. Only Aurue, the youngest, still remained at the water's edge, she noticed, looking back.

Ileth looked at the burned remains, and the joy of the moment turned to ash, ash as cold and wet as the philosophical old dragon's remains. Leave it to life to squeeze the triumph she should feel at this moment out of her spirit. She was a dirty dishrag passed from fate to fate, wrung out and tossed.

The line of dragons came in one after another, tails waving about as they balanced at the last moment for the landing, slapping them down to absorb the shock of alighting. Most stalked straight through the wide tunnel to the Rotunda but two males stepped off onto the wide plaza before the tunnel entrance to scratch at their scale like giant dogs and shake off the ash before going inside.

As promised, Taresscon set down so gently Ileth hardly knew they were on the ground until the leathery rustle of her wings folding in on themselves tipped her to the fact. She felt dazed.

"Just slip off, girl. No, other way. Off side, remember? That's it. Start your habits well, dear, and you'll save yourself trouble."

"Th-Thank you for your advice," Ileth said, back on the ground again, her legs a little wobbly from the unaccustomed work of gripping a dragon's neck. Now she was physically wrung out as well as emotionally.

"I've had enough practice," the senior dragon said. "I served six years sort of attached to the Assembly. Speaking for the dragons. *Humph.* I'm for my shelf. It's been one of those days where the joy and sorrow keep changing places, no? Anytime you want more practice, girl, look me up. I get tired of all the meetings."

She brought her head in close. "Just between rider and dragonelle, so to speak, you did well. I've had riders in saddles who almost tipped off, and there you were hugging tight as a scale nit even without a saddle. Be proud of that, and thank Ottavia and the cooks for the strength in your legs."

Ileth realized she'd left the blanket Galia had brought her back on the beach. She couldn't face the long walk down to retrieve it. She just couldn't.

Too tired to even take the extra hundred paces to the kitchens, she went straight to bed.

You look terrible, Ileth," Ottavia said as the other dancers rose the next morning. "I'm excusing you from drill today, to spare myself from facing a jury on a charge of witchcraft for reanimating the dead. There's ash everywhere. You smell like the sampling lounge of a tobacco house. Get rid of the shambles you're wearing, then wash your body, hair, and linen. Report to me this afternoon when you're fit to be seen in public as one of the Serpentine's dancers."

Ileth decided to eat at Joai's house. Joai wasn't the best of company;

the sudden onset of winter, as if to pay back the warmest Feast of Follies in recent memory, had brought with it a cold. Her face was red and her nose even redder as if her nose considered the coloration of her face a challenge it had to answer by doubling.

"Word is you rode old Taresscon. Bare-skin," Joai snuffled.

"You make it sound like a circus attraction," Ileth said.

"Ooo, I don't. *Are-choo!* It's just overturned half the apple carts in Jotun, you might say. There's rules and traditions about when to ride dragons, as you're no doubt about to learn."

Joai limited the rest of her communication to sniffles and sneezes. Ileth walked back to the Beehive and her interview with Ottavia feeling that she'd planted both feet in the muck. Again.

"Am I in jeopardy?" she asked, as soon as she passed through the curtain and entered the Dancers' Quarter.

Ottavia smiled from her little desk, where she folded and laid down a note.

"I wouldn't call it jeopardy, Ileth. I wish you'd spoken to me before doing your death vigil down on the lake; I would have happily excused you and made sure you had warm clothing for winter's arrival. As it is I can't find fault with your instructions, other than missing drill. You were assigned to the Lodger, after all, and you carried out your assignment. But remember, we dancers are a team. You can't just go off on your own hook like that, despite your grief. But I'm ready to let the matter be forgotten. It was a mad night, with the feast and the fire and the Lodger's death. Just communicate your needs to me in the future."

"And Gorgantern."

Ottavia's dark brows came together. "Gorgantern? What does he have to do with it?"

"He's the reason the fire started. He was in the Cellars. He meant murder."

"You mean arson, no—oh, I see. Well, rough justice, then. The fool." She shuddered. "I've a horror of being burned. Strange for someone who works around dragons, I know, but that's the Wheel of Fate.

"Oh, more sad news. You missed Peak's farewell. We had our winter rice pudding with brandy-raisins early. Santeel ate your portion. She claims the drills are famishing her. Peak told me to tell you good-bye. She said she'd never forget your memorable entry to full womanhood with your skirt over your head in a horse stable. She meant it as a compliment, I believe. I shall miss her brass more than her skill at dancing."

The wheels in Ileth's brain stopped turning. "Santeel was at ... the drills?"

"Yes, she joined us. I made it strictly probationary. We've never had a society girl, much less a Name like Dun Troot. What is her family going to say, I wonder? You and I know what goes on here, but that's not how they see it in Sammerdam or Asposis. Not yet, anyway. But the good news is the next time Preen eats too many of those cat's-catch-of-the-day disguised as sausages from the dragon kitchens, you don't have to clean up. You had a quick spell as scour. Assuming our new scour Santeel doesn't fall out, then you're back to scrubbing out the sluice."

Ottavia ended the interview by informing her that she needed to visit Caseen, the Master of Novices, in his office after dinner. If she wished, she could take her dinner privately in the Notch or anywhere else she might find convenient.

"A final word: sorry about the Lodger, young lady. I heard you two were a fine match. Taresscon herself spoke to me. She was quite moved by the way you stood by him, in bad times and good."

Ileth polished herself in the washroom to the best of her ability. She noticed a new bed partition, Santeel's, obviously, and a special lacquered sort of carry-all that she'd seen carpenters and such use filled with brushes and soaps and balms in the washroom. One of the cases in it was beautifully inscribed silver.

Clean with her singed hair clipped even closer to the scalp—she took care to remove any of her own hairs and rinse off Santeel's brush before she returned it—and with a scalp glowing from the gentle caresses of the quality bristles, she dressed in the better of the two shirts she owned (they were always swapping places as they wore down) and her mended overdress. She steeled herself for another encounter with the Master of Novices.

She had to wait; he was dealing with two boys who looked as

though they'd been in a fistfight. The cat that prowled the hallway took the opportunity of her waiting to leap into her lap. She idly scratched it.

The boys left and she made her presence known.

"Nothing unpleasant today, Ileth," Caseen said. "Please sit down."

Ileth took her little seat opposite the desk. The room smelled like boys and blood. They'd dripped a little on the floor.

"I'm sorry for this loss. I understand you quite liked working with the old dragon," Caseen said.

"He enjoyed my dancing. I enjoyed learning from him. I wish . . . I wish we'd had more time."

"Remember what I told you about time at the door? About nothing on earth being able to retrieve a lost hour?"

She nodded.

"I'm sorry you had to learn the lesson this way."

They looked at each other in silence for a moment before he spoke again.

"You've also had your first flight, earlier than most. How did you like it?"

"Joai said there would be some trouble about me riding Taresscon?"

"Ah. Well, no harm you knowing that's the sticking point before you walked in here. Yes, some trouble, but not—don't look at me with those eyes. No need for tears, girl. I'm not going to reprimand you. If the dragons ask you to do something, and you can do it, you can't ever go far wrong here following their instructions. Awful as that night was, I know the Lodger had a horror of just going to sleep in his room and never waking up. We weren't going to cut him up no matter what, though. To tell you the truth, the plan was to just seal off that room of the Cellars and turn it into his tomb. This whole place wouldn't have been built if it weren't for him, so his bones might as well lie in it. Still, he went the way he wanted. Few enough of us have that privilege. Do I have to tell you that little of this would have existed if it wasn't for him?"

"He didn't talk about himself much. I know he took pride in the Beehive. Why did he live in secret?"

"I'm not sure anyone, even Taresscon or Ausperex, knows the full story. He made some powerful enemies in life. I suppose some of them, or their descendants, might be after him still."

"So how, so how do I have to fix matters with flying on Taresscon? Or are you opening your Blue Book?"

"Ach, no. Riding a dragon, well, it signifies that you've reached a certain level of achievement. You broke with tradition, Ileth. That's not always a bad thing. Doesn't hurt to test a tradition now and then to see if it's worth keeping. Usually we wait until spring before making any of the previous summer's mob apprentices, so the first rides can be carried out in pleasant weather. But you've forced us to move up the schedule a bit."

"I didn't know . . ."

"I told you, a dragon invites you to do something, do it—as long as they aren't telling you to murder a clumsy groom or something like that. That's the difficulty, though. I can't make you an apprentice. There's a lot of talk associated with your name here. The duel. There's that unfortunate party. The fire. Not that you are being blamed for the fire. If I made you an apprentice, every girl who keeps her sheets clean would be at my door asking why I couldn't make her an apprentice if I did it for you. Do you understand?"

Ileth nodded.

"Now. My other difficulty, just to show I don't just have to think about you novices, has to do with satisfying our partners on the other side of the bridge. Taresscon and her two fellow seniors who act as sort of a three-dragon jury in running the Beehive have made it known to me that the Lodger spoke to them about you shortly before the night of the Feast of Follies. It seems he persuaded her—and if there's one thing the Lodger could do it was persuade you so you thought his ideas were yours—that you were to be put into flight training at once as a thank-you for what you did for him and also for your bit in sniffing out those thieving scale-rats in the Cellars."

Ileth rode a surge of emotion as best as she could, keeping it off her face. The crest of the wave being that she would fly again, certainly and soon, and the trough being that nothing, not even flying, could fill the hole in her life left by the Lodger.

"It would take a braver man than me to tell Taresscon that the last request of a dragon like the Lodger would be ignored. Honestly, I'd sooner face a hooded jury. So I'm stuck between the traditions of the Serpentine, a request that might as well be an order from the dragons, and my own efforts to make sure my novices are all justly treated.

"After speaking with all concerned and the Master of Apprentices— I was a busy man while you were standing vigil over the corpse of the Lodger—here is what I have decided to do. I am promoting five novices to apprentice. You are not one of them. I am giving flight training to six of the Serpentine. You are one of them. Your second in the duel, Santeel Dun Troot, is one of the names I am promoting, I'm sure you will be happy to hear. I am explaining, should any of you lot have the temerity to question me, that we need a dancer for special duty with a dragon, and since you had experience with the Lodger you are up for the job, assuming you can handle the training. I'm not going to ask you if you think it's fair one way or the other. This is the only way I can make all those currently bothering me about one Ileth of the Freesand quiet down and give me peace. So I hope you are looking forward to marking some time on dragonback among your other duties. I've already dropped a hint about what's in the offing to Ottavia; the rest is going in this note."

He sealed the paper with a dribble of wax and handed it to her. The Captain could probably run the Lodge for an entire year on what the Serpentine spent on paper alone, never mind ink. She laughed at herself as she thought this—northerners had a reputation for keeping their purse close and the drawstring tight, and here she was, totaling up the price of paper in her head.

"Oh, speaking of training, guess who is at the top of the roster. You won't guess, so I'll tell you. It's that little curtain of a boy with the impossibly long name—Sifler. He learns fast and he's already tutoring some of the slower apprentices in navigation. Master Saiph told me he worked out the Coverix Method on his own. He'd never heard of Coverix and still worked out how to figure latitude. Amazing. Anyway, he's the first from your group to formally go on dragonback. Be sure to congratulate him. I think there's some tradition about shining his boots."

For once, she had heard of this tradition. The first novice to fly would get a brand-new pair of boots paid for by everyone in his swearing-in group and have said boots shined by all the other novices in turn. Various traditions had grown up about what he won as a bonus when getting them from the girls at the Manor. Ileth thought of his embarrassment when he walked in on her that day at Joai's house and decided to arrange something especially embarrassing at the Dancers' Quarter when he went there to pick his boots up from her. She could probably rely on Zusya to come up with something obscenely embarrassing to do to him.

"One more thing, Ileth. Kess, at the archives in the old temple, needs you to see him. The Lodger had some old books and scrolls there. He won't be there now. He rises early, but he's out like a shot when the dinner bell rings."

That gave her another mystery to think about after she delivered Caseen's note to Ottavia. The dancers were busy, with their numbers reduced by the brides' departures. Ileth was scheduled to dance with the troupe the next day for some kind of debate that was to be held between two teams of males, and the dragons had requested a show.

Ottavia didn't see any difficulty. "But since Kess is an early riser, you can rise even earlier and see him in the morning."

In the morning, in name only, Ileth knocked on the door of the archives.

The archives were in the jumble of buildings at the up end of the Serpentine. For a temple it was a distinctly uninspiring building, squat and dug into the earth. The new Great Hall had probably been sited to obstruct it from being viewed from the gate. It was a tiny, almost light-less temple that she'd been told was of the Old Hypatian style, seeking their gods down in the cool, unchanging earth.

It took so long for the heavy-timbered, iron-reinforced door to be answered that Ileth feared she'd be in for another wait on the doorstep.

A face like a rain-worn statue, all pocks and fissures, looked down at her.

"You are that Ileth," Kess said gravely. His Montangyan had an odd cadence to it. She vaguely remembered him from her oath ceremony. He'd been watching the novices sign on to the roster of the company.

"Yes."

"I have a statement for you and some letters. They require your attention."

She followed him down a short, narrow few stairs into the archives. It had a domed ceiling painted with symbols, scattered across the surface like stars. The paint was scored and badly flaked, faded mystic secrets from long ago.

Kess's archives held shelves of papers, scrolls, and books on one side and a collection of war trophies ready for parades and such on the other: some in cases, some hanging from the ceiling, and some simply piled against the walls. She marked a wide set of stairs leading down to another level.

The archivist had a small table with a folded piece of paper the size of a medium painting canvas unrolled on it. He brought over a lamp from a far more cluttered table. Ileth realized there was not so much as a stool to sit on.

"May . . . may I have a chair?" she asked.

"Sitting too much is bad for the health," Kess said, setting the lamp down so it illuminated the paper.

He took her through the statement. It noted that the Lodger had named her as his heir in the Vales (he had left other heirs elsewhere, it seemed, and Kess was at his wits' end over how they would even be notified of his death) and that she was in charge of the practically nonexistent personal effects he'd left in the Cellars, in the form of his bedding and an old tool he used to ream out his ears and nose. There was also a dragon-mounting hook of the kind that riders did not use anymore (if you weren't careful with it you could catch it under the scale and wound the dragon).

Kess's apprentice, an unfortunate-looking young man with ears that stuck out, put a piece of paper down next to Kess. "I copied that list of titles. It's Hypatian."

"This dragon—he liked to write and read," Kess said, waving off his apprentice. "His collection wasn't stored in the Cellars. A good thing, as it turned out, or the fire or water—*fwoosh*. I have some of his books here; the rest of his titles are registered in the old King's Library in

Asposis. This letter listing the titles will get you in if you ever need to retrieve the documents he stored there. The list my apprentice, Gowan, just brought is a copy of the works from his collection preserved there."

"I see." Actually she didn't. She understood only a few of the titles; the rest were in some sort of Hypatian shorthand, as far as she could tell. Her education had many gaps.

"Sorry about the Hypatian," Gowan said. "Lawyers. They use it to keep the rank and ordinary puzzled."

"Excuse my apprentice's impertinence," Kess said. "He was forced on me. His father is a former dragoneer who wanted him here, but somewhere safe, not floating dead in the river next to the Scab, as his letter put it. Not in the best Serpentine Dragoneer tradition but practical. He's very well off, if you're looking for a husband, girl."

Ileth wasn't sure if Kess meant the father or the boy. Gowan had a face suited for a long-course voyage, as the Captain used to put it, tolerable enough if you didn't have to look at him every day.

"My Charge just lost two dancers to marriage. I'm afraid she'd put a curse on the betrothal if I left too," Ileth said.

"You need to sign where I've laid that red ribbon, right below the physiker and the Master in Charge. Put your name or mark right before where it says *heir and assignee*. All three copies, please."

Ileth nodded and took up the pen, carefully writing her name in her best script. Kess knew his quills; it wrote magnificently.

"Some of them fake it to get in here. You'd be surprised how many we catch out the first few months. That's done. Would you like me to store the library letters and such here, or does your family have an archive?"

She thought of the cabinet full of mismatched volumes in four languages at the Captain's Lodge. "Here would be best, sir."

"It is safer here. I close for dusting and sorting and travel to distribute and collect for a month every spring and fall. Other than that, I'm here or in the Masters' Hall."

"Could you help me with s-something, sir? I need to use a Drakine translation. *Vhanesh luss*. I . . . I think."

"*Vhanesh luss*. That's not current Drakine, at least as they speak it

here. It's an imperative. *Sh* is always an imperative ending. Dead Drakine, I expect. Something to do with fire or light. I have no volume that
will help you; you would have to go to Hypatia—or places even less
accessible."

Well, that was the end of that, for now.

"Oh, one other thing. A piece of correspondence that they brought
here, by mistake I suppose. It is a receipt having to do with a music box,
showing the price paid in full by proxy in Sammerdam. It was supposed
to be delivered some time ago. I hope it wasn't destroyed in the fire.
Ivory. Expensive stuff. You wouldn't—why, whatever is the matter,
girl?"

The announcement that the first of their group of novices would
become apprentices, with all the privileges, duties, and honors en-
compassed by the title, caused a stir. "Just five," was the general lament.

Speculation flew around at the news like birds greeting the dawn.
Negotiations weren't going well with the Galantines; they'd soon be
fighting over the Scab again and they needed trained dragoneers to
feed into a renewed war.

Others figured it to be Names putting pressure on Charge Deklamp.
Quith was one of them.

"If it's five a year I'll have gray hair before I'm apprenticed," Quith
complained to her at one of her rare meals in the dining hall.

Ileth put a comforting hand on Quith. "I don't think the rest of us
are delayed. They're just early."

Ileth thought of telling her that she was heir to a dragon, inheritor
of a couple of old grooming and dragonriding tools and some books in
an archive in Asposis. She'd been carrying around the old mounting
hook after giving it a good cleaning whenever she had to walk about at
night, just in case Griff decided to follow Gorgantern's example and
sneak into the Serpentine. Rumor had it he'd departed downriver. Instead she spoke of the wingman with the sideburns Quith was so keen
on. She'd seen him in the Beehive in a striking new uniform, talking to
Santeel.

"Wouldn't you know," Quith said. "Santeel would be first up for apprenticeship. I'm sure letters arrive weekly: *We're counting on our beloved daughter making progress and getting the recognition she deserves. Like the Serpentine is the Queen's Own Graces and Arts Academy for Dignified Females in Their Second Decade instead of a factory for dragon mlumm.*"*

In the wake of the posted apprenticeship announcement, the first flight roster made no splash at all. For one, it was posted in the flight cave at the clerk's desk and not the Great Hall. So the fact that Ileth was tacked on to the list of those due for their first dragonback training escaped notice save for whoever drew up the list and presumably the Master of Apprentices, who signed it, and the clerk in the flight cave, who stamped it—when dragons were found willing to take new fliers up and risk having to have vomit scrubbed off their scales.

Ileth couldn't resist making excuses to go look at it anyway. More than once, in fact.

---

* One word every novice learns their first days in the Serpentine is the Drakine term for excrement.

10

My Dear Falth,

I hope this letter finds you well. Thank you for your own note and more paid paper. It was kind of you to include that bank draft as well, but in truth I have little chance to enjoy your generosity. Novices are not allowed outside the walls generally, so I have nowhere to spend it, and on market days I always seem to have duties. I did manage to resupply our quills and ink and paper among the girls with a portion of it. If you really wish to do me a favor, I would be grateful to you for a small everyday set of the Liturgies in Ordinary bound in book form. I was told by a learned friend that studying them would improve my natural style in Montangyan and Galantine so I can write without (as I do now) resorting to phrases copied from books of formal correspondence.

I enjoy the fortune of seeing Santeel (she has insisted we be on a familiar-name basis, as we are thrown together in our duties a good deal) almost every morning, noon, and night and can assure you that she is in excellent health and her spirit is good, though not quite as good as it might be on mornings when our washroom requires extra cleaning.

You may make the Name Dun Troot happy in the news that the honorable young Santeel Dun Troot has been made apprentice, in the first group so promoted, five in number out of a novice group that numbers some ninety now, as a few novices have left to seek other opportunities. The rest of those promoted were all boys so she is the only one of her sex so distinguished. She has taken to the distinction like an eagle to the skies and reminds the rest of the female novices of her achievement of evenings in the dining hall when she takes her natural place at the head of our company and sets the social order and conversation to her liking.

We are both dragon dancers now. If you are unfamiliar with the art, acquainting you with it is too much for a letter such as I have time to write here, but it is important though exacting work. I believe Santeel has never had to put such consistent and taxing physical effort into anything, for at first she was quite easily exhausted and constantly requested breaks for physical comfort so she could catch her breath. The efforts we put into our movements and poses! We make and wear canvas slippers that require much toughening of the feet, especially Santeel's dainty ones, which were the envy of all the rest of us until they became toughened and callused. I understand some dancers use softer slippers of chamois. Perhaps you can acquire her some in the city.

We frequently perform together for the dragons and those human members of the Serpentine who appreciate the art, and of course getting over our natural modesty in moving to music with nothing but light material between our audience and our natural selves. As we are both fairly new to the art, there are sometimes minor collisions, and one routine with a third dancer named Vii, also new, became unintentionally comic when we accidentally struck each other with our arms and matters escalated from there in time to the music. Our musician kept playing, even more enthusiastically to cover our mistake, and we did our best to get through it despite the exchange of palms, elbows, and heels. But a good laugh was had by all afterward, and the bruised eye sockets and bleeding noses soon healed! My own nose was broken in my early years so I'm not much worse off than I was before.

This letter must be brief. I wish I could report that my own health is as good as Santeel's, but I am coming off a bout of digestive issues caused by, I think, certain spices I have been trying on my food. I have found, like some of my fellow dancers, that I enjoy exotic peppery blends of late to fight the dull winter chill and tasteless cabbage, but they take some getting used to and I find some mornings I am in digestive distress. I am *told I will soon grow used to them and their effects won't be quite so spectacular.*

> *Your servant, sir,*
> *Ileth*

The first-flighters would have to wait for good weather after the winter solstice. Ileth was told that after the initial blast of winter storms that came with the solstice, the Skylake valley would often get a few weeks of clear, cold weather. After hunkering down through the storms, there would be a flurry of activity on the flight deck as the backlog of dragons as couriers and such were distributed to the districts of the Republic, and when other dragoneers and their wingmen who'd been waiting on the ground for better weather returned.

It gave Santeel Dun Troot a chance to retrieve and show off her flight ensemble. She did so in the main room of the Dancers' Quarter, gathering them all one evening for the full effect. Except Preen, who said she was ill and retreated to her bed.

The Serpentine did not insist on strict uniforms when it came to flying gear; the dragoneers each had their own ideas for what to wear on dragonback to fight off the cold or opponents. So Santeel, or perhaps her family, had opened their purse and let fly with the haberdasher.

Santeel Dun Troot's flying outfit could be called many things, but Ileth would have chosen *formidable*. It made her look a bit like a dragon herself. It combined the ladylike lines of a riding skirt with the necessary usefulness of trousers—the skirt had what looked like a decorative seam that you could open up when forked in the saddle. It was mostly dark, bluish leather, with a few flashes of red decorative trim and white fur with black tips visible at the collar and cuffs. From what little Ileth knew of the fur trade that came in through the north, she knew it must be fantastically expensive. The top was two layers of jacket that hid horizontal armored fittings sewn in, wind-cutting leather of the supplest lambskin on the outside, and more fur on the inside. The jacket, cut in the equestrian patrol style, reminded her of a dashing horse-lieutenant she'd met on the road, though he'd been wearing a warm bearskin hat instead of a flying cap. Santeel's flying cap had a long white silk scarf she could wind around her face and a button-closed windshield. The cap itself was topped with a sort of fringe evocative of that of a female dragon, with a fabric cockade of her family colors fitted jauntily on one side. There were riding gauntlets that went high on her arm as well, also trimmed in that thick white fur with black tips on the collar and cuffs.

The new leather made so many squeaks and wheezes as she walked about in her polished riding boots that it sounded like her rig was filled with outraged mice being pinched whenever she turned and tried a different pose.

"I'm not entirely satisfied with the fit," Santeel said. "I believe my figure has altered a little since joining the troupe. It's a little loose about the seat and thighs."

"You'll be grateful for the room on long flights," Dax said; he was more excited than the rest of the dancers combined to see her Tyrennan-designed and -fabricated riding outfit finally worn. Dax knew a rich girl who enjoyed having a court when he met one, and they'd become friends.

"How would you know? You've never flown," Shatha said.

"No, but I've known plenty of dragoneers. They like a lively tune much as you dancers."

But Santeel's flight trunk reveal gave Ileth pause. She had little she could wear against the cold weather outside the Beehive, let alone what she might encounter if the dragon took her up to "test her teeth for high airs," as the dragonback veterans put it. Yael Duskirk in the kitchens was little help. He was slotted to do more flying as well and hadn't acquired much more than a long, thick scarf and an old fisherman's coat. His gloves were in a sorry state as well. The fingers had started to wear away and he'd chopped them off last year.

She put the question to Galia when she had a free hour to track her down. She confessed, wretchedly, that she had nothing and no money that she could spend on attire. Galia sympathized but had no old clothes suitable for riding, was taller and broader than Ileth, and needed her own riding rig, laboriously built up over the better part of a year, for her own frequent rides. Galia hadn't even been able to afford a proper purple for her wingman's sash and had to make do with her own mixture of cheaper dyes.

Novices had a clothing issue, but it wasn't suitable for flying. Even cold-weather coats were almost impossible to obtain. If you couldn't afford to buy one at the now-rare winter market days, you were out of luck and had to go about in layers of cast-off laborer's jackets. Anything too worn out went to the rag room; otherwise the girls of the Manor, desperate for anything that could be called "new" to wear, took them off her hands. But Galia promised to take the matter up with her new dragoneer.

Ileth could still lose her concerns in her dance. She was performing more often for the dragons now. She even had a couple of sister females who shared a cave in the Upper Ring who specifically requested her to entertain them on the long winter evenings when there was little else to do but sleep ("the tiny one with the male hair who bucked up Old Stripes" was how one put it to Ottavia).

Ileth had just finished a long after-dinner dance, a mixture of performance and conversation, with a garrulous old red named Falberrwrath. She found him tiresome because she couldn't just dance, thank him for his attention, and say she looked forward to next time—he kept her up talking when she wanted to sleep. He tended to tell the same story each time, about the four-day battle where he had four riders "shot off from atop me, one after the other—I never even learned the last one's name but you can look it up, I suppose. It went into the histories."

Stuck one evening hearing Falberrwrath's stories again, pinching herself in the arm whenever she nodded into sleep, she had a visitor. The towering scarecrow figure of the dragoneer she'd heard called the Borderlander walked by. He looked in, met her eyes—the color of his were hard to define, blue but so pale they were almost a steel color—and cleared his throat.

"Pardon, Falberrwrath, I've come to collect Ileth," he said.

Falberrwrath ground his teeth in annoyance at his story being interrupted. "Usually she stays until I'm ready to sleep."

"It's her night for the bathtub and I won the draw to wash her, for once. Been looking forward to it all day, sir." He grabbed her by the forearm for emphasis.

"Ah. Yes, yes. Quite. Don't let me keep you, young man."

"Thank you, Falberrwrath. You're the Tyr's own in my book."

He walked her out of the room. Once they'd walked a safe distance down the passageway, he released her.

"Thank you, sir," Ileth said. "I could hardly keep my eyes open."

"I saw you slumping." Ileth liked his Montangyan. Its casual approach to grammar and the accents reminded her of the Freesand sailors. "Tell you the truth, I am too. Catherix was in a mood tonight. Took forever to get her wings greased so she thought them acceptable. They can crack in this cold weather if you don't do that, you oughter know. But it's not just that."

"What is it?"

"Come back with me and I'll show you."

He took her to Catherix's shelf in the Upper Ring. The grayish-white dragon—Ileth had never seen her up close, though she'd passed through the Chamber a few times when they were dancing—was chewing on a thick bone that must have come from a large ox or something like a moose or elk. What Ileth could see of her wings gleamed with fresh oil. It occurred to Ileth that she never saw the Borderlander with grooms or wingmen or much of anyone when she passed him. Always alone, unless he was hanging about with Dun Huss or the flamboyant Dath Amrits. He was an odd fellow.

He found a key on a small ring and led her over to a battered trunk. A variety of clothing buttons, some in precious metals and finely designed, were glued atop it, covering perhaps a third of the surface in no particular design. He unlocked the trunk. She was curious enough to angle for a better view inside the trunk and saw just an old belt and boots, a few books, a closed personal portrait case, a thing that looked like a rolled-up carpet, and a big sack tied off with a leather cord. He extracted the sack.

"Here you go, girl," he said, tossing her the heavy sack. She wished he'd said *brace yourself* or some such before he tossed it to her. She just managed to catch it—a dancer's body-sense was good for something—without falling over. It was bulky but not horribly heavy.

"Open 'er up," he said. She decided his rustic accent would be snickered at even in a backwater like the Freesand. Here, among all the Vors, Duns, and Heems, it was refreshing.

She untied the cording and opened it. A mix of cloth, hide, fur, and finished leather tumbled out onto the floor. It smelled a little musty, but there was no rot or mold to it.

"Huss said you needed a rig. Nicer than what I wore on my first flight. I know what it's like to go up in nothing but a bit of sheepskin with old bulletin-paper wrapped around your chest to keep out the chill."

Ileth's knees buckled. This was fine flying gear, as fine as she'd seen. Not dashing, like Dun Huss's, or the inspired work of Tyrennan artisans, but better than she'd dreamed of when talking flying coats with Galia.

"I will return it in per—"

He shook his head. "No. It's yours now. It's my old gear from Typhlan. Haven't had the heart to wear it since she died. Bit stale, air it out and get some musk oil on it first thing. Too big for you, mostways, but that can be amended, and cuttin' it down will give you plenty of extra bits for alterations. Too big's fixed easier than too small. You ever work leathers?"

"This . . . this is wonderful."

"I respect what you did for Old Stripes down there. The man who taught me the job, well, his grandfather rode alongside him once. In the war against the Snowspot Blighters, and was rewarded by the king at the time, one of the good ones, I think. Good dragon. I wouldn't die in a hole if I could claw my way out, either."

She bobbed out her usual obeisance, happily clutching the bag to her breast.

"None of that, now," the Borderlander said. "Where I come from, deeds sort folks out, not names. You wear it in health and don't feel bad about whatever cutting you have to do to make it your own."

"May I . . . may I ask you a question, sir?"

"Spit it out, girl."

"Do you . . . know why he had to hide in the Cellars?"

"No. Didn't have anything to do with the Snowspot Blighters; there's hardly any left these days. They can still fight, though. Don't let anyone tell you the blighters are dumb, if you ever have to go up against 'em. They know warfare."

The trouble she had getting the dragonriding rig to properly fit her was a story in itself, woven in and out of her life in the next few weeks. Dax wouldn't help; time was pressing and he already had Santeel Dun Troot under his wing. He suggested Vii, whose mother worked in clothing and textiles and had done work for famous names in Sammerdam. Vii grudgingly agreed when Dax pressed her, saying that if she could turn Ileth out properly with a sack of old leather and sheep hides cut to fit for a man in such a way that it could take some of the starch out of Santeel's collar, it would be worth it. And it was an interesting challenge.

Two other novices, encouraged by Santeel's joining the dancers, had added to the number and Ottavia breathed a little easier. She grumbled about Santeel and Ileth taking time away for their first flight training sessions—"Be a groom or a feeder if you want to fly off all the time"—but Santeel pointed out that they might get more novices wanting to dance if a female dragoneer came out of the dancers. Ottavia thought it over and quit grumbling.

Ileth worked on her riding rig nightly, with Vii helping when she could, or at least checking her work and offering suggestions.

Dragoneers tended to wear gray, a dark blue known as *patrol blue*, and once in a while black. A few flamboyant ones dressed completely in their dragon's color, and there was a famous female dragoneer they'd heard stories of in the Manor who wore whites, but the Borderlander's old rig was mostly a sort of sulfur color, too dull to be called yellow but not exactly a tan either—it was something in between. Vii called it sulfur so Ileth did as well, feeling like a little girl playing dress-up in the heavy canvas overcoat covered in some kind of waxy material to keep out the wet. The first thing Vii took out were assorted belts and weapons harnesses.

They built from the ground up. The boots she'd arrived in were still the only ones she had—she had no coin to buy another pair, but she'd managed to get them resoled with a little of the money Falth sent her. There was sort of an armored plate in the Borderlander's kit made of dragon scale that protected the front of the lower legs and kept the wind out of the laces. They wound bandaging material around her legs, a trick she picked up from Galia, who said it kept you warm and helped your circulation, and turned the oversized leather pants into protective leggings that laced up at the sides—Vii labored over those especially, stripping an old pair of men's lace-up riding boots in the process. They split the long riding coat up the back and shortened it at the arms and arranged it so it went over the shoulder armor the Borderlander had worn (in his case, hardened leather cups reinforced with metal bands). There wasn't much to be done with the chest plate, so they left it for now.

"You're not going into battle," Vii said. "Just learning to ride."

The Borderlander had an assortment of scarves and kerchiefs, tattered and worn, and Vii mated them up and turned them into a sort of fitted cushion that went around her neck (another suggestion of Galia's) that trailed off into a scarf. The big leather gauntlets worked without modification once she put on a pair of thick wool gloves under them, though it made her hands look enormous. The hat was lambskin, tied down over her ears with a chin strap so the fleece warmed her and the leather cut the wind. It had a hint of the fore-and-aft-style decorations, though shorter and smaller than the Guard versions. It was her favorite part of the flying rig; the little details looked fetching and she felt a bit guilty as she admired herself a little too much in it in front of the mirror wall than was proper for a stolid Serpentine dragoneer.

One of the Captain's old maxims was "To learn, do." Ileth left the hard work of the leggings to Vii and learned a good deal about working with leather by going up to the tack workshop and making her belts and closures fit.

At last it was more or less done, through hours of effort put in between dancing duties.

"I don't know how to thank you. I have a little money left from when I bought that paper. Can I give it to you?"

Vii frowned. "Ileth, just giving a friend money for a favor—it's a bit crass. Especially in these circles. I know you're northern, and I suppose they do things a bit different up there. If you can't do a favor in return, get them something they like."

"I see. What do you like, Vii?"

"A good night's sleep, which you can't get in the blasted alley between your wind from all that spicy food and Preen's mumbling in her sleep."

Ileth smiled. "I've stopped taking peppers. It was getting boring."

Vii leaned back against the wall of their bedchamber alley and thought.

"I miss swirl. Have you ever had it? It's a sort of drink, made from ground pod-beans that have been dried in the sun with cinnamon and sometimes salt added. It's from way south. It's bitter, but hearty in its way. Very satisfying."

She'd never heard of it. "Do they sell it on market days?"

"Not here. No. Too expensive or hasn't caught on, I don't know. You don't see it outside Sammerdam. At least I haven't. Oh, I know what I need, a nice sheath. Something I can wear under my dress when I'm not dancing. I keep ruining my good ones because I forget to change before drill. Something in a startling color."

The sheath seemed doable. Ileth would keep her eyes and ears open about the swirl. Maybe Amrits or one of the others would know where to get some.

11

The day of her training flight arrived. They had, as predicted, a few days of milder, storm-free weather as the winter collected itself after the solstice before truly settling in. The flight cave was a flurry of activity.

The listed boys had gone for their first flights, and there was a great to-do about it. Idlers lined up on the Long Bridge to cheer them on their way in, and the dancers whispered about some of the rude, painful, and embarrassing rituals they'd been put through by the wingmen and apprentices the night before. She found it hard to believe they had walked to their first flight across the Long Bridge with a squab's egg clenched between their buttocks, but it was a good story. Each went up on an older, experienced dragon, a dragoneer flying with them, exercising his mount and showing them how to read arm signals.

Santeel and Ileth were to go the next day, and there was no to-do anywhere. Ottavia said that there would be no rituals, because so few of her dancers had taken flight training. Though they were free to invent one. Santeel joked that they could brush each other's hair before the flight, but the joke hung in the air of the Dancers' Quarter without a single laugh. Ileth's hair had put on only another finger-width or two. Her body seemed content to wait on the hair while it built dancing muscles.

Ileth suggested, in her halting way, a ritual from up north. In the Freesand, the first time the young men go out, each buys the other their first drink of spirits. They are bought and poured in the morning and remain on the bar all day until they return. In the north, boys were allowed only small beer until they came of age and took up work.

Santeel made a face, but her republican politics perhaps got the better of her. "Well, it will warm us up after being up in the cold air."

"I have just the thing," Ottavia said. She returned with a bottle of clear liquid. "Lifewater. And two glasses. Vii, on the shelf there. Get them. Pour each other one, and don't stint."

Ileth poured first, it being her suggestion, and then Santeel poured hers. They left the glasses on Ottavia's little table and went off to change into their flying rigs.

Santeel was scheduled first, but Ileth went up to the flight cave with her because sitting around waiting to go would just make her nervous. In the back of her mind, she was thinking that it would be amusing if Santeel lurched about when the dragon took off, as a couple of the boys did yesterday.

It was wickedly cold in the flight cave, thanks to an unusual and brisk north wind. Ileth flapped her arms, hoping the chill wouldn't make her stupid. It was easy to get mentally dull when you were cold.

She waited in the back of the cave while Santeel reported them in, and then one of the apprentices staffed to the cave pointed Santeel to a dragon: none other than Auguriscious, the dragon who liked ale after a flight and belched into Duskirk's face. Ileth watched her tighten her gloves, then climb up into the learner's saddle after being corrected on the on versus off side (a learner's saddle had an extra belt to hold you and a tight front tether—actual dragoneers often flew with just a long rear tether so they could hang off the dragon at various angles and employ their crossbows and such, or move down the dragon's body to saw off a highpoon). Santeel had no dragoneer to fly with her. It disturbed Ileth enough to ask one of the apprentices. She knew him by sight as he was always passing the dancers but not by name. He was on the older side for an apprentice.

"Oh, she's on Auguriscious, she'll be fine. He's gentle as a cloud and they've got the learner's saddle on him. Nothing but the best for a Dun Troot. It's a joyride, anyway. One is often enough for those Name girls. They get scared. Had one pee herself one time. A dragon's not a hunting horse, after all."

Ileth, waiting, suddenly had doubts about her bladder, and rather than worry about the *what ifs* went off to use the sluice. Galia hadn't mentioned *that* in her little talks.

When she returned, having had to get half undressed for the operation, as she was putting her gloves back on, a different flight cave apprentice whom Ileth didn't know but who had directed Santeel to her dragon pointed her to a waiting green. She was not a large dragon, but broad-backed and muscular. The females were supposed to be faster fliers. The males, weighed down as they were by thicker scale and heavy horn, usually couldn't keep up.

"Vithleen is impatient to go. Hurry up, apprentice! Are you ill too?"

"No, sir!" Ileth wondered at the last. If Santeel had been ill enough for it to be visible from the ground, it must have been a spectacular event.

She didn't bother to correct him that she wasn't an apprentice. Her thoughts were on the dragon. She hurried over to the green and clambered up on the extended leg.

The apprentice double-checked the saddle girth and some other fittings. He gave her a hard slap on the shoulder. "Enjoy!" he called, and hurried off, after one final check of the back tether for her. A lodge-girl from the north didn't rate a learner's saddle. There were several hooks and attachments at the front of the saddle, but she couldn't find the short tether trainees used. All she found were bags and cases.

"At last," Vithleen said.

Vithleen, anxious to be off and done with it, it seemed, scuttled out of the cave with an odd lizardlike scramble and jumped.

Ileth yelled "Wait!" as she hadn't found the front tether yet. Vithleen had a wicked sense of humor, for she kept her wings partway closed and plunged through the cold down toward the bay. Once she felt she'd picked up enough speed, she opened her wings and Ileth felt the earth pull at her stomach as the dragon shot up into the sky like an arrow, riding her dive speed and the north wind, leaving Ileth's stomach somewhere over the bay.

Once Vithleen ceased her acrobatics and fell into a steady flight, Ileth found a safety tether at the front of her saddle, neatly tied under the front horn—it would have been decent of someone to point that out to her—and hung on for her nearly fifteen years of life while she fiddled with the knot. Vithleen liked to fly fast. As soon as Vithleen leveled off, she managed to connect the tether and attached it under the vent in her riding coat to the thick bracing girdle at a metal ring.

With the short safety tether on, she felt better and looked about.

She saw Santeel on her gold doing a lazy circle above the Beehive, using the lighthouse as the circle's center. (Did the center of a circle have a name? She felt like she should know that.) "V-Vithleen," she called. No response. "V-Vithleen!" she shouted louder still.

"Yes?"

"Aren't we . . . forming on . . . that gold?"

"I don't understand you!" It was easier for Ileth to understand the dragon; the words were carried back by the wind.

"THE GOLD!" she shouted, stabbing her arm toward Auguriscious and Santeel.

"What about him? Nothing to do with us."

Ileth was already feeling a chill from the wind. She wrapped her scarf around her face and hunkered down. If she got down low enough, like a racer on horseback, the wind wasn't so bad; the female's head and fringe channeled it over her.

"Thank you," Vithleen called, picking up speed. She didn't look like she should be fast. She was as wide as the males, who were probably twice her weight, but it seemed to Ileth they were going up the coast like an artillerist's missile. The Serpentine was receding from view. Santeel on her gold was increasingly hard to pick out against the sky.

Still, it was flight, and it was even more glorious her second time, as the weight of the Lodger's death and funeral wasn't pressing her heart flat. She could take—what was the word the apprentice in the flight cave had used? She could enjoy.

After what seemed like hours of flight—but the sun didn't shift much; Ileth was learning that dragon flight seemed to throw off your sense of time—Ileth began to wonder if they were ever turning around. Her legs were achy and the cold and fresh air blasting across had given her an appetite. Vithleen turned west. Ileth saw, looming far off, the range of mountains divided at the Cleft Pass.

"Going up the south side. Looks like there's weather piled up north," Vithleen said.

Ileth hardly heard the words. She was lost in the rhythmic beats of the dragon's wings. Her mind worked over the statement, looked at the mountains, and sure enough, there were some clouds at about their— oh, what was it called—altitude, but they were on the other side of the mountain range.

"Shouldn't we turn back now?" Ileth shouted, taking down her scarf and leather windshield. The gusting wind at this altitude smacked her face like a slap.

"Why? Weather's great!"

Well, the dragon was eager to press on. As she'd been often told, their job was to keep the dragons happy.

It took a moment for Ileth to recognize Jamus and Elothia, the mountains on either side of the Cleft. She was used to seeing their north sides. She'd passed between them on her way south from Freesand. She'd just about kill for a big steaming mug of Freesand tea, even a muddy serving of the Captain's all-dust, no-leaf blend he supplied to the Lodge. The sun seemed to be speeding up as it sank toward the horizon. They would miss dinner at this rate, and her legs were very, very tired. She was glad Vii had helped her make tight the fabric strips under her hose and leather leggings.

"Not fighting the wind anymore," Vithleen said. "Going's easier from here. I can catch it on my quarter." Ileth was glad of it but not quite sure what she meant. A ship could be pushed along by wind from its side, every direction save dead ahead, she knew. It might be the same with dragons.

"Hungry," Ileth shouted.

"We both are! Just a little bit longer now. I can see the Cleft. How are your eyes?"

Ileth could see the general outlines of the Pass but couldn't make out the buildings of the way station where travelers could recover from the fatigues of the mountain road.

Vithleen began to lose altitude. Ileth felt sick to her stomach. Something must have gone dreadfully wrong. This couldn't be a training flight, unless they were trying to break her confidence and teach her a lesson by sending her out for hours. The other possibility was that she'd gotten on the wrong dragon, but the apprentice in charge of the flight cave had directed her to this one.

No, this had to be some kind of prank. It seemed the sort of thing Dath Amrits might organize, both as a test and for the wicked fun of it. That would be just like him, though she was surprised he'd go so far as to deny her a learner's saddle. She might have been killed. She suspected Caseen would go along with taking her down a peg. Falth was right, they were always testing you. But why her in particular? The boys, despite stories of eggs clenched in their nethers, were up and back between breakfast and the midday meal and still exchanging toasts of spiced winter wine in their honor at dinner! What had she done to deserve hours in the cold?

Despite her fatigue and unease, it was fascinating to see the Cleft from above. It was a sliver of a settled valley with a widening and narrowing river (currently frozen) that couldn't decide whether it wanted to be a lake flowing out to the north. At the south end, the highest point of the Pass, there was an old fortification that was mostly just a wall.

A cluster of buildings huddled next to the wall on its north side, and her dragon set down next to the largest of the buildings save the tower, a great barnlike structure.

Some humans in cold-weather coats and heavy fur hats ran out to meet them.

Vithleen circled twice, testing the wind in the confused airs of the Pass, then glided in. She set down lightly, letting her tail absorb most of the landing. Ileth concentrated on remembering to dismount from the correct side.

Men in thick gray felt coats and soft boots came to meet her. "Vithleen! I had a bet you would come yesterday." One of them went to work on a case tied down at the bottom of her saddle girth.

"Mail delay," Vithleen said. "We had a courier from the Galantine border expected. They decided it would be better if I took the lot; who knows when the weather will turn foul again."

"Mail?" Ileth asked.

"I got it. You must be new. The Cleft doesn't look like much, but 'if there's mail you're in civilization,'" the man quoted to her.

Ileth climbed off with difficulty, but she did remember to use the off side. She looked around.

"It's behind that wooden wall there," said her helper, detaching a heavy hooked pouch from a flare behind the saddle. She hadn't seen them when she mounted and wasn't able to see them once on the dragon without leaning far enough out for the wind to catch her badly. She promptly followed his directions.

She returned from the rude privy, stiff-legged and with no small amount of soreness in her lower back. Her flight mask was off.

"Why, you're nothing but a girl," the man who had taken the mail bags said. He was attaching another one to the off side of the saddle. "Vithleen, you have a new wingman?"

"Apprentice this time, I was told. A promising one," Vithleen said. "He took ill; I think this girl's his replacement."

"What's your name, girl?" The man had the gray uniform of the Auxiliaries.

"Ileth," she managed to say, working the knots out of her legs. She resisted the urge to massage her buttocks in front of this man.

"Ileth. Ileth." He thought for a moment. "Ileth!"

The last repetition of her name sounded ominous.

"Where are you from, Ileth?"

"The-The-The dragoneers of the Serpentine, sir. M-May I have a hot drink?"

"We have dinner in the small house for you," a man with the felt boots and the flat gray hat of the Auxiliaries said. "I'll tend to Vithleen here. You might want to give her order to the inn up there first. Building with the big orange door and the moon hanging over it." He rubbed a salve into the junction of wing and skin at her shoulder.

"A thin gravy with plenty of shredded meat," Vithleen said, as the man applied the salve to her snout. "Don't skimp on the salt. Phew, I need it. A honey roll would be welcome, too. They usually have some. Two if they're small. Oh, Stanthoff, you're a blessing, whatever are you doing in the Auxiliaries? Why aren't you at the Serpentine?"

"Oh, you know their lordships there. Got to be able to construe Old Hypatian so you can mix with the quality. I sign my name with my inked thumb, old girl."

Ileth found the inn, gave the order with some difficulty ("On account, I expect," the innkeeper said; she nodded dumbly, since there was no other way for her to pay, unless the saddle had some coin secreted in it along with the mail bags), and returned to the barn. Vithleen was stretched out in the center of it on a flood of straw. Ileth found the small house previously mentioned and sat by the fire and ate a stew and bread. They gave her a choice of wine or hot tea. She told them to pour the wine in the hot tea. It was dreadful, she'd never ask for that again, but she needed both. Then she slept. Before she knew it she was being shaken awake.

"Time to be up and in the air, dragoneer," the one Vithleen had called Stanthoff said.

There was still sunlight in the western sky, but the sun had disappeared behind the mountains.

"Again?" she asked. "Well, I asked for it."

"What's that, dragoneer?" Stanthoff asked, following her.

"Just t-t-talking to myself."

"You know," he said, "we had one of the North District Governor's assigns up here last summer, asking about a girl named Ileth. Young, small for her age, a stutterer."

"Hmmmm," Ileth said.

"Just making conversation. It's a name you don't hear much. Ileth. None of my business, I'm just an Auxiliary man."

Ileth thought it strange that one of the Governor's officials would be looking for her. The Captain never mentioned the Governor but to curse his taxes. She didn't believe any favors were owed between the two.

She didn't have time to think it through.

Vithleen was out of the barn and pawing about anxiously again, eager to be off. She lowered first her forequarters, then her hindquarters, raising the other end. She stretched her tail out like a great tree trunk and let out a titanic belch that Ileth felt in her boot soles. "Now you can tighten the girth, Stanthoff," she said to the Auxiliary.

"We're going up again?" Ileth asked Vithleen.

"We'd better, or we'll both have to answer for it."

Ileth let out a little moan. But she got on.

"Express is in the white tube," Vithleen said. "Front of your saddle, where you can see it. They attached it while you were resting."

"Express . . . white tube," she repeated. There was a leather cylinder like a map case on her saddle now. She found the fastening latch and opened it. There was a white cylinder within, big enough for a rolled-up painting.

"Winds help us," the man who'd handled the bags said, shaking his head.

She relatched the tube. It was in front of her knee where she could see it. At other times, a weapon might go on the fitting.

She mounted with some difficulty and numbly latched herself in.

"Ready?" Vithleen asked, sounding fresh as new snow. Which was blowing up the Pass now, actually.

"Yes, thank you," Ileth said.

"I have a terrible time with your accent. Don't understand a word you say. Ready?"

"Yes!" Ileth shouted.

The dragon glanced around to make sure her wings were clear. "Up and off!"

This leg was hard, painful from the start. Ileth clung to the dragon's back, low, and fell into kind of a trance, where there was nothing but wind and growing darkness.

She was convinced now that this wasn't a trick, or a joke. She'd gotten on the wrong dragon. Been directed to the wrong dragon, more precisely. They didn't mess about with the courier pouches. Were it a joke, someone would be not just kicked out of the Serpentine but probably handed over to an assign for a jury. She had no business being involved with the Republic's correspondence. You could be hung outside a posthouse for robbing or otherwise interfering with the Republic's mail. She wasn't robbing the mails. She'd do her level best to help Vithleen get them through, but she dearly, fervently hoped she wouldn't have to explain that to a jury.

Best not to even think about whether a mix-up like this would mean getting a line drawn through her name in that blue leather ledger of Caseen's.

The stars were still out and the weather seemed to be holding north of the mountains. They proceeded southwest now. She knew her maps; the most sensible destination from the Cleft in this direction would be Sammerdam. She'd always wanted to go there. She lost herself in the rhythmic wingbeats, finding that if you relaxed into them, your muscles felt better. Almost as good as a massage, if you just let the dragon's contractions flow through you. She even drowsed.

"Still with me, girl?" came a voice from what felt like a pillow.

She roused herself. Her eyes were full of gunk, and she had trouble blinking. Directly ahead of Vithleen's nose were spiderwebs of street lighting. Only one city in the Republic had this much public lighting: Sammerdam.

The city of Sammerdam sprawled across a river delta. The only topography provided was that of rooftops and parks. It stood on a horizon inland from the open western ocean, behind a series of sandbars and confused inlets. She knew it was a vast engineering project started by Gant the Third, the Last King-Victor of the Vales, but not completed until decades after his death. It had only grown since then.

Jealous neighbors like the Galantines called it the world's largest open sewer. But it was, at the moment, the beating commercial heart of the western continent; the Vales sat astride it like a tiny rider atop a vast horse.

"Light," the dragon called.

"I see them."

"Blue light. Light it and keep it upright to let them know a courier is coming."

"Uhhh—I don't have blue lights."

"Right," the dragon said. She spat out a small gob of flame, waited a few wingbeats, then spat another, and another after that at similar intervals. They puffed out long before they reached the ground.

The moon had moved across the sky.

A sprinkling like tiny flowers in a burned field, the lakes and waterways about and running through Sammerdam reflected the moon. Far to the west was a faint smear of light. That had to be the Benthian Ocean. The Captain had never sailed on it, though some of his friends had.

The lights below resolved themselves into hundreds of little glitters, most of them emanating out from a shape that reminded her of a crab for some reason. It had seven legs, though, and two thick, uneven arms reaching around something octagonal and dark.

Vithleen circled down toward the dark thing, tipping her wings so she slipped toward the ground.

Ileth made out a vast plaza. In the center of the plaza, behind them, the giant building loomed. It was the tallest structure she'd ever seen save for the Beehive.

Vithleen set down in a great open plaza made up of what must have been a million cobblestones in front of a whitish building raised up off the cobblestones on a masonry mound, making it look like an old tooth in the lamplight. She had a horrible moment when she didn't see the map tube with the vital white cylinder, but found it; she must have accidentally nudged it so it lay out of sight over the front lip of the saddle. She checked the catch. All was secure.

A team of six men hurried to take their places around the dragon. One of them held a lantern, lighting up Vithleen. The others were armed with pikehooks, save for one who cradled a long meteor, a weapon that instead of firing an arrowhead or bolt launched a lead bead by way of explosive dust.

Ileth took out the white tube, slid off, and patted the dragon's neck as if she'd been carrying mail for years.

She'd been half considering confessing her status as a novice, but these huge, formidable-looking men made her cautious.

"The one with the brass buttons," Vithleen said quietly, gesturing with her snout. "Give the express to him."

Ileth looked around. A heavyset man with a thick, bristling mustache, a tunic closed by shining great buttons, and an even bigger buckle at his waist, carrying the lantern, looked at her expectantly. He saluted her, felt something amiss in the salute, and tucked back a shock of hair that poked out of his hat. Perhaps he'd been sleeping.

"Express," she said.

"For—" Brass Buttons asked.

"I was taught that it's . . . it's impolite to examine others' letters," Ileth said.

Brass Buttons harrumphed, said, "Of course," and studied the tube. "House Heem Roosvillem, better take it now. I'll have those," he said, taking the two heavy satchels. He expertly hooked their straps and hung them over his shoulder.

"Haven't seen you before," Brass Buttons said as he shouldered the bags.

She didn't care how big he was; if he would be rude, she'd be rude right back. She had the honor of the dragoneers of the Serpentine to uphold. "No."

He waited for an explanation, but when none came forth, he rubbed his mustache.

"As you're new: there's a warm bed in the backyard, right in the enclosure. The stove is lit. I'll wake the old woman and send some soup. Tea is ready right now, or would you prefer an infusion? The escort will water the dragon. They're used to her."

She thanked him. She wasn't sure where she stood, as a dragoneer-courier, with such officials. Vithleen, restless despite the long flight, eagerly moved off toward the back of the white building. She followed the dragon around an iron railing and over more cobblestones. A lonely-looking tree stood in the back in a little patch of garden with a stout block dome-roofed building that would have been one of the finest houses in the Freesand, but it was evidently a dragon stable. It stood with dragon-sized sliding doors open, an inviting orange glow from the stove within.

Vithleen settled down by the stove on a thick mat woven out of what looked like ship's cable. Ileth looked around. There was no bed near the stove, but some sort of hinged panel was folded against the wall near where the stovepipe rose to the ceiling. She found a latch and opened it, and a shelf with rope webbing came down. It was rugged enough to hold six girls her size. She shrugged off the heavier parts of her flying rig, then warmed her muscles and stretched a little. Ottavia had repeated that it was when your muscles were most exhausted that you needed a quick stretch to keep them from seizing up on you in the night. With that done, she climbed in, putting her feet closer to the fire, grateful to be able to stretch out. It smelled a little greasy, but she was too tired to mind. In an instant she was asleep.

Light. A hand shook her awake.

"Why are you sleeping on the ham rack?" the young man who'd taken the express tube asked. "There's a little apartment up the outside stair, you know. Bed, sheets, blanket."

"Didn't see it," she yawned.

Vithleen was eating out of a wheelbarrow that looked like it had a detachable pan. Ileth smelled roasted pork.

"Your soup's on the stove," the post-assistant said. "Would you like bread? It's yesterday's, sorry."

"Yes," Ileth said, getting to her feet, sore from her ears to her toes. "Do you have a market nearby that is open yet? I need to bring back something special."

"The markets of Sammerdam never really close. But yes, it's a fine morning."

"Here's the thing—I left my p-purse behind at the Serpentine . . ."

"Umm—" the assistant said, "I don't mean to—"

Vithleen looked up from her meal. "Oh, for my egg's sake, put it to my keeping. Say I asked for it and put it to my account. For her first run, she's not complained at all. She's been up there like another parcel bag. Go and run get whatever she wants and if you're not back by morning bells I'll wing-whip you."

Ileth gave him exact instructions and he hurried off with an apologetic bow to the dragon.

"Bureaucrats," Vithleen huffed, watching him go.

"I don't feel like I've slept at all," Ileth yawned, wearily sniffing at the soup.

"We got in at the evil hours, so I'm not surprised."

"I forgot to find you water."

"There's some in that lovely ceramic trough against the wall. The boys here filled it fresh."

She washed up in the dragon trough, then drank—the water tasted a bit odd after her months with the clean mountain water of the Serpentine—and some more of the couriers came out with the inevitable bags, this time four of them.

"Rich city," Vithleen said. "I vouch they just like the look of the wing stamp. *Ohhh, look here, darling, the Heem Twits sent us an invitation by air courier . . .*"

The young assistant returned with her parcel. "Charged to the Serpentine's account under Vithleen's courier run," he confirmed as he handed it to her.

Ileth thanked him, enjoying the fact that the young man was out of breath from his run to do a lodge-girl's bidding, and stretched again before turning back to the dragon. "Do you need to settle your stomach before I tighten the girth again?" For some reason words came easier when she spoke to dragons. Her speech flowed almost evenly, with just a short halt now and then such as was usual in most people's conversation. Curious.

"You learn fast." Vithleen walked out into the courtyard; the building they stood behind shone spotlessly white, formal white with black storm shutters flung open. Some old women swept the cobblestones and the stairs leading up to it, ignoring the dragon and rider. The Guards—Ileth couldn't tell if it was the same group as last night—leaned about the black iron fence chatting.

Vithleen reared up, hopped about a bit, waved her tail, and then belched again, loudly enough to rattle the rows of small square windows in the dragon stable.

"Your cheering section is out front," the assistant said. "I think old Vor Gorts went back to bed. Or he's eating one of his breakfasts and reading the newssheet. Sorry he isn't seeing you off."

Ileth was curious about that ritual. She'd heard Santeel complaining about newssheets, sort of a long gossipy letter everyone could get, but had never seen one. She kicked herself for not asking the assistant to pick one up on her errand. It would be fun to know all that happened recently among the important personages of Sammerdam. Quith would treasure it.

They moved around to the front, alerting a few children who'd snuck into the alley to peep to return to the others and let them know the dragon was coming. All sizes and standards of clothing were represented in the mob, here to see a dragon take off. Ileth hoped they weren't expecting her to throw coppers or something; she didn't have so much as a fig on her. The excited shouts and talk from the children washed over her like a surf.

"Good crowd for a winter day," the assistant said.

It hardly seemed like winter here, a bit chill and damp, but then again Sammerdam was chosen partially for its climate.

"Give her room, would you," Ileth said, making waving motions.

"They'll back up once I start beating my wings," Vithleen said. "Mount up."

Vithleen rustled her wings out and the children scattered. Then she seriously warmed her muscles and Ileth felt the familiar force of the air buffeting back at her. Vithleen gathered herself—

"Out of the way, out of the way," the assistant said, running ahead of them . . .

And with a leap they were off. Ileth looked back. The assistant had sensibly flung himself to the ground. He appeared to be the only one who needed to pick himself up; she couldn't see that they'd bowled over any children.

As they rose, Ileth had a good view of the huge, multistory building in the center of the plaza. It was some kind of arena-amphitheater, with two balconies and a stage. The center of it was bigger even than the Beehive's Rotunda. She'd heard that the people in Sammerdam loved the circus; maybe this was where they exhibited.

Smoke rose everywhere, making its own weather above the rooftops. Streets crossing canals filled with sliverlike boats stretched out in all directions with parks making up blocks of gray, dead winter branches. The delicate network reminded her again of a spiderweb, provided the spider had a few drops of wine before weaving it.

"Where now?" Ileth shouted.

"Asposis—then home."

"Fates be with us, then." They'd made a rough sort of diamond through the heart of the Vales.

The excitement of taking off wore away and the muscle ache had returned, with a stiffness layered on top of the pain that made riding difficult. She couldn't even relax into the dopey trance she'd managed last night. But she kept on. Maybe she could put a balm "on account" at the next stop. Asposis wasn't terribly far from Sammerdam.

Though the day started out well, it turned into a nightmare. Less than an hour into the flight Ileth had to ask for her to land, and quickly . . .

"First time in Sammerdam?" Vithleen said, sympathetically.

"Yes."

"The water. First couple times you drink it, it's a bit—unpleasant. I forgot you were new. Here's a tip—bring a good flask of white vinegar and mix some in whenever you drink it. Vinegar cleans water just as well as it does wounds. You'll soon get used to it."

"Vinegar. I'll remember that."

She'd heard that the Republic's standing armies and Auxiliaries got vinegar rations whenever they were on the march to put in their water. It was also good for washing wounds and making cool compresses.

They put down in a winter field and Ileth took care of what desperately needed taking care of. The rest of their journey was slowed by three more breaks until Ileth clung on, foul and empty.

"You'd best just have tea at Asposis. Maybe some salty boiled broth," Vithleen suggested. Ileth smiled wanly, though Vithleen couldn't see it. She was supposed to be taking care of the dragon, not the other way around.

Asposis, tucked in mountains just big enough to be picturesque, wasn't as big as Sammerdam, but it was stately and the views were splendid from any angle on the ground and doubly so from the air. There were two frowning rocky hills at the south end of the box valley, shaped like two great cats who had settled down to keep an eye on each other, one with a few ruins, and the other a fortress that was known as the "old castle" (though she did not know at the time that the actual "old castle" was the ruins on the smaller rocky hill across the way) according to Shatha, who'd grown up there.

Ileth had learned a good deal about Asposis since coming to the Serpentine; about a third of the dragoneer apprentices and novices called it or the villages around it home. Most swore it was the most beautiful spot in the Vales: a mix of mountain scenery, cultivated gardens, and tended waterways. A curving lake not quite in the center of the valley had the city (though it wasn't much larger than Vyenn) of Asposis at its southern end. The rest of the lake had many fine homes around it and a finger of land with an old observatory tower, and a wooded area with an impressive castled house where the king had lived until the Republic. Some of his family still lived there, she knew, and were among the most important society in the Vales, but they took no part in politics and only occasionally acted to set the tone for manners. Quith often talked about them and the families close to them, speaking of them collectively as the "old guard."

Not all was ideal around Asposis, however. She saw untended gardens and houses that had fallen into disrepair, with trees growing right up to the windows.

They only stopped briefly, in the courtyard of the fortress now flying the red-and-white flag of the Republic, and saw nothing of the city itself, beautifully set along the lake and the most famous promenade in the Republic. There were no Auxiliaries here, just men in splendid, spotless uniforms each with a sheathed sword or a Guard's pike, their arms matched up and held properly. They conducted elaborate marches and countermarches and shifting of columns as Vithleen arrived. She would have liked to stay and examine some of these male specimens up close, clean-shaven save for a carefully groomed mustache or two, for she'd never seen such brilliantly turned-out young men and wouldn't have minded watching their military evolutions until she was entirely recovered from the fatigues of mail duty, but perhaps it was just as well. She couldn't imagine how she looked, and she felt sweaty and dirty indeed after the pell-mell activity and digestive illness, without a chance to even change her sheath.

She and the dragon stayed only an hour to rest and refresh themselves before taking off again, this time with two satchels of messages. Ileth felt fatigued by more than the flight.

"The Headwaters, and home!" Vithleen said, by way of encouragement.

They reached the Antonine Falls where the Skylake emptied into the Tonne just as the weather turned on them. They touched down just long enough for them both to take a warm drink while mail satchels were exchanged. She couldn't see much of the famous river. The Tonne flowed down all the way to the Blue Ocean in the south, and the bit of it that looped through the Galantine lands—Reester, as in "the Reester Question"—and the midriver fortress known as the Scab had been the subject of the suspended war the diplomats were trying to bring to a close.

They hurried to get into the air again, fighting time. The laden clouds that had piled up north of the Cleft had escaped, over or around the mountain barrier at the Cleft, and flooded the south half of the Vales. They were an ominous, flat-bottomed expanse heavy with promised snow.

"We shall have to go low and slow getting home. Thank your egg—sorry, figure of speech—thank your mother we're at the river. All we have to do is follow it home."

They took off into snow.

It was slow going, against the wind, and even Vithleen tired on this final lap. Her wings seemed to need to gather themselves between each beat. Or perhaps she just had to put more effort into it with the wind and snow in her face. Both flew with their eyes scrunched up, not seeing much but snow and the lakeshore.

"If it gets much worse we shall land," Vithleen said. "I have to see the lake. Too many cliffs to risk it."

"You're the one who has to cope with it."

"Again? Your words . . . I'm just not getting them."

"Your decision!"

She'd seen far worse storms, from the safety of the Lodge, fortunately. The blowing snow confused everything. She wondered how much daylight was left; all she could do was guess at the location of the sun. Ileth kept watching the shoreline, looking for landmarks.

A flat cliff loomed up in their path. Vithleen didn't seem to be turning; perhaps she wanted to fly close to it so the snow wouldn't be in her face for a few moments, but—

"Vithleen!"

Ileth yanked her dragon whistle out of her bracing vest and shoved the cold metal end in her mouth.

TWEEEEEEE!

The dragon startled, tipped her wings, and closed the left one a little so it just brushed the cliff with an audible scrape.

"I'm more tired than I thought," Vithleen said. "I was lost in fatigue." She rattled her *griff* hard and shook her head. "I'm glad one of us was paying attention. Good for us we're close. That's Heartbreak Cliff."

They were well over the Skylake, almost home.

She had heard more than one girl in the Manor talk dramatically about leaping off Heartbreak Cliff when discussing their (mostly imaginary) romantic successes and failures, but as far as she knew no one had actually done so; it was just a silly expression. This was the first Ileth had seen of it except as a distant break on the horizon at the south end of the Skylake. Had Vithleen struck it head-on it might have been changed to the Dragonbreak. Ileth's first viewing had nearly been her last!

Plowed her dragon into Heartbreak Cliff on her first flight, they'd be saying years from now, retelling old stories of lost dragoneers. Imagine the wild stories that would grow up around that! Ileth giggled. The illness and fatigue and the close call must be making her mad . . .

The wing-brush with disaster gave Vithleen energy, it seemed; she lengthened her neck and the pace of her wingbeats picked up. She put on a little more altitude. Ileth made out a lighter spot in the snow; it must be the glow of the lighthouse atop the Beehive. Home.

In another moment or two they were over the forested stretch of land south of Vyenn, the trees looking odd and foreshortened from above, and then at last they saw the lighthouse atop the Beehive. Its light, though blazing brightly as ever, was next to useless in a snowstorm. The Serpentine looked vast and strange with snow on it, seen from above Vyenn.

Vithleen didn't want to risk a landing at the Beehive end of the Long Bridge, it seemed, because she swung around over the up end of the Serpentine. Ileth made out the little red door where she'd sat, what seemed like years ago now. It looked like a piece of a dollhouse.

After surveying the landscape, the dragon set down on the main gravel path, crunching snow and gravel as she came in with the Pillar Rocks looming just ahead. Snow made the Beehive beyond an immense, gray shadow.

"Stars, it's good to be home," Vithleen said, folding her wings. She stretched like a cat, low in front, which made Ileth's dismount (she remembered even in her illness and exhaustion to use the off side) easier.

A member of the Guard in a heavy gray coat with a decorative pip on his fore-and-aft-rigged cap ran up to her. He held his hat on with the storm. Ileth didn't recognize him.

Ileth used the words she'd been rehearsing since they'd left the Antonine Falls.

"Novice Ileth, reporting with mail," she said, saluting as she'd seen the Guards at the fortress in Asposis do. She had no idea if that was the proper form, but it seemed to suffice.

"Thank you . . . novice?" the officer of the watch said, peering at her keenly. His eyes widened as he finally put the face together with the strange, snow-covered flying rig. "At changeover they said there was a mix-up with Vithleen and to keep an eye out for her coming in from any direction, but . . . a novice?"

"May I see to m-my dragon, sir?" Ileth asked.

"Certainly," he said, snapping into formalities with ease. He directed another apprentice pulling guard duty to take the satchel to the Master in Charge.

"Look after your dragon, dra—er, novice," he said.

It was fun to trip someone else's tongue up!

She realized he was waiting for another salute. "Yes, sir," she said, bringing her hand up again.

"I thought there was something amiss," Vithleen said, as they walked toward the Beehive. "So you're just a novice?"

"I was directed to you. I think someone wrote the wrong name down someplace. Or nobody recognized me in this getup."

"It looks like, oh, what is his name? I have a hard time keeping track of humans. The tall one, Catherix's man. His old getup."

"The Borderlander, we call him."

"I doubt anyone's mistaking you for him. He's twice your size."

"Not that much!"

"I'm too tired to argue," she said. She huffed out a snort. "Why does it feel so much colder on the ground? Ugh, let's hurry. You rode me; you can get this saddle off and put some salve on if we ever make it to the warming room."

The warming room would have to wait, though. She was told upon entering the Beehive that Master Caseen wanted to see her as soon as she returned. A team of grooms under a wingman she didn't know by name came up to take care of Vithleen.

She reminded them to use plenty of salve.

For once, Master Caseen did not seem aggravated by her. He was amused. But not right off. When she was summoned to his office he stood up and placed his fists on his desk.

"Ileth, I am beginning to be of the opinion that I have to hold your hand or things go wing-over and tail first. Every time you walk out of my office and I can finally have my supper, you seem to get in trouble before it's even digested properly."

She felt her mouth go dry. Vithleen had promised she'd give a good account of their flight, but there was no way for that to reach the Master's ears yet. "Am I . . . am I—"

"No, your name is still not crossed off the ledger," Caseen chuckled, dropping the blood-and-thunder face. "We had a good laugh about it, imagining what must have been going through your mind when you set down in the Cleft. We figured Vithleen would return for a new rider and set out the next day."

Ileth massaged her sore fingers. "She wanted to hurry a-a-along her route, I-I think. She didn't like the look of the weather to the—to the north."

"How did you like it?"

"My mind was most on how sore my back and legs were. I wondered if I'd done something wrong."

"Oh, I asked some questions all right," he said. "It was a mix-up in the flight cave. You weren't supposed to go until Santeel returned. You disappeared, our wingman running the cave had to deal with a broken girth, the courier who was supposed to fly Vithleen—it was Duskirk from the kitchens, by the way, his first commission—was ill and a re-placement was found but he wasn't ready yet, and you showed up in an unfamiliar getup. All Vithleen knew was that she was to have a new rider. Not that she needs one, but it's safer for dragons to have a drag-oneer with them in case of the unexpected. So off you went on Vithleen with no one the wiser until Santeel returned covered in her breakfast and asked where you were."

"Covered in—in . . . ?"

"She got airsick. It happens. That rig of hers will need some cleaning to get it out of the fur. She'll go up again in a couple days. It's natural, the dragons sometimes do a few fancy moves if they think a new rider is getting a little too full of themselves."

"Santeel can give that impression," Ileth said. "Am I to get a new training flight?"

"I think you've proved you can be taken up without falling off. Oh, did it make your teeth hurt at all?"

"No, sir." She didn't add that everything but her teeth hurt at the moment and she risked toppling over asleep standing in front of him.

"Then I can safely promise you that barring accidents you will fly again. Perhaps if I don't see you in these quarters again until spring, hmmm? That is, if you haven't decided to leave flying for the birds."

"I came here to travel and see more of the Republic. I just didn't think it would happen all in one day."

"Don't go adding a dragon rampant to your family seal just yet. It seems we must be careful with you. If this is what you do your first time up, I'm a bit afraid on your second you'll fly off and start a war. But knowing your luck, you'd come back with three captured banners and a signed surrender. We're done here. Go get some rest."

"Yes, sir." Ileth saluted.

"Novices don't have to salute the Masters, Ileth. This isn't the Guards."

She nodded and left. She'd never heard anyone call her "lucky" before. "Lucky" Ileth. Ileth "the Lucky." No, it was awful no matter how you arranged it.

She hurried back to the Dancers' Quarter as quickly as her sore legs could manage the trip. She was eager to see if her celebratory drink was still there. Not that she needed the help being eased into sleep, but it might loosen up her stiffening leg muscles.

12

With the story of her courier run told and retold back in the Dancers' Quarter (once to Ottavia in the common room, again to the dancers settling down around Preen's tea), she was able to thank Vii in proper form. She handed her a bundle with a tenweight of swirl from Sammerdam itself. Vii looked at it like she might a paper bag of fairy dust and gold nuggets.

Vii sniffed it and sighed. "Ground and seasoned and everything. Did your man say where he bought it?" Ileth shrugged.

That aroused the troupe's curiosity, so she made some after a search for some milk they could steam and honey they could add. "You can do it with water and add a little butter, but milk is the best," Vii explained. They passed it around.

"At home we'd stir it with a sprig of sweetmint," Vii said. Ileth had no idea what sweetmint was but nodded along with the rest until her turn to try it came. It was warm and rich and satisfying and she felt almost immediately restored.

"It's like witchcraft!" she squeaked.

"I know," Vii said. "I feel like I should brew it in a cauldron. Some of the Names show off by offering it to guests instead of tea."

"Take it slow," Santeel said. "It grows on you like ardent spirits." She was fuming at Vii being in her element, explaining the combination of flavors and ingredients and the spices you could add. Some people liked it peppery, others added mint or cinnamon, and there was even a delicate, hard-to-obtain sort of brown bean pod . . .

"Speaking of which, what happened to Ileth's lifewater?" Preen asked.

"Ottavia put it up after I drank mine," Santeel said. "When no one could find you we thought—we thought the worst. The flight cave men figured it out eventually."

Ileth yawned. "If I have it, I will be out like a plunged torch. I feel like I've been gone a week."

"If only," Santeel muttered. "I'll get you your drink."

Ileth looked longingly at her bed, four curtains down. "I should eat, but I'm too tired."

"Sorry, some dirt must have fallen into it while it was on the shelf," Santeel said, handing her the drink.

"'Though the Serpentine crumble, our dragons won't fail,'" Vii quoted, to general acclaim, casting a look at Santeel.

Ileth tossed it back in the manner of the sailors she'd seen at the end of a hard day on the water. It burned on the way down, and it burned on the way back up when she started discreetly burping it. Perhaps it wasn't settling down in a friendly fashion with the swirl.

She decided to let the swirl and lifewater fight it out without her. She staggered away from the swirl party, collapsed on her bed, and fell instantly to sleep.

There was little to do over the next few days but drill and rest. The weather closed in around them and they ate salted and dried food. The Serpentine slowed to a near stop like a hibernating bear while the snow flew.

Ileth was in the main room working on her flying rig, calling in Vii for advice when she was in difficulty, but mostly just listening to Zusya's chatter about the coming Fast of Ashes. Over at the other end of the room, where Zusya was somewhat muffled by the cushions and carpets, Ottavia and Dax were talking music for choreography involving all eight dancers currently present. Shatha was working on a wig, using Dax as her model head, when Santeel crashed into the room like an escaping thief looking for a hiding spot.

"My father comes! Ileth, thank the gods you're here."

"What do I have to do with it?" Ileth said. How had Santeel found out about the letters? She'd worked on them in great secrecy and had snuck them out through Galia. Galia would be the last person to go to Santeel.

"Advise me! You are a runaway or something, right? Once you're oathed into the Serpentine, can they pull you out?" Santeel asked.

"Where is he?" Ottavia said. "He can't just storm in here; I don't care if the whole Dun Troot household is marching across the Long Bridge."

"He's in the Visitor's House. He's found out I'm a dancer! He means to take me back home. Ileth, what should I do?"

Santeel, in her panic, didn't seem to be wondering just how her father found out. Maybe she was so used to him discovering her secrets and stratagems she no longer asked why.

"Ask Master Caseen. I don't know any-anything about legalities. Said the oath and that's it. Same as you."

"I shall speak to him," Ottavia said. "I've had to explain dragon dancing to worried fathers before."

"He doesn't listen to women," Santeel said.

"Perhaps if I spoke to him," Dax said, adjusting the voluptuously curled wig Shatha was touching up. "Man to man."

"If you don't have a title to your name and ten thousand in property it won't do any good," Santeel said. "If a brass god came alive and climbed down off a temple monument and told him to sacrifice a chicken, he wouldn't listen to it, either, just point out that gold is more valuable. Suppose he has Falth beat me? He traveled in *winter*, Ileth. Through the snow. On a *road*. My father doesn't visit a decorative garden unless he can do it from his traveling barge."

"He just needs to understand what we do," Ottavia said. "Let me reason with him."

"Reason? Litus of Hypatia himself couldn't reason with him. He's like a scale that will tip only if you put money or Names on it. He doesn't care six figs' pocket money for art. Unless it's reading the prices paid at auction in the *Quarterly Record*."

An idea came to life in Ileth's head. It wasn't on its feet yet, but it was sitting up in bed and calling for some porridge. She needed to occupy Santeel so she could think in quiet.

"Santeel, go put on your riding rig." Ileth grabbed her hand and pulled Santeel toward her sleeping nook.

Ileth moved the quarter-trunk to the floor and opened the main trunk. There it was, beautifully cleaned and folded. Not a trace of spew.

"Why should I wear my riding gear?"

"Because you look st-stunning in it."

"Stunning?" Santeel asked. One corner of her mouth turned up, the other down. "You think so? In truth?"

"Yes. Whoever d-d-designed it and fitted you out is a genius. You look like you could . . . command an army in it, leave off chasing around atop a dragon."

Santeel was never so happy as when she was dressing, and the ritual took some of the fear out of her eyes. "Powder your hair. It looks fine with the black." Ileth threw a scarf around her shoulders and handed Santeel her powdering mask.

Even Preen got into the spirit of the thing and worked laces and buckles. "Tight enough?"

The conelike powdering mask nodded from the fog of hair-powder.

"Let's go," Ileth said, after throwing on her overdress. Good, it was thoroughly pilled and wrinkled. The contrast would help.

"What are you going to do?"

"I'm going to lie like a Galantine High Inquisitor has caught me at midnight under a blood moon bearing a black cat on my left shoulder, that's what I'm going to do. Play along."

It wasn't the entire Dun Troot household, but it was the illustrious father in a heavily brocaded coat, in person, with two servants, one at the door holding an overcoat and the other holding a decanter on a silver tray; a clerk standing at a portable writing desk; an elegant powdered woman, with a female servant, who must have been Santeel's mother (so alike in features that they might be mistaken for the same woman at two different ages); and Falth. Falth, despite standing nowhere near the fire and there being a winter chill in the still-warming

Visitor's House, wiped his forehead and looked as though he'd prefer to be clamped in the public stocks at the end of the sorry tomato harvest.

Various supernumeraries for the trip were still waiting outside the gate. Ileth had seen them standing about a great wagon-carriage with real glassed windows. It had sleigh fittings on the axles that could be swapped out for wheels—at the moment the sleigh tracks were on.

The Visitor's House was a cottage with a large fireplace, currently lit. Selgernon, the Master of Apprentices, and the Charge of the Serpentine Deklamp himself were entertaining the guest. Quith had managed to free herself of her duties and was peeping in the window with another novice from the Manor.

Falth brought Santeel and Ileth in with the relief of a besieged garrison that's just had reinforcements cut their way through to the gate. Santeel's mother smiled at her daughter in dragonriding attire, but other than Falth the men ignored her.

"There's no argument, sir, that you have the right to take your daughter away," the Charge was saying. Ileth thought he looked even more owlish thanks to a scarf wrapped about his throat. The senior Dun Troot still looked now and then at the taller and more impressive Selgernon as though he required some convincing that this small, odd man was responsible for the whole of the Serpentine. Dun Troot kept glancing at Charge Deklamp's plain black uniform and ordinary shoes. Ileth had to admit that he looked like the owner of an accounting house who wanted to give the impression that he wouldn't overcharge you for his services to support his lifestyle. "It isn't a question of *rights*, but it is a question of *right*, if you understand me. Santeel is a very promising young dragoneer, just elevated to apprentice."

"The honorable young Dun Troot is the first young lady of her draft to make apprentice. It is an honor, sir," the Master of Apprentices assured him. "What she *does* is not material. It's an honor if she were bristling out the chimneys or pushing fish up from the Basin." Ileth hadn't come across the Master of Apprentices often. Like Charge Deklamp, he didn't look fierce at all but had more elegance to him, like some of the tutors she'd seen giving lessons in the Great Hall.

Dun Troot, stiff as a statue, spoke: "Sir, I would understand my daughter being put to such work, even chimney sweeping, provided she was instructed and supervised so it could be accomplished safely and allowed to wear gloves to save her hands. Common labor is an exercise that benefits several virtues. No, sir, I am strongly in favor of that! Dancing for an audience is not work, sir. It is performance. Dun Troots entertain but they do not perform, sir! And dancing of all things—well, you are men who have been in the world, certainly. I say again, it is not fit, not for a maiden of her Name who hopes to enter into respectable marriage and social life. I could perhaps, *perhaps*, just see it were she singing to the dragons."

"That's just it," the Charge said. "The dancing is for the dragons. It is in no way public. Nor is it entertainment. If anything, it is a ceremonial ritual of great antiquity, going back to the first days of human and dragon cooperation."

All the while he spoke, the clerk took notes on the paper at his portable desk and then looked at the Serpentine officials expectantly.

Santeel's mother moved up next to her husband. "Why can't we just see them dance for these beasts and then make up our minds?" She spoke with the air of having said it several times before and in little doubt that she would have to say it again.

"Santeel," the father said, turning to his daughter. "These men tell me you asked to be taken off the duties they'd assigned you and become a dancer?"

Santeel's lips trembled. "Yes, Father."

Her mother took a deep breath but said nothing. Falth wiped his forehead again.

"Excuse me, would you introduce me to your friend, and explain her presence in such an intimate family matter?"

"Father, this is Ileth. She is . . . she is my best friend here. She grew up in a lodge. She is also a dragon dancer, and an experienced dragon-rider who has been charged with delivering the express to Asposis and Sammerdam. Ileth, I have the honor of introducing you to my father, of the Name Dun Troot."

"Thank you, Santeel. I am happy to meet you, Ileth." He didn't particularly look it but gave her a nod of recognition, then turned to the company as if he expected acclaim.

"Well done, sir," Falth said. "You display a true egalitarian manner."

Ileth bobbed an obeisance.

"Santeel," her mother said, "if you bring a friend in the hope of keeping us from speaking plainly to you in front of her, you are mistaken. Just because dancers exist and you have one as a friend does not make it right for you. I wish to know a great deal more."

"This determination of yours," her father said. "I am willing to indulge you in your service here up to a point, accept that there are certain dangers involved in flying about on dragons, and even acknowledge that you have met with more success here than I—than anyone expected." He looked at the Masters and nodded. "All that is a credit to our Name. But if it became generally known that a Dun Troot was dancing... Well. There are lines one does not cross, marks that cannot be erased, debits to character that money cannot pay up. Santeel, if you can't keep your Name clean, it's up to your parents to do it for you, in the interest of your brothers and their futures as well as yours."

Ileth burst into tears and quickly covered her face with her hands. Falth ran forward with yet another handkerchief.

"Young lady," Santeel's father said. "I was speaking of and to my daughter. There is no need for you to carry on so. I bear no reprimand for you and would not think of speaking for—" At this he stopped, perhaps remembering that his daughter had introduced Ileth as a girl from a lodge.

"Oh, S-S-Santeel, all y-your hopes. Gone!"

Santeel looked uncertain. "Ileth," she said, patting her on the forearm. "Don't cry. I cannot defy my parents. No matter—no matter the reason. The reason. The reason being—"

"He will be so dis-disappointed," Ileth put in quickly.

"Who will be disappointed, girl?" Falth asked.

"Rapoto Vor Clay-Claymass," Ileth cried. "I'm n-not s-supposed to say, but it was all arranged. The painter Heem Tyr—" For once the stutter worked in her favor; it made the tears sound more convincing.

"Sir, shall I assume she is talking about—" the clerk began.

"Would those be the Jotun Vor Claymasses?" Santeel's father asked the Masters.

"One of my apprentices is Rapoto Vor Claymass," Selgernon said, after a nod from the Charge. "Yes, he is of that renowned Name and line. I have seen him walking about with your daughter a little. In daylight, to be sure."

"He's one of our better young men," the Charge said. "I expect him to remain here as long as we are fortunate enough to have him."

Selgernon nodded. "He's working in the Masters' Hall. Page duty, keeps track of work schedules, that sort of thing."

"What did she say about the painter?" Dun Troot said. "She did mention Heem Tyr?"

The clerk nodded.

"I believe his paintings sell at fabulous prices," Dun Troot said, displeasure leaving his face as though rinsed away.

The Charge cleared his throat. "Yes, Heem Tyr was here a few years back to paint one of our dragons. We've usually no objection to visitors. We have experts of various kinds visit now and again. There's an architect here at the moment, as a matter of fact. But Heem Tyr spent a season here. He found the dancers fascinating."

"I'm sure he did," Santeel's mother said, arching an eyebrow. "I met him—years ago, when he had his old rooftop studio."

"You never told me this," Santeel's father said.

"If I listed everyone I'd met in Zland before we courted I should have to have the pages bound as a book, husband. The society there is quite lively."

"I understand he did several studies of our dancers," the Charge continued. "I think we have a sketch or two still in the Serpentine. I should have to ask the Charge of the Dragon Dancers. He spoke of coming to do more, but I never heard anything definite. One of our dancers, lovely young girl, ended up engaged to him. She left us before this last solstice."

"Well, girl," Dun Troot said, glowering.

Ileth feigned terror and pursed her mouth tightly.

"You aren't in any jeopardy, young woman," the Charge said. "You are not giving evidence to a jury. This is simply a misunderstanding, not an inquisition."

"This was all to be a secret," Ileth cried. She fell to her knees and clutched at Santeel's riding skirt, sobbing into it. (It still did smell a bit like sick, up close.) "Rapoto spoke of g-g-getting your picture done alongside his. It was all arranged. And a study of you dancing. He wanted to know if we would write Peak in Zland for him, so that she might get a price for the commission. I'm sorry, Santeel. I'm so sorry. It was to be kept secret. This will ruin everything."

Santeel managed to look confused, and a little stunned. She opened her mouth, thought better of it, and closed it again. She patted Ileth on the head, then squeezed her shoulder.

"Oh, come now, girl," the Master of Apprentices said. "Don't carry on so. This is easily remedied. There is no injury here."

Dun Troot paced the length of the room and back, muttering the name *Heem Tyr* a few times with arms clasped behind him, chin down in thought. He halted, as though an idea had come to him.

"Perhaps, before we make a final judgment, we should see your dancers perform," Dun Troot said to the Charge. "One should examine all pertinent evidence before making up one's mind."

Santeel's mother sighed quietly.

"Excellent idea, sir," Falth said. "I'm sure Santeel would not be a member of the company if they were doing anything immoral. She was raised better than that." Falth added emphasis and distinction to each word of the last as he looked at Santeel.

"Get up, girl. Stop carrying on," Dun Troot said to Ileth, who was still clinging to Santeel's skirt as though it were the only thing between her and a headsman's block.

Ileth shot to her feet at the order as though on springs. "Then Santeel's hopes are safe?" she asked, covering her stutter with sniffles.

"I—well, let us leave the matter as suspended for now, awaiting re-evaluation as necessary," Dun Troot said. "All shall remain as though we never spoke of her leaving. This is a social call, to drive away the winter doldrums, and see how our daughter is progressing among her new friends."

"Thank you, Father," Santeel said. Her father gave her an encouraging smile. There was a gentleness to his eyes when he looked at his daughter. Ileth couldn't help but feel an empty ache in her chest. Lucky Santeel!

Santeel's face worked, and for a moment Ileth feared she was going to confess. Instead she turned.

"Ileth, you *are* my best friend," she sobbed, clutching at her and burying her face in Ileth's shoulder. "You are!"

"Didn't she just say that?" Dun Troot said, nonplussed.

The clerk checked his notes. "Yes, sir."

"Girls. Come, my wife," he said, extending his hands to his wife and daughter. "We should spend some time with our dear Santeel. I believe she is taller." He turned to the Charge as the servant helped him on with his coat. "Perhaps, Heem Deklamp, you might indulge us with a brief tour, as long as we are visiting."

"With pride and pleasure, sir. You might be interested to know that Santeel lives not far from the dragons. Anyone wishing to threaten the safety of your daughter will have to go through them first," he said as they walked out the door. "As it is a quarter exclusively composed of young ladies, even I must make a formal request before entry, so we can't visit until I get her Charge's approval. But I'm sure there are other points of interest and sights you would find as more than compensating your journey."

"Like that lighthouse! I saw it once, touring in my youth before I was married, and always wished a closer look. Come along, Santeel," her father ordered. Santeel hurried through the door the servant held open. Her father and the Charge exited, the Charge already pointing out landmarks.

The Lady of the Name Dun Troot looked Ileth up and down and slowly, then silently applauded, if such subtle motions could be called applause.

Ileth grabbed each side of her dress and bobbed an obeisance in return.

"I am glad Santeel has found such a reliable and, well, *resourceful* friend here," Santeel's mother said.

"I should hope if she ever needs someone to stand by her, she will find Santeel and the rest of us equally resolute," Falth said, exchanging a glance with his mistress.

Ileth gave a deep obeisance, as though just finishing a dance to general acclaim. Though it took no small effort to keep the smile off her face.

PART THREE

THE GOLDEN LAND

The Galantines are extraordinarily
pleasant people,
right up to the moment their dagger bites.

—SPEAKER OF THE ASSEMBLY PETYR HEEM KALFF
OPEN ADDRESS ON THE SCAB QUESTION 2967

13

The Dun Troots toured the Serpentine and met the golden Aussuntheron, their most courtly dragon, and the dragon dancers' patroness Shrentine. Between them, they did more than even Ottavia to reassure the Dun Troots of the importance to the dragons of the dancers. Several tons of armor-plated manners, eloquently discoursing on the vital role their daughter was playing to oil the machinery of the Serpentine, left even such a personage as Dun Troot overawed. He was quickly reduced to nodding in agreement as he rubbed his hands together like a shopkeeper with a demanding customer.

They were properly impressed by the Beehive's Rotunda and the dragon alcoves in the Upper Ring, and finished their visit when chairs were brought out so they could sit through a performance that would live on as the most sedate dragon-dance exhibition in Serpentine History.

Some of the less flamboyant dragoneers of the Hael Dun Huss style, rather than the Dath Amrits mode, were invited as well. Rapoto Vor Claymass was given a front-row chair, center, right next to Santeel's father. Fortunately Ileth was able to have a private moment with him before the performance and whispered a warning that if Santeel's father hinted at anything or mentioned a painter, he was to act in a reserved manner and say that even young men expected a certain measure of privacy.

Rapoto, who had somehow caught wind of the purpose of the Dun

Troot visit, complimented Santeel on her dancing, said it was the high-light of his week, and hoped he would see her and the troupe perform on those rare evenings when his duties spared him. He expressed a desire to meet her family again with leisure to get to know each other. Santeel's father pointed out that it was possible to go from the Dun Troot home to Jotun entirely by water with all the comforts and conveniences such a trip in a well-appointed barge could afford and extended an open invitation.

The Dun Troots departed for the principal inn down in Vyenn, and those remaining, even the Master in Charge, breathed a sigh of relief.

"Santeel, you never told me your family was so charming," Dax said, once the last servant had grabbed on to the back of the great carriage. "One usually has to stand by a pond full of ducks to enjoy such lively conversation."

With Santeel's crisis past and the brief stay by the Dun Troots in Vyenn over, the winter season settled down into bleak meals of salted and pickled foods and indoor work. There was a minor tragedy when they lost a novice to the icy exterior stair going down to the Catch Basin. It was cold enough for the body to be conveyed home, wrapped up and borne in honor on a dragon. Ileth found the whole thing distressing, and it put a pall over the most enjoyable winter she'd ever spent. The boy lost was the one who'd replaced her at the fish-gutting table.

Illnesses were passed around and overcome, and with the off-and-on beginnings of a thaw the correspondence became more frequent and the first fresh green foods came up by river from the warm Blue Ocean coast. Among the foods was a well-wrapped, waterproofed, and cushioned gilt-edged set of *Liturgies in Ordinary*, which the Lodger had encouraged her to study to improve her natural style.

Ileth couldn't help but feel a sense of satisfaction every time she looked at the volumes, arranged next to her little pamphlets on simple Drakine and those few classics the Lodger had around. But now she felt guilty whenever she looked at Santeel. She wondered if she should confess that she'd reported her affairs to the Dun Troots.

She threw herself even more into her dancing. Ottavia was giving her more difficult choreographies, keeping her dancing on the edge of her ability, as her Charge styled it. She and Santeel were called away to flight training sessions, strictly on-the-ground talks about weather and signals and map reading and such, just often enough to keep the dancing from growing stale.

With the fresh food there was talk that the river trade wouldn't last long, though; the peace would shortly be confirmed with the Galantine Baronies and the river either lost or given trade duties so heavily where it passed through what would end up being the Galantine lands that it amounted to the same thing.

Two more novices were promoted to apprentice when they successfully hunted a fox that had made a home within the walls of the Serpentine and was feasting on the chickens, more as a way to liven up the winter and give the Academy something to talk about than because it was such a coup. Hael Dun Huss was called away on an urgent mission with his most experienced wingman, leaving Galia and his other wingman to get on as best as they could with their training.

Dun Huss was gone for so many days without word that Galia began to fear for him. At last, his wingman returned with news that he was well, and that same night Galia and Ileth were both summoned to the Master in Charge, Heem Deklamp.

He lived and worked in isolation in a low, old tower that dated back to the earliest days of the Serpentine's peninsula being of strategic importance. At the time it had been built, a king had briefly had a domain encompassing the land between the lake and the mountains of the Cleft. The kingdom didn't last, but the stones did, and though it wasn't comfortable, the Master in Charge restored it and made it his own. (The previous Master in Charge had spacious and comfortable rooms in the Masters' Hall, now a study and meeting room for when all the Masters gathered.)

Both Caseen and Ottavia were called to the conference as well, but Ottavia allowed Caseen to speak for her when it came to Ileth. The dragon that Dun Huss's wingman had flown on was exhausted, having fought hard winds and weather the entire trip, and Ottavia and a team of physikers were attending to him.

So she, Galia, and Caseen met with the Master in Charge, Galia and Ileth sharing a reading couch, while the Master in Charge examined a long letter by a reading lamp set on his desk. The room was otherwise unlit.

The Master of Apprentices arrived late, making excuses. He looked red-eyed and ill.

"Dark night," the Charge said, once everyone was greeted and seated. Deklamp kept a heavy shawl about his shoulders in his quarters. His owlish gaze went from one face to the next, nose following his eyes. "Dark nights for dark business, is the general rule. This will be an exception that proves the rule, I very much hope."

"I'm relieved to hear it," the Master of Apprentices said.

"More bad news from the Galantine lands, I'm afraid. Fespanarax seems to be on a decline," the Master in Charge said.

Ileth knew enough now to recognize a dragon name and know that he was probably darkish gray to black in scale.

"Galia, did you know his rider, Heem Zwollen?"

"No. They were captured just before I came here. Dun Huss spoke highly of him," Galia said.

"Yes, he was a wingman under him, years ago. Galia and Ileth, Heem Zwollen and Fespanarax commanded anywhere from three to twelve dragons when the Galantine War was, shall we say, more active before the armistice and peace negotiations began. Fespanarax was wounded and he and Zwollen were captured before the armistice. Zwollen could have gone away with Dun Huss but he rightly refused to leave his dragon. I know there are a lot of stories of downed dragons and their riders dying back to back, fighting as it were, or committing suicide, but those sorts of heroics don't happen that often in practice. Heem Zwollen and Fespanarax surrendered and were taken to an estate that volunteered to support the dragon during their internment. I'd like that to be a lesson to you two, Galia and Ileth, if nobody else has taught it. Your first duty is to keep your dragon alive. *Alive.*"

Ileth felt a silent thrill that she and Galia were named in the same breath as being responsible for a dragon.

"Now there's no particular reason you need to know this, but

Zwollen's captivity led to the first peace negotiations. We haven't come off well in the war. The Galantines are powerful; they scored a coup early on, and our diplomacy failed and we found ourselves without allies, but that's for the history books to sort out. There are certain problems with the situation now I must address. Zwollen caught an infection last fall. He survived it, but he was so weak this winter that he succumbed to illness and died. Dun Huss went out there to see about getting the body returned and to see if something could be negotiated about Fespanarax, whom the Galantines are understandably loath to release; he's one of our best dragons even if he is a bit greedy for coin. They have but few dragons, and the ones they do have are, well, second rate and a bit chary of risking their lives, so it's one of the few areas where we have a decided advantage over them.

"Once the war is officially over, which we expect anytime now, prisoners will be released. Fespanarax will be able to return here. But things with diplomats are never certain. One incident, one fiery speech, and it could be back to the fire, blade, and crossbow for the whole bunch of us."

Ileth was curious as to where this was leading. What particular reason was there for her to be briefed on prisoners and negotiations?

"In effect, Hael Dun Huss is now a prisoner of the Galantines, as he is reluctant to leave Fespanarax without proper care from the Serpentine. What I am proposing is to send Galia, we've already spoken about this, to take Dun Huss's place and care for Fespanarax. Ileth, I know what you did for our Lodger. I'm hoping that if Fespanarax is in decline, you'll have similar results with him. Maybe some human women about are all he needs. I understand few Galantine women go anywhere near dragons; they think they've been hurled straight up from Inferno."

"Ileth, I believe you said you speak some Galantine," Caseen said.

"A little. I r-read it well enough," Ileth said.

"Oh, it's better than that, unless you were unusually lucky—even for you—when I tested you," Caseen said.

"Then you can teach me," Galia said. "I learned how to demand surrender: *Quar-benth!*"

"That's the spirit," Heem Deklamp said. "But hopefully the situation won't come up. Peace is in the offing, remember?"

He turned his attention to the young women. "You need not fear the Galantines. They're stiff enough on the battlefield, but their conduct toward prisoners is irreproachable. If I am ever captured, gods grant it be by the Galantines. They are also famously courteous toward women, so you two will probably have it about as well as Dun Huss and Heem Zwollen did, if not better."

"It is a commission of great responsibility," Caseen said, stressing the word *commission*.

Galia's hand reached for Ileth's and they squeezed each other's palms. A commission. Commissions were for assigns of the Assembly, important dragoneers, and such. Successful completion of an important commission would be reported to the Assembly, perhaps printed in those newssheets in Sammerdam that Ileth had not yet seen.

The Master in Charge gave that a moment to sink in. "You've had the honey, here's the vinegar: there's no absolute guarantee we'll see you again before an old-age release as a mercy. We would be turning you over to them as prisoners. The war could start again and go for thirty years, and you'll already be prisoners without ever having a chance at your glory. I don't mean to be dismissive, but if that happens, I'll need every man I have, and I'll sleep better knowing Galantine custom and manners are making things easier for you because of your feminine birth. You might be there three weeks, three months, three years, or three decades. Therefore this is not something I can order you to do, you understand."

"I'll go," Galia said. "I've had enough time to think about it."

"I'll go with her," Ileth said. Galia had volunteered, after all, and hadn't she been told to imitate her? She instantly regretted it. The Captain had often chuckled to his roustabouts that when the call passes through the cabin for volunteers, one should duck into another cabin before they know you've gone. Then she argued with herself again—a trip to Galantine, the sunny Golden Land. Manners, traditions, a place where lordly men rode out for their king . . .

"Thank you," the Master in Charge said. "You lived up to my expectations for the two of you."

He swept the others with a look, and then his face followed his eyes to the two holding hands on the couch once again.

"There's one other matter, again. Obey any and all restrictions the Galantines put on you. For Zwollen, I understand from his letters he was free upon the grounds of their host's estate—he stated the lands were extensive. He was allowed to go into the village that supported the estate, and the host family invited him along for such village feasts and religious ceremonies that were appropriate. But within those restrictions, learn all you can. You never know what insights might come of an observation. They are a traditional culture, in some ways almost Hypatian. I'm not asking you to be spies; that's hardly a job for two women in their second decade. But we're all dragoneers—or we want to be—and one of the first duties of a dragoneer is reconnaissance by observation."

"How will we get there?" Galia asked.

"I've given that some thought. Galia, you will ride Cunescious. He's young, and he's never been over the Galantine lands. I'd like him to have the experience. Ileth, you don't weigh much; you ride behind her on an attached saddle. Bring no more than will fit in one small bag. That's one of the reasons I'm sending you two; neither of you are trunk-fillers. Makes it easy to shift you about."

"Poverty keeps no great wardrobe," Galia said.

"You'll be guided there by Dun Huss's wingman, Preece. He will escort Dun Huss back, the sooner the better. Keep your wits about you. I don't expect the Galantines to try a coup, with you flying under flag of truce and negotiations so close to conclusion and with their advantage on the ground, so to speak, but if they could find some excuse to bag Mnasmanus, perhaps our best fighting dragon these days, and your young dragon along with Fespanarax the Reckless, it would be a stunning move and a hard blow for us. So be on your guard."

Ileth made light of the trip with the other dancers. They all gave her little voyage-gifts and a light basket to take them in on her stay in a foreign part. Ottavia lamented her loss and expressed hope for a recovery by Fespanarax. "If all else fails, suggest that they give him a few gold coins to eat. Silver might do. The Galantine lands have a great deal of silver, do they not? Fespanarax I remember as something of a coin-hound."

Santeel thought that the Galantines were devils incarnate who would whip her unless she joined their "incense-fogged idolatry" and seemed ready to give her up for dead, burned as a heretic, and even Vii regretted her going because she had an idea for a bracer for her (used but once!) flying kit laced at the back that would be better than the hip-pinching leather girdles the men wore.

They didn't have long to prepare. While hurrying to what probably would be her last dinner in the hall for some time, she passed through the darkness under the loom of Mushroom Rock. The wind was blowing from due northeast, an unusual occurrence, and a lamp that hadn't been hung properly had fallen and smashed out, leaving a long stretch of darkness.

"Hullo, Ileth," a voice said from the shadows.

It startled her. For one moment there was Gorgantern, mountainous, reaching for her—

Rapoto Vor Claymass gave her a tentative smile. "May I speak with you for a moment?" He lit and hung up a replacement lantern.

She felt more than a little like a frightened cat that needed coaxing down from a tree. "I . . . I suppose."

Awkwardly, he thanked her for her little ruse with Santeel. "She's the sort of woman my family would like me to marry as well. Old name. Old lands. Old wealth."

"It seems you're-you're coming to a *but*."

"Old customs. Dun Huss won't marry until he's retired. He's my model of a dragoneer. He told me he didn't think it was fair to a woman to make her a widow. When he's too old to fly he'll see about a marriage and a family. I was thinking of following his example."

Ileth, in her tongue-tripping way, made much worse by her fright, started to say that if this was his way of bringing up his old, panicked offer of marriage—

"Oh, no, just—I don't want you to think the worst of me if I don't end up making an offer to Santeel. But that's not why I wanted to talk to you—I was actually on my way to the Beehive to have a word, but I thought I'd better get this light working again. "

Ileth nodded.

"I've heard you are off to the Galantine lands."

Ileth wasn't sure if she was supposed to talk about her commission, but since Ottavia had told the dancers, it must be all right to speak with Rapoto. "Yes."

"You and Galia. Be wary, there."

"What do you mean?"

"They gave some of us who handle letters and so on a long lecture about Galantine spies. They stressed that the Galantines have a strong group of spies in the Republic, better than ours, I was told. They probably have managed to put a spy or two in the Serpentine. We were warned that they always want to recruit people who work with dragons."

Ileth hadn't thought much about spies or traitors, but she could see how it would be so.

Rapoto was satisfied with the light and left off working with it. "They told us the Galantines don't use many women. They don't think much of women, believe they can't keep secrets, rot like that."

Ha! Ileth thought. She had trouble keeping track of her secrets, she had so many.

"I'm not so sure," Rapoto continued. "Just—if they come to you with some kind of offer, money or a title or something, just remember that they're probably lying. We were told of several unfortunates—a couple from the Serpentine, even—who played the Galantine game and their only reward was a quick stab. I'd hate for something like that to happen to you. Turn them down. Or better yet, make them think you're a fool. I know you have a certain talent for—playacting."

"Why are you telling me this instead of—instead of Caseen or the Charge?"

"I don't know enough about you, Ileth, but it seems the Republic hasn't given you much reason to love it."

"The Serpentine has," Ileth said, emotion smoothing her words. "I wouldn't fail a commission for Galantine gold."

"Take care of yourself, Ileth." He leaned in to kiss her on the cheek, but she shifted, her nerves still on edge from the scare.

"Oh," she said. "I don't want another misunderstanding."

"Understood. Then let's have arms. Ever done the Dragon Grip?"

"No."

"It's supposed to be for dragoneers and their wingmen and such, but—" He took her arm, sliding his forearm against hers to nearly the elbow, where he opened his hand wide and gripped her forearm, thumb tight against the pulse point at her elbow. He arranged her fingers so she did the same. They squeezed each other.

"You have some muscle," he said, surprised. "Bit wiry; reminds me of a rabbit hound."

"You have some fine mat-material for a shirt," Ileth said. "When it wears out I'd very much . . . very much like it to make a new sheath."

"You can have it now," Rapoto said, taking it off and rebuttoning his quilted winter coat. "Never let it be said a Vor Claymass wouldn't give you the shirt straight from his back!"

She did find time, at dinner, to say good-bye to her one remaining friend from her Manor days. Quith being Quithier than usual had to run through all the iterations of possible combinations with Ileth and Galia both gone, leaving Rapoto entirely within the webs of Santeel and Yael Duskirk without the female companionship of either Galia or Ileth. Ileth wasn't convinced Rapoto had an interest in anything of hers that didn't jiggle or flex when she danced, and as for Duskirk, their talks were entirely innocent and she thought Duskirk's tilt toward Galia was more from her being the most promising young woman in the Serpentine and a person from whom he could learn something other than the best way to please her so that she might kiss him. But to Quith, unless there were layers of motivation behind every encounter and exchange like a candlestick-high holiday serving of sliced tenderloin in pastry, she had nothing to think about and would fret. So Ileth at least indulged her and admitted that Rapoto had told her to watch herself in the Galantine lands and write if she could.

Speaking of writing, she sent off a quick letter to Falth updating him on Santeel's flying (Santeel had been up three times since her introductory flight, an unusual number for an apprentice) and the number of times Rapoto had been able to get away from his other duties to watch them dance or to take tea in the Dancers' Quarter.

The precise day of her departure depended on the fluky late-winter weather. Ileth suggested they consult the innkeeper's wife, but the sagacity of their own scryer, who combined the talents of an astronomer, astrologer, calendar-keeper, and weather-reader would have to do. He was an old man, and if Serpentine folk tales could be believed, five major dragon-fighting campaigns had gone ahead only once he made a determination of a stretch of fair weather long enough for the operation. But that was the Serpentine, a great machine where sometimes a small cog had to turn before anything else would move.

The cog turned one morning and Galia came to collect her. Galia, dressed in her flying leathers and a heavy riding cloak, helped Ileth get into her rig and the pair met Preece in the flight cave. The whole way Galia was tense, silent. Ileth had a feeling there was something she hadn't been told. Preece had a round rustic's face and ears that jutted out like dragon wings. Ileth, had she met Preece in a market, would have taken him for a vegetable farmer who had a half-filled stall because he couldn't bring himself to send his dogs out after rabbits, so mild was his manner. But he knew his business. They went to Joai's little house and shared the traditional Serpentine precommission meal of cave-aged beefsteak, eggs, and fried slivers of potatoes cooked in a good deal of butter, with Preece explaining the chain of landmarks they would follow to the border, which they should reach by the afternoon, unless the weather changed.

As she walked across the Long Bridge one last time, gauging the weather, she saw Santeel waiting with a little bundle at the other side. Preece wished her good morning, Galia just nodded and said "Apprentice," and Ileth was about to say that she'd miss dancing with her when Santeel thrust forward the bundle. It was heavy.

"You forgot your music box. How are you going to dragon dance if you don't have your music?"

Ileth would have kicked herself. Dax had checked the mechanism to make sure it was sturdy enough to travel, and after he gave it his approval she'd put it in the little alcove by her bed where the monks or whatever had put their religious icons, so she'd be sure to see it and not forget, and she hadn't seen it and had forgotten.

Gratitude tumbled out of her mouth in its usual stop-start fashion, overlain with emotion. She'd miss Santeel. She was like a mirror or a measuring stick that told the truth about you whether you liked it or not.

"Oh, get in the air, Ileth. Good flying. I'll miss having to dodge those clothes-tree arms of yours." Santeel blinked quickly and her smile trembled, but just a little.

The three jointly inspected their dragons, saddles, emergency food and water, and each other's flying rigs before climbing into the saddle. "The more thorough you are on the ground, the better it goes in the air," Preece said.

They also took two wheel-cocked crossbows that could be aimed from a support stuck into the saddle. Ileth hadn't had any weapons training yet, just a single lecture where they learned the names of both small and large weapons, but understood that the missiles fired by the devices flew with enough force to pierce a dragon's scale if it hit at the proper angle. There was often talk among the dragoneers about crossbow bolts and meteors and how best to thwart them or reduce the chances of a hit.

Galia said a quick farewell to Yael Duskirk in the flight cave as Preece, Ileth, and an experienced apprentice inspected the gear on the dragons. Duskirk had been hanging around at the edge of the cave attempting to look busy, waiting like a faithful hound. Ileth got the impression the farewell was too long for Galia and far too quick for Yael, but neither of them was particularly easy to read. They did exchange an embrace. Yael might have kissed her on the ear; Ileth did not have the best angle on the farewell and was standing by her dragon.

Charge Heem Deklamp popped his head in just long enough to give Ileth and Galia a quick flying salute and sent the embarrassed Duskirk back to his duties.

"Anyone want to burn a feather?" Preece asked once Galia returned. It was an old superstition to bring good flying weather.

Ileth wasn't particularly superstitious. At the Captain's Lodge you knew when your luck was going to turn by the rattle of knocked-over bottles and drunken oaths. Galia just said, "I'd rather be off." She muttered something about the sooner they got to Dun Huss, the better.

Ileth was happy that the copper Cunescious didn't care for Vithleen's alarming takeoff method. He spread his wings wide, angling them to catch wind like a sail, and did a quick jump into the air, flapping hard up behind the huge Mnasmanus.

They followed the great river south, past the spectacular Antonine Falls, roaring beneath them like a chorus of dragons, and on into lands new to Ileth. Cunescious bore his riders and their small bag-rolls and bundles attached to cargo fittings along his back to the border without complaint or apparent difficulty, but the dragon did stretch out his wings and limbs a great deal after they landed and asked for some wine to warm his chilled wings.

The border post where they alighted wasn't much: a watchtower overlooking a road that crossed a creek that was called a river only because it served as the border between the Vales and the Galantine Baronies in this part of the foothills. A few cavalry scouts kept an eye on the creek and road, mostly watching out for smugglers and, according to them, on entirely friendly terms with the Galantines opposite, trading salutes now instead of meteor-shot and crossbow bolts. The only indicators that it might have once been an army camp were some stone foundations, a large empty corral, and a vast supply of firewood, former cavalry obstacles that had been broken down when they started to rot and collapse. There were comfortable huts for them. The dragons stretched out on the woodpile and ignited a bonfire with the plentiful wood. Preece warned them to prepare for a predawn rise the next morning. They would have a long day's flight to reach Dun Huss on something called *Ves Verdus* (which Ileth translated as "the Green Crossing" or possibly "Greenbridge"). They all, even the dragons, recited and memorized a new set of landmarks.

The scouts overheard that Ileth was a dancer. They produced an impeller, a fife, and a drum and asked if Ileth would dance. Though she was tired and sore and had no costume, she did her best in a loaned set of Galia's woolen longhose.

The dance succeeded. The scouts stamped, applauded, and whistled. The dragons, ostensibly the beneficiaries of the performance, complained that they could hardly smell her over the sharp wood smoke.

In return for the dance, the scouts tended their fires, fetched them water, and cooked their meal. The meal was rough camp biscuit—flour, water, and salt cooked in grease—but it filled one up.

"They'll be talking about you for weeks, young dragoneer," the scouts' grizzled chief said.

Ileth glanced over at Galia, wondering if she should correct his promotion of several levels of Serpentine distinction, but she just smiled in return and gave a quick shake of the head. "No need to point out his ignorance," she said later, in their hut, and they chatted about the scouts and what they might see on the flight tomorrow. Ileth was glad she was her old self again. Maybe the responsibility of her first real commission as a wingman had weighed on her.

Early the next morning they tied white streamers, strips of sailcloth about the size of a bedsheet torn in two, to their dragons' wings. It was a traditional symbol of peaceful intent or a mercy commission. The dragons grumbled that since it was the humans who were actually fighting each other, it would make more sense for the humans to wear the signals, but a grumble that was hundreds of years old had earned its right to be said through repetition.

As the day before, they ate a light breakfast. Preece discoursed about "concentrated" foods to them. He was interested in meals not as a gourmet looking for new tastes but as a rationalist who had studied physikers who believed you could avoid disease and swiftly heal an injury by eating foods that concentrated vital elements; the more concentrated the food, the better it was for you and the less you had to eat, reducing digestive difficulties. Neither Ileth nor Galia had much opportunity in their lives to pick and choose what to eat, but they listened politely to his talk of the livers of cold-water fish and vegetables drawn fresh from volcanic or otherwise improved soil and fermented milk.

His enthusiasm for the subject carried them along until it was time to depart.

The dragons, with red-painted wingtips to identify their origins from the Republic (Ileth thought it contrasted nicely with the white streamers), warmed their wings and then launched themselves down the hill, brushing the gorse-bushes with their claws before rising again. It would be a long day flying, so they conserved energy on the ascent, following the hills until they found an updraft, and then turned east across arid grasslands toward their first landmark, the ruins of an old castle on a lake that had belonged to both sides over the years. Now it flew the orange-and-blue Galantine flag. Some wooden buildings and shelters made of rubble and tenting among the ruined walls with campfire smoke showed that it was occupied, and they circled the place until a signal sheet was rolled out, a long white carpet of fabric. Preece had told them that if the ground signal was parallel to the border, they needed to stop and explain themselves; if it ran perpendicular, they could fly on. With the truce being of long standing, and perhaps the Galantines' recognizing Mnasmanus, the signal pointed toward the heart of the Galantine Baronies and they flew on.

They crossed a line of mountains that had a winding road going up to a red-roofed barn and yellow inn, their next landmark. From there they passed through the mountains, a thin chain hardly worth the name *range*, and came to a greener, warmer land.

Ileth felt the welcome change to the air immediately. They were just in cold air now, rather than frigid with ice from their breath building up on their scarves.

They overflew many herds and planted fields and roads winding this way and that. The Vale folk liked reliable roads, and the Republic had been merciless in their land reforms in the early days so that their roads might run in that manner. The Galantine Baronies let old cow paths become roads and didn't do much in the way of drainage ditches that Ileth could see, but perhaps their lands did not have to deal with the runoff of the mountainous Vales where clouds piled up against the peaks. Or maybe the Galantines liked staying put and traveled seldom.

The next landmark was a blue-roofed baronial estate with a long rectangular decorative pond surrounded by a white path that conveniently marked where they would turn. They were to follow the direction of the pond toward a thick forest that showed first black in the distance and then bluer as they approached. From the forest you went to a little pile-up of three low mountains, one of which had a lonely observatory atop it that could be seen far off as it was capped with brassy, shining shingles that almost always reflected the sun.

After they made yet another minor turn, towering white clouds ahead indicated trouble.

"Thunderstorm," Galia said over her shoulder.

Preece put out an arm and rotated it like a wheel. His dragon increased speed.

They'd talked it through when planning their flight. Though they were expected at *Ves Verdus*, they were still members of the Republic's military arm, a vital and powerful one at that. They couldn't just set their dragons down at the nearest inn and order dinner and beds, at least not without a great deal of trouble from the locals. According to Preece, it would be a good way to get a mob up, howling for dragon blood to avenge old injuries. An aristocrat's house might be a possibility, but the famous Galantine hospitality applied only to invited guests, not members of an enemy camp in wartime, whatever the armistice might say. The safest, but least comfortable, would be to find something remote and make camp under the dragons.

Ileth had asked about religious orders, but they were an even riskier chance than an aristocrat's house. The official position of the Galantine High Church was that dragons were incarnations of wicked spirits sent to test and torment the faithful. There was an order of monks dating back to Old Hypatian times that took a different view (Preece said they cared for the Galantine King's few dragons), but there was no way to recognize them unless you met one on a road and studied his vestments.

There were still five more landmarks to go and the clouds piled skyward. At the rate they were passing, they'd be under the storm before two more had been passed. Clouds boiled up all along the storm line as though it were reaching out arms.

They passed over a river, a wide, sandy sort of mess of a stretch of isle-dotted water. There were many islands with trees at the bends of the river and here and there in the straights. Preece gave up and angled toward them. Even if a contingent of peasants took to pike and bow and came after them in a storm, they'd have to swim to be much of a threat, but judging from the rooftops, the nearest village was some distance away and there were no roads along this part of the river.

The air was warmer. Spring was already well on its way in the Baronies.

They set down. Thunder sounded in the distance and the sun disappeared behind the thunderheads.

They chose one of the smaller islands, well away from the banks with only some small farms scattered about, well away from the river. A larger island stood just a little distance upstream, its banks more crowded with trees overhanging the water, sometimes the trunks leaning over it as though to take a look. Ileth thought she saw some raggedy shapes with unkempt hair looking at them from the thick growth, but whoever they were they didn't care to venture into the open.

The river had a different smell than the mountain flows and coastal washes Ileth was used to, different from the vast lake around the Serpentine. It smelled rich and green and full of life but vaguely rotten, like lichen on a wet old stump.

Lightning can be a bad business for dragons with their metal scale, but Preece was prepared for that. He tied a flexible wire to a special crossbow bolt and carefully shot it into a tall tree, then pegged the wire into the ground with a metal peg. It, and the top of the poor tree, would draw the lightning away from the dragons.

"We're being watched from that island there, I think," Galia said, when Preece returned from setting up his lightning trap. Another blast of thunder, louder.

"Really?" Preece said. "I don't think some curious fishermen or whoever they are will be a threat. Not to dragons, anyway. We might as well eat."

While she and Galia readied the food and Preece told the dragons to sleep, if they could, and the humans would keep watch, a blast of wind and thunder hit and it began to rain. The dragons settled down, back to front like two horses standing in a field so they could swish flies from each other's faces, and stretched out their wings facing each other, forming sort of a tent. The dragons put their heads down under their other wings and soon were breathing deeply and regularly. Ileth couldn't see their *griff* to know if they were truly asleep or simply resting.

Three figures, all teenage boys, Ileth guessed, emerged from the other island and swam, paddling like dogs, to their sandy stretch of ground. They didn't have to swim far; they waded unsteadily through the flow and up onto the sandy, tree-lined island. Their clothes were crude, in tatters below the knee, and their shirts weren't much better, utterly frayed at the collar and sleeves. Their hair was thick with dirt and she could see rib bones through rends in their shirts. Hungry, wary eyes looked from dragon to dragon.

One of them spoke. All three held out their hands, palms up in supplication, bowing and bobbing.

It was Galantine, Ileth thought, but a dialect she couldn't begin to understand, except for the word *we*.

"I think they're hiding from the conscription agents," Preece said. "One of them said *army*. Don't know if he meant theirs or ours."

"They're begging food," Ileth said, picking up the word *meal* in the requests. "Meal?" she asked in Galantine, holding up her wrapping paper full of bread and nuts and smoked fish.

"Meal, meal," they all said, nodding. She could see saliva bubbling up on one's lips, even in the rain.

Ileth wondered how awful service in the Galantine army must be if it was better to be dirty, cold, wet, and half-starved in the middle of a river.

Galia looked them up and down. "That one's not over twelve. He can't be hiding from the conscription agents."

Preece shrugged.

Ileth stood up and divided her meal between the three.

Galia sighed. "Ileth, they'll just be starving again tomorrow."

The three boys squatted down in the rain, bolting the food like dogs, watching the dragonriders and their resting dragons. One of them pointed to the wing tenting and said something and the other nodded.

Preece got up. "I can't sit here and eat with them staring at me like this." He handed each of them some bread and nuts.

"Turn your back if it bothers you," Galia said, tearing off another bit of smoked fish and eating it with relish.

"Maybe they're escaped p-prisoners," Ileth said.

"No," Preece said. "Galantine prisoners have ink drawings on their faces. Dug into the skin, like, so it can't wash out. Stands out. I've seen the work gangs on reconnaissance. They fell trees and build roads and whatnot for Galantine army camps."

"Galia, you're just going to—going to sit there and eat in front of them?" Ileth asked.

"I didn't invite them over here. They can strain my crap for walnuts after we leave."

"Galia, what a thing to say!" Preece said.

"What?" Galia said. "I've done it. I grew up in the gutters. My brother and I would hunt rats. We'd eat 'em and collect the bounty on the heads. But they were scarce in winter. Rich folks have crap full of seeds and shells."

"I don't believe it!" Preece said. "Your handwriting, it's an educated hand."

Galia shrugged. "So I learned to write fair and round. Doesn't mean I didn't grow up eating rats."

Ileth couldn't reconcile the accomplished, confident Galia with a child starving in the gutters.

The smallest of the boys crept closer to Ileth. He began to talk, slowly, pointing to the dragon.

"Now what?"

Ileth still wasn't getting much of it, but she thought she got the gist with the help of the boy's pantomimes. "He wants to come with us. Leave with us. He thinks we're going back to the Vales. Says he'll be a servant. Fix shoes. He's not bottom? No, not heavy. Light, easy to carry, I think he means. On the dragon."

"Doesn't know we're going farther into the 'Golden Land,'" Preece said.

Ileth shook her head no. The boy looked crestfallen but perked up when she retrieved a sack of dried apple slices.

The thunderstorm passed but the rain continued, light and steady. Galia wondered if the river ever flooded, and Preece assured her that the dragons could fly or swim them to safety. Lightning struck nowhere near them, and the boys repaid them for the food by finding a few sticks of dry firewood. It wasn't much. They'd picked the sandy island pretty clean on other explorations, it seemed. It was too dark to continue by the time the rain stopped, so they bedded down for the night.

By morning, word had gotten around that there were dragons about, and they had a few curious locals lining the riverbank to watch them take off. Their audience neither cheered nor threw stones as the dragons took off, using the river as a flightway. They just watched. The wretched boys went back into hiding.

The sky spanned bright above them, nearly windless, and they were all sore from the previous day and an uncomfortable night in the wet. They had changed a few items of clothing to keep out the worst of the wet, but it was still uncomfortable for Ileth thanks to her damp stockings beneath her boots. She flexed and pointed to keep circulation in her limbs. But she was learning that flying came with a certain determination to reach your destination, and she faced her soreness and discomfort in the same way an athlete running a long race might—just a price that must be paid in order to finish properly.

They crossed more hills, saw a lake shaped like a bent key that was another landmark, and crossed high, piney hills that some might call mountains. Ileth expected more dry plains on the other side as this seemed to be the Galantine pattern: well-watered farming country full of meandering roads and little villages and dry high plains with herds and sparse forests alternating, but on the other side of the mountains they came to a land that seemed a little of both.

Preece put both arms up with elbows out, the signal for *destination in sight*.

They passed over a land that reminded Ileth of a bowl. High mountains, ranges that rivaled those in the Vales, ran to the north and curved down the east and smoked a little—those must be volcanoes, which she'd heard of but never seen. The center of the bowl was a deep, green swampy area full of little tufts and stands of timber, and in a ring around that were thick fields of what looked like grain and grass. She guessed it was cattle country. Herds thick enough to color the topography themselves made splotched patterns like spilled paint on the grassland. They overflew cattle of a breed unfamiliar to Ileth. She was used to smaller brown-and-white milk cows. These were mountains of muscle and hide and horn and looked as though they might turn and charge a dragon rather than run. They passed over a town with three plazas—their last landmark before the destination itself—and turned north toward one of the volcanoes.

Ileth saw a winding loop of river coursing around a rich, green spot of land, with lines of trees forming a tremendous X away from a long stone house with a flat roof and several barns and outbuildings discreetly shielded by another line of trees. There was a small pond near the house and she spotted geese and a few swans. She had a good view of a formal garden near the house. It had a fountain, walls, and squared-off walkways, all neat and well tended.

They circled and circled again, then descended toward a vast green field near what looked like an oval arena roofed with canvas tenting. There were barns and grain enclosures near it. She wondered if it was a theater, or perhaps a bear- or bull- or even convict-killing pit such as appeared in stories of Hypatia in its decadence. It wasn't a large enough arena for even a good-sized town, but it seemed out of place on the grounds of even a manor house such as this.

As they came in to land, Ileth saw the outline of another dragon behind a roofed horse arena. Greater even than Mnasmanus, the dragon must be Fespanarax: the object of their trip.

Hael Dun Huss watched them set down. He appeared relaxed and tan from the sun. He said a few quiet words of Drakine to Mnasmanus, then looked at Preece.

"You made good time, Preece," Dun Huss said. "Hello, wingman. Cunescious, enjoy your first trip over the Galantine lands? More peaceful than mine. Ileth, you are a pleasant surprise. Did you make apprentice yet?"

"No, sir," Ileth said.

"Well, we shall have to see about that one of these days, won't we. Watch, here comes our host."

A strange sort of riding contraption pulled by a high-stepping horse wearing a woven sunbonnet with holes cut for its ears approached. Its two wheels were huge, the largest Ileth had ever seen unless you counted mill wheels grinding out grain. A man of indeterminate but not elderly years in a bright green coat with black lapels and a shirt with a high collar of snow-pure white that matched his equally white wig drove the thing, and drove it well, albeit at a sedate pace. As it approached, Ileth saw a hunting dog and what looked like some kind of spotted wild cat up on the wide, couchlike seat of the riding cart with the driver. The dog looked happy, the cat bored.

"The Baron is fond of animals," Dun Huss said quietly. "Indulge him."

She saw something else behind and wondered what else might be in the cart menagerie but realized it was just the heads of two servants. The cart wheeled up and the driver had the huge horse perform a pretty turn on one wheel. Ileth was fascinated by the double springs connecting the axle and the seat. It looked well balanced and the stays were arranged well to make things easy on the horse. The horse's tall body was combed and almost gleamed in the sun, without a trace of collar or saddle sores, and the small amount of dirt on the hooves just served to show off how well tended they were.

The Baron stepped onto a metal foot-vault hanging off the side of his cart and jumped to the field. His servants dropped off the back at the same instant and moved around to hold the horse and keep the reins out of the way. He turned to them, looking as though meeting a group of his country's enemies and their fire-breathing dragons distinguished the happiest moment of his life.

"You have arrived," he said in Galantine that Ileth, fortunately, had no trouble understanding thanks to his measured and precise manner of speaking. "How very, very good."

Dun Huss stepped in between the two parties, carefully standing so that he faced neither the Baron nor the visitors but aligned himself in between, and gestured toward their host. "The Baron Hryasmess, Knight of the Ancient Mounted Order, Guarantor of the—"

"Oh, this isn't the Court Exalted, Dun Huss," the Baron said. "You can dispense with all that."

Dun Huss continued in his slow Galantine.

"My aide, Preece, you have met. This is my other aide, Galia of the Serpentine"—it occurred to Ileth that it was interesting that Galia had no surname; before this she just thought she didn't use it—"and with them rides Ileth, a . . . dragon care apprentice and, please forgive me, contortionist?"

"Maid of the Dance," Ileth supplied in Galantine. She had looked it up before they left, but the Serpentine volume on the Galantine language in the archives was over a hundred years old. She bobbed to the Baron. He seemed pleased by the gesture.

"I am happy to meet you," the Baron said, in what sounded like carefully rehearsed Montangyan. "And your magnificent dragons."

Something moved under the Baron's wig and Ileth squeaked.

A gray-faced rat blinked at her.

"Oh, do not take alarm. He is of my household, not vermin, young lady," the Baron said, back to his Galantine.

"I am sorry," Ileth said. She spoke slowly, trying to keep her tongue under control.

"I'm honored by your skill with our language. I shall provide someone to coach you on your pronunciation, if you would accept the offer in the spirit offered. A Maid of the Dance! I must have you meet my daughter Taf. She is about as grown as Galia here and she so loves a dance. Her master calls her a prodigy, but one never knows if the praise is genuine or something to keep the lessons coming. Perhaps you can tell me if I'm throwing my money away, Ileth."

Ileth doubted the Baron would let his daughter stretch her leg against a doorjamb wearing nothing but her sheath.

"I've never met anyone who kept rats," Galia said to Dun Huss.

"I'm not understanding?" the Baron said. Ileth did her best to translate.

"Ah, well, they actually make excellent companions. I believe the rat is the smartest of my animals," Baron Hryasmess said. "It's also the only one that isn't afraid of the dragon—dragons, I mean. The dog whimpers and hides behind my legs, and as for the cat—she simply seizes up and I can do nothing with her."

The dog in this case was under the cart, not that a wooden cart would make any difference to a dragon.

"I am afraid we cannot all fit in my two-wheeler. I use it to get about my estate and always have it ready. When I saw I was happy in the increase of such interesting guests I had to hurry and greet you. If you have no objection, sir," the Baron said to Dun Huss, "I will walk alongside you, and the young ladies may ride. Or I can send for a cart so you may all ride together. Or do the dragons need tending to?"

Dun Huss and Ileth passed on the invitation, which prompted a short conversation.

"I think they will be content to sleep in the sun," Preece said after Ileth gave everyone the gist of the Baron's comment. "We were stuck in a storm last night and spent a cold and wet night. But I will stay with them as I expect they'll wake up hungry. I know my way about."

"I will visit Fespanarax," Ileth said.

"Young Ileth, there are two men there who know something of dragons after all this time. You all look like you need a meal and sleep."

The Baron helped Ileth and Galia up into his cart, showing them where to put their feet. "So, you both ride dragons. How exciting for you," the Baron said.

"Our . . . order," Dun Huss said in his labored Galantine, "was builded of woman significant and we nourish them since."

"Your skill in our language improves daily!" the Baron said.

Ileth enjoyed the view; you were as high off the ground on this cart as you would be on the back of a smallish dragon, but it was much more comfortable. The seat was a sort of couch with upholstered leather with the tufting held in place by fine buttons.

The Baron led the horse, which seemed a gentle and compliant creature; he barely touched it, with Dun Huss walking beside.

They approached a beautiful sort of fortified house of three stories. It was as long as the Masters' Hall but decorated with fanciful frills and flourishes you'd never see in the north. The windows and doors were heavily reinforced by decorative wrought iron, and the top had fortifications and statuary that could, in a pinch, Ileth supposed, shelter archers or crossbow men or meteorists. The house itself was set upon a low rise, about waist-high above the leveled grounds about it. There was a substantial stone wall running around its yards and gardens of over man-height, with firing steps behind here and there disguised as benches and lamp-lighting steps, and an inner protective hedge that girdled it with what looked like narrow paths within.

Nothing about the house suggested it had ever seen the kind of battle that required such defenses.

The Baron helped them down while the servants moved around to steady the wheels of the cart.

"This is my home: Chapalaine on the Green River. I am also Mayor of the Green Crossing, our village, and patron of the common-house and chapel. I am honored to have you stay with me for the duration. I can offer you any of the traditional amenities while you remain wards of my estate in the custody of my person. As an enforced guest you have nothing to fear and a good deal to hope for in terms of education and entertainment. Your visit will last until your representatives at the negotiating table acknowledge that you have lost the war and see reason about the new realities."

"We all wants over negotiations brief," Dun Huss said. Ileth wondered if his atrocious Galantine was as hard on the Baron's ear as it was on hers.

"Before we can receive you properly," the Baron said, bowing briefly to Dun Huss, "you no doubt wish a respite and a chance to wash away the fatigues and weather of your journey. I'll take you on to your rooms; you are on your own out there, where you won't be troubled by all the coming and going at the great house. I'll send one of my sons to call on you and bring you to the house itself for a dinner, if you find that agreeable. I hope you don't find it too severe a prison."

Their "prison" was manifestly better than the Lodge. It was cozier than the Manor attic or the alleylike angle in the Dancers' Quarter of the Beehive. Dun Huss introduced them to a building off the garden that stood alone between the outer tall stone wall and the inner hedge that had once been some sort of storage building, with a loft reachable by a tiny staircase. It had been the residence of the head gardener and his wife, who were removed to the village when the dragon and rider arrived for safekeeping.

In the Freesand, it would be considered a sizable house, the sort of place a prosperous fisherman who owned several boats might install his family. Dry and airy, it had a tiny kitchen that had a nook for a bed and closet for a servant, a tiled water-room for bathing and washing fed by a good hand pump, a sitting room, an extra room known as the warm room because the bricks from the kitchen fireplace jutted into it, and two upstairs bedrooms on either side of the narrow staircase. The only thing against it was that it had only a single door and the windows were small and set high, offering light but little view. And it was chilly, but fortunately the Galantine climate was mild, with summer heat more of a threat than winter snows, according to Dun Huss.

One of the bedrooms had a few personal effects, clothes, and loaned books of the dead dragoneer Heem Zwollen placed in a wicker chest, light but surprisingly stout. Galia lifted a flying cap from within. The leather wasn't quite black. It had a sort of steely blue color to it that reminded Ileth of a predawn sky just before the sun appears.

"I am sorry for your loss, sir," Galia said, reverently returning the cap. "I understand he trained you."

"He was the best dragoneer I've ever known," Dun Huss said, his voice heavy. "I've tried to follow his example ever since. Just as I hope you will follow mine. None of us know the number of our days—it's why we have to do everything we can to see that those following us are ready to take our place in turn and prepare others to do the same. I'm glad you have Ileth on your wing in the same manner you're on mine."

"I don't know how I could go on if you—" Galia said.

Dun Huss smiled. "None of that. I am certain you could, and will. You've triumphed over greater losses than one wind-burned old soldier. With Heem Zwollen gone, I suppose I should start thinking of myself as one of the old wings."

"How long before you return to the Serpentine with Mnasmanus?" Ileth asked, trying to find a happier subject.

"When I am satisfied I can do no more here. Then I shall return."

"What is there to do?" Galia asked.

"Heem Zwollen was murdered. Careful when you speak, even in our own tongue. Trust no one in this place."

A young man called for them as the sun touched the western mountains. "My father the Baron Hryasmess of Chapalaine and its lands hopes you will join him for dinner," he said, with the gravity of a thirteen-year-old charged with escorting prisoners of war. "He understands that formal dress in your circumstances is impossible and will therefore greet you in clothes ordinary."

They bowed to him, and only then did he return the courtesy in a perfunctory manner.

"Little swine," Galia muttered.

"Is there some difficulty with the unsexed prisoner?" the youth barked.

"I've praised the roast pig the kitchen productions in the commanding of your father," Dun Huss said after a moment's thought. "She is entirely an appetite in anticipation. Lead on, bastard."

The boy's eyes widened in shock.

Ileth supplied in Galantine to Dun Huss, "Boy in precedence or son of a noble father."

"Oh, have I erred?" Dun Huss said. "*Son of a noble father.* I am still the clumsy with your elegance language."

The Baron Hryasmess had a thriving and innumerable family. Ileth met only a few that night at dinner, which, the Baron said, perforce had to be intimate and limited to sixteen. There was awkwardness at first, with the family eyeing Galia's and Ileth's clothing in disbelief. Galia wore an ill-fitting uniform of a wingman that she had purchased used from a man and altered, and it looked every inch the tragic story it was, with clogs of the sort worn by a fisherman's wife when she was out haggling for vegetables. Ileth's only clothes were her same old men's work shirt, rough overdress, cotton hose, and homemade canvas slippers.

But once the visit-by-destitute-relations awkwardness was over, the introductions proceeded, and the dinner party found each other interesting company. The Galantine women had bright bold eyes and great skill at making the best of whatever beauty, great or small, they had, and managed to make the visitors feel their sisterhood, whatever their poor dress, odd accents, and foreign ways of arranging their hair.

The Baron, introducing his wife, noted that she had produced twelve children (as of the date of Ileth's arrival) and ten of those lived past infancy. He had two younger brothers living alongside him at Chapalaine, along with their wives and their combined children, and some adoptees from a widowed sister who died in childbed. They were attentive and affectionate to the entire population no matter which pair produced them. Ileth never did, in her time there, get an accurate count of the throng or quite straighten out the nieces and nephews. If they'd all been lined up in a field like soldiers, babes in arms to near-adults, she could have done it with the aid of a tally sheet, but they would never be still and there always seemed to be neighboring children over visiting, or members of the combined brood departing for some party. Somehow the mothers and nannies and governesses kept it all straight. It would have been interesting to set Rapoto and his page skills against the task of tracking their presence, comings, and goings, just to see if he could accomplish it without being driven mad.

The house that accommodated this small army consisted of two long wings jutting out from a domed central social area they called the Gallery. The Gallery was open between all three floors, and the dome above was made of frosted glass supported by wrought iron. It admitted a great deal of light. Lamps on chains could be lowered to whatever height the Baron and his (expecting again! Ileth surmised, when the Baroness stood in profile) wife desired. The Baron's family had one long wing with its own dining room, his brothers and their throng the other, and the chief adults of the family often met in the Gallery to play cards or hear singing at night once the children retired, along with anyone over fifteen who did not have other occupations such as studies or duties around the house.

Unlike the Vales, where one tended to retire indoors once the sun went down, the Galantines enjoyed their evenings outside if at all possible, even if it did bring bugs only partially discouraged by foul-smelling tallow lights placed at the edges of the verandas. On this first night the family and their guests wandered in and out at will.

Later, she came to know the Baron's grounds as well as she did the Beehive. In the Vales such an estate would have pheasants or possibly deer in the woods for hunting, but the Baron hated such sports, though his few other "significant" neighbors indulged in them (just not on his grounds). The Baron rose early, accomplished his work in time to have a midday meal with one of the local officials who seemed to visit almost daily bearing letters and other matters for his attention, and then he would walk about in his woods and gardens with a pocket full of nuts and seeds that he would distribute to the squirrels, birds, raccoons, and groundhogs that found his garden and lands as congenial as he did. About every third day he would mount his cart and ride about his tenants' lands or visit the homes of his neighbors of significance.

Ileth learned that the word *significant* was something of a shining line in Galantine society. You had significant wealth or you did not. You owned significant lands or business concerns, or you did not. You came from a significant family or you did not. There was no contempt for the insignificant; she never heard the word uttered. But the significant only mixed with other significants.

The two *significant*—at least to Galia and Ileth—members of the Baron's brood were his senior daughter but one (she hardly spoke to his eldest daughter, as she was eternally involved in the younger children's care and education), a raven-haired girl named Tafista, or Taf as she preferred to be called. Her rich dark hair reminded Ileth of Peak's, but Taf's was straight as a plumb line and almost always hanging free. Ileth wondered if a servant brushed it every time she sat down, for it always looked tended. The hair matched the girl: well-tended, free, and spirited. The other Galantine girls and women only traveled in groups with their own sex, but Taf liked to wander about on her own. The other notable youth was the eldest son but one (the eldest was at a military academy), a shy and soft-spoken young man who had the duty of seeing to the more mundane needs of the "guests" such as fresh breakfast eggs and soap for their linens. He was more errand boy than jailer, and Ileth judged him to be about her age. He had a long and distinctive name full of tongue-tripping consonants she could only get out of her mouth with great difficulty, so he let her call him Young Azal of Chapalaine (by Galantine custom, young women could be on a first-name basis with young men only if they were siblings, cousins, or being formally courted, an impossibility in this case; otherwise the youth's name had to be accompanied by chaperones of title and geography).

Taf, on the other hand, regarded Ileth and Galia as cousins if not sisters. The Master in Charge had been right about Galantine manners and tradition of hospitality, but he didn't know that the Galantines hadn't much experience with female prisoners of war, and often they had to invent custom on the spot. Before they set out, Galia had told Ileth some hair-raising stories of female dragoneers who were captured by ordinary soldiers without any of their better-bred officers about. Ileth suspected most of the details had to be made up because the unfortunate women were always executed at the end of the ordeal. Did one of the brutes write it all down and toss the story into a Vale encampment?

The Galantines had traditions for women in wartime, but the dragoneers fit none of them. Had she and Galia been wives or children taken in a conquered fortress they would be fed, sheltered, and swiftly repatriated under honor guard, but the Galantines had to acknowledge that they and their dragons were legally combatants.

Perhaps the Baron had told Taf to make the young ladies feel a little less cut off from home; he seemed to think women would run mad if they didn't have news of parties, babies, weddings, betrothals, and illnesses to discuss all day long, so he tended to redirect conversation to such matters in their presence. Taf invited them to spend time with her in the Chapalaine Gallery sewing or enjoying music, or, best of all, dancing.

Back in their house that first night, as soon as they had said good night to Young Azal of Chapalaine and the servants with torches who had lit their path home, Von Huss had them all pull their dining chairs close together.

"You think Heem Zwollen was murdered?" Preece asked.

"I asked Fespanarax what he knew. He told me that it was sudden. He was recovering from his illness—which in itself is strange, I never saw him seriously ill, but this is a more southerly land and they say they suffer more from plagues—and seemed to be in perfect health. The rest is mostly according to what the Baron and that son of his who brings the eggs and milk told me, so believe it or not as you will. They told me one night he complained of a terrible cramp. He took a salt flush, and though it purged him, it did not help at all. He was dead by morning. Our host had two doctors in to look at him, I am told, and both pronounced him dead of a plague that he'd seemed to have recovered from but that suddenly returned stronger than ever. They both wrote letters to that effect, that they'd seen similar deaths. Personally, I think he was poisoned."

Ileth felt her belly harden. Little pains shot across her stomach. She hoped she imagined them in sympathy. Galia and Preece both looked thoughtful.

"Sadly, I know little of poisons," Dun Huss continued. "By the time I arrived here, he'd long since been burned as a plague victim. That is what they have to do, you understand, because even the bodies are dangerous for most plagues. Fespanarax burned him himself and told me he saw blue spots on his neck and face, and even more oddly, his gums had gone blue as well."

"Spots mean blood plague, do they not?" Preece asked.

"Yes. But Fespanarax told me one more thing, quietly and in secret. The spots on his face wiped off if you rubbed them with a little saliva. Which he did right before he burned him, under the pretense of covering his face so he would not have to look at his rider when he spat his flame."

"Poor Fespanarax," Galia said.

"Poor indeed. He's been unlucky with his riders. He was worried they were going to kill him as well, so he pretended to be so grief-stricken he didn't eat save a few nibbles and the odd rat until I arrived. I believe he overdid his act and that is what put him in a decline."

"From what I know of the Galantines, they will release someone they think is likely to die as an act of mercy. Could we petition or whatever they do here to get Fespanarax released?"

"The Galantines don't really think of dragons as fully reasoning beings. To them, even though they know they can talk—as you know, they even employ a few—mentally they put them in the category of circus ponies that can do astonishing tricks. An animal talking—they think of dragons as animals, or worse—no matter how sensible, is just a kind of stunt to their way of thinking."

Judging that he had warned them sufficiently, Dun Huss, as senior, changed the subject of the conversation to the Baron, his family, and what they should offer and expect in the way of hospitality. He was convinced no harm would come to them. His judgment of the Baron's character was such that he might just be capable of murder on direct orders of his king, but he'd swallow his own poison before intentionally doing harm to Galia or Ileth.

Ileth spent more than her usual time in front of the palm-sized face-mirror Santeel had given her as a voyage-gift, looking at the color of her gums.

Ileth made it a point to rise early the morning after their introductory dinner—she sometimes thought the dancers were the most disciplined of the Serpentine's groups, except perhaps for the watchmen—and, taking her music box just in case, visited the dragons. Someone had risen earlier than she, for there was fresh water in portable troughs, and a big platter held aloft contained the head of a cow. She supposed they put the meat up off the ground to keep rats off. Didn't they know dragons preferred their food cooked?

"We have to scorch it ourselves," Cunescious said. His Montangyan was as good as, or better than, Ileth's. "I am resolved not to complain about the Serpentine kitchens ever again."

"I'm sorry," Ileth said. "They gave us dinner last night. Everything cooked."

"If this is what they give Fespanarax, no wonder he's dull."

"Have you . . . talked to him?"

"*To* is the word for it. Not much talk comes back. I don't think he's quite as bad as he lets on. He did say something to me about suggesting that they give him some coin. They gave him some silver when he first arrived, I understand, to get on his good side, but they've been short with it of late. Perhaps he's faking a serious decline in the hope of starting the flow of coin again. Well, he's not the first devious dragon and he won't be the last. Still, shouldn't play with your health."

Cunescious took the cow head and began to chew it. Ileth heard the bones snap in his powerful jaws. "My mother always told me cow brains are good for you. I wanted more liver, but she insisted I eat the brains first."

Ileth left him to chew and stepped into the big barn.

She wondered if *barn* was even the right word for it. It was more of an indoor arena, a vast thing, solidly built, and the strong dragon smell hadn't quite eliminated all the horse. There were mortared walls on either side of the arena entrances at the ends, and someone had installed three rows of seats built on stands such as she'd heard about in theaters and stadiums but never seen, unless you counted the amphitheater in the Serpentine.

Fespanarax lay in the center, on a thick bed of wood chips—well, larger than chips, bark and shards of wood that reminded her of the lumbering camps that harvested, and planted, and harvested again the tall straight pines that grew on the mountains in the frequent rain of the Freesand.

He was quite the largest dragon Ileth had seen to that date, bigger even than the Lodger (she'd always been told older dragons were larger; they kept growing like trees, albeit slowly after the first hundred years or so), but did not seem older than her ancient departed friend. His color was as unique as Mnasmanus's purple, in this case a steely blue not that different from the spring-steel arms of a crossbow rubbed with an oily substance to protect it from the elements. He had something of an underbite. His chin jutted forth just a little ahead of his snout and the white teeth showed plain there. He had heavy, horny brows and it was hard to make out his eyes in the shadow underneath, but maybe it was just because he was gaunt from not eating as he should. There was something about the way his wings lay, spilling down his sides and partially on the ground, that suggested a dead bird.

"Sir, may I approach you?" Ileth said in her best voice.

The dragon's jaws worked. She heard teeth grinding.

"Certainly, girl. You're from the Serpentine. I can tell by your speech." He didn't bother to raise his head to speak to her.

Ileth came down from the edge of the seating gallery and started across the hippodrome. "My n-name is—"

"I don't bother with names. When I address you, you'll know it."

"I'm a dragon dancer. The Master in Charge sent me here to attend to you."

"Good of him. Thinking once in a while of those of us in durance vile. It would seem simpler to arrange a suitable exchange of prisoners, less trouble feeding mouths that aren't doing much, but I suppose the Republic knows its business."

"I haven't done my drills yet this morning. May I?"

The dragon snorted. "Go about your business and I will go about mine." He curled his head away and tucked it under his wing.

She cast about until she found a chair that she could use as a support for both her body and the music box. She draped her overdress on the chair and went to work warming up.

She kept at it most of the morning. Mnasmanus and the other dragons made room for each other about her, watching as they stripped the bones of their breakfast and noisily crunched them down.

Mnasmanus offered a comment now and then to the others, but in Drakine, and quietly enough Ileth couldn't quite make it out. "You're right," Cunescious said to him in Montangyan, "not quite the same without proper costume. And the open air is taking all her scent."

Fespanarax took it in but never raised his head, apathetic as a sick dog.

Tired, but the enjoyable sort of tired she experienced after dance, she returned to their "prison" and found Galia and Taf sitting on the floor of the sitting room together with a sea of clothing "talking" through pantomime as they held up items. The apparel had a stuffy, medicinal smell to it.

Taf jumped up. "It's a rag party. Join us, Ileth. Sorry about the smell, it's to keep out the moths."

"A rag party?"

"Yes. I hope you don't think I'm being rude, but, well, I felt sorry for all of you last night. It's one thing for the men of your Vales, I don't believe they care about anything with their appearance as long as they've shaved their necks, but I know you two must have felt it very severely, coming into a house like Chapalaine in . . . I'm sure your attire is fine, perhaps necessary for the Vales and your mannish work, but, you know, families of our significance have a certain standard. I consulted Father and he agreed and we did a collection of some clothes from my mother, my aunts, and the older girls. Not fancy attire, plain as you like things in the Vales, which we wear for cooking or tending to the house or sewing or gardening. Father said nothing above your station and not to insult you. Have I insulted you?"

"No," Ileth said, head swimming from all the Galantine. "It's . . . appreciated."

Ileth wondered if the remaining matters in the peace negotiations couldn't be solved by putting Taf and Zusya in a room and deciding that whoever quit talking first would have to relinquish the claims still at hazard.

"I'm sweated through," Ileth said to Galia in Montangyan. "I'll have a wash first."

Making similar excuses to Taf, she scrubbed herself quickly in the water-room with the flowery Galantine soap, which produced a fine lather but disappeared quickly, then dressed in her clean shirt and put on her overdress, which chose this moment to have a strap-button break again. The truth was, it didn't fit her that well anymore and her muscles were strong enough from all the dancing to rupture the seams. She should join the rag party. After food.

She ate some good soft bread but wanted eggs, and they seemed to be out. She returned to Taf and Galia. They were back to pantomime—mostly.

"We're playing Lovely and Hideous," Taf said. "It's the only two words in Galantine your friend knows, and I'm very proud of myself for beginning her education with them. We're having great fun at Lovely and Hideous. Seems like that's all we'll need."

"I am hungry. Are there any eggs left?"

Galia made a face. "Preece finished them off."

"Is there a problem?" Taf asked.

"Just hunger," Ileth said.

"There's farina," Taf said, jumping up and opening a crock filled with milk-colored grains. "Ever had it? Nothing like Galantine farina."

"It's porridge?" Ileth said.

"Yes. It's the traditional first meal for a good Galantine baby. Once the babe eats its first farina, the mother and baby—if she's still alive—get their congratulations from the extended family and neighbors and such. But we hold off on an introduction party until they're four just to be on the safe side. As you know, a great deal can happen between taking solid food and four."

Taf showed her how to make it, heating some milk on the stove. "It's best with milk. I love it. When I have babies I'll eat it with them. We give it to wet nurses, as much as they like, because their bodies are taxed so. I imagine dancing is similar."

"You want lots of babies?"

"Why shouldn't I? My own grandmother had eighteen that lived. Then she started young. She was married at fourteen and Father says he doesn't want to hear the word *swain* until I'm sixteen and a half. Why the half? Maybe because it will be in summer and there are more parties. Still over a year away. People still get married at fifteen all the time, but Father says you need the extra year for more mature judgment. You only get to enjoy courting society once, so why rush it?"

"We must be near the same age," Ileth said. Come to think of it, she would be turning fifteen. If someone had told her a year ago she'd be turning fifteen on a Galantine estate like Chapalaine—well, that could be said of a great many things.

"How interesting. How many did your mother have?"

"I grew up in an orphans' . . . home."

"Oh. How tragic. But you've triumphed despite that. I mean, riding dragons about. I thought only people like your gallant Dun Huss were allowed to do that."

Ileth wondered if she should tell the dragoneer that he was spoken of as a Galantine gallant. He'd probably find it amusing.

"No, anybody. The dragons do much of . . . much of the work, a-after a-all."

"But aren't you supposed to sit atop and shoot—oh, I'm terribly sorry. Father said I was not to speak to you of military matters. I think it violates some terms of your captivity if you're questioned about those. Oh, he'll turn white if he finds out. Don't say anything."

"We were just talking. You didn't ask for the keys to the Serpentine."

It didn't have keys, but there was no harm in letting the Galantines think it did, if Taf had been asked to find out what she could about the dragoneers. Taf's friendliness did seem a bit forced at times. Reconnaissance through rag parties? Or perhaps she truly was just silly.

Eventually, Taf left, though her conversation never faltered even if her energy did. "I should have a long nap," she said on the way out. "I'll send someone over for the baskets. Keep whatever you like. If you need scissors and needles and such, we have plenty." She embraced them each and kissed their cheeks as though they were about to depart again.

"Oh, faith," Galia said when she left. "I am sick of trying on clothes. I hope it's not all going to be like this."

"You l-learned *lovely* and *hideous*. A bad start is still a start," Ileth said.

"Ha! That's one of Caseen's favorite sayings."

"The food's good," Ileth said. Taf had been right about the farina; it was excellent and filling. Ileth felt renewed. Which was just as well. She'd hoped to try dancing for Fespanarax again that afternoon. "I don't know when I've tasted milk like this. I wonder if it has something to do with the grass?"

"Eh, never much cared for it. You know, they say travel is supposed to broaden your mind. I don't think that's true at all. I can't wait to get back home to the Vales. I hope the diplomats work it out soon. Sewing parties and nannying isn't my air."

"Too . . . too bad. You have the . . . have the clothes for—for it now." Galia threw a blouse at her.

Her afternoon session with Fespanarax went no better than her morning one. But that evening she did sort out five reasonably good outfits from the prospects. The only problem was they were all a bit bright in color and overruffled for the Serpentine. But they'd do. She wasn't strictly out of uniform; she did still have her novice's pin. And her silver whistle.

I f the Baron owned his own version of Caseen's Blue Book, Ileth went into it that first week.

As the awkwardness grew into familiarity with Chapalaine routine, Taf begged Ileth to dance with her "if you are not too fatigued by your travels." Ileth was later to learn that for women from significant families, a trip around the garden might require a short spell with supported feet on a "respite," the specially designed chair-sofas distributed about the place for use by the women (especially when pregnant). There were respites everywhere, indoors and out, in Chapalaine.

Ileth agreed. One of the Baron's sisters-in-law went to a keyboard instrument hidden behind one of the curved stairways and played a sedate parade-dancing air. Ileth took Taf's hand and followed the fairly easy steps, just marching back and forth across the room and turning properly to return with an obeisance thrown in here and there.

"It quite looks something when there are hundreds of couples lined up doing it," Taf said. There was some argument over what to play next and they had a livelier tune. Taf danced well and the foot placement and poses were similar to what she'd been taught as a dragon dancer, except the leg movements went no higher than little kicks and extensions and heel-or-toe to ankle movements. They were merry enough, though, and being able to dance raised their spirits.

"My father tells me you are some manner of specialist in dance?" Taf asked.

Ileth did her best to explain, in her taxing and limited Galantine, that the dragons enjoyed watching humans dance for them.

"Like my father watching the dogs run after a thrown fur-sock?" Taf asked, accepting from a servant on Ileth's behalf a second small glass of the syrupy wine they offered after dinner. "He does so enjoy doing that and the dogs are happy to occupy him all afternoon at it, if he lets them."

"Something like that. They don't . . . join—take a part. Just view. Sometimes they . . ." She was tired from travel, rich food, and wine, and trying to form her words into Galantine and keep her mouth limber was exhausting, but for some reason her stutter lessened a little in the foreign tongue. "Sometimes they call for more speed by slapping their tail. Or shaking limbs—wings. Like applause, in . . . in music-time."

"We should like to see how you dance for them. Do we not, Father? Shall she dance, Father?" Taf asked.

The Baron, engaged in a conversation with his brothers, turned his head. "By all means, enjoy."

Ileth looked over at Dun Huss, and he nodded.

Well, they'd requested a dragon dance, so she would offer one to them, as a good guest . . .

"A court-dance tempo would be best," Ileth said to Taf, who ordered a tune from her aunt.

She definitely couldn't dance in the overdress, so she passed the straps over her arm and let it drop. The men's work shirt hung low on her in any case.

A startled squawk from one end of the room was followed by the Baron's wife covering the eyes of the boy who had come to call them to dinner.

Ileth started to dance, legs free in her shirt and sheath, but she'd barely warmed her muscles with some turns on earth leg, low kicks, and jumps when the Baron, seeing her attire, or rather the lack of it, put a stop to the music.

"My dear," he said, smiling at her and picking up her dress, shielding her from the audience with it and his own body, "your presentation is very—uhh—naturally athletic. But your talents are, your talents are talented, and such talented—such a performance is wasted here, since we have so little experiences against which to judge it. Like performing music for an audience of the deaf. Perhaps we can arrange your exhibition, an exhibition of your dance, that is, in the dragon-shelter, so those creatures can benefit from your skill. My, what they do teach you in the Vales. I knew your Republic cast away certain traditions and institutions, but—well, you perhaps should have warned us," he finished quietly, his smile as gentle and unmoving as if it had been painted across his face.

Five more days passed, much as the others had. Fespanarax ignored her, but more and more often he ignored her with his nostrils pointed in her direction. He hardly ate. She wondered if a minimal appetite was a worse sign than no appetite at all. Supposedly as part of their training at the Serpentine they'd rotate through the physiker's, if the Masters judged you smart enough to handle such work, but that was for apprentices. Galia didn't remember much about appetite issues from her training—"it's all stitching and feeling for broken bones"—and wasn't much help.

She did pass on the request for precious metals, through Young Azal of Chapalaine. Both Ottavia and Fespanarax had suggested them.

She received an answer from the Baron himself, with a request to put on a formal exhibition of her dancing. He was doing what he could to get some coin together, and it would help matters to have something novel to show his guests arriving with offerings.

In the end, she agreed. In her later years she didn't much care to think about that night. For one thing, excepting Galia, the only women to attend were the Baron's wife and two women of the household staff who'd heard stories and were curious. The rest were men, not just men of the family, but it seemed every significant man and elder son from the Baron's lands had been invited.

It wasn't the fault of the music, either. She worked out the music ahead of time with the Baron. When she asked if there was someone who could play an impeller, he chuckled. "Oh, those things. No, they're not much used among families of significance, just the tavern singers. Young lady, why have one instrument doing three jobs badly when you can have three proper musicians?"

Three proper musicians he did hire, and Dun Huss joined their company with a borrowed drum.

She couldn't dance on a proper floor. They talked for a bit about taking one of the great winter doors of the barn down, but that seemed like a good deal of work and she suspected she'd just get splinters. So they raked the surface of the hippodrome out as well as they could and put down fine fresh sawdust. If the horses didn't trip on it, she wouldn't. She was a bit worried about the floorlights setting the whole place alight and spent some time arranging them on old platters and serving trays, so even if she lost track of where she was and knocked one over it wouldn't roll into the sawdust.

The Galantine ladies had some simple cosmetics and she used them as Ottavia had taught her, when they spoke of court dancing. Ileth did her best, highlighting her eyes and cheekbones, exaggerating the corners and sockets of her eyes so they showed up more to the audience, but in the little mirror it looked amateurish, nothing like what Santeel or Peak could do with the same tools.

"Be the performer, be the performance," she said, repeating one of Ottavia's predance encouragements. The idea was that someone else took your place onstage; it wasn't you at all, but a different—far more confident—person who handled your body while you were in front of the lights.

The reflection frowned at her. The performer didn't care for how she looked.

She grabbed a rag, wetted it, and washed the paint off, and instantly regretted it. Her face was pale and nervous, her eyes wide and scared.

"Shows how m-much you know," she said to the performer in the mirror.

Summoning the most courage she'd needed since the morning of the duel, she marched out to the great barn-arena. She tried to ignore the fancy carriages and chariots parked outside, patient horses munching at nosebags from loosened harnesses.

In the end, she did only three dances, though they planned out music for five. Ileth blamed it on Fespanarax, who took the invasive audience as an opportunity to look even more pathetic than usual, despite an excellent dinner of roast pork. But it wasn't Fespanarax who put her off so much as all the staring men. She tried to concentrate on the dragon, tell herself that she'd been watched before, but it was so much easier with the whole troupe about her. It felt ugly.

If only Fespanarax had roused himself and shown a little interest. She could have had him as her audience and ignored the Galantines.

She tried not to think about what must have been going through their minds as she went through her evolutions in her dancing sheath. At times, even the musicians seemed to lose track of their instruments, when the music would break down as they watched. Dun Huss pounded away at his drum until they picked up the tune again. She concentrated on Fespanarax. He was the audience, even if he couldn't be bothered to look at her.

In the end, she gave up. She ran lightly over to the Baron, smiling as brightly as she'd been taught, and explained that the dragon wasn't responsive after three dances, and her troupe's tradition was to stop so as to save their feet and not annoy the dragon overmuch.

The audience applauded and the musicians thumped their instruments. Ileth picked out three different men in the audience at three angles, made eye contact, and bobbed a deep obeisance, smiling.

Then she fled, before they could see the tears.

The next day the Baron himself called for them. They received a note with the first sun and the milk that he would visit them early.

"There's something I'd like you to see. Young Ileth, especially. Don't be alarmed, it's a *very* pleasant surprise for you."

Their first thought, when he took them toward the barns, was that the negotiations had concluded and there was a courier from the Serpentine bearing a message that they were free to return.

There were no strange dragons, so a message was unlikely, unless a courier had dropped it tied to a rock.

But there was a stout gardener standing there next to a large bucket. They approached it, the Baron giving a little chuckle. Ileth noticed that it reflected the morning sun.

Silver coins filled the bucket right to the brim.

"Well!" said Dun Huss in his slipshod Galantine. "Your generous stench overwhelms us, Baron Hryasmess. I appall and salivate you."

Galia, whose Galantine was improving by the day in dragon-sized leaps and bounds, did not follow the talk but her jaw dropped open at the amount of coin.

"That's just . . . the Baron's relatives and friends?" Galia asked.

The Baron either didn't understand her or pretended not to. "You are too kind, sir, it's the least I can do. There's enough left over to give the other dragons a mouthful in memory of their visit here. As, sadly, I believe it must become a memory all too soon, except for those two of you who make me and my family so happy by remaining. If I keep you from your duties any longer, your diplomats can fairly accuse me of plotting against the Republic by delaying its gallants."

The Baron produced some bowls from his overcoat and carefully counted out coins into each one. "I imagine it's the tradition for the dragoneers to give these to the dragons. I don't want a Galantine Baron accused of trying to bribe your dragons!"

Mnasmanus flapped his wings in eager anticipation, and the others joined him. "Go ahead," the Baron urged. Dun Huss led the way, with Preece and Galia following, each bearing silver to their dragon.

"Our young Ileth, as your exhibition provided the alchemy that filled this feed bucket with silver instead of corn, I believe you should present this to our resident. Who knows, this may be an omen of your future! No, I can do better. May *this* be an omen for your future." He reached into his pocket and produced two heavy gold coins. "One for you, and one for the bucket." He pressed the coin into Ileth's hand.

"Very generous, sir," the gardener said.

"I shall not forget your aid in your wage account this month, Leafway. But perhaps I won't be as generous as I might have been, as you're breaking in on my conversation with our young performer here."

The Baron gestured to his gardener. The gardener's thick shoulder muscles bulged as he picked up the bucket.

"What, my dear girl, is this the famous republican stolidity? You smiled wide enough last night. Perhaps you are still fatigued?"

Ileth stared at the coin. It weighed more than the little mirror Santeel had given her. "I don't see how—"

"Didn't you know? You were dancing at an almsgiving event. Do you know the phrase?"

"The words, yes. I'm . . . I'm not sure of their significance, Baron."

"Significant families from my and neighboring lands gathered to see an exhibition of your dragon dancing. Word of your—art got around quickly and arous—*hmmm*, inspired curiosity. A combination of pity for our languishing dragon and interest in seeing you perform opened purses and accounts for a halfday* all around."

They walked into the hippodrome. Fespanarax stirred and rolled his head so he could eye them. Baron Hryasmess, speaking of the Galantine tradition of charity that was as famous as their tradition of hospitality, paid no attention to the giant creature that could blast him

---

* A Galantine unit of distance, about fifteen miles.

out of existence and continued speaking to Ileth as though they were the only two present.

"Your performance was quite a novelty. I hope you don't think I indulge in self-flattery often, but we did rather well out of it. Charity work is not the least of my delights. I'm sorry we couldn't have you into the house, but it was elegant dress and the talk would have bored you in any case."

Their roundabout way of talking certainly made Ileth dizzy. Ileth stopped the procession near the door. "Close enough," she said. "If he wants it, he can come and get it."

"Fespanarax," she called. The gardener set the bucket down and hurried away with a strange walking-jogging gait that made it seem like he had three legs.

"I'll leave you two alone," the Baron said.

She lifted a handful of the silver, then let it trickle into the bucket again. She could buy her own squadron of fishing boats in the Freesand with the coin next to her foot. Used, but still . . .

"It's me again, Ileth. We have a little gift for you."

"You're going to be a bother about this, aren't you?" Fespanarax said, raising his head. He had a groaning sort of a voice, like a heavy door on old hinges. "I don't find you or your bird chatter charming in the least."

"Well, I like dragons, even grouchy ones. Good thing for you, since we're stuck together here for a . . . for a while."

"Grouchy, eh? You're a bold one."

Dragon baiting might be fun, but she didn't want to push it too far. "I just think it would be good for you to be on your feet."

Fespanarax sniffed the silver. His mouth began to slime up, an effect Ileth had been told about but hadn't seen yet. "Just because you're human and about as old as a summer dandelion, doesn't mean you can't be right. I should get up."

And he did, grinding his teeth the whole time. The slimy saliva dripped, reminding Ileth of clear syrup. He trundled forward, a little stiffly, and extended his enormous tongue and began to take up coins, curling his forked tongue around them almost lovingly. He swallowed them, slowly, as a human might relish olives or some other delicacy.

He took short breaks in his slow, methodical eating, letting the slime in his mouth build up until it dripped.

Ileth backed up a little so he could work the bucket better. He dropped a coin here and there but retrieved each, artfully. Then he ate the bucket itself. They must have a powerful digestion.

"Just one gold coin?" he asked.

She hadn't even seen him eat it.

"Yes," Ileth said. "I think it was supposed to be dessert."

"There's another coin in your shirt pocket." Why did they never put pockets on anything for women but aprons? They were so useful.

"Which is a gift from the Baron. I intend to keep it."

"That gold is worth a lot more to me than your life, girl."

"Are you threatening to kill me?"

"Hmm. Let me think." Fespanarax spoke Montangyan with no attempt to sound human. He was more difficult to understand than most. He spoke each word as if he were treading out corn, pounding it out his mouth and not much caring about the shape. "No. Just teaching you an important lesson: don't flit about strange dragons with the smell of gold on you. You don't know me."

"I know you are a dragon of the Serpentine."

"I was. I hope to be again. What I am now, though, is a prisoner in a conflict I find I care increasingly less about. I'm starting to think the only thing keeping me here is habit."

"They would miss you at the Serpentine if they never saw you again." She took out the coin. "Sir, if it means that much to you, I'll show you the loyalty of—"

"Oh, girl, noble gesture. No, you keep it. I know you danced hard last night. I could see the heat on the men's faces. I never felt more than an academic interest in such displays, but I did appreciate the break in the monotony, and for that I hope that coin of yours attracts some friends."

The silver had improved his mood, it seemed. His eyes looked around with new interest. "Huh, Cunescious has grown. You know, it feels good to be on my feet. I might walk around a bit so the coin moves about and settles in my metals gizzard."

Stepping so slowly that he reminded Ileth of one of the ruptured old sailors on the Freesand fish docks, the dragon went out into the morning air. He walked toward a pond, setting all the geese to alarmed honking.

Dun Huss, usually so measured, hurried in to speak to her after he departed. Had she ever seen him run?

"You know, Ileth, I'd have to check with Ottavia. Two sick old dragons up on their feet. I don't know which was more remarkable: the ancient Lodger, or the notoriously obstinate Fespanarax. He can be stubborn, and you've got him up and strolling about."

Praise from the dragoneer warmed her more than the satisfaction of seeing the dragon up and about, as she hadn't yet developed an interest in Fespanarax beyond duty. It even let her brain and mouth cooperate. "I think Fespanarax just went into a decline because he was bored. This morning, he finally became bored with being bored."

Dun Huss decided that night to depart early the next day, unless the weather turned unusually foul. He and Preece paid a brief call on their host at his house to thank him, leaving Ileth and Galia to their quarters. It gave them a chance to decide how they'd divide the house with the men gone. In the end, they both decided to be upstairs, but to share a bedroom for the companionship and security.

Galia, oddly, seemed to be losing her nerve about the dragoneers leaving. She asked if they could perhaps negotiate for a little more time to be sure of their position with the Galantines.

Dun Huss shook his head. "Our host has dropped more than one hint about the expense of feeding so many dragons. Now that Fespanarax at least seems on the mend I can't delay. I wish they would let us change Cunescious with Fespanarax, as Galia is being accepted in exchange for me. Cunescious is young and the experience might do him good. I'm not sure I like Fespanarax's attitude of late. He was never the easiest dragon, and I'm not at all sure that he won't give you difficulty. Getting a message to the Serpentine through the Galantines could take weeks. I asked the Baron about a swap and he declined, politely, but very definitely."

"Why not Preece, then? He is senior to me. The Galantines do not seem to think much of women."

"It's not that I do not trust Ileth and Preece, but two young people, stuck in a foreign land with little to do." Dun Huss chuckled. "The Galantines would never allow it. No, it is as the Charge said, we can count on the women to be treated more like company than prisoners. And there is just that odd chance the Galantines will take pity on two women and let you go as a gesture of gallantry, with some sort of solemn promise that Fespanarax will not participate if hostilities resume. They can be quite sentimental, as you see from the Baron and his animals."

It was a cloudy, windy morning, but they decided to risk leaving in any case. If the weather forced them down, it forced them down. They could return in easy stages, and the Baron had weighed them down with gifts of food for both humans and dragons.

The Baron and his wife rode out, with the cat perched in her lap and the dog running beside the high two-wheeled cart. The rat might have been left home on the chilly morning, or content to remain in the Baron's wig. Ileth wondered that the household staff, usually so considerate of women in general, let the Baroness up on the cart, considering her condition. She suspected it would overturn easily.

"Whatever the outcome of the negotiations between our two nations, you may always rely on your friends at Chapalaine, my dear Dun Huss," the Baron said. He'd descended to say his farewells; his wife remained in the cart, smiling at them with the cat in her lap.

"I shall improve it one day," Dun Huss said.

"Improve what?"

"My Galantine. They say it is hard to learn a new language at my age, and I appear to be proofs."

"Well, the way these wars go for your Republic, you may all end up learning it eventually."

"Come and try to teach me some, at your leisure, sir," Dun Huss said, steel in his eyes. "I am always ready for a lessons, whether given and taken."

"Well, sir, you show more color than I thought you plain citizens of a republic possessed. I wonder that they give you women to serve under you. Sparks such as that should land on a warlike tinder, not under-skirts."

"Then I am happy I am leaving Galia and Ileth with you, so that you can see for yourself what kind of women our mountains produce. But don't expect to inspect their underskirts, unless you wish to see some sparks."

The Baron laughed. "I will not delay you any further, pleasant as this kind of talk is. A speedy and safe journey, sir."

"If I stayed to thank you for all your kindnesses, sir, we should not leave until dinner. Give my compliments to your beautiful wife and hopes your family increases in size and health." Dun Huss's Galantine was much improved at the end, or perhaps he'd rehearsed this with his tutor. Then to Preece, in Montangyan: "Ready, wingman."

"As ever, sir," Preece said. "Galia, Ileth, we will return for you soon, I hope."

Galia's jaw trembled, but she said nothing. Ileth had to speak for them. "We . . . we look forward to that. Fates make it soon."

"Write us often," Dun Huss said as the dragons warmed their wings and turned into the wind. "Even if the news is only that you are weary of farina. The letters will be slow, but they will get to us."

"Yes, sir," the pair said in accidental unison.

They exchanged vigorous Serpentine-style salutes and the dragons dashed into the wind for an easy lift, wings flapping madly, like geese taking off. The dragons circled once, with humans waving and Cunescious cracking his tail, and rose into the sky.

"I will leave you to watch them as long as you like," the Baron said. "But I should get the Baroness back under a roof; it looks like rain. Please come to dinner tonight, if you feel up to it. We will understand if you do not and send out a tray." He climbed back into his cart and turned it away toward his house.

The two young women stood there, together in the wind, and watched the dragons and their riders until the outlines became dots with wings. Soon there was only wind and clouds the color of the sea.

"I love him, you know," Galia said.

Ileth couldn't have been more surprised by a slap. Her face probably looked much the same. "What? Preece?"

"Scale, no. Ileth, it makes me happy to hear that I hid it even from you, here. Hael Dun Huss. I love him. I have for years."

Ileth could only gape.

Galia tilted her head and touched it to Ileth's in a friendly fashion.

"Unreturned, but then it could not be anything but, with his standards," she continued, blinking tears until she gave up and wiped her eyes. "I confessed it to him once. Only once. Let us get inside."

As they walked back to their congenial prison, Galia continued:

"You know, he's the one who found me? Rescued me, more like. Found me on the streets of Sammerdam. It was after my brother died. A rat bite, we got them all the time. Thought nothing of them. But this one, his arm grew red and the veins stood out. He spoke of great pain. I got him medicine, expensive medicine—don't ask me how—to cure it, but it did nothing. He said it tasted like dry starch. It had plenty of opportunity to work; I dosed him and dosed him every hour. The next morning, he was stiff and cold. I was alone. So alone. Scared. I was more scared then, with him lying dead next to me, than I've ever been, before or since. I became brave after that. Recklessly brave. You see, the man who sold me the cure swore on his right hand that it would be effective."

Galia's jaw clenched and she ceased speaking for a moment, looking at the ground. Then she gained her voice again.

"Hael Dun Huss found me a few years later. I was chalking, then— decorating the steps leading up to the homes of the wealthy when they had parties. It was the rage for a while, and I'd learned to write beautifully. Announcements of babies born to the house. *On the occasion of Sedalia's betrothal* and lots of drawings of flowers, stuff like that. Or just decorations for holidays. He came early to a party and saw me finishing up, asked questions about where I learned to create such wonderful blossoms. I told him by watching other artists at their easels, running and getting them cool water and getting a word of advice in return. I never told him I stole my first run of chalk. I remember sometimes that it was me that did all those things. But it was a different me. Like a sailor's lucky knife that has had two new blades and three new handles.

"Well, I must have interested him because we spoke for a bit. He said with a hand like that I could write letters or be a clerk to some great lady or even be an artist. I had sewage all over my skirts from sleeping in the gutters; I can just see me showing up at some society woman's door smelling like sock wet with a wee: ''Scuse me, sira, you be needin' a bookkeeper?' As if.

"He said a talent like mine could be, *should be* trained. 'You can be so much more, Galia,' he said. He actually brought me to the party and asked the host if they could find a bed for me. They did, in the end, and I bet they boiled everything afterward if they didn't burn it. I think he was going to set me up as an apprentice, but then there was an emergency. I believe he thought he would lose me again in the gutters of Sammerdam—it is a place where it's easy to become lost, whether you want to or not—so he just brought me with him back to the Serpentine. He looped a line about me so I rode in front of him, cradled in his warmth. His smell. I can still feel his stubble on my forehead when I think of it. First thing I knew I was in the air above the city looking so clean and orderly—oh, how everything looks better from a sounding or two up—and the air was cold and fresh and smelled like rain. It was like being carried off at the end of a story. Beginnings, endings, they're kind of the same thing, aren't they? I'd barely eaten my first fried fish in the Serpentine when he was called away on a commission. I ended up making myself useful as long as I was there, and the next summer I oathed in with a group just as you did. He hired tutors for me, improved me in my Montangyan, gave me lessons in history and geography and all that.

"When it seemed the time was right, when I was fully a woman and able to marry without anyone's permission but my own, I did confess my love to him. In the greatest privacy, to save him embarrassment. If only I'd known how much shame it would cost me! I'm embarrassed to think of what I was wearing and how I acted. Silly. And you know, I think now that if he'd taken it, I'd have quit loving him. Gods, I belong with the madwomen in a locked lodge. He refused, rightly and properly and heartbreakingly. 'You can be so much more, Galia,' he told me, just like on that doorstep in Sammerdam. The first time he said that to me I glowed. It stung this time.

"Yet he still looks out for me. Won't touch me unless it's through flying gauntlets and then just on the arm or the leg as he checks my saddling. It's torture for me to see him, but torture I don't want to stop. Him making me a wingman was just another turn of the rack. And now he's gone and the rack's turned again. I think I may snap. So there we are. I love him, impossible though it is. So now you know the heart of the Serpentine's leading young dragoneerix."

Ileth couldn't think of anything else to do but hug her. "I'm so sorry for your . . . for your brother. As f-for the rest, well, endings and . . . endings and beginnings. Who knows which this is."

14

The days passed slowly. Ileth would rise early, warm up by running over to the dragon (the first time one of the Baron's household saw her running, they rang the fire bell but they soon accustomed themselves to her strange brand of femininity), and do her drills and fatigues. Fespanarax slept, or pretended to, through them. After asking Fespanarax whether he desired food or cleaning that day she would run back with hot muscles, wash up in cold water (in the Freesand, few had the time and money to set up hot baths), and breakfast with Galia. Then it was back to the dragon for the two of them to see to his feeding and appearance, where they spent most mornings with Fespanarax attending to his teeth and scale.

Ileth used the time to improve her knowledge of dragon care and grooming. Galia, while not exactly happy to teach her as she felt not nearly enough of an expert herself, instructed her in the art. In return Ileth improved Galia's Galantine (Ileth's own was being improved simply because it was in use constantly, as the servants and family relayed messages to both of them through her), and often Taf or Young Azal helped her by speaking simple commands and giving her old scrawled-up copybooks the smaller children used. Galia found the latter quite interesting, as each page was about one third filled by a woodcut illustration full of intricacy, intended to teach as many moral lessons as the artist could cram into it.

The tools involved in dragon care were closer to those needed for a smithy than, say, horse care, other than some stiff bristle brushes for scouring the dragon off and cleaning his teeth. There were files for taking burrs off a piece of scale that might irritate the dragon and a big gripping sort of thing such as was used by farriers to pull horseshoe nails that they used to pull scale. The Baron was allowed to keep any scale removed from the dragon and do with it as he liked according to the captivity agreements. Dragons regarded a scale being pulled as a minor pain, perhaps comparable to having a hair plucked, judging from the mild wince it evoked. Ileth always made sure to get the dragon's permission and show the scale that needed pulling before doing so. They had a little sewing table with some probes and tools for removing parasites, and needles and strands of gut for rends in the wings (which he didn't get because he could fly only under special circumstances). The only tool the Baron lacked was a reamer for the ears and nose, but they made do with a brush handle that had some soft pads such as Galantine women use as their monthly dressings stapled to it and soaked in white vinegar.

Fespanarax bore it with his usual humor, which is to say little.

Sometimes they helped out in the gardens later in the day after the sun passed its meridian. Spring seemed in a rush and there was a tremendous amount of work to do in the flower beds and herb garden, the traditional areas of the soil allotted to Galantine ladies of significance. The rest of the family played lawn games if the sun was not too fierce, and most of them wore broad hats and gloves when outdoors. The babies had sun tents. Galantine children could get sunburned only between the ages of five and puberty.

More often than not they ate with the family, and they dined in a far more extravagant fashion than they would have in the Serpentine, unless they cooked for themselves or quietly ate bread and cheese during the mysterious Galantine fast days, which came every ten days or so.

Galantine dinners for the immense family were generally served by setting up the dishes at one long side table, filling the plates from the platters and tureens, and then sitting down at another table to eat in shifts. The Baron served his wife or they had their plates brought by servants, the husbands served their wives, the older children served the younger, the governesses and nannies and nurses served the still

younger children, and winds only knew who served the servants, perhaps the cats and dogs prowling about the place who would then be
served by the mice, Ileth fancied. In any case, the remaining food
would be brought out to Galia and Ileth most nights (the rest was
carted off to the pigs, dogs, and chickens), sometimes with a decanter
with a little wine left. Ileth was always careful to wash and return whatever was brought out to them by the time their cold breakfast (if there
were suitable leftovers) was finished the next morning and the routine
began again.

The ample, quality food seemed to start something in her body.
Everything was growing out and up, from her hair to her toenails. She
felt it first in her house slippers; she had to ask for more canvas to make
new ones. Her reliable old traveling boots, which had been pinching in
the Serpentine, finally became impossible to get into.

Most nights she would walk out to the dragon and dance. These
events were more often than not attended by the servants, who leered
less and applauded more when she leaped and spun. Many of them,
men and women, could play little hand organs or cheap pipes and
drums of one kind or another, and they knew so much lively music that
she would only hardly hear the same tune twice from fast day to
fast day.

Galia watched a performance now and again and tried some drills
out of boredom. Sometimes Ileth could convince Fespanarax to take a
walk and they would circumnavigate the great field where the dragons
first landed. But Galia seemed to be suffering the boredom of captivity
more than she did (Galia had never been cooped up in anything like
the Captain's Lodge) and fretted by starting and abandoning sewing
projects, Galantine novels thought suitable for young ladies, and letter
writing. She would avoid the wine for three days straight and then, in
one night, ask Ileth for her share and make an unsteady walk to the
great house and claim that they'd spilled theirs and could they have a
little more.

Ileth didn't know what to do to offer relief from the boredom.
Growing up, Ileth had often heard that boredom would lead to trouble,
one way or another.

It was on one of the Galantine fast days that the Baron sent them a note shortly after dawn that he wanted to show Galia and Ileth the village and some of his tenant lands, and introduce them to not one but two visitors who would hopefully stay through the fine weather of the summer.

Galia put on her Serpentine wingman uniform for the occasion and even broke out her fore-and-aft-rigged hat. Taf had been fascinated by both and improved the fit by suggestion and even considered it her duty to put a new lining in the hat, as the old one was badly stained by men's hair oil designed to hide gray.

"And they say women are vain!" Taf had laughed, sniffing at the inside of the hat. "I'm glad to see that men are much the same all over. My father wears wigs more and more as his hair thins and changes color. Don't tell him I said so."

Ileth suppressed a giggle when the Baron pulled up in his two-wheel cart wearing a new and much thicker wig. The horse seemed happy in his work and gave Galia a friendly nicker as she approached.

"Hop up on my high-wheeler. Galia, would you rather squeeze on and one of you hold my traveling-cat Raffleth, or ride in the back? I do have a way to attach a seat back there."

"Sir," Galia said in her improving Galantine. "I have a, have a digestive difficulty. A ride often improves it, I find. I can ride a horse. But if my condition worsens, would I be allowed to return to Chapalaine on my own?"

Galantine women had, or pretended to have, delicate digestions and could get out of almost any activity by suggesting their food wasn't sitting quite right.

"I am sorry to hear that. I shall have a tonic brought to your larder at once," the Baron said. "I will give you my gentlest horse. My son is accompanying us so he can see you home." The Baron turned to Ileth.

"You are quite safe up here, and there's room. The dog can run, lands know he needs the exercise, and Raffleth here will sit between us. Raffleth, this is Ileth, our companion today."

Ileth dutifully climbed onto the high cart, the cat was shifted, the dog was deposed and forced to jog alongside, and the Baron took the cart. Only a single servant rode behind, leaving room for Galia to be borne for the two minutes it took to reach the stables. There they met Young Azal of Chapalaine, already mounted and in a handsome riding helmet, and a horse was introduced, saddled, and handed over to Galia in a trice. They also tied a spare horse with a saddle to the cart.

"Our first stop is the village inn," the Baron said. "We have distinguished visitors from Court who arrived late last night and did not wish to awaken the household. We go to retrieve them."

They rode around the front, down through the yards of Chapalaine, past an orchard, and through the encircling wall. A gardener tending the road took off his hat as they passed.

He paused in the road to let Azal and Galia move ahead so he could drive behind them. "Interesting name, Ileth. I suppose you know it is of Galantine origin. Not much used now. The name has fallen into, well, disfavor."

"I had . . . a relative who came from here. It's how I know a little . . . of your language. He had some books of letters."

"Well, I'm sure you'll forgive my patriotic prejudice, but I am pleased that you are kin of sorts and kept the language in some small way. There is no better tongue or more useful tongue west of the Inland Ocean, whether your bent is toward the arts or diplomacy. The Wurm, well, less said about them the better, though their royals are fair people. They speak Galantine as well as I do. I will not opine on your own plain good people of the Vales, though they do seem to be trustworthy and reliable in issue of money and commerce, which makes up for a certain lack of polish. I like to think the best parts of the Hypatian Ideal live on in Galantine culture, though the Elletians would dispute me. You know, I went across the Inland Ocean in my youth. There are some good people scattered about here and there, but between what's left of their great cities, well, the pilgrimage had to travel with guards."

Azal and Galia broke their horses into a canter. Galia had to clap a hand over her cap to keep it from flying off as she rode. The Baron urged the horse on to keep up. The dog left off his occasional sniffs at the verge and ran alongside, tail whipping in excitement. As the road came to a turn, they slowed and saw the beginnings of the village.

"I should have liked to show you my village before now, but I had to wait for the mud to dry up. Our roads are generally very good, save for a short span in spring and fall."

In the Vales it would probably be called a town as it had more than one street. But most of the houses and establishments were low and humble and much the same sort of thing as in villages everywhere. There was a silversmith. In the Vales you had to go to a very large town to encounter a silversmith.

The Baron's arrival in the village set all the boys in the streets in an uproar. Some left, others arrived, and nobody did anything at less speed than a run, though it seemed to be more from excitement than employment. The road widened toward the center of the village, where it turned to cobblestones surrounding a magnificent decorative fountain before a thin and solemn temple, washed white in the Galantine fashion. Women stood up from their washing to wave and nod at the Baron.

The Baron called out names and made inquiries about the health of children and livestock. All the news being agreeable, the Baron passed on his well-wishes to fathers and husbands.

The inn was the most substantial building save for the temple opposite. It had benches in front of it. Ileth thought it strange that there were no older men about; in every inn in the Vales that put out benches about the center of town you'd see men too old for work hanging about the inn, happy to give strangers direction and tips for the best table and beer.

The two riders let their horses breathe, reins idle.

A fleshy man made of smiles and anxiety, whom she presumed to be the innkeeper, came out, along with a well-dressed man with a monocle. Unlike most of the Galantine men she'd seen, the monocle-man wore neither wig nor hair tie. Instead his hair hung loose about his shoulders as in the style of the Vales. Ileth was interested in the monocle, but something else seemed off about the man and she realized he had only one ear. There was also a scar on his chin on that side, so she guessed he'd had a close call in a battle—or duel. She believed the Galantines also dueled.

"Cousin!" the Baron called.

"Cousin!" the visitor called back, raising a walking stick.

The Baron descended to greet his guest, as did his son, who did not seem overeager to address his cousin. Ileth was not told what to do, so she remained seated.

"You must tell me all that's happened at Court first chance you get," the Baron said.

The visitor clapped him on the shoulder. "I can do that now. A great deal always happens at Court. But it's always exactly the same great deal whenever you go, so just imagine that and you will be up-to-date. It's good to be away from it." Ileth found him easy to understand, but he pitched his voice high and loud, as if he was used to talking over crowds.

"Hi, Ransanse, leave the servant to her duty and come out and meet my cousin," the monocle-man called into the inn. The innkeeper glanced through the door and frowned.

Griff emerged onto the threshold. Elegantly dressed, fashionably wigged, bright buckles on his shoes, but unquestionably the same Griff she'd last seen being taken away in a fishing boat over his scale-stealing scheme. Ileth let out a small squeak.

"You!" Griff said. "In-In Chapalaine?"

Griff wore a light blue uniform coat with a great deal of piping that hung down to below his knees and riding boots. Underneath the coat she could see a single red crossbelt, but she didn't know enough about Galantine uniforms to place him with a particular order.

"What's this, Ransanse?" the man with the monocle asked.

"This is Ileth, a girl from the Serpentine," Griff said, in better Galantine than Ileth's. He licked his lips. "I quit the Serpentine shortly after she came in. How exactly she was admitted into the Serpentine is a mystery, but I do know that after they ascertained her character, she was put in with the dancers. Does the Baron know he's sitting next to a public dancer in that flier? I have heard her called a jade."

"That's enough, young man," the Baron said. "King's uniform or no."

"He was called Griff in the Republic," Ileth said in her best Galantine. Griff startled. "He's a thief, and this last speech proves him a liar as well, what-whatever he calls himself now."

The monocle-man scowled. "Cousin, I hope your daughters don't—"

Griff stepped up. "I'm entitled to the name Ransanse—I stand to inherit the estate, in time. It's Galantine custom that you may use the property name."

Galia jumped off her horse before the innkeeper could reach her to help her down. "What on earth is Griff doing here, Ileth?" she asked in Montangyan.

"Faith, is this another Vale girl?" the monocle-man asked. "Savage manners."

The Baron rapped his walking stick hard on the boardwalk he stood upon. "I must assert myself to restore order. I won't have arguments in the street in my village. Galia, Ileth, quiet now."

Everyone froze. It was easy for Ileth, and probably Griff, they were each so shocked at meeting the other again. Ileth had heard some talk about Griff having family in the Baronies; evidently he'd gone over to them. Gone over in many ways, as he was now in some sort of uniform. Ileth wished she had something sharp and discreet to stick in him.

The Baron made introductions. The visitor with the monocle had a long surname that began with Dandas, so to Ileth he would always be Dandas in her head and the Baronet Dandas when she addressed him. The Baron contrived to introduce them in such a way that Dandas knew they were here to take care of the "interned" dragon, intimating yet avoiding the label *prisoners* when it came to the women. Galia, the senior of the two, was still progressing with her Galantine, and her underling Ileth was an excellent dancer though not in the tradition that one usually saw at parties. Griff was introduced as Young Ransanse of the Air Squadron who had come to see the dragon on the Baron's estate and make "an estimate of the situation."

"Yes, I heard you were feeding a dragon," Dandas said. "Aren't you afraid it'll go mad and burn Chapalaine down? They often do, you know."

"No, no, no," the Baron replied. "You speak from an unfortunate ignorance. They're not like that at all, not if you feed them well and let them sleep. Given those two conditions, they behave in a way that could be called reasonable.

"Which reminds me," the Baron said. "How are things with the armistice?"

"Completely collapsed," Dandas said. "Not the armistice, that's still in place. It's the garrison question on the Terraslat* all over again. We gave on the matter of a flag, but that wasn't good enough for them; they want the island occupied only by a religious order, not even a small honor guard for the cemetery. You'd think the Grassway had never been fought by their attitude. Well, what could we do?"

Ileth suddenly felt a little ill. Imagine years here. Or a lifetime. She wondered how much of the conversation Galia had understood, but she appeared to be studying Griff's uniform.

"Oh," the Baron said, casting an apologetic look at Galia and Ileth. "Well, I am fortunate in their continued stay, then. I hope your visit will not be cut short, Dandas."

"I am entirely at liberty, cousin. Unless we get called up to the banners again, but I don't see that happening." He made a gesture at the nearby religious edifice.

Ileth translated for Galia. Galia took it well, her face a mask. "Baron, may I return? My sour stomach."

"I am sorry to hear that. Azal can take you back."

"Please, let me assist you," Dandas said. "I expect there's somewhere we can get you some rising soda to settle your stomach, or a tonic, here in town."

Galia said, "I'm sorry," and turned her horse back up the road. Azal hurried to follow her.

"Well, devils, that's a bad start to the visit," Dandas said. "A sick woman. Perhaps I'll call on the priest and offer up for her."

The Baron looked grieved and wiped his forehead with a pocket

* The Galantine name for the midriver fortress known to the Republic as "the Scab."

handkerchief. "It's my fault, cousin. We should not have spoken of politics in front of ladies. I am sorry, young Ileth."

As Dandas spoke, Galia mounted and urged her horse into a canter, despite being still in town. She was a skilled rider, thanks to dragon-hardened muscles. She veered the horse around a parked wagon with skill; Azal struggled to keep his seat as he tried to catch up.

Dandas squinted through his monocle. "Well, I'm riding after her, my fault or no. I shall see you at Chapalaine." He tightened the girth, then mounted the spare horse the Baron indicated and was off in a clatter of hooves on cobblestones.

"Just follow Azal to the house," the Baron shouted. "Don't risk your neck, man!"

"How am I to get to Chapalaine?" Griff asked.

"It is a pleasant walk, especially for a soldier, Young Ransanse," the Baron said, climbing into the cart. "Or I can send for a horse, but I don't expect to return for some time, as I have another errand."

"I'm to walk while this enemy jade rides?"

Ileth started to stammer out a response but quieted herself. The Baron had asked her to be silent, and silent she would remain. Besides, she was getting the feeling that the Baron didn't much like Griff, and that sort of language with no response from her would only increase his disgust.

The Baron resettled his wig with a hand that trembled, just a little. "Sir: she is a guest of my family. She dines with the Baroness. Just one more insult to anyone under my roof and you will find the gates of Chapalaine closed to you."

The Baron turned the cart and rode off without any sort of farewell, just a wave at the innkeeper, who bowed his head in return.

"This morning is off to a poor start," the Baron muttered. "I'd hoped for lively company but I grossly overshot. Forgive me, Ileth."

Ileth decided that a young Galantine lady probably would not want to speak of the recent unpleasantness and shifted to a happier subject.

"Your cousin . . . your cousin Dandas seems a g-good rider," Ileth said.

"Second cousin, actually," the Baron said. "He's excellent company, though I understand he gambles. That is a most dangerous habit, but he won't be able to indulge it here unless he's content to play for pins and buttons. I thought he'd cheer you ladies with all the news and stories of Court. He wrote me that he was bringing some sort of dragon expert. I didn't know he'd have bad news the instant he stepped out of the blasted inn. Forgive my language. Galia took it hard. Are you quite all right, Ileth dear?"

The Galantine thing would be to say that she was happy she'd spend more time at Chapalaine in the company of the Baron's excellent family and surroundings, but she didn't feel she owed him a speech. "I am well. The news about the negotiations upset me. But it is a matter I have no ability to change. So I sh-shall try not to dwell on it. Does that make sense?"

"You're a philosopher, Ileth. Yes, it does make sense. It's the right way to take news like that, I think. Perhaps you can give my daughters lessons. Have you ever tutored?"

"Thank you, sir. Only little children with the usual reading and such."

"Well, let's try to follow your philosophy and make the best of this day. Shall we, Raffleth?" he said, scratching the cat between them.

"Our first stop is the village cobbler. I am going to buy you a new pair of shoes. My daughter won't give me a moment's peace until you have something presentable. She wanted to gather up unused shoes from the family, but giving away some old clothes is one thing; shoes—it's just too dismal, don't you think? I don't know a lot about you uplanders, but I know you're not fond of taking charity."

"Good sir, I can buy my own shoes. I have that gold coin. Surely that's enough to pay for a pair of shoes."

"In a village like this, dozens." The Baron laughed.

He pulled up to a shoe-mender's that looked as though it catered more to the townspeople than the Baron's daughters. The place was mostly house, sharing walls with other houses, with a small selection of shoes and a workbench in the front. The Baron helped her down, but almost immediately a man accosted the Baron with a tale of a bull that had gone astray. The Baron begged her forgiveness and sent her into the store.

The cobbler had seen the cart pull up and left his workbench and took off his cap to give her his complete attention. She bought two pairs of shoes, some laced walking ones that just covered the ankles for going about the estate in the manner of a Galantine woman and some social slippers with a hook closure she could wear in the great house that would also be good for dancing. Though she asked to see them, just to look, he didn't have women's riding boots at the moment, but he could create a pair in a few days, and the Baron's daughters had them if she wished to evaluate his skill. Ileth temporized on the riding boots; it seemed she'd probably be stuck in the Galantine lands for the foreseeable future. Upon seeing the gold coin he tried to sell her a little silver clasp for the slippers, but she declined. He had to venture upstairs to get enough coin to balance the account. She glanced out the window as she counted her change; she didn't quite understand the coins she'd been given. The Baron seemed to have some business with men outside.

She relented on the matter of a polishing cloth she could use to wrap up her shoes and even made him happy by buying some shoe-keepers filled with pine chips to tuck in the walking ones if they should become wet. Then she went out, her purchases carefully wrapped in plain sacking, and found the Baron speaking to a group of men. A burly, booted fellow who had the arms of a blacksmith held an unshaven man with disheveled hair forward so the Baron could examine him. A few townspeople, both men and women, were watching from a respectful distance. But not so respectful they couldn't hear what was being said.

"Ah, but what is the evidence?" the Baron asked the pair as Ileth approached.

"He was drunk last week after the collections and was heard to say he'd poison the dogs if he could find some gravesleaf anywhere around here," the burly fellow said. "It grows out on the river sandbars, you know, sir."

The Baron repositioned the cat on his lap, looking into its eyes briefly. "Hmmm. Anything other than words? A bloody knife, blood on shoes or clothes, cleaning rags, handprint on the door?"

"Nothing like that. His fire had quite a lot of ashes in it."

"Hollows, I'm not going to have a man executed and hung up next to the notice-wall because he hasn't cleaned out his fireplace. The dogs had their throats cut, they weren't poisoned. Peppertree should buy fiercer dogs, or more alert ones. Vimes, you are free to go. I hope you'll learn to stop issuing threats, Vimes, and spend your nights more productively from now on. Don't give in to the temptations of wine and beer. Go to bed and get up with the sun and show a good set of Galantine manners; that'll keep you out of nine troubles out of ten, I always say."

"Yes, Baron, thank you, Baron, you're—" Ileth wasn't exactly sure what the man said; his Galantine was thick, but it seemed to be a flood of praise and gratitude.

"You should thank Raffleth. He always liked the look of you. Don't you, old beast?" the Baron said to the cat. "Ah, Ileth, and with our cobbler happier in the sale of some shoes today, I hope."

Ileth nodded, looking at the men warily.

"Hollows, we'll talk about this later," the Baron said as the crowd broke up. Ileth wondered if the trials were carried out so quickly and informally, what the punishments were like. She wasn't eager to find out.

The Baron's servant handed her up as the Baron calmed his cat.

"Well, now you have some idea of the heavy cart I pull around here. My tax collector had his dogs murdered two, no, three nights ago now."

He started to drive and continued.

"My tax collector is the problem, I believe, but it's hard to find a reliable man for the position. The dogs are supposed to be for his protection, but he likes to frighten people with them. They've bitten a child and have killed household animals. Nobody likes a tax collector, but I believe Peppertree goes out of his way to be as unpleasant as possible. The ordinary think just because I'm charged with collecting the money, I get to keep a great whopping share of it. They think it all should be spent on public feast days and the poorhouse and whatnot. I get next to two feathers over nothing for the duty; it goes to the King of course, and out of the two feathers I have to pay Peppertree. And buy him some new dogs now, I suppose. My man who collects my rents is much nicer. He cut off a few fingers when he first took over the job but didn't add insult to painful injury, and now everyone is prompt and accurate."

Ileth, glad she was living at the estate rent-free, studied the cat.

"I think Raffleth decided the matter correctly. He felt Vimes is guilty of nothing more than having a bad head for ale. You think I'm mad, I suppose. I'm not, I'm quite sane, I just trust my furred companions more than I do people. Now, if I'd referred the matter to the dog, then you could have called me mad. He's quite a silly creature and it would be the height of irresponsibility for a man of my significance to ask him about any matter of import."

With his mind cleared he inquired about her shoes. He commended her for sensible purchases. "I too often buy one or two little extras, even if my wife could produce far superior sachets to keep the shoes fresh. Why not let a hardworking, honest man like our good cobbler be happier with some small increase in his sales. You know, speaking of shoes, in the Aventis they have lovely shoes for dancing with satin ribbons. Have you ever seen satin? It's too bad I don't have an excuse to go, haven't gone anywhere since I took on that dragon for the King. He has freed me of tax for the duration, but given the expense of feeding him and all the scrap iron I have to scrounge up I'm wondering now if our good—my own good King is getting the better deal of it."

Ileth said she'd seen satin bows on fancy dress, on his own daughters. It was hard to make small talk. This talk of poison had put her in mind of Dun Huss's warning. But why? The Baron seemed exceptionally correct in his behavior, even solicitous to the point where milk curdled. She couldn't see him poisoning someone he'd been charged by his King with feeding. And she doubted anyone on his estate would take the step without his explicit approval.

"Oh, you are a bright young thing, aren't you? I did enjoy your dancing even if it wasn't to the taste of people of our station. It must make one extraordinarily healthy and vigorous. You could probably have twenty children before your age catches up with you. If only there were a way for you to be courted by a man without having to speak. If you had a rich father, it would be nothing; it could all be done by correspondence. But as soon as you talk, it sets a man thinking that he'll have to listen to that every morning and night. What I should do, if I were you, is show him your dancing first, then move on to conversation and restrain yourself to polite phrases. He will think you modest, and that may even compensate for the, uh, hmmm, vigor of your dancing. You know, less than two hundred years ago they'd probably have drowned you as an agent of the infernal regions for that stutter. I am glad we live in enlightened times."

They turned off on a little track that led to some hills in the east. In the distance, she saw the line of mountains, the two volcanoes there steaming. Ileth couldn't help but wonder what Griff's presence meant. Maybe it was nothing; he'd gone over to his Galantine relations and the Galantine King was making use of his experience around dragons. He seemed unknown to the Baron. If she'd learned that he visited around the time of the dragoneer's death she would suspect him. Griff, so far, was the only person she'd met in the Baronies who struck her as a potential murderer.

"Where are we off to next?" Ileth asked, speaking slowly so as not to awaken her stutter and risk a drowning in the nearby Green River.

"Oh, we have some more visitors to the Barony. Not as distinguished as my cousin, and definitely not accepted at Court, but I'm sure you will find them interesting. I'm looking forward to this."

They seemed quite far from Chapalaine. From a rise she could just see the dark of its forest. She was wondering about a midday meal, then remembered the Baron was fasting today.

Certainly, Fespanarax was valuable to the Republic. The Galantines would not want to restore him to their enemies. Griff was low and clever in his own way. Just the sort of person you'd send to discreetly kill a dragon. She wondered if she could manage to keep him away. The Baron was halfway to throwing Griff off his grounds as it was.

"Sir, I've been . . . I've been thinking. I hope I don't have to see that Ransanse person again."

"Oh, my dear," the Baron said. "Have you been worrying about that this entire drive? In such nice weather? Set your mind at ease. I will give you plenty of warning of his visits. I have already decided he won't sleep under my roof. We have some canvas shepherd's camps that will do, if he won't stay in the inn. I will have one set up outside the gate for him. The wet ground may teach him to control his tongue. I will tell the

Baroness that you will withdraw whenever he is present. I wonder just how much I should tell her of his accusations."

"You know best, sir. It is nothing to me if you give her the details in full. Lies don't trouble me."

"To think he said those things while wearing his King's uniform. Raffleth, what should we do about that?" The cat didn't answer, as it was sleeping. "Should Baron Ransanse be—no, no, I would not care for someone else intruding on my family arrangements."

Ahead, Ileth saw a rough pasture with a collection of perhaps fifteen wagons in a circle. They were curious sorts of wagons, round like giant logs or barrels on wheels. This was some manner of encampment.

The Baron took his cart off the road and had to concentrate on his driving.

"You're about to meet some people who share your enthusiasm for dragons. Not that I don't like them; they're fascinating, but they are expensive, aren't they? Don't misunderstand me. I am relieved that the dragon rallied and regained his health. Losing one prisoner is bad luck. Losing two, well, that brings with it a whiff of carelessness, do you not agree? But it was a terrible plague that took our dear Heem Zwollen. I'm not sure three infants survived in the village altogether and the old people, well, they fell in windrows. In the end I had to order that anyone suspected of illness be driven away, so they didn't even have the sacramental niceties. They died in the woods in little hovels or just by the side of the road. They were burned just as they were found. Horrible business."

The people they approached were dressed in black, with splashes of red and white here and there, unlike the Galantines, who seemed to enjoy bright orange, lemon, and grape colors.

"They're not even Galantine, but they do enjoy our protection. We call them the Tribals. There are some Baronies where Tribals are most unwelcome, but mine is not one of them. They are an odd sort of society. The men and women spend most of the year apart. The vast majority of the men go into the mountains with their horses and goats; the women roam about the flatlands selling their balms and trinkets. They only spend the winter together. Sometimes a baby is a full seven months old before it is presented to the father."

The dog seemed tired, so the Baron halted and had his servant hand him up. The dog lay down between the Baron and Ileth, and the cat, shifted to the Baron's lap, glared at the dog.

While that was happening, a procession came out to greet them. It was almost exclusively female, as the Baron had described. Ileth saw only one boy with them, and two men moving about the improvised corral their circle of wagons had made.

"Oh, Ranya, good to see you again," the Baron said to the assembly of black-clad women. A tall woman in a red wrap inclined her head. It was difficult to tell on them what was dress, what was skirt, what might be blouse or vest and so on, for the garments were all dark and seemed intertwined and buttoned or hooked together. "Well, people, the dragon, I am happy to say, is much better, but I invite you to tend him as long as you like this summer. You may stay in this field as you did last year, but you may find it inconvenient to be this far from town. I invite you to stay on my lands. You may inhabit my theater if you wish an increase in your comfort, and beneath the seats it is cool and pleasant on even the hottest days.

"But please, no games of chance. Not even if my locals ask for it. I know they did last year and there was trouble. I simply won't have gambling. The priest doesn't like it and I don't either. As long as we understand each other on that, you may sell your potions and such as you like."

"Agreed, sir," the tall woman he'd called Ranya said.

"I would like for you to meet a sister of sorts to you. You know, I always thought you all were unique, but it turns out she dances for dragons as well. You may find you enjoy each other's company. This is Ileth of the Serpentine in the Vale Republic."

Ranya looked puzzled. "Ileth. I hope to know you better. Perhaps you can teach your countrymen hospitality. Baron, will you take tea with us?"

The Baron looked uncomfortable, and then he brightened. "Ah. Not just now, Ranya. I am keeping fast, you see. I am sorry, I have other calls to make."

He said a few more farewells and offered compliments on the condition of their wagons and turned his cart about.

"They are a curious lot, but my people seem to enjoy their entertainments. Don't show them a coin you wish to keep," he added quietly as he sat down again.

That night Chapalaine held a dinner party to welcome Cousin Dandas. The Vale ladies in the converted storeroom were "especially invited." The Baron added a private note that Young Ransanse would be in attendance but had been warned by both the Baron and Dandas that he was not to approach or speak to Ileth or Galia, and he hoped the Baron's own guarantee would be enough for them to feel safe attending.

Ileth, special invitation or no, considered begging off with a malady, since she had any number of real ones to choose from: mental exhaustion from hours of overpleasant chat with the Baron, sore muscles from being bounced around in his tippy cart with a dog panting on her, a headache from the sun—whatever the excuse the Baron would be certain to understand, as Griff, or Ransanse as he was now named, would be in attendance.

"You're going," Galia said. "Because if you stay behind, saying you are ill, they'll wonder why I attended anyway when my friend is sick and needs nursing. They'll think I must want to be there for some special reason."

"They're Galantines. If there's nothing to speculate upon at their table, they'll just talk about the neighbors, or the village, or their p-precious Court," Ileth said. But she went. She had new shoes to wear, to go with her Galantine hand-me-downs.

It turned out to be an unexpectedly large dinner party, as everyone was eager to be introduced to this Dandas. Ileth wondered if he wasn't a more important person at Court than had been let on. They'd brought in several additional tables and set them up in the Gallery, allowing the guests more room to mingle. Even more astonishingly, there was soup on each table instead of the usual Galantine buffet, covered and kept warm by tiny candles. One small meal table held a selection of breads and rolls. Ileth thought it strange, but the Baron's wife explained that it was traditional to dine lightly at the end of a fast day with thin soup.

They made a small table for six, featuring Dandas, Azal and Taf, one of the Baron's nephews to balance things, and then Galia and Ileth. The Baron called it the "young guests" table, and if there was an "old guests" table, she didn't know the faces of the Baron's friends well enough to recognize it.

Griff was seated on the opposite side of the room, in a seat arranged so he was blocked from view by a trio of musicians, and from the very little Ileth could see of him, he didn't seem happy about it. The musicians were good.

Dandas was in great demand and effortlessly bathed in the interest, hardly sitting at the young guests' table. He reminded Ileth of a bee going from flower to flower to flower, collecting and dropping introductions.

Ileth was tired and raw from the long day and bad news. Hungry too, and the soup wouldn't be consumed until a certain hour had been struck. Adding to her discomfort, with all the great ladies about, her hair couldn't get up to much. It was at an awkward length, neither long enough to do anything much with nor short enough so it could be just swept back or to the side and ignored.

Dandas had spread the news that the negotiations had broken down.

"Oh, more fighting won't be necessary," the Baron said to his brothers and most significant neighbors. "It's a Republic. Their finances are a mess. Republics always fall. Always. No financial stability. No social stability. It's as I've always said, the egalitarian rearranging of natural order that brings the whole lot down. You can take a whole pail of cream and throw in a cup full of sewage and mix it up—you'll end up with something that tastes much more like sewage than cream."

At last the hour of the end of the fast arrived. The soup could be uncovered.

Dandas took his place at the table and shifted the conversation to dragons. Both Galia and Ileth stayed quiet. Galantine manners for this sort of introductory affair seemed to be that you focused your attention on the new guest. Ileth assumed he was trying to be polite and include the prisoners in something that would interest them.

He inquired about the number of dragons they typically had to feed at the Serpentine and received nothing more than "it changes" from Ileth and a stony stare from Galia.

"Naturally, I'm no expert. Only dragon I've seen up close is a dead one," Dandas said.

"Truly?" the Baron's nephew asked. "In the war?"

"Yes, years ago when I was first with the Fencibles. We'd got the rider on a low pass, knocked right out of her saddle—we didn't know it was a she until later. We were aiming for the dragon, which shows you how rattled we were, everything went high. Well, the dragon, a great silver beast, it landed to try to recover her body. Can you believe it? A beast like that. Didn't fly off in terror at all, set down and picked her body up as gently as if she were sleeping."

Ileth felt the room lurch.

"Perhaps she had coin for it with her," Dandas continued. "We put thirty or so bolts into its chest as it lifted her, and it dropped stone dead atop her."

"His ch-chest," Ileth said. "Silver dragons are m-m-male."

In a flash she was seven years old again, sitting atop a silver dragon with Annis beside her, having been told her stutter was because she had too much spirit in her.

Dandas said something that Ileth hardly noticed. "What?" she asked.

"His, then," Dandas said, exasperatedly. "His head is sitting with our banner in the trophy hall."

Ileth saw red. She'd heard the expression before. Perhaps she'd read it in an adventurous romance. But it had never happened to her despite her temper, not even in her duel with Gorgantern or the fight in the kitchen or when she was grabbed in the Cellars. She didn't think; her body moved so quickly that later, looking back on it, she was astonished that so much action could take place so suddenly apparently without the brain willing it . . .

In the time it takes to drop a spoon from your hand to the floor she was on her feet. They told her she screamed but she didn't hear it. She pushed out her hands, connecting with the soup tureen, upending it with purpose so a wave of soup splashed out, flooding across the table toward Dandas. The hot tide struck his glass, utensils, and own soup bowl in a steaming surf of creamy vegetables. The wash drenched him from shirt front to thighs, though a few ambitious droplets managed to reach his eyebrows and hair, including one bit of broccoli that hung on his nose like a desperate mountain climber.

"You mad—" Dandas sputtered, jumping up with soup running off him, teaching Ileth her first truly vile word in Galantine.

Fortunately for Ileth, Galia, and most especially Dandas, they did not break their fasts with a serving of roast beef and carving knife and fork.

She might have climbed straight over the table to get at him, except Galia flew to her. "Ileth, what on earth—"

Talk broke out as she and Galia fled. Ileth realized she was sobbing. She heard the words *seizure* and *attack*.

Ileth wasn't completely rational until they were safe in their little house with the door bolted.

"Oh, Ileth, you always have to be the center of attention." Galia fell back in her chair with her forearm over her eyes for dramatic effect. "I'm Ileth, I dance around half naked. I'm Ileth, I'll get into a stupid duel with a stupider man. I'm Ileth, I'm just a frail little nothing pressed up against a stable wall, and tonight it's Ileth, who just can't bear to hear of any precious dragons killed in a war we've pumping *lost*!"

Galia drew a few breaths and looked at her coldly. "Caseen told me he thought you were lucky. I think your act just works on him better than most."

Ileth slumped. Galia thought all the events of the past months were an—*act*?

"Suppose they decide we've violated the terms of our surrender or whatever and they chuck us somewhere else? We can't fight the Galantines, not just the two of us."

"Two of us and a . . . and a dragon. We could escape."

"Oh, I think he's had the spirit knocked out of him by all this. All he wants is a mouthful of coin now and then between his regular meals. He's not Fespanarax the Reckless anymore; he's just a creaky old dragon. I can't believe I ever suggested bringing you on this. I thought it would be jolly and a spell in Galantine country would mean you'd be made apprentice for sure. Serves me right."

Ileth, overwrought and on edge, felt the tears coming. But if she let them go, Galia would just accuse her of being overdramatic again. She looked at the floor, as she used to when getting a dressing-down from the Captain.

"I lost my temper," Ileth said. "I met that dragon. And his dragoneer. Once. When I was a little girl."

"I'm sorry, then," Galia said. Her temper ebbed and she rose and put her arm out, clasping Ileth's shoulder. "We've been cooped up together too long. We've never lived together, not close. Bound to get on each other's nerves."

"I suppose I should . . . apologize."

"We'll see how it looks in the morning. Look at it this way, they'll be talking about that party all summer."

Dandas and Young Azal arrived shortly after they had breakfasted the next morning. Well, Galia had breakfast; Ileth was still too upset to eat. She just nibbled at a crust of bread and drank water (one of the Baron's several cats had gotten in and spilled the previous day's milk and for some reason none had been delivered that morning). Dandas bore a small wooden box.

"You missed a good deal of apologizing last night," Dandas said from the smoothed area of gravel that served as their doorstep. Azal nodded behind him. "I have one more to do, to the party I've most aggrieved," he said, as they stood aside to let the men enter.

They refused to sit.

Dandas had long since removed the soup from his eyebrows. "I won't delay any more. It was unforgivable of me to bring up what I saw on the battlefield. My mind was on what I'd heard at Court and how it contrasted with what I'd seen with the Fencibles. All I can offer by way of explanation is that you two are so charming I completely forgot your origins and acted as though you were just Galantine ladies interested in an anecdote about dragons."

"I am sorry as well, sir," Ileth said. Galia squeezed her hand.

"The only apology you should be offering is that you didn't dump the soup where it should have gone, atop my thoughtless head. My stomach committed no offense I know of beyond growling in hunger."

Galia laughed at that. Ileth just smiled.

"By way of apology: I understand you mountain-breds love tea. I have a small chest here of fine tea that was intended for my hostess, the Baroness Hryasmess. I am willing to temporarily injure her—until I can find an appropriate replacement—in order to make it up to you. What do you say, dragoneers? War, an armistice, or a peace treaty?"

He bowed, perhaps a trifle too expertly, as he presented it to her. Looking back on it later, she wondered if the whole performance wasn't mechanical, much in the vein of Ottavia's music boxes.

"A peace treaty," Ileth said, taking the box and bobbing an obeisance. "Thank you, sir."

"Justice!" Azal said. "Best of the three."

"They should send you to the negotiating table, sir," Galia said in her improved Galantine. "If you can soothe my dear Ileth, you can persuade anybody."

They broke into small talk over the weather and the cat's accident with the milk.

Galia expressed an interest in taking in the morning air, and Dandas offered to walk with her. Ileth said she'd remain behind and enjoy her tea, though she'd have to make it camp-style in a boiling pan as they had no kettle. Azal looked as though he'd like to remain behind and have some tea as well, but being alone with Ileth in the house would be inappropriate, so he walked with Dandas and Galia.

Ileth was glad to have them gone. She felt oddly like a passenger on a boat going with the river current, rudderless. She needed to rest and think.

But she had duties to do. She dressed and saw to Fespanarax. Griff had beaten her there and appeared to be in a conversation with

Fespanarax, albeit in the dragon's usual style of discourse, which was to ignore you until you gave up and wandered away. She smelled hot grease. Someone had brought breakfast. Ileth pretended to turn away, but she circled around to the other side of the arena and did her best to listen.

Fespanarax's tail twitched. He was irritated, but whatever they were saying to each other was blocked by the dragon's bulk as effectively as if the conversation were taking place on the other side of a fishing boat.

With little to do but think, Ileth went over in her head last night's events. No, she doubted she'd been deliberately provoked. She was pretty sure that you weren't supposed to build a plan around the reaction of your enemy. But given the circumstances, Dandas could have told Griff that he would keep the foreign "guests" occupied with his apology, giving Griff a chance at a private conversation—

"Enough," Fespanarax said in Montangyan. "Rotten breakfast and worse company. Mount up on your promises and ride them away, see how far they take you."

Ileth changed her position so she was just behind Fespanarax and watched Griff stalk away, head bowed, hands clasped behind him.

Fespanarax settled his hindquarters. "Girl! Don't go poking around a dragon's flanks. You're liable to get your back broken by a tail that way."

"Sorry," Ileth said.

"Can you believe what that fool brought me for breakfast? Come look."

Ileth ventured out around the dragon. A barrow filled with the remains of last night's dinner rested there, mostly untouched.

"Slops! Last night's leavings, as if I were a pig to be fattened cheaply."

"Shall I get—"

"I'm in too bad a mood to be hungry." He dropped his head between his forearms and snorted. "I want nothing more to do with humans today."

"If I may ask, sir, what business did he have with you?"

"Nothing I cared to hear. You're not usually this slow, outside your speech. Go off. Dance for the birds. I want none of it. Keep your plans and your wars, or better yet, keep at them until you kill each other off and we dragons can enjoy some peace again."

That afternoon the entire Tribal encampment was at the grounds of Chapalaine. They did use the old theater, parking their wagons around it and driving the horses into its sandy expanse at night. During the day the horses grazed the fields within smelling distance of the dragon, which surprised Ileth.

The Baron was right. They half worshiped the dragon. They tended Fespanarax from nostril to tail tip, doing many of the jobs the staff at the Serpentine performed, and did them even better, if a good deal more slowly. They collected filings from his scales when they smoothed them and inspected his droppings for bits of bone that had passed through. Anything that fell from the dragon, including saliva, was collected.

They also would dance for him. It seemed a religious rite to them. The moon had to be in its proper phase: visible and increasing. Dancing for a dragon in decreasing moonlight brought all manner of ill fortune, one old Tribal who could no longer dance whispered to Ileth in an accented Galantine so strange she could hardly be sure what she said.

They certainly improved Fespanarax's mood. Maybe that was what was missing, an army of people attending to him. He became positively conversational. Even Galia, who visited the dragon for only a few moments each day, noticed.

One morning, after Ileth finished dancing for him (he still only occasionally glanced her way, though he did take a deep breath of the air about her now and then), he talked to her about their dances.

"So are they different from the Serpentine dancers?" Ileth asked.

"Yes. Their dances aren't as exacting. I know they don't sweat as much, unless it is warm. They'll work in shifts, as you do, usually in groups of three.

"I'm lucky they don't ask to bleed me, not with you around, anyway. Last year they asked several times for blood, whenever Zwollen and the Galantines weren't about. I refused. There was too much of that in the past, and it didn't end well for the dragons or the people who drank of it. Though I haven't heard of Tribals drinking it themselves; I think they use it in potions and whatnot."

"You're familiar with these people?"

"Oh, yes, they've been here for ages. They're the descendants of Hypatians who served dragons as slaves. We used to call them"—and here he used the Drakine term for *thralls*. "The tribe is older than I am. They don't visit the Vales. I think the people are unfriendly to them."

As he'd been obliging in conversation, Ileth pressed her luck. "May I ask you s-something else, nothing to do with the Tribals?"

"I'd welcome a change of subject."

"Why don't you ever watch me dance?"

Fespanarax chuckled. "I am an old-fashioned dragon, in some ways. There is an old adage against giving attention to your kind. I was taught to beware of humans of your age and sex. The way some humans won't touch a snake, poisonous or no. You can cast bewitchments on dragons and send them to their doom."

The idea that a dragon might ever be afraid of her would take some getting used to. Or perhaps he was just teasing. "Doom? Never."

"You do not need intend any wrong—it is, well, the idea is difficult to express in human terms. You attract the fate just with your presence, the way a flower draws the bee."

Ileth explained, haltingly, that she hadn't heard of any other dragons of the Serpentine fearing the dancers.

"Ahh, but no dragon monopolizes any one dancer, do they? That is what brings the fate down. And that is why you dancers never become dragoneers."

If she was getting closer to Fespanarax, things moved in the other direction with Galia. Galia stayed friendly toward her, but they rarely spent time in activities just the two of them, save for eating and sleeping. With the Tribals taking care of the dragon they didn't groom or feed him together, and all their plans for Galia to tutor Ileth further in being a dragoneer seemed forgotten.

Galia spent more time with the Baron, and especially with his cousin Dandas. She was often in the village with the Baron and Dandas, or riding horses with Azal and Dandas, or at a game with some of the younger children with Dandas watching and teaching her how to play.

Their Galantine continually improved, Galia's through practice and Ileth's through a great deal of reading, both aloud and to herself. Taf especially took it upon herself to tutor her and improve her manners, and slyly, in moments when she was positive her father was far away, she had Ileth show her some elements of dragon dancing, which apparently had kindled something in Taf's imagination the way meeting Annis Heem Strath and Agrath had sparked Ileth.

Taf would go silent when questioned about her cousin and Galia, as though ordered not to reveal anything.

She finally got something out of Young Azal of Chapalaine, though. Usually reticent, she saw him limping back one afternoon from riding, carrying a muddy helmet and looking as though he'd been dragged through a hedge. Or six.

"Are you injured?" she called as she hurried out from Fespanarax's arena.

He waved, and she fell into step with him. His horse didn't like it much; she must carry some of the dragon's odor with her.

"I'm fine. Just a fall. I was brushed by a branch trying to catch up to them. Your friend Galia and Dandas left me chewing on the clods flying from their horses' hooves."

"So your cousin is with Galia, alone?" Ileth sensed they were doing something improper, unless Dandas was formally courting her. That couldn't be happening, could it?

"He's not my cousin," Azal said.

"Well, your father's."

"Girl, everyone with the title *Baron* in this land is related in some manner or other. They're all cousins. The first time I saw him was in the village with you. All the girls in my family are mad over him. I'm done talking about the fellow. He's as transparent as that monocle of his."

"Lucky you," Ileth said slowly. "I have a feeling I'm not."

Her prediction turned out to be entirely correct. Ileth spent most of that night discussing Dandas with Galia over some of the gift tea (Ileth was carefully rationing it out). Or rather, Galia spoke of him and Ileth just put in a word here and there. Those were her favorite kinds of conversations to have, unless the subject was Riefense Dandas. Even more frighteningly, Galia had several of his titles memorized.

"Chapalaine isn't at all impressive compared to his estates. There are several," Galia said.

"How do you know?"

"He told me. It wasn't brag. I asked him whether the Baron was typical of his peers or not. He said he was on the lower end of the scale, where property is concerned, and this was one of the smaller Baronies. Then he described his estates. Well—his family's."

"He's Galantine."

"Yes, I've noticed," Galia said, scowling.

Ileth sipped her tea. Whatever else he might be, Dandas knew his tea. Invigorating yet soothing, with just enough bite to make you notice the flavor.

"I'm not falling in love with him, if that's what you think," Galia said. "He's likable, courteous, and knowledgeable. Yes, he fought against us, but I fought against him, even though the last time arrows were flying I was a novice."

Ileth wondered if Galia was arguing with her or herself.

"Does he ask you about . . . ask you about our dragons, or the Serpentine?"

"Never. Remember that time he asked how many dragons we fed? I gave him an earful, and he said he'd watch his conversation in the future and not probe on matters military, even by accident. The closest he came since was when he asked me what it was like to fly. I introduced him to Fespanarax. He touched his scale, ran a finger across the trailing edge of his wing, and said nothing. No, he did say he's large. Or maybe mighty. Not sure of the word he used. Fespanarax tried to get coins out of him through me. Odd that out of all of us, the dragon is the only one that hasn't learned any Galantine. He's been here years."

Ileth tried to picture Galia, who hated Santeel Dun Troot and everything her family stood for, falling in love with a Galantine aristocrat. "Wh-What do you talk about?"

"Oh, life. Views on art. Status. You know, in some ways, the Galantines are more equal than us. People like us, we're always scrabbling, trying to make a name for ourselves. If I were a Galantine girl, the fact that I'd grown up eating rats wouldn't matter a bit if a man like Dandas married me. I'd instantly be elevated to his status, and he wouldn't be reduced at all by mine. Not like the Vales."

Ileth felt like there was a flaw in that, but she wasn't clever enough to pry it open. She tried to think of what a better intellect, say the Lodger's, would say to show her she was wrong. Well, the Lodger liked to hold a mirror up to an argument sometimes.

"What if you were a wealthy Galantine girl and-and-and he the rat-eater?"

"I don't think it ever goes that way," Galia said. "How would they court? The family wouldn't let him in the door."

"You might want to consider the reasons for that."

"You're in a nasty mood," Galia said. "Just because you're having an awful time here doesn't mean I must."

Ileth finally saw the Dance of the Tribals, and it was far from an awful time. It turned out to be one of the highlights of her stay at Chapalaine.

Their routines were intricate and geometric. They danced close to each other and whirled as though they were interlocking gears. One turn out of place and they'd lock arms and go down like the Baron's cart with a tree stuck in its spokes.

Fespanarax accepted the performance with his usual relaxed disinterest. His ears did flick about in time to the music here and there.

The music played was mostly percussive. Sometimes they danced with cymbals on their fingers, so they made their own music or accompanied the instruments. With time to study it, Ileth figured out that the lead dancer in each group was passing off cues for what series of moves to do next; one gesture might mean four different turns and a change of dancing positions, another a series of arm movements up and down above their heads. Brilliant dancing, all in the spur of the moment.

Their dress was heavier than that of the Serpentine's dragon dancers, but in some ways more provocative. They bared their midriffs, which Ileth found surprising in the relatively staid Galantine lands.

She later learned it was something to do with their umbilical attachment to their mother and the moon. Or the moon was their mother. They were cryptic about it and both were speaking in tongues foreign to them.

She, in turn, exhibited Serpentine-style dragon dancing and they delighted in it, applauding some of her extensions with an enthusiasm only another dancer would have. She found the Tribal music enjoyable to dance to; it was wild, improvised, varied. The musicians watched the dancer and threw out little challenges that she, as the dancer, either accepted or refused. She felt that the music was seducing her into pushing herself to leap higher, spin more, express herself with hands or face or torso.

Later, looking back on it, she decided she went a little mad, especially when she tore open her dancing sheath to reveal her belly button. But the music *was* seductive, and what's the fun of being seduced without a memorable climax to the affair?

After that the Tribe accepted her as a sister in dance if not a member of their clan. They let her practice with them, which took some of the sting out of her increasing distance with Galia. Which led to a bigger surprise.

Taf secretly danced with the Tribals.

Ileth wondered how she engineered it to trick Chapalaine, where everyone seemed to know everyone else's business. But there she was, barefoot and bare-bellied, with cymbals on her fingers dancing as if she were a member of the Tribe herself. She even wore black clothing altered so she could be mistaken for one of them from a distance, had her hair wrapped back in a kerchief, and wore a thin veil under her eyes with little brass rings sewn into it.

"Ileth, you'll say nothing to my father!" Taf said, when Ileth recognized her. Maybe it would have been better if she'd pretended she didn't recognize her.

"I certainly won't raise the subject with him," Ileth said. The Galantine language was conducive to equivocation, she'd give it that. "In return, I'd like to ask a favor of you."

"Well, anything, Ileth dear!"

"What is our good Dandas up to with Galia?"

"Ileth! Really, just because she's the prettier—"

"That has nothing to do with it," Ileth said, in her halting, careful fashion when speaking Galantine. "It seems . . . strange to me that he'd lavish so much attention on, well, a prisoner."

"All he's said about it—not to me, this is something that I've overheard—is that he finds her intriguing and a different, oh, what's the word he used . . . challenge, I think it was. He says he can't get the way she speaks to him out of his head. He doesn't care whether she's talking about dragons or dandelions, as long as she's talking. I wish someone would say that about me."

Did he keep her talking so he had to talk less himself? Was he afraid of giving something away? Ileth was sure she wasn't the only one who knew that trick. "I'm happy to listen to you, Taf."

"I mean a man, silly. Why, if some swain with Dandas's property spoke that way about me, well, they'd have to revive me with oiled salts."

"So he does have property."

"His family does, much more than our family. I'm sure if he asked for *my* hand Father would be beside himself."

"Has he asked about marrying Galia?"

"Not in so many words, no. Well, not in any words. But his interest is pronounced, and he certainly needs a wife. It's not like men are about to start having babies without us."

"If they can f-f-figure it out, they're welcome to it, for my share," Ileth said.

"You are a strange one, dear. Don't tell me you don't want babies."

"Never met anyone whose babies I'd like to have. I want a place in the world. Or above it."

"Do you Vale folk *always* make the simple so difficult? If you marry well, you do have a significant place in the world. Even if you just marry, well, it's still a place. You've clearly just not been around decent people enough. Oh, I don't want to argue. The music is starting again, and I rarely get a chance to let myself go. Come, let's dance."

The Tribals were early risers, even the morning after the dancing under the moon. They'd spent all night roasting a pig they'd purchased in the village, and Fespanarax ate it with gusto. The one dragon need they couldn't fill, however, was precious metal. They had some bits of scrap iron they gave him, but Fespanarax hated it. "It's eating to live," he said. "I'd rather live to eat."

Galia, in one of her now-rare sessions teaching Ileth the ins and outs of dragon care, showed that his scale was showing some signs of long-term metal deficit. A white chalky substance had formed at the outer edges of the scale. Galia used a thumbnail to scrape some off and showed it to Ileth.

"Scale rot," she said. "It's not bad. He's getting enough to get by. He could use a few months in the Serpentine eating ore. Or another charity gala where you swing your leg up and give all the significants a glimpse."

Ileth thought of throwing back a mildly obscene answer in the style of Zusya, who could match any of the Captain's roustabouts for ribald talk, but Galia was teaching her something for once. Best not to provoke her.

She took the matter up with the Baron. Summer was coming on more strongly than she'd ever experienced in the Vales, and the Baron was out with his daughters, helping set up netting that would shield the more delicate berry bushes from the worst of the sun so the berries would remain plump and sweet.

The Baron listened carefully to her suggestion. He didn't think another party to raise money would work, so soon after the last one.

"If you desire silver in quantities that would satisfy a dragon, there is a mine to the north. Two mines, one abandoned, and a much poorer one on a plateau that is difficult to get to. The Cowshead we call it, not sure why because I've never seen a resemblance."

"I should mine for it?"

"Oh, heavens no. I would think you commercial republicans would jump at a solution right away. There are hundreds of strong backs there digging away. But as I said, the plateau is high up, nearly a desert. They bring up corn and salted pork and such, but the miners have plenty of silver to trade for other things. I understand beer is very popular. Kegs are awkward to carry up a difficult trail. Bearers are often falling trying to get loads up to them. The trail can't even be walked by a donkey; there are too many places you take your load off and climb, then pull your burden up behind with ropes. If you could convince that dragon to carry some up, you could sell it for silver ore at a handsome profit. With summer they will want beer up there."

The Baron offered to set up the arrangement with the brewery on the Green River and pay the starting expenses, if Ileth could convince Fespanarax.

She decided to take it up with him after the Tribals had made a great to-do over him the night before, as it had been a full moon. Ileth and Taf had both discreetly danced as part of the party too.

Ileth was still nervous about approaching Fespanarax. He was so mercurial. Sometimes she could address him and he'd pretend she wasn't there. She missed the Lodger's easy, friendly manner. Imagine what she could have learned from him, with months to spend on a pleasant estate and little to do but talk.

She waited for an afternoon when he decided to cool himself with a dip in the duck pond. He emerged, dripping and covered with water plants that he mostly shook off, and accepted her offer to pull the rest where it was trapped in scale and horn. He remarked that the dip had done him some good; he felt so fresh he'd like to fly, but the Baron forbade it.

"I have an idea on how we can get you in the air and earn some silver for you to eat at the same time."

Fespanarax yawned. "I like the eating silver part. A flight would be a welcome relief from the boredom. *We* and *earn*, however, I'm not so keen about."

"You'd have to work, yes. I think the exercise would do us both good. You especially. You've been stuck on this estate for years."

"Five summer solstices and six winters, I think. I need to establish a calendar for myself. All over a human affair."

"It's not far. There'd be some flying in the mountains."

"Where, exactly?"

"By that volcano to the north. There are silver mines there." She explained the rest of the scheme to bring them kegs of beer.

"Hmmm. Fairly easy. The prevailing winds will be on my rear quarter, which will help a great deal if I'm flying with a load. Well, if you can arrange so nobody gets the wrong idea and starts shooting crossbows at me, we can try it. Let's hazard it and not think about the catgut."

The mental activity of the plans ended up doing Ileth and the dragon good. The Baron had to send letters to his "cousin" in the north who had the lands around the silver mines, which led to further complications involving that Baron, who had another one of those complicated Galantine titles that Ileth reduced to Blue Heron because that animal was named in one of the orders he belonged to and she found it easy to remember. Anyway, the Baron of the Blue Heron something-or-other thought if the dragon was bringing beer for the miners, he could also bring some spirits from a distillery on his own lands, with the dragon getting the same percentage of the sale that he received from Baron Hryasmess. Baron Blue Heron could send an agent to the plateau who would receive the shipments and pay out the dragon's share of silver. Baron Hryasmess, in turn, wanted to send his own agent to make sure everything was correctly recorded and fairly done, which led to an argument over letters with the Baron Blue Heron threatening to go to Court and get a royal warrant to have a King's commissioner sent to the plateau, until Ileth offered to copy all the tally sheets and verify them and let Baron Hryasmess inspect them himself. The Barons found that acceptable.

"It's not me, so much, it's the brewers," the Baron said. "They have to order smaller barrels than they are used to using, and the cooper is complaining to me that he needs a new guide for bending wood. At least Taf is being sweet about the streamers."

The streamers were in Chapalaine's own colors, turquoise and green, with a long white tail. They'd identify Fespanarax as being on the Baron's business, on the off chance they ran into one of the Galantine King's dragons.

In the midst of this activity Griff returned, still in his uniform, and did some riding about with Dandas but apparently had no other aim beyond enjoying summer weather and the Baron's cuisine. There were new icons on his collar and shoulder, and his coat seemed to be cut of a thicker material. Ileth wondered what he'd done to earn a promotion, or if the Galantine half of his family's money was buying him promotions. Galia had been making much about the fact that after his first commission, Dandas had never had to purchase higher rank in the Fencibles; he'd been promoted "on distinction," as they phrased it.

She spent extra time with Fespanarax, but like a spurned suitor, Griff either had lost interest or was good at pretending that he had.

In the midst of the beer-delivery negotiations, with the Baron riding his couriers hard, she and Galia received a packet of letters from the Serpentine. They'd been carefully opened and resealed by Galantine agents, she knew, as was their right for the correspondence of prisoners, and they contained nothing of importance beyond names of those at the Serpentine. Caseen joked that things were quiet without Ileth about and that he would soon be busy with a new batch of novices. Some books the Lodger had requested for Ileth had arrived and were waiting in the Serpentine's archives. Santeel wrote that her father was complaining about the bills for her flying leathers and dance costumes (he'd been under the impression that with his daughter installed at the Serpentine there would be a reduction in expenditures on her keep and had been proven wrong). Rapoto was now a wingman for Dath Amrits. Rapoto wrote a short, colorless letter saying that he thought of Ileth often, missed her dancing, and hoped she would be allowed to return soon, as it didn't seem fair that one Serpentine person in the form of Heem Zwollen had been replaced by two captives. Galia received a whole packet of letters from Yael Duskirk.

"Same old Serpentine," Galia said, having read the letters, leaving the Duskirk bundle unopened—at least while Ileth was with her. All but Duskirk's were addressed to both of them, after all. "A big crab pot with everyone scrabbling for position. The weather here is much nicer, don't you think?"

Ileth shrugged. "The sun gives me a head-headache when I'm out in it too much."

"I sit patiently through your stuttering, and when it's done it's usually a complaint," Galia said.

"Sorry," Ileth said. The letters would need answering and she'd have to beg the Baron for paper and ink.

At last, the day for the test run arrived. There was so much excitement that Fespanarax was going to fly, even Galia took an interest and made sure the dead dragoneer's saddle was still safe to use. It was.

The only landmark Ileth and Fespanarax needed to remember was a small plateau about halfway up to the main one, on a little saddle that joined the volcanic mountain to its eastern neighbor, which was this Cowshead plateau with the silver miners. She could just see the outline of it from the Baron's estate. There was a good road up to the saddle, built in the days of the thriving mine, and only a precarious trail up to the plateau after that. The saddle had a posthouse, red roofed and otherwise painted white as so many Galantine establishments were, a place where they'd once changed teams of horses bearing loads. It was the only spot near the mine where there was any sort of meadow, built up gradually over the years from horse droppings. An agent of Baron Blue Heron would meet them there with his cases of spirits, and up they'd go.

With Galia's assistance they'd managed to fix Fespanarax's saddle so it held two full kegs of beer under his chest, using netting reinforced by a pair of chains. Fespanarax, testing the weight, thought he could carry perhaps two more, but for the test run they limited it. Ileth would carry the spirits on the saddle behind her (with the proviso that Fespanarax had the last say on his flying burden). They hung a couple of goatskins of wine from the saddle as well. Apparently with a certain class of Galantine, wine fermented in the scraped-out-and-sealed skin of a goat was a traditional drink at celebrations.

Galia and Dandas wished her luck, jointly. Their couple-ish manner of speaking troubled her, but she was too busy to think much on it. Galia lent her an additional cloak, big enough for her to wrap herself up in if she had to spend the night atop the plateau. They were warned that it was chilly up there. The Tribe gave her a little good-luck charm, some semiprecious stones and an old silver coin with a hole punched in it and a small feather from a bird she didn't know threaded onto a loop that went around her ear. It felt odd at first, but she wore it. She'd learned the value of a little luck.

"Here I go," Fespanarax said to Ileth, as he put himself in what he judged the best spot for his takeoff. Fespanarax wasn't the kind of dragon to say *we*. "You do all the talking, I do all the flying, and the silver is mine. Right?"

"Right," Ileth said. "Minus expenses. I receive only the pleasure of it." The dragon eventually understood that they'd have to give most of the silver to the Barons and the brewer, but he could look at all the expenses written down on paper.

Fespanarax, who had been doing circuits over Chapalaine to reawaken his flying muscles so often that the village kids no longer ran all the way to the gates of Chapalaine to see him, did a running takeoff into the wind, then turned for the saddle between the volcano and the plateau.

He was fast. Nearly as fast as Vithleen, it seemed to Ileth, though she didn't have much experience at flying dragons, even with his load. Maybe they all flew at about the same speed, though the dragoneers didn't talk that way in their chats about speed against thickness of scale or strength climbing or ability to carry an awkward load.

The volcano drew her interest and occupied her mind as they approached. It steamed, but the prevailing winds carried the vapors off to the northeast, over Baron Blue Heron's lands. There didn't seem to be much in the way of planted fields near the volcano, and she soon saw why—there were ash clouds falling. The volcano gave off a steady series of belches and tossed about rocks now and then—she could see one now, rolling down an ashy slope, sending smaller rocks on its journey with it.

"Tricky things," Fespanarax said. "Don't believe the legends about dragons being born from them. I'd just as soon stay well away."

He added a name in Drakine that she knew to be a place. Ileth had never heard any of those legends, of volcanoes giving birth to dragons or this other unknown word that gave birth to it. Which gave her a thought.

Their first stop was an old posthouse.

The posthouse was in disrepair—part of the roof had fallen in and there were cracks everywhere in the masonry. It looked like there had once been constant repairs to it, but now they left well enough alone.

The Baron Blue Heron's man met them. He had two cases of ceramic jugs with stoppers and wax seals. Ileth helped him tie the ardent spirits behind her saddle. There did seem to be some kind of diggings at the volcano.

"They look for ore with silver that others have missed," the agent told her when she asked. "It is not as futile as you think. There are often quakes. Sometimes silver nuggets even turn up. There are silver veins all through these mountains, but mining is hard because of the earthquakes."

Ileth asked him about the miners on the plateau. He said they found silver at a slow but steady rate. Few got rich quickly.

"But once or twice a month, there is a big silver find. A few times a year, someone becomes rich and returns home to buy land or a business or found a mine elsewhere—that hope keeps them up on that hell-in-the-sky."

While she made to remount, Fespanarax was lively and talkative in anticipation of some delicious silver, so she decided to ask him.

"Now that . . . now that I'm thinking of it, Fespanarax, what does *vhanesh luss* mean?"

She had to repeat it twice more, her pronunciation of Old Drakine was so bad.

"If I'm hearing you correctly, which I'm not sure of, it means *more sun*. *More light* might be the closer meaning in Montangyan. Where did you pick up Old Drakine?"

"Can't remember, quite," Ileth said. "In the Serpentine, anyway."

"Well, I hardly expected you to hear it in whatever kennel bred you."

"Ah. Well, let's go seek some more light. The kind that shines off silver." Fespanarax was so pleased with that he let out a *prrrum* like a gigantic cat. Then it was up to the plateau.

Ileth didn't know what she expected to find, but the mining colony reminded her more of a giant colony of scattered gopher or rabbit holes, with bits of canvas stretched to shelter those who set up housekeeping just outside their holes. Not much would grow, as it was cold and dry. Her improved-by-reading vocabulary settled on *desolate*.

There were perhaps two hundred miners, she guessed, and an indeterminate number of women and children, dwelling among their holes and rain-catchers. According to the agent at the old posthouse, the women allowed life to exist on the plateau. They would make the day-long trek to a market some distance below (on the Baron's side of the mountains, as it was considered more safe from the volcano), spend the night there, and bear a week's worth of supplies back up, plus a little charcoal and whatever else might be most needed. They worked out schedules and rotations and somehow scraped out an existence. It seemed bleak to Ileth, but the children played happily enough among the piles of tailings and she heard laughter and songs from the women.

The dragon made a stir. Children who'd been digging with broken bits of tool jumped up, left their works, and came to see Fespanarax land.

It was unusual to see so many bearded Galantines in a land where the men were generally clean-shaven or wore artfully trimmed mustaches. Then the wind hit her face as she came around the dragon's side.

They had been right. It was cold up here. Ileth wondered how the Galantines stood it. None of them were dressed in anything like her riding rig, mostly rough vests and cylindrical wool hats with flaps that came down over the ears.

They met a big man in an apron who also wore a Galantine-style collar under his fleshy jowls. She'd been told he was the Tentkeeper and would take the beer delivery and give the agreed-upon silver, if the count was correct. He and a pair of associates carefully removed the kegs, spirits, and sloshing goatskins and placed them where Fespanarax could keep an eye on them.

The Tentkeeper tapped the beer barrels suspiciously and inspected the seals on the bottles. He stuck a reed through the main stitched closure on one of the goatskins and sucked out some wine. He smiled as if at an old memory and tied off the opening he'd just made. Only then did he hand over two rags tied with a broken old bootlace. One was much heavier than the other.

"Big for you. Small is cut for the Baron's Tightneck waiting down below," the Tentkeeper said. "Understand?"

Ileth nodded. She let Fespanarax sniff at the silver. When he was satisfied and his mouth was running with thick, clear liquid, she stepped to the saddle.

"Ready to return?" Ileth asked the dragon, back in the saddle with her safety lanyard on.

"What, and leave this garden-spot of the Baronies?"

The dragon trundled over to the edge of the cliff. A dragon's steady gait ate up a fair amount of distance in a few moments. No wonder the Auxiliaries would gladly use a grounded dragon. Fespanarax didn't even bother to ask her if she was ready when he jumped off the cliff.

Just to add to her thrill, he only opened his wings when they were three quarters of the way to an end upon the rocks at the base of the cliff. He whipped around and, still using the momentum of the dive, rode cliffside air currents toward the old posthouse.

"Feels good to be rid of those barrels!" the dragon called back to her. He came in for a neat landing in the field. The agent stood up from where he had been reclining on an old bench and hurried over.

"That was quick. That journey would take a strong man much of the day, up and down, with a tenth part of the load."

Ileth handed over the smaller of the two pouches, as instructed. The agent tossed it in his hand speculatively, then concealed it in his undercoat.

Airborne again, and homeward bound with their silver.

"How much of that is mine?" Fespanarax asked in Montangyan.

"Our sh-share," Ileth replied, "is about—about a third. To your health, Fespanarax."

"That's hardly a mouthful."

"Well, you had some exercise, managed to leave the confines of Chapalaine, sharpened your wits on me, and have some silver. I'd say you came out well ahead on the b-bargain."

A dizzying distance below, the Baron's Green River began its journey to his lands. No wonder growth along its banks was so rich; it carried rich volcanic soil downstream.

They were back at Chapalaine in time for Ileth to interrupt a tea. Galia and Dandas, with Taf there as a chaperone, were all enjoying some of her small store.

"Just help yourselves," Ileth said. "Taf, is your father at home? I have something I must give him."

"Oh, he's about," Taf said. "I know he walked out twice to see if he could see your return. I think he suddenly grew afraid you'd just fly off."

"Ileth only embarrasses her friends; she doesn't desert them," Galia said.

"That is unkind!" Dandas said, shooting Galia an accusing look. "We have poached your tea, Ileth of the Serpentine, but I've ordered a quarter-chest of the stuff for my cousin here and I shall restore the portion."

"It's . . . just tea, sir," Ileth said.

"I've heard you republicans were . . . ahem . . . reluctant and judicious in your hospitality. I don't want you to think I'm trying to steal anything away from you."

The Galantine summer, all sun, stillness, and heat, came on in full. Whenever she and Galia said anything about the heat, the Baron's family said that their guests didn't know heat—the true heat was on the coast to the south, or in the islands. That was their response to most conversations about the weather—it was always worse somewhere else. To hear them talk, the Vales were a frozen wasteland of snowy mountain passes and avalanches.

Ileth continued flying beer to the plateau. As the summer baked on, they developed a system where they went once every six days. The one change to the system that had been developed by the Baron and his cousin in the north was that Fespanarax never had to fly empty kegs back. Wood was so scarce up there, it was used for shoring in the mining tunnels or turned into cooking charcoal. The Tentkeeper paid them for the barrels instead, and the Baron allocated the precisely weighted silver nuggets and dust to the cooper and the brewer in the village, who were enormously satisfied with the increased business.

The Tribe stayed in residence, grooming Fespanarax, with extra attentions on his flight days. Now and then one or two of them disappeared into town or left with a cart on one of their mysterious journeys, selling the potions and medications cast off by the dragon. Ileth thought it was profiting off superstition, but Fespanarax said there could be something to it, as in his father's time dragon blood was still being drunk by people—with appalling results to humans or animals who made it a long practice. Fespanarax, more conversational now that he was eating silver every week, told her what he'd seen with his own eyes: jungle jaguars transformed into terrible striped creatures twice their usual size with a great round face gone white. They were set up in the Realm of a Thousand Princes (wherever that was) as holy temple guardians. Some escaped, and they appeared to be thriving.

From just about any other dragon she would have assumed she was being teased, but Fespanarax cared so little for what she or any other human thought of him, she decided it must be true.

"What happens to humans who drink dragon blood?"

"The first time, very little, except excellent health and vigor. That's all, if you have it only once every few years. How long do humans live again? The ones I know all die young. Sixty or seventy years? Then say six or seven times over the course of your life. Insofar as I know in the Serpentine, they would have you drink it when you became a dragoneer, but I'm unsure if that tradition continues. I haven't asked lately. If you drink it more than that—you don't want to know."

Even as Fespanarax grew more social, Ileth began to have doubts about the deliveries. The miners and their families lived in holes, their children went barefoot on a chilly plateau, everyone's ribs were showing, and she was flying in not plump chickens or sides of pork but beer and spirits.

"If they would pay for pork pies for what they pay for drink, I would have you fly in pork pies," the Tentkeeper said, who was now looking like someone was, in fact, flying in pork pies. Although she knew a great deal of beer could also fatten you, pigs in the Freesand were fed on the tailings from brewers and thrived on it. "It makes no difference to me. Beer and spirits are what they are willing to give over their silver for, so that is what I sell them."

Ileth still felt a little guilty. Perhaps she could bring in some sugar candy for the children.

The Tentkeeper must have caught her smiling at the thought. "While I am on the subject of what they will pay money for, I have an offer for you."

Ileth went suddenly wary. "Oh?" she said.

"I know you are a dancer. A good one, who performs for audiences. Audiences who pay."

"Who told you that?"

"Your dragon."

"I've never seen you talk to him!"

"It was two runs ago. You had to—the necessity."

"Ah, yes." There were filthy holes scattered about for such purposes. Perhaps, in time, the collective waste of the miners would build up the soil enough on the plateau for a few crops to grow.

"How does this concern him?"

"Oh, we were talking as men do. I swear he is not—you know what I mean to say. What do men ever talk about? Women! There aren't enough up here. So he told me of your dancing and the bucket full of silver *vits* you earned."

"I only dance for audiences of dragons."

"Well, your dragon said otherwise. Take it up with him. When he told me you do it nearly naked, and with your youth and figure, I knew that you could make some extra silver. Not a great deal, but you never know. If it doesn't work out, forget it ever happened. But if it does, you may buy yourself a new, modest dress to impress the Tightnecks. You need not be afraid. The dragon said he would be there."

"Did he?" Ileth wondered if a dragon would feel a slap.

Ileth was in a foul mood the entire return trip. The dragon was already eating all the silver. She was flying for the exercise and the joy of it, so she didn't mind, but for him to want to increase his haul by—well, it was a good thing he was a dragon with a thick hide.

Her mood, only somewhat mellowed by the free air and sunshine of the flight back, did not improve when she returned. The Baron waited for her.

As usual he ignored the purse for the moment. He had to take care of the courtesies before matters as distasteful as counting out coins could be addressed.

"I have some news for you, Ileth. I'm not sure if you will take it as good or bad."

"More problems with the . . with the negotiations?"

"No, they are to return to the table this autumn. I expect the matter will be swiftly concluded now. This has to do with our arrangements. I want you to hear it from me rather than at the inn so you understand: I had to send the brewer's son off to the islands, convicted and sentenced."

"You were right. I'm . . . I'm not sure I understand," Ileth said.

"You know, the brewer has been cheating me this whole time. I only found out because I was talking to the cooper about making barrels more cylindrical along the lines Fespanarax suggested. He showed me what it would cost, and I happened to see what he was charging the brewer for each cask. Something looked wrong about his figures. Well, the brewer has been doubling that in his accounts to me!"

"What—the brewer's son was taking the difference?"

"No, the brewer. But I couldn't send him to the islands, could I? Have the village inn, and our little concern, lose its source of ale? No, under Galantine law I am allowed to scapegoat—are you familiar with that concept?—a close family member for bloodless crimes. Hard for the son, but it's not my fault I was being cheated. I'm glad you wouldn't do anything like that, would you, Ileth? You're not protected by our excellent Galantine law, just military custom and my own sense of hospitality. Though I do feel your Vales have cheated me a bit; I had the distinguished Heem Zwollen, and after he died they replaced him with someone who's just a Dun, then I got these two girls for him, and now it's just you. Not your fault, but you Vale folk deal sharp, if you'll forgive me for saying so. I shouldn't wonder wars start all the time."

"What d-do you mean, now it's just . . . it's just me?"

"Galia has departed. She left you this note and asked me to give it to you. I hope you don't find it too upsetting. Please let me know if there is any way I might soften this distressing turn of events for you. Perhaps some brandy before you read it?"

Ileth fled from him, sought refuge in what had been "their" house, now quiet, so quiet, lit a candle, and tore open the fine cotton-paper envelope. The seal spun off into the darkness.

Oddly, it was in Galantine, though in Galia's own beautiful hand. Ileth wondered if Galia had consulted with Dandas on the message it contained. She had to hold it close to the light to read.

Ileth,

I must leave you with a note. A good-bye would be painful and today is no day for pain. Dandas has asked me to be his wife and I have said yes. We will depart Chapalaine at once.

I know I'm leaving you and our people behind in doing this, for we must build a life here. Do not fear for me. He is an excellent man and there is nothing to hold me in the Vales but the Serpentine. You may think that I'm deserting you to live a life of luxury, but it won't be like that at all. Dandas goes to an important new command, and it shall be a camp life for a while until we can find somewhere a person of his significance can take as a house for me. It will be a great adventure, but what better time to go on a great adventure than when you are in your bloom and with a man you love?

Oh, my friend, I have treated you badly since Dandas arrived and I realized I have feelings for him. I'm no philosopher, but I believe I struggled with myself and treated you as the part of me that wanted to be at the Serpentine and fly and believe all the egalitarian nonsense that's wrecking our land and causing us to lose wars. I do not know yet what fate will decide for me, but I think it has matched me with a man who will take me there with the wit and wisdom and manner I've come to appreciate this last beautiful summer of my youth and girlish silliness. As the Galantine High Church says, there is a time for everything, the seasons of life begin and end, and we must accept that. This part of my life is at an end.

If someday, when you return to the Serpentine, as I hope you will soon, take with you my hopes for you to pair with an excellent dragon and rise to be a dragoneer as great as your Annis. Should Hael Dun

Huss ask after me, tell him I finally decided to be something more—a Baroness.

> *I sign my name, for the last time,*
> *Galia of the Serpentine*

Young Azal and Taf knocked quietly, Azal looking discreetly away as if he expected to find Ileth in rent garments wet with tears. Taf set down a tray with her dinner and a small decanter of the syrupy Galantine brandy considered fit for ladies. Taf offered to keep her company, but Ileth dismissed her.

She opened the door again to thank them but closed it again halfway through the Galantine courtesies, rereading the letter.

Alone. She thought back on all the times in the Captain's Lodge that she'd longed to have a warm little house, all to herself, only her own dishes and washing to do.

She opened the brandy, sniffed it. "To love and havoc," she said, raising the decanter and putting it to her mouth. She made it through only a third before bringing it back up.

15

The wedding would take place in the late fall. Ileth, perforce, could not attend, as she had neither the freedom nor the money to travel. And in any case, she hadn't been invited. She doubted it was a deliberate snub, especially after rereading the letter. Galia knew her restrictions (Galia's own were lifted with her betrothal and assumption of Galantine citizenship and entry into the Galantine King's church).

She missed Galia's presence, keenly, and would have had her back, even the moments when they frayed each other's nerves down to the last thread, if it had been within her power. She left a lonely ache that was hard to fill.

She did try to fill it. Galantine literature; volunteering to do little tasks for the Baroness, whose increase at the waist meant a decrease in how much she could do for her family; even working on her flying rig. The runs with Fespanarax gave her hours of experience in the air learning the shortcomings of her flying attire. Taf showed a surprising interest in and flair for helping her solve the issues.

Taf being Taf, she couldn't stop talking about the wedding. Her father would take her and her brother Azal to the Court Exalted at Dymarids. Galia would wear Chapalaine's colors at the ceremony. She and Azal would be presented to the King! Unless he was indisposed that day, in which case she would bow to his royal representative. One day they were in the little, now roomy and quiet, house, and working in the warm room, which Ileth had turned into a flight suit workshop, when

Taf quit talking about the upcoming wedding and asked about how the Serpentine taught one to fly.

Ileth told her the truth that she hadn't had that much formal training yet, just a good deal of informal experience.

"I wonder if I could fly on a dragon. I think I could. You seem to do all right even though you're a woman and haven't gone through all that training."

Ileth asked how so.

"It would be easy, like my trick with the Tribals when I dance with them. Put on your clothing—our builds aren't that different now that you're getting good Galantine food instead of sheep tripe and sturgeon—wind a scarf around my face, and get on the dragon. He does all the work, yes?"

"All I do is hang on," Ileth admitted.

It remained just idle talk, however. But Ileth's flying rig improved in fit, if not in style (Ileth did not take any of Taf's suggestions for adding a bit of Galantine "dash" to the ensemble).

The summer heat waxed and waned but mostly waxed. The Baron and his neighbors ceased all pretense of work and spent the hottest part of the year hiding from the heat during the day (if there was not a picnic or a barbecue on the schedule) and going around to outdoor dinners at night. Even the Tribals briefly joined the community when they invited the Baron's coterie to a performance in the little outdoor theater. Both Ileth and Taf danced with them, Taf incognito, Ileth in a patchwork blend of her own dancing sheath and a Tribal dancing skirt.

But just when Ileth was feeling well disposed to Galantine society, they would do something she found appalling. They had a custom of calling a "horn hunt" where a single rider would pick a spot in the countryside and blow a horn from somewhere secretive until he could hear the sound of hoofbeats. Then he would ride off to a different spot and blow the horn again. Ileth saw the damage wrought from the back of Fespanarax. Crops about to be harvested were flattened, overdry grazing round was torn up by hooves, vegetable gardens were trampled, and even laundry drying on the line was knocked off and trod upon if the course of the chase took them through a gap between the dwellings of the nonsignificants.

On another one of her visits, she saw a criminal's body hung up on display at the edge of town. The Baron explained that he was a vagrant who broke into a house and stole food. "Long ago the body would be coated in pitch and left to rot," the Baron told her on their way to the brewery to try a new summer ale he was testing. "Now we just leave it up three days. I think anything longer than that is unhealthy, don't you? I mean, there are children in the village."

After seeing the body, she avoided the Baron and his family. She simply said she wasn't feeling well and excused herself from all social activity with the family. Galantine tradition accepted any failing in the health of women as sacrosanct, so she wasn't questioned, though Taf discreetly hinted that if she needed a draft to help with cramps, there was a reliable remedy from the family physician kept constantly in stock.

Her absence from the family turned out to be fortuitous. The Baroness gave birth at last, and the child, a son, had the house in a flurry. She sensed, through Azal and his deliveries, that though the child was healthy, something was odd about him, but since they allowed her privacy, she didn't press the matter.

In the morning two days after the long-awaited birth, the Baron himself came to visit as she sat in the garden reading after her morning drill and check on Fespanarax. The rat was out of his wig and riding on his shoulder for a change.

"Ileth, my dear, how are you feeling?" he asked.

"Much better, sir. How is the Baroness?"

"Robust as always. Nursing. She doesn't believe in wet nurses for the first three months of life, and I rather think she's right about it, but it exhausts her. She is keeping to the birthing room."

Ileth was sensitive enough toward Galantine custom to know not to inquire after the newborn, as she wasn't family.

"I was hoping I could get you to come into the house today. I have a visitor who wishes to speak to you. No, it's not Galia or any of your countrymen, I'm sorry to say. It's that Young Ransanse."

Griff! What could he want?

"I'm—I'm at a . . . at a loss as to why he would wish to speak to me."

"He said he wished to offer an apology."

She started to say that Griff could take his apologies, roll them up, enclose them in a map tube, and . . . but it wouldn't do to use that kind of language in the Baron's gardens.

"Sir, just send him out here."

"Ileth, I'll confess, I don't much care for this young man. He's the sort of grasper we have too much of at Court these days, no refinement or sense of duty to the common people, but I'll allow that I could be wrong about him. If he does offer an insult to you, a girl of your age, in my house, under my roof, well, there are certain nuances to Galantine social life that could ruin him, at least in the eyes of the Baron Ransanse. Just because he is in line to inherit doesn't mean that matters couldn't be changed. I intend to have him speak to you in the library. I shall retreat to my study, which is connected by sliding doors. My two biggest servants, the ones my wife charges with moving furniture about and hanging sides of beef, will be outside the door. Either one is capable of launching Young Ransanse over the estate wall by himself; together they could throw him into the next Barony, I imagine. So you need not fear for your physical safety."

Ileth agreed, mostly because the picture of Griff being sent flying without benefit of dragon appealed. She changed into her more presentable housedress but made no attempt to do anything else with her appearance for the interview. Her hair could remain in its sweated dance-bun.

She followed the Baron into the house and to his library at the far end of the Baron's family wing. As the Baron had promised, two enormous footmen in work vests and loose, long-sleeve shirts sat on a wooden bench in the hall. They stood up and took position to either side of the double library doors, now closed. Either one looked a match for even so tall a dragoneer as the Borderlander, never mind a not-yet-twenty boy such as Griff. Their thick arms and wide shoulders were reassuring.

The library itself had tall windows of many panes of good glass. You could see right through them and out into the front grounds. There weren't many books, just one case, glassed off, and a map table with several wide drawers beneath. The few books that were in the case looked to be very expensive. Ileth had been in the house's sewing room and writing room, and each of those had many more books than the library, though they were cheaper volumes meant for leisurely reading.

Someone had set two nice, round-backed chairs in the center of the room, facing each other.

Griff was still in that light-blue uniform. He had immaculate white breeches this time, tucked into gleaming black boots. Other than that, he was the same old chap-lipped Griff, though his hair looked better cared for and his skin healthier.

"Young Ransanse, here is my Ileth," the Baron said, before retreating toward his desk in his study at the corner of the house. "Remember your promise, now."

"Sir," Griff said, standing at attention. "Ileth," he added, giving her a short bow.

The Baron personally closed the two sliding doors to the well-lit little nook, and the muscular servants closed the double library doors.

Ileth wasn't sure of Galantine custom, so she remained standing opposite him. He wasn't his usual sneering, shifty self. He looked as though he'd taken great care of his appearance for this interview.

"It is customary for ladies to sit," Griff offered. "I'd like this to be a friendly call."

Ileth thought it over and sat in one of the two chairs at the center. Once she was comfortably seated, hands in her lap, Griff sat down opposite. He put his hands on his knees and leaned toward her a little.

"How are you getting on without Galia?" he asked, speaking Montangyan.

"Well enough, thank you."

"Is the dragon giving you difficulty?"

"None," she said.

"Ileth, we got off to two bad starts, one back in the Uplands, one here. For my part, I'm sorry."

"F-For my part, I can't imagine why you came all this way again to tell me so."

"Because I believe I can make it up to you. I was a foolish boy back in the Serpentine. I've grown up since I knew you there."

"I am happy to hear it."

"You see, I'm not such a bad sort to get along with, given a chance."

Ileth, half-revolted, half-interested to see where this was heading, shrugged. It seemed an especially inappropriate gesture for this sunny room full of expensive books, but it kept her from having to talk.

"Ileth, I know certain things. You would do well to follow Galia's path and associate yourself with the Galantines. The Republic's doomed. Financial trouble, society's a mess, just lost a war, and with one wrong step they'll get into a bigger one they'll also lose. I don't mean to be harsh, but you've hitched your cart to a sick horse, as they say."

"We still have the dragons," Ileth said.

Griff lowered his voice. "The Galantines have dragons too. I've seen them. Indeed, I'm playing an increasingly important role with them. You could too, a far more important role than you ever could at the Serpentine. I heard the apprentices and wingmen talk about you. They think you're entertaining but not destined to do much before you're tossed out on your ear like most female novices. I know you've got your name in blue ink in Caseen's office."

"So what if I, if I do?"

"I made a change for the better. Galia did. You could too."

If the Galantines did want her to come over from the Serpentine and take up a new nationality, they chose a poor agent to make the offer. But then Ileth had been specifically charged to learn what she could here, keep her eyes and ears open. "I'm—I'm listening."

She concentrated, attempting to remember every word of this conversation. Griff might let something valuable slip. He'd been sloppy before.

"Ileth, you have an advantage over even Galia, beyond anything she can dream about. Some of us young Barons spent some fifteen days at the King's residence, invited for riding, birding, a formal ball, that sort of thing. I saw the King's gallery. There's a private room where ladies aren't invited. You know he has some studies of dragon dancers? Four paintings by Risso Heem Tyr himself, do you know who he is?"

Ileth nodded.

"You would be a sensation at Court. I could get you an audience with the King. You'd barely have to speak. Galantine women say 'yes, thank you' and 'thank you, but no,' and list the number and gender of their children. You could get posted to the dragons, not in uniform, but in a similar role to Ottavia. Form your own troupe. They've tried bringing Galantine women around the dragons and they about die of fright. They're no good at all because of the way they've been raised. Those Tribals, we don't trust them; they're not even Galantines. You speak it, look it; sometimes I wonder"—he lowered his voice even further—"well, I don't know enough about the Directist purges but we may have to be careful if they ask about your family background. Your name's a bit of an obstacle, but it's out of living memory now about."

Griff slid to the edge of his chair. "If you would join my fliers I can guarantee you a title as lady. A property—not a big one, but it would be all yours. You would see Galia again."

"I would like . . . that, but I've . . . but I've reconciled myself to never seeing her again."

"You can do better, much better, with me. That man of hers, he's with the Squadron, in a way. He's a good man, doing his duty to his king, but"—Griff spread his hands—"no ambition. I shall rise."

"It's . . . it's good to have—to have ambition. How high does yours go?"

"I have learned something since coming here. Every time I think I have gone too far, I find I can go further."

He reached across the space between them, then took her hands in his.

"We could go further still together."

"The two of us?"

"Three. With Fespanarax. I've spoken to him, and he's agreed to come over to our side. It would be a brilliant coup for us."

There it was again. *Our. Us.* Did he mean the Galantine nation, or Griff and Ileth?

His hands felt strong. But not so strong she couldn't grab them and fall to the floor, pulling him on top of her, and yell for all she was worth. The Baron might have been hinting to her that she should do that exact thing. Griff would fall just as quickly as he'd risen in the Galantine lands.

No. Even if Griff was an enemy of the Serpentine now, even if she disliked him, even if he'd called her a jade or worse, she wouldn't resort to *that*.

"Fespanarax will leave the Serpentine?"

Griff stared at her hands in his. "You know him."

She withdrew from his touch. "I do. I am . . . I am surprised he's throwing over his friends for . . . for Galantine silver."

"You know dragons. One bunch of humans is much like another to a dragon. The Galantines can give him gold and silver instead of waste ores, beef and pigs instead of fish."

"For me?"

"Gowns instead of sacking overdresses. Shoes instead of slippers. Servants instead of duties. Featherbeds instead of mats. A great house instead of a shaft."

"As your wife, I suppose."

Griff raised his eyebrows. "So you do think of such things."

Ileth shrugged. "I just believe that before coming to an agreement, you see . . . you see all the terms laid out plain."

"Marriage. Not right at first. All I propose is an alliance between us. I will introduce you at Court. Get you a role with the Squadrons at the Trifall."

Trifall. Trifall. Trifall. She'd never heard of the place. Three falls?

"That sounds pretty. Three waterfalls?"

"It's lovely. Two of the waterfalls are beautiful. The third fall isn't much, but there is a pool beneath it that is excellent for swimming in the summers."

"I should like that. The summer heat gets to me."

"The Court Exalted is on a low plateau. It's even more pleasant in the summer. Chapalaine here is in the wallows. But I didn't come here to talk geography, I came here to get you out of that grotty little hole and put you on my arm at the most glittering court in the world. What do you say?"

She thought of Ottavia's talk about how young noblemen liked to have a dancer on their arm as a sort of ornament.

"It is too much to think about now. I have certain commitments to the Baron."

"Your silly beer barrels? I will not repeat this offer again after this interview. Rise with me or fall with your Republic."

She was tired of probing him. He wasn't giving anything else away, not without much more from her—and she was in no mood to give him anything but spittle.

"It's your Republic too, Griff. You have family there."

"They will be taken care of. It's why the family divided to begin with. The Republic would prosper, and the family with it, or fall, and the rest of the family would be there to pick up the pieces. My family plans for eventualities."

"What is your eventuality for me refusing you?"

He stood at her question.

"I appreciate your offering to put the past behind. I took an oath that gave the Serpentine everything but my honor. Both my honor and my oath make agreeing to your offer of an alliance impossible. Last year I took you for a villain, when you were just a boy who—"

"You've been in the Galantine lands long enough to know that a young lady doesn't lecture her superiors."

He let that sink in, then continued, ice in his words. "I thought that despite your tongue you were clever, quite clever. That scheme I had with the scale, you sniffed it out, turned me in, and attracted the notice of the Masters. Brilliantly played. There are women at Court with twice your years who couldn't anticipate and adjust all the angles you did. I thought, once I placed what I have in mind before you, you'd be smart enough to agree at once. I am sorry to be mistaken."

Apparently he'd finished.

"Aren't you going to . . . threaten me or something?"

"Would it change your mind? Ease your conscience? Then I'd be happy to. We're not on some stage acting out a drama for shopkeepers.

I made you an offer. You declined. We are finished. I hope you will accept that I alone, out of all those you've met since you came to the Serpentine, am the only one who discerned your talents. I wanted to give you the opportunity to make the fullest use of them. When the wheel of fortune begins to turn and crush, as it inevitably will if you return to the Republic, and you find yourself dirty and hungry again, I hope you do not lose yourself in regret. When it all comes down, mention my name and I'll see that you at least have bread in your stomach, Ileth. You still have my esteem, even if we shan't have an alliance."

With that, he left the interview. Ileth sat in the chair, listening to footsteps, and didn't rise until she saw him leaving the house and mounting his horse.

The Baron appeared and asked if she was all right, whether she needed some tea or perhaps even a little brandy to recover from the encounter, but Ileth made her excuses. She hurried to Fespanarax. She found him idly gnawing on a steer's head.

"Sir," Ileth said. "I just had an interview with Gr—Young Ransanse, of the Dragon Squadron or whatever they call it. It astonished me."

"I should think if I were astonished I'd sit down a bit until the sensation passed, rather than go bother a dragon enjoying his digestive bones."

"He insulted you, sir."

"The birds insult me every morning with their chatter. At least that grasper had the courtesy to do it out of my hearing."

"Aren't you curious?"

"Just tell me and get it over with, girl."

"He said you were—you were leaving the Serpentine and going over to the Galantines."

"Then by your account he insulted us both, because he told me the same thing this very morning. As though that would convince me to fly for these peacocks."

"Then you —"

"Girl, I'm ready to quit your bunch and your filthy little wars entirely. I'm finding I care less and less about them as they wheeze up and sputter off over and over again. That fellow was just playing the old game, telling each party to an agreement that the other had already gone along with it."

"So you refused him?" She took a certain satisfaction in knowing that she and Fespanarax the Reckless had acted alike.

"The Galantines are poor managers of dragons. They think we're big armored horses. I talked to one of their dragons once. Stupid fellow."

"I'm glad to hear it, sir. I'll let you finish your bones." She started to withdraw, but the dragon spoke again.

"One more thing, girl, in the interest of you enjoying a future. Suppose I had gone over to the Galantines and you found me out. Rushing right off to tell me about your discovery is not the wisest move. I might decide to burn the evidence of my guilt."

"Burn me, you mean," Ileth said.

"I don't see anything much stopping me."

"If your honor isn't eno-enough, then I would think such a scoundrel would be worried about the questions that would come. Your dragoneer is dead, Galia has gone over to the Galantines, and your fifteen-year-old dancer burned. One might call that a pattern."

The dragon glanced sharply at her.

"Well, such a scoundrel, as you put it, would be playing a deep game indeed. I'm sure he could explain away another death easily enough."

For some reason this speech frightened Ileth more than talk of setting her alight.

"Calm yourself, girl. I can't say I'm fond of you, but I'm now enough used to you that having you replaced would be more annoyance than it's worth. Same with going over to the Galantines. For a start, I'd have to learn another yapping little human tongue. I don't want to bother with more than a few words of any more human languages if it can be helped."

Galia's wedding took place in due order, once the heat broke and people felt like moving about again, but before the fall rains became more than a nuisance.

Upon Taf and Azal's return from the wedding, Taf did most of the talking. She invited Ileth to join the other older daughters and nieces to hear the events of the day.

It took some telling. Significant Galantines have not one but three weddings: a religious one so that the High Church can sanctify the couple; a Court wedding where they are presented to the King or his chosen representative (in Galia and Dandas's case, it was a representative), who asks them if they wish to be married and then gives his permission; and finally a family function where representatives of both sides come together and arrange matters of presents, residence, presentation of first servants, and so on. The exact order for the three could vary.

"I was only at the family one, though I did wait outside for the Court one; only Father was allowed into Court," Taf said. "The family one was a little strange. Father and Azal and I served as her family. The Dandas side did not send many either—I don't know if they disapprove of Dandas marrying outside the King's lands, perhaps? As for the Court, they had to wait behind three other couples, and ahead of only one, the last being an old man who was marrying the daughter of his steward so the steward could assume his assets. He must have been a decent man. Right afterward he took poison and just fell asleep, they tell me. Very decent man. Went with a smile on his face—his teeth were blue but he couldn't help that, could he? As for the church one, it took a great deal of time because Galia had to enter the church and go through volitions and all that. It was the longest of the three, so naturally it was closed to the public. But I did see a great deal of interesting sights outside Court while Azal and I waited."

This led to a long discussion of the latest styles of dress and carriage. Ileth had her mind on poisons and only half listened, even when Azal spoke up with an experience of his own, until she heard that a young as-yet-unwinged dragon drew their wedding carriage after the church service, which was left to last because they were unsure as to how long it would take. She assumed it was one of the few Galantine dragons. Nice tribute to Galia, if that was what it was, but she wondered at a dragon being tasked to pull a carriage. She couldn't imagine any of the Serpentine's dragons doing it, unless perhaps as a special and spectacular favor for a beloved dragoneer.

After the three weddings there was a party at the Dandas family residence at the Eternal Court's home city of Dymarids.

"It wasn't well attended. I was more than a little disappointed. You'd think with our dear Dandas, a man of great significance at Court, more would have been there. Do you think it's because Galia is from the Vales? Maybe it's because they expect another war."

"Another war?" Ileth asked. Azal turned from the water table—he'd been complaining of a headache from the journey and seemed to be undergoing some kind of spasm.

"Yes, I heard Dandas's father—or was it his uncle?—saying that they just needed a provocation and the Court would rally and convince the King." Azal's glass shattered on the floor, but Taf didn't seem to notice; children were always breaking things at the Baron's.

Taf continued, "The King, apparently, said he's sick of throwing men into the mountains and never having them come back, all over something that happened before he was born. Baroness Sefeth herself told me that. I shouldn't worry, Ileth, you'll be quite safe here. I asked Father and he—"

Taf looked at her brother and her face went blank. Azal had his face in both his hands.

Ileth pretended she wasn't the least disturbed. "What did your father say?"

Taf's mouth worked like that of a landed fish: "That. That—"

"That there probably won't be a war, so why worry," Azal supplied.

There wasn't a war. Nor did peace come. The Baron's prediction of a quick consummation of negotiations proved to be wishful thinking, or a white lie to get Ileth through the difficult period of Galia's loss.

It seemed too much like captivity with Galia gone.

She could still escape into the air on Fespanarax, on the beer flights that made everyone but Ileth so much richer (well, the brewer wasn't quite so much richer and was down one son banished to some kind of labor on an island). The dreary conditions of the miners and especially the children continued to depress Ileth. She asked the Baron Blue Heron's agent why the landlord didn't improve things for his miners.

"On a map, yes, it's his land, but they pay him no rents. As this station shows, once upon a time, before the Cracked Cauldron woke up, his father kept the roads and mine in perfect order and drew handsome rents off it. But the Baron has declared the lands around the Bald out of his jurisdiction. If there is a murder up there, the miners must handle it themselves. Even if they did, he could do little because of the difficulty of getting anything up there. The trail is a terrible, precarious thing, and the constant quakes sometimes close it until the miners can clear it again. They lose people on it all the time, a dozen a year or more."

It would be easy to be lost on that cliff, much higher than Heartbreak Cliff near the Serpentine. Ileth had thoughts, sometimes, that if the war resumed she would jump and end it all and let her bones remain a prisoner of the Galantines. But then she remembered the Lodger's training to not let events that are out of your control trouble you, and think only upon that which is within your power, *and one's attitude was always within one's power, was it not?* came his voice from the dead.

When the "darks" came (as she called such hopeless thoughts), she increased her dancing until exhaustion drove them out of her mind. She lost herself in it almost every night. She danced on her own, she danced with Taf (who sometimes secretly joined her in her drills), and she joined with the Tribals in their practices, though she was barred from their rites. She managed to save a silver nugget here and there (the Baron knew that she gave hers to the dragon and sometimes gave her a nugget that she would then conceal in her work room) and used the biggest one to buy the finest riding boots the Galantine cobbler could make.

Some nights a few members of the Baron's household would watch her dance for the dragon as he settled down to sleep. The Baroness, once she had her baby and needed an escape from nursing (she passed the babe on to a wet nurse only after he took his first solid food), grew to be a bit of a fan and would show up now and again to just sit and watch. That, or she had found out about her daughter's interest in the exotic and highly improper practices of both dragon dancers and Tribals and was worried.

Perhaps it was the madness of the heat, perhaps it was the boredom, but she agreed to perform for the Tentkeeper on the Silver Plateau. She refused to call it the cow plateau; it wasn't shaped like anything on a cow unless you counted its udder. The Tentkeeper became so excited he asked for three extra barrels of beer. She'd been practicing, without thinking about it, to a worker's song she'd heard a few times at the Green River ford near the Baron's estate, combining some of the Tribal movement of shoulders and hips with the outstretched arms and dramatic leg extensions of dragon dance. It became stuck in her head, probably because it reminded her a little of the sea chants she'd heard in the Freesand. The melody was similar, with hard beats when the men would pull together and a counterpoint as they regained their footing and grips and got ready for another pull.

The Tentkeeper had expanded his tent for the event. Bits of rug and cushions made out of old rags or little canvas folding chairs were arranged for the audience. Ileth had a small circle in front of her musicians to dance in, marked off by footlights she had brought, spirited out of the stores left in the old theater by the Tribals.

Fortunately, on that trip, she brought up extra goatskins of wine. She begged a mouthful from the Tentkeeper to steady herself. He cautioned her that drinking wine from a bladder was a learned skill if she'd never done it and directed her to open her mouth so he could send a short jet of wine into the back of her throat. She swallowed—the wine was quite tart but warming—asked for one more, and was ready.

All the bodies crammed into the tent made it warm, at least.

The miners knew the tune. Her "musicians" (no less than eight men had received free admission in exchange for playing) rolled pebbles around in pans or shook them in old spirit and wine bottles, or rattled two spoons, but she hardly needed them because so many in the audience hummed, clapped, or sang along.

She should have been embarrassed by the nearly all-male crowd, or frightened. Each of these men was undoubtedly stronger than her. Perhaps she would have been reluctant to dance for just one of them, but for the mass of them, almost undifferentiated in their beards, grime, and shaggy hair (those who'd cleaned up for the event had their faces shining like moons, reflecting the footlights), they transformed into a necessary extension of her dance, a partner, waiting for her next flourish so they could respond. The connection with them felt strange and new and powerful. Dancing for the dragons in the Serpentine, or for Fespanarax, was like dancing for the stars; you had very little back. As for the Baron's leering friends, she couldn't wait to get away from them. These miners drank in her movements like she was their ale and they lifted her into the air with their applause and cheers.

The miners gave off a thick, crowded-animal smell. But their appreciation, her love of the tune, and her skill fed her dance. Looking back on it in her later years, she considered it one of her favorite performances.

As she changed behind the privacy screen of drying laundry, she felt oddly like she'd stepped across some kind of threshold, conscious of a strange new power in her body. It was an interesting thing to possess; she could even take pride in it, but she couldn't see herself using it in this manner often. Whether she would end up taking more satisfaction in having such ancient magic to wield or in letting it remain quiescent remained to be seen.

Several unsettling thoughts competed in her head. Had she been around the Galantines so long that she thought these common folk were half animal, and she could perform as easily before them as she would a field of cows? Or was it that they reminded her, sweating in the tent and wiping their foreheads or noses on their shirtsleeves, of the fishermen and the sailors of the Freesand she'd been born among? Was she looking down on the herd, or was she of it?

Afterward, the Tentkeeper showed Fespanarax the silver collected at the performance.

"This, dragon, is all. I give you the largest nugget for putting the idea into our friend's head. A quarterweight I give to the dancer. I keep the rest."

"You mean your wife keeps it," Ileth said, smiling.

"Yes. We save for a real wooden tavern. Home above, tavern below."

Fespanarax, who had followed the conversation with some difficulty, swallowed his nugget but grumbled the rest of the night at the unfairness of it.

Winter approached at last and broke the warmest fall Ileth had ever known. The Tribals departed while the weather was still agreeable. They would take a roundabout route back, selling their potions and remedies and charms as they zigzagged back to reunite with their men. It didn't matter if it rained; their wagons were well designed, ruggedly wheeled, and not heavy.

Winter in Chapalaine passed comfortably, with frequent rain and rare snows that left quickly. The Baron's family had feasts with such frequency that her stomach only just recovered from one when the next came along. She gave unusually energetic performances for Fespanarax to tamp the food down in her digestive system.

In her imagination she was roaming the Beehive, sitting in the audience as a new class of novices were sworn in. She even felt a little nostalgic for the Catch Basin and the grunts of the fishermen as they carried their tubs and trays to the gutting tables.

The Baron reported to her that negotiations were started fresh with the Vales; new sets of diplomats, in a new location so that their conference could continue despite winter weather, seemed to promise much. It gave Ileth hope that she might be but one year in the Galantine lands.

The only change spring brought was less feasting and heavier rain. Often she would be soaked by the time she made the walk to Fespanarax.

One night, late, as she reread a Galantine novel from the Baron's library more for the improvement of her Galantine than because it interested her, listening to the rain pour down outside, she heard a tap at one of her high windows. Then it was repeated three times, then once again: *tap ... tap tap tap ... tap.* The windows were too high and narrow for her to see outside without getting a chair. She double-checked the bar at her door and moved a chair over to look out the window.

A snarling brass ogre face rose up at the end of a wooden shaft and tapped again. There was no mistaking the walking stick of Dath Amrits.

She was still in her housedress. She jumped into her shoes, picked up a waxed canvas rain cloak, unbarred the door, and, after first checking the grounds to make sure no one was about on this rainy night, swiftly walked around to the side of her domestic prison facing away from the great house.

It wasn't Dath Amrits holding the walking stick after all, and she startled, until she recognized the man as the Borderlander. He put his finger to his lips and gestured for her to follow. Ileth almost asked if the negotiations had been finally successful, but that hardly seemed likely or he would have flown in the sunlight to retrieve her covered in streamers acquired at the border.

She followed him along the garden hedge and to the wall. He moved well in the rain and the dark, passing here and there to survey the grounds, and when he paused, pressed against a tree trunk or a gap in the hedge, he became next to invisible in the shadows. For such a gangly great man, he was as stealthy as a cat. Finally, they came to an old gate in the wall. The lock had been worked open, it seemed. Dath Amrits and Hael Dun Huss stood there on the other side. The Borderlander handed the walking stick back to Amrits.

"Ileth, you've grown!" Dun Huss said. "No one would mistake you for a child at the gate anymore." Ileth smiled, though she wondered how Dun Huss knew about her first application to the gate. Paired dragoneers didn't stand guard duty unless they were being disciplined for some reason.

"I'm happy to see you all," Ileth said. "I may cry!" She had a difficult time suppressing the urge to hug them.

"A dark night for dark business," Dun Huss said, weirdly echoing the Charge in that meeting in his quarters so long ago. "We're taking you out of here, Ileth."

Ileth, so shocked that her stutter hardly allowed her to talk, said that she'd given her word to the Galantines. No leaving Chapalaine except under the specific direction of the Baron. "It's a question of honor," she finished.

To their credit, none of the men cut her off during her stumbling speech.

"No, there's no honor involved," Dun Huss said. "We've consulted, and they weren't to use the dragon for any military, courier, or exhibition purposes, including parades, circuses, and displays in menagerie. Well, it's not military correspondence, but bringing beer up some mountain so his jailer can make money off it is the act of a courier, whether it's a bag of letters or beer."

She'd mentioned her flights with Fespanarax in her letters back to the Serpentine. She'd wanted to reassure them that he was restored to health. "But it was my idea, to occupy him with . . . with something other than sleep. Get precious metals in his diet."

"Still, they plain broke the terms," the Borderlander said.

"Most girls my age dream of a handsome dragoneer carrying them off. I know I should thank you to the day I die that all three of you showed up, but I fear you've wasted your time."

Amrits rolled his prominent eyes. "Tripe! The Serpentine's a dull place without you. Nothing's burned down or boiled up in months. We must have you back."

Dun Huss ignored him: "We needed a small enough group to go in quietly, but a large enough flight to handle anything the Galantines could put in the air against us. You may not know it, Ileth, but the Galantines have two of their dragons posted with a view of your valley, just in case Fespanarax gets out of hand."

He went on to say their dragons were concealed on the riverbank. They could submerge and hide everything but their nostrils and be invisible in the dark if anyone walked along the banks, as unlikely as that was on a wet, chill night.

"These are the orders of the Serpentine?"

Amrits nodded. "We took it to the Master in Charge. He agrees that the terms of your confinement have been violated."

"Not even your parole. You're here on a dead man's promise," the Borderlander said.

"Be honest, Amrits. He didn't tell us we could do *this*," Dun Huss said.

"Don't be a stick, Hael. He didn't tell us *not to*, either, when we presented him with the plan, eh?" Dath Amrits said. "We were able to leave with our mounts and supplies without interference. Did they think we were going camping, with winter coming on?"

"Are we going to talk, or are we going to fly?" the Borderlander asked.

"I must refuse. If we go back, it could restart the war," Ileth said. "I think they're looking for an excuse."

"If they want an excuse, let's give it to them," Dun Huss said. "If we escape, it's done and we can confront them at the negotiating table with your account of Fespanarax being used for profit."

"Pure venting," Amrits said. "Ileth, I've been six years a full dragoneer and I've never, not once, rescued a maiden. To be honest, they're beginning to talk down at the Cock and Stack." Ileth had heard that the dragoneers frequented the High Rooster, a beer garden in Vyenn with a sign of a rooster atop a haystack.

Dun Huss looked at the Borderlander, who shrugged. "If they break negotiations and invade, our people will rally. The Vales don't like making war, but receiving it is another matter."

"We're at full strength again," Amrits said. "If we can get Fespanarax back, we might even be better off. But starting the war again. That's not my line at all."

"How do you know they're looking for an excuse?" Dun Huss asked.

"The Baron. His daughter can't tell the difference between gossip and Court affairs. She let slip something she heard. It's a long trip back. Suppose something goes wrong and you have to fight." She continued on to say that if they hurried back now and were spotted, they could plausibly explain that they'd become lost in bad weather, apologize profusely, and return to the Serpentine. But dragoneers carrying away a prisoner who had been paroled to a pleasant estate and a powerful dragon . . .

"Blast it, I think the girl's right," Amrits said. "But I feel a fool having come all this way just to leave her here."

"They'll still take your coin at the High Rooster, Amrits," the Borderlander said.

"Sirs, you've done more than you realize," Ileth said, tears welling up. Luckily the rain hid them.

"How's that?" the Borderlander asked.

"Seeing you three. You are all important dragoneers, yet you came just to bring me out. I am happy, very happy to know I am missed, even if it's just by you three. It couldn't have come at a better time, either."

"What," Amrits said. "The rain this time of year gets worse than this?"

"I am sixteen! I'm not sure of the exact day, but the season's right. From now on my birthday shall be this date, each and every year, and not one will go by where your gesture won't be remembered. I will never forget this party."

"Good heavens, maybe we should get her away," Amrits said. "Even if we have to tie her across Fespanarax. Birthday parties! She's going Galantine on us."

Ileth spent a few moments relating the details of Griff's defection and Galia possibly being of help to the Galantines. Also that she'd heard of an old man taking poison that left his teeth blue and that Fespanarax seemed ready to quit human affairs altogether. They listened attentively, seriously, and asked a few questions about young men being pressed into the King's service or purchases of horseflesh for cavalry. She'd heard talk of neither.

They decided to go and find a more remote spot to rest their dragons. The Borderlander shook her hand, Amrits gave her a quick kiss on the forehead and joked that if she grew much more he'd be guilty of dallying with the apprentices, and Dun Huss, perhaps best of all, accepted and returned a formal salute, taking care to do it with the same precision he'd use on Charge Roguss Heem Deklamp.

She hugged the thought of the respect on his face. It drove away the fear that she'd never see the three of them again.

16

Charge Ottavia,

I write you in the hope that what little news I have will be relayed to the rest of the troupe. I also write to exercise myself—I am so used to speaking the Galantine tongue I wonder if I need to use my native language so as not to forget it entirely. Fespanarax has taught me enough Drakine now so I can follow simple commands in his feeding, grooming, and care, so I hardly use it with him, either.

First, I must relay some news for you to pass to Hael Dun Huss and his wingmen who were friends with our Galia (when she was ours) and whoever else might ask of us. I received one letter from the Baroness Galia Dandas (as she is now and I won't trouble you with the other titles) with news that she is happy and in good health. She had hopes of starting a family quickly but has not yet been blessed. Her life has other interests, but unfortunately she couldn't be explicit as they are military in nature, I understand, having to do with her husband's command.

As for me, I am glad the winter has passed. The trips on Fespanarax will resume soon, as the plateau with the silver mine I mentioned is hospitable again with winter over and the miners shall return. As for this pleasant valley, the only complaint is tedium. One grows tired of the same walks, the same society, the same conversations. The view has altered slightly, however. The volcano to the north opened up a new fissure on our side of the mountain range, and on clear nights you can *sometimes see the fire, which looks to me like a ship burning signal-candles, but bigger.*

I am entertained in the late afternoon as the dinner is being set out whenever I wish to be by the many children of my host's family, but perhaps you have to actually be related to them to truly delight in their exhibitions. I long to dance again with the troupe. It's too bad the costumes and style are still a little too foreign to the Galantines than to audiences in places like Zland, as some of the social dancers are skilled and I have never heard better musicians. It would be wonderful to have a few here to break the monotony and let me truly dance.

Long live the Republic! The censors may ink that out, but they can't remove it from my heart.

> *I leave you now, having filled up the piece*
> *of paper my host considers sufficient,*
> *Ileth of the Serpentine*

The glow of the visit from "her" (as she liked to think of them) Dragoneers warmed her until the balmy spring sun returned, earlier than she'd ever experienced. She welcomed it. In the north, sixteen was an important year in a girl's life. Some took jobs and started earning for their families, some courted with a serious eye toward marriage, a few took religious orders, but most everyone thought it the year to do the first trial swim in the deeper waters of adulthood.

She did leave one detail from Galia's letter out of her own. Galia had asked her about drinking dragon blood and fertility, not for her, but for her husband. Galia was contemplating a visit to Chapalaine and Fespanarax for that express purpose. Ileth, speaking in general terms in a return letter, professed ignorance of the exact effects on men (true!) and warned her against its use save in infrequent circumstances (also true, unless Fespanarax was lying).

She suspected the Baron had either received a similar letter from Galia or been told by his wife. Ileth believed Galia corresponded regularly with the Baroness because she sometimes relayed some small bit of news like the fact that Galia had found friends among some of the wives around camp, saying they were quite agreeable but not the least bit stimulating. The Baron relayed in a conversation, seemingly out of nowhere, an anecdote of a former game warden on his lands who had been caught trying to bleed Fespanarax, and had escaped a conviction of witchcraft only by being publicly lashed before volunteering for service in the Fencibles. Ileth, who still knew little about the Galantines on the battlefield, did understand thanks to the unfortunate scene with the soup on that fast day with Dandas that the Fencibles had the most desperate and dangerous work of all the Galantine companies, as they were charged with taking down dragons.

"Could just as well be called a death sentence. Chances are you get burned either way," the Baron had sighed, scratching his dog's ears.

The first visit to the plateau to deliver kegs of beer went much as the others. The Tentkeeper spoke of a supply of wood he now had enough money to have conveyed to the plateau, so he could have the beginnings of an actual tavern. He had begun to lay out big stones for the foundation. He was hopeful that if he could get it built, Ileth would perform again as a ceremonial opening to get the place open with an appropriate spectacle, even some real musicians instead of men shaking pebbles in pans and clacking spoons.

She and Fespanarax were descending to Chapalaine after the first run when she noticed much of the Baron's family outdoors, looking at her. No, not at her; she looked behind her and saw great clouds of dark smoke boiling up from the mountain, dark and different from the usual steam. Arcs of lava splashed up from the Cracked Cauldron like a heavy surf hitting a boat.

She decided it would be best to land nearer the Baron's family and asked Fespanarax if he would set down by the grounds there.

Once off Fespanarax, she felt the ground tremble. It was unsettling.

"The Cauldron's erupting. We're quite safe," the Baron said. "Still, it's lucky for us the wind is from the southwest today. If it were a winter wind, some of the ash might even reach Chapalaine. Too bad about those miners. I suppose we won't be selling beer to them anymore."

"What?"

"Oh, they're doomed," the Baron said. "They're right downwind."

She begged the Baron for some good rope. She had to produce tears, but once he finally agreed, his livestock people were summoned and instructed. She hurried back to Fespanarax. "We have to help the miners."

"We?" Fespanarax said. "I don't know that I have to do anything but obey the terms of my confinement."

"They're trapped up there. The path faces the volcano, if it even exists." The Baron's men were bringing lines, twine, old bridle leather, everything they could find. Ileth started sorting through it.

"Hundreds of people? You must be mad!"

"Children, then. As many as we can," Ileth said.

"A pointless risk of my wings. Volcanoes are nothing to mess about with when they erupt."

"I'm quite rich, you know." She was a terrible liar. Well, no, actually she was good at lying. That is what was terrible.

"They don't make rich girls dancers."

"My family gave me this when I left for the Serpentine," she said, holding up her whistle. "Would a poor family have a whistle like this made?"

Fespanarax sniffed it and his mouth started to run with thick saliva. "I suppose not. Consider it a down payment."

"What?"

"Let me eat it and I will fly for you."

"It's, it's not even a mouthful for you. Wh-What good could it possibly do you?"

"It could show me you're in earnest about paying your debts."

There was nothing to do. She gave it to him. As she'd predicted, it was practically nothing to swallow.

"Ample silver. If I don't get it, I'll take it out of your hide, Ileth."

"Bargain," she said.

"Tie some sacking about my snout. You'll want scarves."

They took to the air.

As they glided into the plateau, she could feel the heat, even at a distance, on the wind off the volcano. "Be funny if they're all dead by the time we get there," Fespanarax said through the sack. "Let me know if it starts to get too hot for you. I can take more than you."

Ileth didn't reply. She was trying to see and keep ash out of her eyes at the same time.

The earthquakes were stronger close to the volcano. A smell like a hot stove hung in the air, even at Fespanarax's altitude. Rock was falling off the plateau, either flaking off or breaking in sheets to crash into the more ancient rock pile below. Escape by the path was impossible.

The plateau was a waking nightmare or a preview of some hellish afterlife. Ash was everywhere, so deep you had to wade through it. The miners tied anything they could over their faces to filter out some of the ash—still, everyone was coughing. Some were sheltering in their little pits, but the sides kept collapsing and they had to climb out again. The plateau was hot enough to be unpleasant—the radiant heat of the lava was being carried by the winds westward over the plateau.

She couldn't even begin this task. Fespanarax had to sweep his tail about to keep them away.

"Just the children," Ileth shouted. "Children only!"

Fespanarax only let people holding children near him. The others he beat back with his wings and tail. Ileth couldn't let herself be overcome by the horror; she had to be careful with the knots, far more careful than when the Captain was watching her work. All she risked there was a whipping.

Frantic parents thrust their screaming children into her arms. The tears on the frightened children and babies made clean streaks running down their faces.

It was too much to take. She fixed them at every point she could, to the saddle, to the stirrups; she tied them on her own body.

"More. I can take more," Fespanarax kept saying. Something seemed to have come alive in him. For the first time Ileth saw a flash of Fespanarax the Reckless.

She had fifteen. But there were more. She should have thought to fix the beer barrels on; she could have crammed a dozen more in them.

"We'll be back," she shouted to the desperate, tear-streaked faces. She met the eyes of the Tentkeeper. "Fast, girl, just go!" he shouted.

Fespanarax came off the plateau in something more like a controlled glide than a flight.

"High ground, we must set them on high ground well away, just in case there are slides off the mountain, or lava rivers," Fespanarax said. The heat was not so much of a problem with the bulk of the plateau between them and the volcano. Then they were in clean air; some fluke of wind current kept the ash back. Flapping madly, Fespanarax found a pine-covered hill out of the ash-fall, and they landed and put down the children. Ileth told the oldest boy to keep the younger ones together.

"Dare we go again?" she asked Fespanarax.

His eyes were alight with excitement.

"If you are game. We've begun this, let's see it through." Ileth saw some hint of the great dragon within that Charge Deklamp had praised.

"Then let's go."

"It will be even hotter up there. I might survive—scale has its purposes. Will you?"

"We'll . . . find out."

They took off. The heat was getting worse. It bordered on unbearable.

Maybe she'd die in the Galantine lands, along with Annis and Heem Zwollen and who knew how many others. But better this than sitting around Chapalaine, eternally at the service and indulgence of the Baron or whichever of his brothers or sons took over when he died. She wondered what poor soul they'd send out to doom themselves on Fespanarax the Unlucky.

They landed, right at the far edge where the crowd had mostly huddled to escape the heat. There were already ash-covered bodies on the plateau. Ileth saw an upthrust hand sticking out of a collapsed minehole.

This time they got twenty-six. The miners sensed their doom and had organized themselves while they were away. The children had notes and family icons tied to them. She heard rites and prayers being called. Ileth had the stronger boys, scarves tied over their faces, hang on to each other like saddlebags across the dragon's back. She tied and fixed and fiddled while Fespanarax did his best to shelter them with his wings. She could hear shrieks of pain.

"Hurry, Ileth," Fespanarax urged from somewhere in the hot blowing ash.

The Tentkeeper managed to make it through the press. His skin was peeling. He thrust a scrawled, sealed letter into Ileth's hand. "My wife. Village of Isswith."

"I shall," Ileth said, thrusting it into her shirt.

He helped her tie on the last of the children.

"Don't forget, Isswith. Now go!"

Fespanarax jumped. He wasn't the only one, but he was the only one with wings. Ileth wept and screamed from the pain and frustration.

They lost one of the boys gripping hands. Ileth had a brief, terrible glimpse of the fear in his eyes as he slipped and disappeared down into the fog of ash. She reached back and held on to the other one until Fespanarax glided to the other waiting children. He skidded in hard.

It was a mercy that the ash hid the denouement. The end of those left on the plateau came swiftly.

There was a great deal to do on the little pine-covered hill. Shelter, water, making a count of the children and putting the older ones with little groups of younger ones, pairing those who seemed most capable with babies.

The wind held and kept the ash off them, and the plume of the clouds filled the skies of Baron Blue Heron's lands.

She spent an exhausting night getting the children to a cattle ranch Fespanarax spotted. Ileth would have preferred to wait until daylight, but she wanted to put more distance between the children and the volcano. Who knew what further cataclysm might come? Fespanarax had them keep to a ridge the whole way. The dragon told her tales of cloudy rivers of superheated ash rolling off volcanoes, and Ileth wanted nothing to do with anything like he described. On the way they met an outrider for one of the herds, and Ileth begged him to get a message to the Baron. They got their thirsty, hungry, and ash-covered children to the ranch house, just a long shepherd's cabin, but it fit everyone. Ileth promised the cattlemen and their wives the Baron's money if they would feed the children for a few days until arrangements could be made.

She helped wash and feed the children before flying off for aid from Chapalaine. Fespanarax, with the urgency of the rescue over, complained of burned wings and said that they'd better produce a great deal of salve.

One of the Baron's outdoor staff, a clever man of middle age who was brave enough to work with the dragon and had turned into a decent groom by watching Ileth, fairly danced with anxiety, his sparse hair flying wilder and wilder with each caper.

"The Baron must see you immediately!" the groom said. "Are you both quite all right?"

"Never better," Ileth said, though she didn't feel it. She slid down the saddle and touched the ground. Her skin pained her. She'd been a little scorched.

"Lords and lands," the Baron said, once she made it to his presence. "What happened to you, Ileth?"

"Bad up there."

"I have here a report," he said, looking at some handwritten notes in his own hand, "that you saved thirty-eight children."

"Eleven b-b-babies, a girl perhaps two—"

"You don't need to list them."

"It should have been thirty-nine," Ileth said. "I lost one boy . . . It was horrible."

"Well, Ileth, I'm sure your intentions were good but I'm not sure you understand what you've done. They're on my side of the mountains, you see, so now they're my problem. I could perhaps find homes for a third that number, given the number we lost in the plague before you joined us. Babies can often be fobbed off on someone. Take a couple here at Chapalaine. But thirty-eight! From the lowest sort of sweepings to the north. Miners never have relatives that can be found; they move around too much. I shall have to establish an orphanage! I shall have to buy land and build, or worse, take an established building where I can credibly house over twenty children. Beg the church, with whom I'm not on the best terms currently, as I keep a dragon, a girl who dances about mostly naked, and what used to be a thriving brewery. I am dismasted in a storm, girl, and a whirlpool yawns beneath."

"Send one or two to Dandas and Galia. I believe they want to start a family."

The Baron brightened. "Now *that* is helpful. Good thinking. The Baroness was saying something along those lines. You Vale girls are familiar with the duties of a wife to a husband, I hope? Ahh, if only you'd flown the lot farther south to get them there, then they'd be Baron Alcester's problem. I don't suppose—"

He read Ileth's face.

"No, no, it's too much to ask. Get cleaned up and get some sleep, girl."

The following weeks were madly busy. The Baron decided that since the new orphans were her doing, she should run about finding rooms and shelter for them in the village. Fespanarax, his wings greased with a cow-doctor's salve used to soothe udders, asked her several times if she'd written her family about his reward. The Baron went so far as to allow her to roam about his lands unescorted on one of the horses his daughters shared, and she became something like a Galantine significant as she trotted about on it, enjoying the fact that her ride didn't argue with her about the quality of his grain and water. Both farmers and townspeople greeted her by name with none of the elaborate obeisances they gave the Baron, often pressing a bit of preserved berry spread in a crock or honey cakes on her "for those poor children the dragon saved." All the while, the Tentkeeper's letter sat, still sealed, on her little meal table.

Ileth worked harder than ever, even if it was just scrubbing Fespanarax's scale with a bristle brush. Only profound exhaustion let her escape dreams of the eyes of that boy as he fell from the dragon.

It took no little doing and much more flying, but she'd just returned from tracking down the village of Isswith and delivering the Tentkeeper's letter (with the usual travel permissions and elegant letters of introduction) when the Baron summoned her again to his library. This time he had Azal standing gravely behind him and Taf seated primly at his secretary-desk. He held a gilded envelope to the window light so Ileth could see it.

"We have here a letter from Court under the King's seal, and strangely, I am ordered not to open it until you are in my presence, Ileth of the Vales. Azal, please witness that Ileth is present and the letter is still sealed. I am posted to the Court Exalted, so I may unseal as instructed. Taf, note the date and approximate time, please, and list those present."

Taf wrote a note in a little book the Baron kept on his desk.

He passed a silver knife under the waxed seal and carefully removed it, laying the seal on a small tray on his spotless writing desk. He extracted a sheet of thick cotton paper with a golden foil border decorating it and read it quickly. Ileth could only see that it bore several ribbons. The Baron's eyes bulged. The thick paper made a slight noise in his hands as it began to shake. His lip even trembled a little as he finished it.

A man reading his own death warrant could not look more shocked. His mouth worked, but no words came. It wasn't some attack; he had the sense to hand it to Taf, who scanned it and began to read:

"*Almendaeldess the Third, King of the Galantine Lands, all her Baronies, Possessions, and Colonies on Foreign Coasts; Defender, Champion, and Final Resort and Supreme Enforcer of her Laws and Traditions, does hereby sign and seal this royal release of the girl born to the Freesand of our western neighbor, one Ileth aged sixteen or thereabout, surname and titles unknown or absent, and a dragon named Fespanarax of the same nation currently held by our most favored friend and supporter Hryasmess at Chapalaine in the Green River Country. Our Gracious Sovereign, in considered and public recognition of their bravery in the saving of life, even at the hazard of their own, in the late disaster known as the Eruption of Laterus ('the Cracked Cauldron') on this Month of Memory in the Two Thousand Nine Hundred Sixty-Eighth Year of our Hypatian Founding Sacred announces the following: Be it known that she and her dragon are made free in our lands, all paroles and restrictions lifted at once and forevermore, and may pass and return at will. Ileth, as named above, is elevated to the honorary title of Lady of the Order of Hospitals and Refuges, with Distinction by Acts, and proclaimed and posted to the*

Court Exalted in significance of her bravery. As of the moment of this order being read in her presence, she shall receive any and all respects and courtesies of that title as occasion merits until her death, resignation of honors, or revocation on the decision of the King or his heir.

"It is our hope that this act of clemency and elevation will lead to an increase in friendship and commerce with our western neighbor and banish forever the pestilence of war between the Galantine Baronies and the lands generally called the Vale Republic.

> *"Signed and sealed with Acclaim of the Court,*
> *Almendaeldess the Third,*
> *King Galantine*
> *(with titles accepted as listed in usual form)."*

"Ileth! I am happy for you!" Taf said. "I'm sorry, *Lady*, I am happy for you." She made a deep obeisance.

"You may say 'Lady Ileth'; technically she's of our household I suppose," Young Azal said. "But then again she's foreign and should perhaps be addressed as a visiting dignitary. *Lady Freesand?* Oh, we can always look it up, I suppose."

"Ileth, do you have any idea of the significance of this? Any idea at all?" the Baron asked.

"It means Fespanarax and I may leave?"

He showed no sign of having heard her.

"'Most favored.' Not only does he name me and list Chapalaine. No! And not 'faithful friend and supporter,' as he'd ordinarily write if he were pleased. I would have danced on my roof if he'd just written 'favored.' But he wrote '*most* favored'! Most! Oh, Ileth, if I'd know when you and Galia arrived all that would issue of our meeting, I should have purchased a white cloth runner from your dragon to my door and lined it with every villager I could drag into place to cheer you to my threshold with flower petals. '*Most favored*'! The marriage of Galia must have exceeded expectations. Lucky Dandas! Lucky me! I must tell the Baroness. Oh, where is the Baroness? Find your mother, children! This instant!"

His joy was made a little comical by the rat clinging desperately to his wig as he capered and kicked up his heels, but Ileth felt happy for him.

"I am happy for you, sir," she managed.

Strange, the Baron's mention of Galia and not her apparently talked-about-at-Court rescue, but she could think about that at her leisure. Another matter eclipsed everything, including her peeling skin. She was free to return to the Serpentine just as soon as she chose. Home.

PART FOUR

THE THREE EGGS

If only the future came with signposts.

—*THE BARON'S CAPTIVE* (A THEATRICAL FIRST
PERFORMED IN SAMMERDAM, 3102)

17

Her journey back was simplicity itself, compared to her first trip to the Serpentine. She flew west on Fespanarax, laden with little good-bye gifts from Chapalaine, the clothes and footwear she'd acquired one way and another, and her little supply of silver nuggets and bag of good Galantine tea. Fespanarax flew streamers that were both white, and white with red shields (with a gold stripe running diagonally across the red shield that indicated a Knight or Lady of the Order of Hospitals and Refuges, with Acts—the Baron and Azal had to look it up in a book but once they had the style, Taf and the Baroness had produced them in an afternoon).

Taf had been the only one to look truly upset at their departure, as without a dragon there would be no need next summer for the Tribals to stay longer than it took to scour Fespanarax's bedding for traces and collect the loose scale Ileth had left for them, entrusted to Taf. Taf said she'd miss the dancing. The Baron was relieved to be free of the expense of feeding the dragon and devoting so many servants to his care. The Baroness was suspected to be with child again and looking as green as the riverbanks. All the children could not wait for the ceremony to be over (Ileth was still kicking herself for not counting them, as they'd been all lined up in family battalions for once), and the Baron's head gardener and family were probably looking forward to getting that little house back.

The Baron had adopted into his family one of the orphaned children she had rescued. She was in the lineup with his other children, clean and well dressed, but standing a little apart from the others separated by a nurse. She presented Ileth with a black stick, probably from a birch. It had three red-and-white ribbons tied around it.

"What's your name?" she asked the girl.

"We can't get her to talk hardly, my lady," the nurse said. "She says *please* when she wants something and *thank you*. Sometimes she'll whisper what she needs to one of the other children her size. We don't know her name either, none of us do. We've been calling her Arenis."

"She knows her parents are dead, Lady," a governess next to the nurse said. "Yet still she asks, especially in the mornings. We have to tell her they are dead all over again. Poor thing."

"Arenis is a nice name," Ileth said. "Thank you for the stick."

"It's from a bedtime story," one of the Baron's younger daughters volunteered.

"Say 'Lady' when you address someone of her order," the governess said.

"Sorry, Lady Ileth, Arenis is a little girl from a story who floats down from a cloud. She thinks a herd of goats are her family for a while, until a kind King adopts her, Lady Ileth." The child looked to the governess and received an approving smile and nod.

"The stick is something the village children do," Taf explained. "It's a wish stick. You wave it at festivals and weddings and such, or when an unusually significant person passes. When a wish comes true, you untie a ribbon. I suggested she do them in the colors of the Vales when I saw her looking for ribbons."

Ileth caressed the little girl and hugged her. She picked her up and let her say good-bye to Fespanarax. "He's the one you should be thanking, Arenis," Ileth said. The girl touched the dragon's ear.

"If I get bloodbug in my ear from the little rodent, I will become unpleasant about it," Fespanarax said. But he said it in Drakine.

Ileth thanked the Baron and Baroness for their kindness once more from the saddle. The Baron bowed. "Lady," he said.

They took off and Fespanarax made a slow climb to good flying air.

She was challenged once, quite early in their journey west. A dragon about half the size of Fespanarax rose from the ground as she approached the first low mountain chain west of the Baron's lands. It had two riders in a tandem saddle designed to take advantage of the hump of muscle near the dragon's wings: a man at the reins and another behind seated just a little above him with a crossbow. They waved her down.

Fespanarax was not keen to land after all the effort of getting to altitude, but he did. They found a mountain meadow and Ileth showed them the King's letter. They were both familiar with Fespanarax; word just had not reached them that he'd been freed. They bowed to her and pledged to do whatever they could for a Lady of Hospitals and Refuges, with Acts, acclaimed by both King and Acclaim of the Court. Ileth asked if they would fly with her to the border so they didn't have further trouble, and they announced that they'd be honored. They were as good as their word, though it meant a long and tiring flight.

The weather was good and Fespanarax was magnificent in his speed for such a large dragon. Perhaps his vast size and huge wings helped him along, much as the fastest swimmers were usually tall with a good reach. The Galantine escort fell farther and farther behind. They reached the border by afternoon and set down on the Republic side for a meal with the border guards. Luckily one of them was the same as on her outbound flight, and another veteran recognized Fespanarax. They had a meal with them and as Fespanarax was feeling well (but hungry; there wasn't nearly enough meat for a dragon, as the guards ate mostly beans and pea-potato mash), he seemed willing to try for the Serpentine, even though they might not reach it before night.

When she hit the Tonne, unmistakable in its width, she turned north. The weather grew colder and colder as they moved north into growing darkness. The mountains to the west looked achingly familiar.

"If it's clear, you can see the lighthouse a long way off," Fespanarax said. "I see sort of a haze that may be it."

"Will you be glad to—glad to return?"

"Eating ore and doing odd jobs for humans," Fespanarax said. "I was tired of it before. But perhaps the activity will engage me more than I think. I look forward to being able to dine on the reward from your family for some time."

"About—about that."

"I tease you, Ileth. I know you are poor. Getting me out of the dull routine of Galantine country will have to be enough."

As he spoke, Ileth felt a stiffness coming down from his neck. She wondered if he'd been rehearsing that little speech in his head. It didn't sound at all like Fespanarax.

For a while they had flocks of migratory birds on their spring flight north along the wide Tonne keeping them company, and eagles. It was a sight to remember, the birds in their thousands, hundreds of little wedge formations. They summered somewhere in the flat lake country north of the bay she'd grown up on. Most of them would, anyway. The flocks dropped well below the dragon and avoided the eagles. Some of the eagles came up, curious, drifted for some moments in the dragon's wake, and then went back to their fishing.

They passed the falls, vague but loud in the dark, and the air grew colder still. She was hungry, but hunger was an old friend. You were sharper when you were hungry.

Fespanarax was right. They did see the lighthouse a long way off. They passed the cliff she'd once idly considered jumping from. Who was that girl? *That Ileth* should have confided in more friends and learned the virtues of patience. If her time at the Baron's had taught her anything, it was patience.

"We'll land on the up end," Fespanarax called. "I feel like I deserve a walk across the bridge, after all these years."

They started in from on high and circled slowly down, giving those on the ground plenty of time to know a dragon was coming in. Ileth's flight training didn't go so far as to know how to signal *recently released prisoner returning*, if such a thing existed, but she did know how to wave a stiff arm down, the signal to other dragoneers that she was about to land.

Fespanarax glided and alighted well on the road just outside the Pillar Rocks. A greeting party assembled.

"He's huge. What dragon is that?" an apprentice asked. It was good to see his white sash again. Even the air felt familiar.

"What do those streamers mean, I wonder," another voice in the crowd asked.

"Fespanarax. Has to be," said an older Guard with a sergeant's decorated pike. "I'd know that craggy head, never mind the size. Finally back from the Baronies."

"This is news," another Guard said. The older one gestured at one of the novices, and he ran off toward the Masters' Hall.

"Who's that on him?" asked a wingman who'd emerged from the quarters in the wall to see the arrival.

She recognized the speaker as Sideburns from the party. His facial hair was thicker now and he'd put on some height. "I know her. It's Vor Claymass's little piece of novice from the party, the one who got tossed into the dancers."

"Oh, yes, Ileth, slayer of Gorgantern. I do remember her," the older Guard said.

"Ever seen a walk across the bridge?" Fespanarax asked.

"No," Ileth said. "What is that?"

"Oh, yes. You're young, aren't you? I forget. The armistice. Well, you walk before me. If we had any trophies, you'd carry them. How would you represent surviving years' worth of the Baron's discourse and courtesies with a trophy?"

"A fussy r-rooster?"

"Well done, Ileth. You're developing a true dragon wit. I'd say peacock, but I don't imagine you've seen those. Good eating. Too bad you'll return to your dull humans. Well, as there are no roosters about, we shall proceed bearing only honor."

Fespanarax raised his head. "All right, you scoundrels, you have returning heroes here. A Galantine Lady, no less. Line the Long Bridge and show some leg running."

Novices and apprentices were duly dispatched. Ileth accepted a bucket of water and let Fespanarax drain it. She was thirsty, but she could wait. She'd had a Galantine water bottle for the trip.

"What's in here?" Ileth asked, tapping the case Fespanarax bore.

"Grooming tools that belonged to me and some of my odds and

ends. There are some precious metals so I put them under metal seal. I can break it easily enough."

"I thought it might be silver."

"Too little, alas. There's some in the leather post-case on the other side. But you have found me out all the same. I'm not so modern a dragon that I don't keep a bit of a hoard. For emergencies."

"Perhaps I can—can add to it, Fespanarax. I promised you my fortune. Here it is." Ileth pulled out her bag of silver nuggets, carefully saved over a year. Though she'd promised the silver to him, even if she hadn't, she would have given it away in any case. The memories of that last flight would prevent her from ever spending the nuggets on herself.

"Not much of a fortune, girl."

"I grew up in a lodge. This is rich to me," Ileth said.

"I will take it. What's more, I will thank you. It's the last silver I'll see for a while in this hole."

They made for the bridge in the style Fespanarax ordered, her walking ahead, carrying her stout bag and its nuggets and the odd Galantine coin or two. It was too heavy to hold up for long, so she ended up cradling it in her arms.

It wasn't much of a procession toward the Long Bridge, though a few came out at the news. Dun Huss and the Borderlander were there, uniforms hastily thrown on and hats clamping down uncombed hair. Dun Huss, as she passed, took one of the streamers hanging from Fespanarax's wings. He walked along, looking at the red shield design with the gold stripe across it.

"Truly, Ileth?" he said, smiling. "Gentlemen, we are being visited by a Galantine significant. Straighten up that line, you all! You're not a bunch of housewives at a laundry fountain. Toe it!"

The last was barked with such an air of authority that those few gathering on the bridge fell into ranks lining it to either side. Those among them who were in Guard uniform presented arms. It wasn't much of a line on either side, but then she wasn't much of a dragoneer.

"Eyes on Fespanarax of the Serpentine, aaaaaaaand—render honors!" Dun Huss said over the wind.

"There was a time the whole Serpentine would turn out," Fespan-arax grumbled. "I suppose they didn't know I was coming."

There was some trouble finding a spot for a dragon of Fespanarax's size and importance so late in the Beehive. In the end, they left him in the Chamber with kitchen staff running for their wheeled troughs to feed him. Ileth happily turned his care over to the grooms. She left her bag of nuggets atop Fespanarax's sealed chest.

It was very late. Or perhaps very early. The only two people still awake (or already up) in the Dancers' Quarter were Ottavia and Preen. Preen was reading, Ottavia worked at her desk, and one of the music boxes played. Preen had tea. Maybe it was morning. She hoped she wouldn't be ordered to drill and fatigue.

They both looked some mix of delighted and astonished when they recognized her, standing in her flying gear, grown a bit, hair its usual chopped mess, looking forward to a wash.

"By my mother's blood, it's Ileth!" Ottavia said, standing. "Back at last. Have you grown? You have grown!"

"Vii and Santeel have missed you, Ileth. It's like having two flints with no steel," Preen said. "Can I get you a tea? We have a great quantity of candied almonds, too. Have as many as you want. They might perk you up. Zusya has a suitor, or someone who wants to be a suitor, that wingman with the big sideburns who used to hang about with Peak, Pasfa Sleng. She told him she could eat them every day, and, well, it's been raining almonds ever since."

"Tea would be lovely," Ileth said.

She took her tea, washed up her most noisome crevices, and collapsed and slept until midday. The dancers rising did not disturb her.

Once able to see and think, she discovered she had three letters accumulated. One was from Falth in his elegant hand, and one was a thank-you note for volunteering from the Master in Charge, awaiting her return. She later learned that this was a habit of his. He would write a note to dragoneers flying out on particularly onerous or dangerous tasks. When they returned, they'd find a note of appreciation. If they didn't return, he placed them in a case in his office and perused them now and then before making an important decision.

Though she hoped to rise in the Serpentine, learning that made her think she might not ever wish to rise to his office.

The third was a little confusing, couched as it was in so much formal legalese. It was from some archivist in Asposis written on the orders of a "Practitioner of Laws, Affirmed as Agent" in Sammerdam. It was a heavily annotated paper, only about a third in Montangyan, with Hypatian phrases and reference numbers throughout. It appeared that as the Lodger's heir (in the Vales; he had other heirs elsewhere who were being notified by other agents who specialized in this kind of thing—for rich fees), she'd gained some "listed title-scrolls, held in trust in the following archives (see attached locations)." They were obviously scrolls and books of various kinds, and the titling was obscure. It didn't seem like anything she'd find interesting reading. It looked to be genealogy lists and discourses about boats and engineering and lumber and mining. Well, he'd been a dragon of wide learning and deep interests and had been involved in constructing the Serpentine. This was probably his reference collection from that time, returned to this archivist in Asposis. If such a thing as a history of the Serpentine's founding were ever written, it might be of interest to the historian. It was a matter for Kess in the archives.

She laid them back on her little shelf and used a candle to hold them down. She realized her only real dance sheath was now not fit for service, and she'd given Fespanarax her silver and coin. She'd have to beg one off someone. Well, she'd begged as a lodge-girl; she could beg as a Galantine Lady of Hospitals and Refuges.

The only person around was Santeel Dun Troot, who was eating pickled eggs from the dragon kitchens and writing a letter to her father. Ileth couldn't help but see "allowance" in the text, as Santeel had underlined it. She said she had two old sheaths she could easily spare, or a much nicer one that would require some sewing before it would be fit for dancing. Ileth was grateful for one of the old ones.

"I enjoyed your l-letters. I wish there had been more," Ileth said, when the business was done.

Santeel crossed her arms. "I grew sick of answering questions: *Ileth, Ileth, Ileth, have you heard anything from Ileth?* I could have just as easily gone. Was it hard, eating Galantine feasts and making sure you didn't expose your bosom overmuch in the sun?"

"The only hard part was the boredom," Ileth said. Half-truths were so useful. "How do things proceed with Rapoto?"

Santeel shrugged. "Our official unofficial engagement has excited our families more than either of us. I wonder if I want that life anymore, presiding over prize apple basket judging at the harvest fair and being complimented on my children. I'm still grateful to him—and you, Ileth—for going along with it so I can stay here. I'm supposed to start with the physikers in the summer. But I shall still dance when they have need of an extra body. Not looking forward to doctoring. I about bring up my breakfast when I see blood, but they tell me I'll get over it."

Santeel brought her up-to-date on other small doings of the dancers' nook and let loose a secret that Ottavia was planning on taking a few dancers to Sammerdam for an exhibition, if she could find any who would swear on their souls not to accept any offers of marriage. The talk of travel reminded her of Fespanarax and she decided that she was still technically his dragoneer and should check on his care up in the Rotunda.

She promised Santeel that she'd see her at afternoon drill.

Fespanarax was still asleep. They had found a shelf for him. She went down to see it and after deciding it would fit him easily she walked back to the notch and ran into Dath Amrits.

Amrits smiled broadly at her but his eyes didn't have their usual sparkle. "Good to have you back, Ileth. You set the example and keep us on our toes. Did the Galantines finally grow sick of the old grump on wings? To hear Hael talk, they do away with the inconvenience with poison that turns your teeth blue."

Ileth explained, truthfully enough, that she'd never worried about being poisoned, and she'd been released in hopes of getting the peace negotiations on a firmer footing. Amrits smiled wanly. He wasn't his usual self and she asked after him.

"Oh, it's Etiennersea. She's in one of her moods. Suffers from headaches. Gets her very down. I keep her on thin broths and stay on her shelf with her until she feels better. Sometimes rubbing her neck helps, but dragons have a great deal of neck, so it wears me out. Oh, speaking of worn out, have you heard about the eggs?"

"Eggs?"

"Yes. Vithleen has had a clutch. She's installed down in your old Lodger's digs, since it is so quiet down there."

"Vithleen! Well . . . they'll be fast when they grow up."

"You should tell Fespanarax. I think Vithleen is his niece or something."

"Vithleen—how does it work with dragons? She has a mate?" Ileth asked. "I didn't know."

"Yes, has for years, they've just never had any luck with eggs. I suppose I should go back to a night not long after you left. I remember old Hael had just come back from the Galantine lands and with his obsession with poisons. Anyway, Falberrwrath was down in spirits. Perhaps he missed you."

"What does Falberrwrath have to do with Vithleen?"

"He's her mate, have been for years. Dragons are odd; they often mate but don't spend much time together unless there's a clutch. Falberrwrath fought in the Galantine War; Vithleen raced about doing messages. But back to my story.

"Falberrwrath was down, as I was saying. Said something about wishing he'd gone down in flames in the war like Mnarfemum. I understand they were close. There was talk that he might be fading into a decline. Well, Ottavia really put on the show to perk him up. She spent three whole nights with him dancing herself half to death. At the end of it, he was feeling like a strong young dragon again, and he invited Vithleen up. Did you know dragons mate aloft? At high altitude, I understand. The males have to work quite hard to get up there; not all of them can do it. Falberrwrath must have had some fire lit under him because he caught up to her, the old notch-hound, and a few weeks later Vithleen asked to be taken off courier duty as she was fatigued. The next thing you know, everyone was talking about eggs. It's rare in the Serpentine. Usually a mated pair who wants a family goes off somewhere remote for a while. It's supposed to be an excellent omen for the novices this year. If you put any belief into omens.

"So as I said, when she felt her time was close, she installed herself where your Lodger fellow used to be. Best keep her out of the way. The dragons don't like humans about, especially when the eggs are about to hatch. That's some ways off, though, the physikers say. But when they start to tap, best keep well away. Even Serpentine dragons will kill you for coming near them and beg forgiveness after the eggs are hatched, I'm told. Maybe you're brave enough to go down and see them hatch, but I'm not."

Amrits saw a groom he needed and excused himself.

Well, dragon eggs. That was news. Funny that Santeel or the other dancers didn't mention it. Was it a secret? Amrits might be the sort of fellow to let a secret slip, especially if he was tired and talking to someone he trusted.

She found Yael Duskirk pushing his food cart. His white apprentice sash was worn, sad, and stained. Usually he kept it so bright.

She asked him to find something special for Fespanarax to enjoy for his first meal back in the Serpentine, as the Galantines had been feeding him on cattle odds-and-ends. He agreed, and asked for details of her release. Ileth said that the letter to the Baron from the King said that the release of Fespanarax was partially in hope of getting the peace talks moving forward again.

"The Galantines usually cry peace only when they're about to get their throats cut, or do some cutting of their own. I wonder why now?" He closed his eyes and rubbed the bridge of his nose.

"Are you well?" Ileth asked. Everyone in the Serpentine seemed to be out of sorts today.

"Tired. My new novice is a lazy scat. You'll notice he's not here. His father's a Name in the stock exchange in Sammerdam and he's used to getting his way, being born with a Vor in his name. I'd like to be a big bug for a change. So how did the world seem over in the Baronies? Will there be peace, or will my torments finally end over the Scab?"

"At Chapalaine there wasn't much talk of politics," Ileth said. "At least in conversations with women. They only spoke of food, entertainments, courtships, babies. Always babies."

"Lucky you. Well, they say there's a monster of a crayfish in the kitchens; maybe your dragon would like that. I'll see to it, Ileth."

He moved away, and Ileth let the phrase *your dragon* roll around in her mind. Fespanarax wasn't the sort of dragon she would pick, and he seemed to have bad luck with dragoneers, but it was still an extraordinarily pleasant phrase to hear. It knocked around in her head the rest of the day, trying itself out.

The next day, the Dancers' Quarter had some excitement. A letter from Peak had arrived, and it contained little but the news of prices for paintings and the fatigues of being a muse. Peak made her think of Galia, and Galia made her think of Yael Duskirk. She realized she should have said something to him about Galia. She hoped that he hadn't been too set down by news of Galia's marriage.

She reprimanded herself for not giving him the full story, as a friend to him who saw Galia and the way she changed up close.

At meal break after drills and fatigues—and was Ileth ever fatigued; she hadn't been drilling as much as she should have in the Golden Land—she went to the kitchen for pickled eggs and found him.

It turned out he was there, supervising some new apprentices and novices and teaching them which dragons preferred fish and which wanted fowl. She inquired about his schedule, and they arranged to have a bite in the kitchens that evening.

That night, neither of them had a sudden call. With the weather turning warm, many of the dragoneers were gone on commissions, and the Serpentine had but a handful of dragons left.

The cooks were just going off duty, arguing about the overuse of paprika. Ileth saw Yael Duskirk scrubbing his mobile feed trough. Judging from the vigor he put into scraping out the trough and the scowl on his face, he was having a bad day.

Ileth asked him if something was the matter.

"I've just been with your friend Fespanarax," he said. "He's the moody type, isn't he?"

"You c-c-can't begin to know."

"He's already forgotten your name, or pretends to. He calls you 'the stuttering girl.' Galia was 'the tall one.'"

"About . . . about Galia."

"I've been trying to forget her. Should never have put my hopes into her. I was fine for her until a wealthy man came along."

"You've heard of her marriage?"

"Yes. It was—I'm not sure *scandal* is the word for it, but it's what I want to say. Shocking. We were shocked."

"Yes. So was I."

Duskirk shook his head. "I can't stop thinking about her. Another failure."

"I think she had too many hard knocks. She married to put some cushioning beneath her. And what do you mean, failure? Aren't you a wingman?"

"I'm not specifically working with anyone. I should have had Vithleen, but now she's with her eggs in the Cellars. The chance of a real commission is slim. They won't give me a younger dragon because I'm too inexperienced, and the older dragons have their own lists of humans they like to work with. Everything seems to go wrong for me, in the air and on the ground. If I were wingman to the Borderlander, perhaps. Could you ask him for me? He seems fond of you."

"I don't—I don't think he takes wingmen. I will ask. What about Fespanarax? I could speak to him about you."

He started to scrub out his wheeled food trough. "Falberrwrath will complain if his trough isn't spotless. He's always complaining about his digestion. As for Fespanarax, I don't know. He's a famous dragon. Seems awful high above what I should expect. That and all his riders seem to die."

"I flew him lots and-and-and I'm still standing here. Unless I'm . . . what's the ex-expression you use?"

"The exception that proves the rule."

Ileth nodded.

"Perhaps Vithleen will give me another chance, once her clutch hatches and years out. Vithleen is kind. Never complains if it's fish three meals in a row."

"Of the dragons I know, she's my favorite." Ileth's legs ached at the memory of their round trip. The long trip on Fespanarax was comparatively easy, come to think of it. Maybe she should try to get courier runs if she ever made it that far. Ask to do the difficult and all that.

"Yes, I should have had that commission. Confusion in the flight cave, and things go wrong for me again. Ah well. Pass me the warm water there, the wash-bucket next to the stove. You know, I've never seen eggs hatching, should be interesting, if they let us anywhere near, that is. Have to split them up right away, I understand. I've heard if there's more than one male, they'll fight to death to establish dominance of the nest. Then the remaining hatchlings eat the loser. How's that for a start in life? 'Course, maybe we humans aren't much better; we just drag it out over twenty or thirty years."

It was difficult for Ileth to lift. The tub itself was heavy even without water in it, and she made the mistake of picking it up on the side that had the pour-spout in the rim. She sloshed a great deal of water on herself as she brought it to Duskirk.

"Don't worry, you can dry it by the stove. The fires there can fix it in no time."

Ileth saw the way he looked at her. She didn't want more of that trouble.

"I can dry it in the Dancers' Quarter."

He stepped toward her anyway. "Here, let me help you."

"Please. I can handle it."

He took one end, ignoring her wet work shirt.

She did like him, quite a bit, even if her interest in him was more about the head and heart than the landmarks south of there. Maybe somewhere other than the Serpentine she would have seen him in a different light, but she'd already been written into that Blue Book of Caseen's and she'd do nothing to risk it being opened again.

"I wonder what Galia saw in that Galantine. A title?"

"I think she saw the estate, not the man. I think she liked him well enough, but she didn't love him. She loved—"

Gods, she was worse than Quith.

"She loved?"

Ileth looked down. She couldn't name Dun Huss. Dun Huss had

done nothing to encourage Galia, behaved correctly to her, even in Galia's telling. Stories always got twisted, the way everyone thought she'd fought Gorgantern in the raw. "Someone back here. But it was impossible."

"Impossible because he wasn't rich, didn't have a title?"

"I—I didn't know enough about it. She didn't confide in me. Her betrothal took me by surprise."

He bent to scrub out the feeding cart with renewed energy, a snarl on his lips, and tipped it. A wave of filthy wash water struck him right in the face.

Ileth stifled a giggle.

"Fates!" he said, wiping his face. "I want to be rich enough so I never have to scrub fish scales out of a bin again."

"I'm sure you will be."

"Not rutting likely. Even you think I'm a bit of *mlumm* that won't wash off."

"No. Yael, you're—you were the first person here to speak . . . to speak nicely to me. I like you."

"I like you too. You're of my sort of people, no great expectations. We could go. Cut loose the entanglements here, build a life somewhere else."

She'd been told men went mad around women sometimes, but this was a little too much. She calmed dragons down by being close to them and made men try to rake the moon. "Yael. Be sensible. Neither of us . . . neither needs to go anywhere. Look at what you have. Flying, even. I'm not even an apprentice yet."

"Oh, they must make you one, now. You brought back Fespanarax. You were basically his dragoneer from . . . from, well, whenever Galia found her future."

"Yes, we were stuck together for a stretch of seasons. What happened there doesn't matter much here. I'm a dragon dancer, and you are learning to fly."

"I bet you'd forget about that if someone rich came along. Like Galia." The comment didn't hurt at all; she'd been carved up by expert butchers.

Ileth tried to think of something that would comfort him. "She'll regret her choice, in the end. The Galantines are tiresome and they treat their wives, well, I don't see Galia as a baby farm. She'll wish she were back here, in that hayloft with you, sooner or later."

"Maybe I should go rescue her."

"Maybe you should, dragoneer."

Yael chuckled. "Well, have to get a dragon first." He scrubbed out his bin with renewed energy.

18

The days passed, the first in which Ileth truly felt returned to her life at the Serpentine. She rose, took a quick cup of tea with Preen and the others, joined in for drills, and then took her aching body back to breakfast. (It was Zusya's turn to gather it and serve, so she was briefed on Vii's latest stratagems in the campaign against, or perhaps with, Pasfa Sleng. *Duties before suitors*, Ottavia said, cutting off the talk and giving everyone their assignments for the day. Ileth's were still light.) Santeel Dun Troot was in exceptionally good humor—she'd left Ileth well behind during drills and fatigues and now showed the superior leg extension of the two. Santeel's ability to spot in her turns made Ileth wish she'd practiced more in the Galantine lands. Even Vii had left her behind. Ileth would have a job of it to equal them anytime soon. Once Santeel got her teeth into something, she was difficult to challenge.

Ileth had little to do until the dragons who were having their dinners wanted entertainment as they digested and settled down to sleep. Ileth hoped she'd be spared until she was back in form. She'd thought she'd kept her body in condition in the Galantine lands, constantly drilling on her own and dancing for Fespanarax. She'd been wrong.

She'd been back over a week when one overcast night Ottavia held Ileth back and sat her down on a floor cushion. Ottavia stretched out beside her, bent legs flat on the floor with the flats of her feet together in her usual relaxed fashion that on anyone but a dragon dancer would be an impossibly painful repose. "Ileth, I have news. There's a jury of inquiry forming—you're not in trouble, not in even the most minor way. Some of the Masters and dragoneers and Republic assigns wish to interview you about your experiences among the Galantines. I am told they are waiting for the arrival of a representative from the Assembly. I'm afraid you'll have no choice in the matter; you must speak to them. Would you feel better if I accompanied you? I know I would be nervous, standing before all those men answering questions. I know public speaking is far from your favorite occupation."

Whatever it was, it would be easier than a mob of Galantine nobles leering at her while she danced for Fespanarax.

"Won't be necessary, Charge," Ileth said. "I've nothing to hide."

"Caseen will tell you more tomorrow. He asks that you call on him just after breakfast."

With little to do until the evening, Ileth decided to go down to her old haunt in the Cellars and see the dragon eggs. She could congratulate Vithleen.

She looked in on the kitchens and realized that she was anxious about running into Yael, but she learned he was at a flight lecture and wouldn't be pushing his food cart again until after the humans ate and the more active dragons began demanding their dinners.

Taking a pickled egg for herself and a bowl of fresh crayfish, just in case Vithleen was in the mood for something crunchy, she traced the familiar path to the Cellars. All traces of the fire damage from the Lodger's last fight—it still hurt to think of him lurching down the tunnel, holding his forelimb to his chest—had been removed and the tunnel walls repainted.

The crayfish made the trip for nothing. Vithleen was asleep. Rapoto was there, however, with a few other apprentices she knew from the dining hall. He had a wingman's uniform now, a Guard officer's straight sword, and his fore-and-aft-rigged hat under his arm. Rapoto had grown more handsome as the indolent, wealthy-boy baby fat finally left his face under the hard Guard training. She'd heard that their swordplay fatigues were nearly as hard as anything Ottavia threw at them.

It was hard not to form the sort of fantasies about a figure like that. It was hard to even breathe around him.

"You flatter that uniform," she said.

He smiled. "I was hoping to congratulate you on your release. Yes, while you were gone they rotated me around a bit. I did a spell assisting in the flight cave. Amrits isn't much of a taskmaster. I pull watches on the walls, and once in a while I have charge of the gate if Captain Tellence has something better to do."

"Stopped any m-muddy fourteen-year-old girls from entering?"

"Haven't had that honor yet, no."

Ileth rounded the corner and peeped in on Vithleen. She looked shrunken, compared to the robust, muscular specimen Ileth had ridden by mistake on her wild circuit of the Vales. But her scale was still healthy. No trace of chalky streaks or patches falling out.

"Is she all right?"

"I'm told she's doing well," Rapoto said. "The physikers say it's natural she doesn't eat much these days. You can see one of the eggs, just where her neck is lying across her tail."

The eggs looked to be lying in a little nest of bones. It was hard to tell what might be egg from bits of old bone; they were similar color. After some more guidance from Rapoto, she believed she saw it.

"No danger of the eggs being crushed?" Ileth asked.

"They're not nearly as fragile as hen's eggs. Not that I want to start experimenting," an apprentice with a physiker's apron said.

With little to see beyond a sleepy green dragon and a pile of bones with some eggs concealed inside, the apprentices turned away.

"Do you know Vithleen?" Ileth asked.

"A little," Rapoto said. "I know she did a good deal of courier duty. She has a reputation of being friendly, a good learning dragon. I should like to ride her regularly. My ideal is a fast dragon. Fast will get you out of trouble. But Vithleen is not the sort to seek glory in war. I'm sure she'd defend the Serpentine to the last like the rest of us, but she declined to go up in the Galantine War. Left it to the males."

Ileth thought about mentioning that Fespanarax was fast, very fast, but decided to remain quiet.

"Will you wait for one of her children, then?"

"Oh, I'd have gray in my beard—if I grow a beard then—by the time they have their wings uncased and are thinking about taking on a dragoneer. But they say sometimes, after having hatchlings, the females grow quite fierce and territorial. So maybe she will end up flying to glory after all."

Ileth, having heard Dandas's description of a glorious ending courtesy of Galantine crossbows, shuddered. Her imagination was eager to supply a picture of Rapoto lying dead under Vithleen. *I wonder what color the males will be?* Ileth decided to ask, and was rehearsing the question before speaking it when Rapoto looked at her.

"I have been forced to learn the virtue of patience when it comes to females," Rapoto said, showing no sign of having heard her. He was staring at her.

It made her so uncomfortable that she forgot herself, bobbed an obeisance, and left.

Ileth had just begun, in the quiet of the Dancers' Quarter, a letter to Falth at Ottavia's writing table when she heard a call on the other side of the curtain, then the sound of running booted feet on the East Stair.

"Stop him!" a voice shouted.

She was just in one of her Galantine night-dresses; they were comfortable, even if they weren't fit for public wear, so she threw the nearest shawl of Ottavia's she could find on top of it and stepped barefoot into the passage leading up from the kitchens.

Preece was trying to get up the stairs; a kitchen apprentice and two dragon feeders were restraining him.

"Murder! Murder!" the kitchen apprentice said.

"We caught him trying to escape!" a feeder grunted, wrestling with Preece.

"P-P-Preece?" Ileth said, sensing that something had gone drastically wrong. "What's going on? Help! Dragoneers!" she called, hoping that Dath Amrits was nursing his headachy dragon or that one of the more sensible ones was on the Under Ring.

"He's a Galantine agent, dance-girl," one of the men wrestling with Preece said.

"He's no such thing," Ileth said.

Other dancers emerged from the Quarter. It felt good to have a few more at her side. If only Ottavia were around! Oh, there was Preen, what rank was she again?

"He's no . . . he's no—" *Curse her tongue!*

"Don't listen to her, she's a friend to the traitor Galia," someone in the mob said.

Preece finally gave up his struggles.

"Who was murdered?" Preen asked.

"Vithleen! And her eggs have been stolen!" the kitchen assistant said.

"One human managed to kill a dragon guarding her eggs?" Santeel Dun Troot said. She had a sleep mask on her forehead. "How?"

"Poison, we think. Her teeth are all blue; the physiker is there now and he showed us."

Ileth felt her stomach go cold. Dun Huss had been asking about a poison that turned the teeth blue. But what kind of poisoner advertises his intent by asking every learned ear for information about the poison?

"Preece, what's this about?" Dath Amrits said, cutting through the crowd. He looked haggard and his eyes were badly bloodshot. "You can tell me. Hael is out on Mnasmanus."

"My dragoneer has ordered me to be silent until he gives me leave to speak, and silent I will remain, even if it costs me my life," Preece said. "Let me get to the lighthouse. Everything depends on it! The murderer will get away with the eggs if I can't signal. Oh, if only we'd guessed!"

"I tell you, he's a poisoner," the cook repeated. "Everyone knows he and his dragoneer have been trying to acquire the stuff."

"It makes no sense," Amrits said. "What sort of poisoner asks every herb grower and physiker in the Serpentine what they know about a substance that turns the victim's teeth blue, then uses exactly that poison?"

"Exactly!" Ileth said. "If he needs to go to the lighthouse, let him."

"It may be a signal to his co-conspirators," Preen said.

"Oh, gutterwash," Amrits said. "This must be the act of a madman.

How's anyone going to escape with three dragon eggs? It would be like running a race while carrying watermelons."

A deep note passed through the air above and the rock beneath. The assembled humans felt it in their bones. Ileth had never heard the like; it was like the moan of the earth itself giving birth.

"That's the Dragon Horn! It's 'dragons up,'" Amrits said. Whistles sounded, three long blasts, and Amrits pulled his own replacement (this one was brass) and blew a trio of blasts as well.

The argument dissolved.

Dragons up! Ileth had learned of that signal; everyone in the Serpentine had. It put the dragons and their riders on a war footing. Every dragon who could take to the air and fight would be up, and armed humans would post themselves at the entrances. The Beehive buzzed now, as though killer hornets were attacking.

"Look, I'll take charge of Preece," Amrits said. "Dragons up. Fire stations. To arms, now!"

Ileth, when questioned about it afterward, couldn't say exactly what compelled her to hurry and seek out Fespanarax, leaving the drama on the stairway behind. She learned from one of the grooms passing out pikes that he'd hurried down to be at his niece's side. Around her, dragons were moving, and dragoneers, wingmen, and apprentices were hurrying to and fro in increasing numbers, gathering equipment and buckling into flying gear.

"It's dragons up, Ileth," one of the grooms who liked to watch the dancers said.

Ileth decided, on her own, to try for the Cellars. Some sense beyond reason told her she had to be there. Perhaps it was memories of the Lodger's final need. The lift was under guard; it would not move, she heard a Guard say, unless under orders of the Charge of the Beehive herself, until the eggs were retrieved.

There was an argument going on in the kitchen. The cooks did not do battle drill often, and an apprentice was arguing that she was useless with a pike but much better with a crossbow.

"You're on the pike team," the Guard in charge of the little group insisted. "Here's the roster!"

"Stuff the roster! I'm the best in my class at marksmanship," she insisted.

Oh, she needed to think! Ileth used the confusion, and her own trained nimbleness, to duck down the passage to the Cellars. She met only one person hurrying up, a physiker's apprentice calling for water and a hose. He paid her no attention.

She rounded the familiar intersection. A splash in a corner reeked. She investigated and saw a great puddle of vomit. The track of a wheel passed through it. A food cart?

Odd that no one was barring her way to the dragon's chamber. But what further crimes could be committed down here? She started down the corridor to the chamber, wondering why Fespanarax's bulk wasn't filling the passage ahead and blocking the light. Why wasn't he guarding his niece?

"Ileth," the Borderlander said, stepping from the shadows. Eerily, he was in much the same spot Gorgantern had used. It was the best spot for lurking, being the darkest stretch of tunnel.

"I'm looking for Fespanarax," she said. "Have you seen him, sir?"

"The whole Serpentine is running with hair aflame. We'll have ten or more dragons in the air soon. Including Fespanarax, I imagine. A rabbit wouldn't be able to get away, night or no. How far is someone going to get with three dragon eggs? Stupid, even if they have a horse or something. I think the eggs are still concealed here. It's the only thing that makes sense. While we're rushing around searching Vyenn and so on, they'll stay hidden. I'm just betting whoever did it, their mind is working and working and wondering if they made some mistake that gives the hiding place away or if they left a clue about their identity. I'm also making sure they don't come back and finish the job on the poor mother."

"Finish the job?"

"Vithleen is still breathing. Barely. But she's unconscious or she could tell us more. Good thing Dun Huss laid in a supply of the antidote to gravesleaf, or she'd be gone already. Preece gave it to her and those fools in the kitchens hauled him off."

Ileth gulped. "I'm down here. Do you . . . do you think I did it?"

"No."

"Why don't you suspect me?"

"I trust my gut. My gut likes you." Northerners and their guts. "Also, if you were about to make a getaway with the eggs, it wouldn't be barefoot and dressed like a whorehouse tart escaping a fire."

Ileth wondered what Taf would think of one of her night-dresses being described like that.

"I think—" At the last second she changed her phrasing from *I think you're wrong* to something more indirect. Once in a while a stutter could save you. "I think the eggs are gone. They went out in a food cart. Yael Duskirk did it."

She grabbed his hand and pulled him down the hallway. Their relative sizes made her feel like an insistent child hauling a parent to a sweet-cart.

"You're sure?"

"There's vomit at the intersection."

They came up to the puddle. He squatted to examine it. "Human. It smells like . . . wine."

"I've cleaned up enough sick to know the smell and look. The s-smell of dragon stomach makes Duskirk vomit. I bet she made a terrible mess in her throes."

"How's he getting away, then?"

"A boat? There's fog on the lake. Or . . . or maybe—"

"Maybe what?"

"Fespanarax. Did he come to see Vithleen?"

"No. Never even heard his step."

"Zwollen in Galantine, and now one here, with the s-same results. Blue teeth. I think Fespanarax brought some poison back with him in that sealed box. Something that turns your teeth blue."

"Yes. Called gravesleaf. Hael told me that tale. He's been buried in herbs and lore on the stuff. Killed a couple pigs with his experiments. It makes sense. Fespanarax was there, and here, and now he and three priceless dragon eggs are gone. And that Duskirk kid's been about him a lot. Seen 'em together."

"What's to be done?"

"We need to fly, and fast. Fespanarax has a head start. You'll have to jump if you've a chance to catch him."

Ileth was forming a reply when the Borderlander grabbed her hand and pulled her along. Now he was the parent pulling a poky child up the passage toward the kitchens. She struggled to keep up with his long, fast strides.

They moved through the chaos, one more loose leaf in a swirling river of activity.

"This isn't the way to—" Ileth said.

"I know. Catherix ain't even in the caves. She's way above."

"Without you?"

"She has brains, more'n me. She's keeping watch, high above, where only she's strong enough to get to—just in case there are some other dragons coming from, say, the Galantine lands to help get these eggs. Catherix likes a height advantage. It's her favorite move. When she comes down, well, it's like getting hit by an avalanche on fire."

"Then where are we going?"

"The flight cave." The Borderlander told her to save her breath for running.

They found Aurue on watch in the cave, guarding the entrance.

"We need you up and after Fespanarax now, Aurue," the Borderlander said. "You're our only hope of catching Fespanarax."

Aurue twitched in thought.

"Me? Fly against Fespanarax?" Aurue asked. His Montangyan had improved while she was in the Galantine lands. "First: why? Second: he's many times my size! Many. Third: you must be mad. Fourth: I'm already at my post."

The Borderlander threw a wool blanket on Aurue's back. "First, keep quiet. Second's also 'keep quiet' and that goes for the rest of the listed items as well." The Borderlander took off his cloak and handed it to Ileth. "This'll have to do."

"He has n-no scale," Ileth as she accepted his overlong coat.

"I am aware of that," Aurue said.

"You should fly on him," Ileth said. "You're the d-dragoneer."

"Well, you have extra brains to make up for that mouth full of sling-stones. He's not full-grown yet, and you're light as a feather. Aurue with you is the best chance we have. Having no scale means he's quick as hot oil and he can change color so's a cat wouldn't see him at night if they were sharing the same tree. Just the thing for following Fespanarax wherever he takes the eggs. My guess is he'll make for somewhere familiar, and that means the Galantine Baronies. You know the Galantine lands, speak the tongue. If anyone can track him there, it's you."

"I don't know the Galantine lands as well as all that. I can find my way to exactly one estate."

"Figure it out as you go along. That's what I do."

The Borderlander found a cable about the thickness of his thumb and tied it neatly around Aurue, expertly putting three loops in it, one for each foot and a third atop the dragon's spine; fortunately he was young and his spikes were still small. He also dug up a cargo net from the flying supplies and tied it around Aurue's neck expertly.

"You're doing it emergency-fashion, Ileth. You've been working your legs two years now. Time to test 'em. The net's just in case you get a chance at those eggs."

"I'm not threaded for reins!" Aurue said.

"Good, she won't be hauling on your ears when you should be listening with them," the Borderlander said. "Catherix isn't threaded for reins. We do all right."

Ileth climbed on and wrapped her dance-slippered toes around the stirrup lines. She didn't feel at all ready to go after perhaps the biggest dragon in the Serpentine, and the most expert fighter.

"What is going on here?" an apprentice with an etching board said, running forward. Dragon departures were scrawled all over it. "Who is she?"

"Ileth flying Aurue, and if you knew your job you'd recognize them." The Borderlander grabbed him by the shoulders, spun him, and launched him clear of the dragon and rider by the expedient of pressing his boot against the apprentice's backside and kicking hard. "Going after the stolen eggs."

The Borderlander returned, checked Ileth's seat, and slapped the gray dragon at the base of the throat. "I've seen you fly. You got speed,

Aurue. Time to use it. He'll probably follow the river south, low, next to the hills while the moon's low, keeping in the moon's shadow."

Aurue blinked. He took a deep breath and warmed his wings.

"Warm them up there," the Borderlander said. "Fly like you're escaping hell, you two." The Borderlander brought his fists up and together in that gesture Ileth had seen. But not to her. He did it to Aurue. Aurue reared up and Ileth clung on, white-knuckled, for dear life. But she still saw the dragon mirror the man with his own front claws, making the tightest fist a dragon could with them.

With that he moved to the opening.

Fly they did. Aurue jumped out of the cave, almost leaving Ileth behind as she tightened her grip on the rope and about his neck, made the turn, and stayed low.

Ileth couldn't help but think it was a fool's errand. They'd delayed too much. Unless Fespanarax had also delayed, he was well ahead of them. Fespanarax was too clever to count on confusion lasting until morning.

Dragons with dragoneers on their back circled over the gate, hunting the approaches to the Serpentine. One swooped low, executing a neat trick as she (at least Ileth thought she was green, it was hard to tell at night) shot through the pillars of the Long Bridge, looking for boats rowing away. Aurue followed her. Ileth closed her eyes as he went through the bridge, briefly closing his wings and turning himself into an arrow.

Aurue was fast, frighteningly so. It was like Vithleen riding a greased fish-chute. The lake slipped by beneath them at a horizon-eating pace.

Then, near the great Heartbreak Cliff south of Vyenn, they both saw a shower of fire. Dragonfire, it had to be, and in its light she saw the flash of a white dragon belly.

Ileth saw her first aerial dragon duel that night and learned two important lessons: first, that they were often over quickly, and second, that you could lose one before you knew you were in it if you were taken by surprise. In later years, those early lessons would save her life more than once. But on this night she was mostly an observer.

Two dragons fought, wings out but not keeping them aloft, as they were clawing at each other. They spun and fell, grappling, heedless of the fall. Just before they hit the water they seemed to realize their danger and broke the embrace of combat. Once separated, she could make out Fespanarax, and another dragon almost as large whom she couldn't be sure of in the darkness but might be Mnasmanus.

Fespanarax turned his fall into a dive. He closed his wings and splashed into the water like a shot arrow. Mnasmanus, who it seemed had the worst of the encounter, tried to bank above the lake but suddenly tipped and went in, throwing up a great wave in the moonlight.

"The one under the water!" Ileth shouted. "It's Fe—"

"I know," Aurue said, so excited that he spoke Drakine.

Aurue was fast, even faster on the descent. Ileth clung on with both arms and legs as best as she could, the Borderlander's big coat flapping in the wind. It was Mnasmanus, she recognized his wings, swimming with Dun Huss clinging to his saddle.

Ileth spotted another swimmer in the water, clinging to a barrel.

"Who is that?" Ileth shouted. "Get me closer!"

It was Yael Duskirk, as she'd suspected, sputtering in the water.

Fespanarax shot out of the water like a leaping dolphin. Hanging in the air at the top of the jump, he opened his wings and began to gain altitude. His saddle hung on his back, askew and empty.

Aurue veered away in shock and turned over. If Ileth hadn't been clinging so tight thanks to not being on a saddle at all, she'd have fallen off and been hanging from her tether. As it was, it took her a moment before she regained her orientation and Aurue was climbing again.

The shriek of a dragoneer's whistle cut the night. Ileth looked back; Hael Dun Huss was clinging to his saddle as he pointed. He shouted something—perhaps it was "eggs."

"Get that barrel," Ileth yelled.

Aurue went for the barrel, grabbed it with his rear limbs, and flapped hard—it began to come out of the water, the wet swimmer holding on for dear life.

Fespanarax turned. Ileth saw him coming, jaws agape and claws out.

They didn't stand a chance. But Aurue refused to release the barrel.

A white female flashed down like a thunderbolt. She seemed intent on flying right through Fespanarax. At the last instant he sensed her and closed his wings to protect them. She raked him across the back and Ileth saw droplets of blood and entire sheets of scale fly as Fespanarax spun from the impact.

But he was a tough, canny old dragon. Fespanarax opened his wings again and beat hard, gaining the advantage of altitude and turning east for the Galantine lands.

The white dragon turned and also climbed, kept turning, guarding Aurue with the barrel by circling. Aurue pulled it into the air, and water poured out—it must not have been closed and sealed, for it had flooded quickly. Good thing they'd gone for it when they did.

Yael still clung to the barrel, somehow. Flapping hard, Aurue made for the western shore of the Skylake.

They made it to the lakeshore under the loom of Heartbreak Cliff. The lights of Vyenn and the Serpentine glimmered in the distance. Aurue set the barrel (and Yael Duskirk) very carefully down as the white dragon, whom Ileth presumed to be the Borderlander's Catherix, circled above.

Ileth dismounted, ignored the sputtering and shivering Yael, and opened the barrel—one end was closed by waxed canvas tied around it, so no wonder it had flooded. Canvas could keep out rain, but not a dunking in a lake.

Behind her, the hurt Mnasmanus emerged from the lake, dripping water and dragging a torn wing. Dun Huss was still in his saddle, soaked to the skin.

The eggs were intact, as far as she could tell, packed in with salted fish. She supposed there were worse cushioning materials.

"I'll get help," Aurue said to the other dragons, in Drakine. "I am the fastest."

"Tell them it's Fespanarax, flying hard for the Galantine lands. He's hurt, they might catch him," Mnasmanus told him. Aurue flew off.

"Duskirk, sit right down there. Don't compound your mistake," Dun Huss warned. He ignored Ileth and bent to check the condition of the eggs and rearrange them in their drenched container.

Fespanarax was a vanishing dot, just visible in the moonlight. He wasn't coming back. Catherix splashed gently at the edge of the lakeshore and walked up to the humans.

"I will not leave the eggs," Catherix said. She spoke Montangyan with a thick accent, even for a dragon. "Not until they are hatched or returned to their mother, if Vithleen lives."

"I don't know what would h-have happened if you hadn't been alert," Ileth said to the dragon.

Catherix just blinked at her. She was like her rider, a little hard to read.

Dun Huss finished resecuring the eggs.

"How did you know the eggs were stolen?" Ileth asked.

Dun Huss finally seemed to notice her. "I didn't. I guessed when I heard the 'dragons up' signal. Unhatched dragon eggs are worth their weight in jewels. Saw Fespanarax with a barrel under his saddle; handy that he just happened to have those fittings. I decided it had to be the eggs in there and went at him."

"Can we catch him?" Ileth asked.

"He's fast, big, and smart. Now that he's been found out he'll be extra careful. In daylight we might have a chance. Not now."

Dun Huss questioned Yael Duskirk. He confessed, and things were much as Ileth suspected. He'd poisoned Vithleen using a tasteless substance he put in her food, but Fespanarax said it was just a sleeping draft. Duskirk believed him; Fespanarax was a relative of Vithleen, after all. Fespanarax had promised him a Barony and all the wealth he could spend in the Galantine lands if they managed to bring the eggs over. "He worked on me—gave me expectations. He said Galia had mentioned me, said I wasn't wealthy enough to tempt her. It sounded believable when he said it."

Ileth regretted all the small talk she'd engaged in with Fespanarax. She thought she'd been cheering him up with news of the Serpentine. He'd been gathering intelligence.

Yael continued his story: when they splashed into the lake, the dragon shrugged him off. Duskirk had kept his wits and clung to the barrel, cutting it loose while Fespanarax turned. It had enough buoyancy to float for a moment, and Fespanarax didn't know it was missing.

Duskirk, having made his confession, seemed lightened by it. "What's going to happen to me?"

"Do you have the knife you cut this line with?" Dun Huss asked.

"I lost it in the lake," he said, pointing out to the deep water.

Dun Huss examined what was left of the line that had fixed the barrel to Fespanarax's back. "I'd say the line parted on its own." Dun Huss took out his own knife, cut the rope, and cast the frayed end into the lake. "There. Now it looks cut. You clung on to the eggs, anyway. That's something in your favor. Hopefully it will go to your credit in front of a jury. The question now is, will Vithleen live?"

For days Yael Duskirk's life stood in jeopardy. Vithleen was in a deep, senseless sleep and could not be roused. The jury, including the Master of Apprentices, a professional assignee from Vyenn with knowledge of the law, and—incredibly to Ileth, who didn't know dragons could serve on juries—the dragon Jizara, pronounced him guilty (no great matter of decision, he had confessed). They suspended sentencing for thirty days to see if Vithleen would recover. If she died, he would die a poisoner's death.

Apparently, it wasn't an easy death. Every time someone tried to give her the details, Ileth clapped her hands over her ears and begged to be spared the particulars.

The Serpentine held its breath, certainly none more so than Yael Duskirk.

Ileth had so many *what-ifs* tormenting her about the whole affair. What if there hadn't been a mix-up and Duskirk had done the courier run with Vithleen? Could he still have poisoned the dragon who flew him on his first commission? The Lodger had taught her not to think about that which she had no control over and instead concentrate on those matters in her control, but in each case, she could have altered the flow of events.

Perhaps she still could. She started rehearsing a speech. If Vithleen died, it wouldn't matter, but if she lived . . .

She danced away the doubts and gloomy thoughts. She realized she was developing a style all her own, in the quiet hours when no one was watching, except a dragon or two lounging after dinner and looking to be lulled to sleep. You were, after all, what you did, and that different version of Ileth who danced didn't spend much time on the *what-ifs*. There was music to follow.

Exhausted from dance, she mechanically ate and mechanically slept and made it through the terrible days of question and doubt. Santeel caught her rehearsing her speech and cautioned her against speaking in favor of a friendless apprentice who poisoned a dragon atop her eggs. Even Dun Huss was only speaking out of tradition; even the most wretched convict in the Republic traditionally had one person assigned to speak for him.

Ileth stuttered out that Yael Duskirk had been the first person in the entire Serpentine to speak to her as a friend. If need be, she'd be the last friend to stand by him.

Vithleen awoke after six days. Falberrwrath was beside her when she did so. Vithleen knew who she was and was glad to see her eggs with the little dragons dreaming quietly within but was otherwise confused; she'd been dreaming that she was flying above thick clouds, and every time she dropped down she couldn't find a familiar landmark, so up she went again; the only odd thing about her dream was that she grew stronger each time she fought her way above the clouds rather than weaker.

It did take her some time to fully recover and remember the names of the humans attending her.

Ileth asked Hael Dun Huss to be allowed to address the jury before the sentencing. It was no great difficulty for him to get her on the roster of people addressing the jury, as nobody but Dun Huss himself was willing to speak for the boy. Selgernon, the Master of Apprentices, was ill; the shock of one of his apprentices committing such an act had shattered his already frail health, so Dun Huss took it upon himself to speak up for the boy.

The jury room was at the up end of the Serpentine, in a very old hall with ornate arching woodwork that got dusty, illuminated by candles that left the jurors looking forbidding and shadowed in their special double gallery with dark stained glass behind. You had to look up at them. The dragon sat below the gallery, her body in a basement chamber and her head looking out from a wide gap beneath the jury balcony.

Ileth's speech was longer than her oath. She stuttered her way through it, just like her oath, but this time it didn't make her feel miserable. Her words and the truth behind them were important, not how she said them, and a foolish man's life stood in the balance. She described herself as a dancer, and talked of how dancers supposedly could bewitch dragons. She believed it could work the other way too; it was hard, when you stood before so immense and powerful a creature, not to be swayed by the words of an ancient creature who could breathe you out of existence. She spoke of how the Lodger had restored her confidence in herself with a few kindly words here and there and given her the desire to bring justice to a thief like Griff. Then she described Fespanarax, a powerful dragon good at getting what he wanted out of humans. She told them of her precious silver dragon whistle, the first token of esteem anyone had given her in her entire life, and how at a few words from him she gave it up to be eaten so quickly he hardly could have tasted it. Fespanarax in his greed was skilled at weaving lies and truth around each other; who knows how he had worked on Yael, used his disappointments against him. She finished saying she couldn't claim to know anyone's heart, but that while Yael Duskirk had failed the Serpentine, he had recovered the eggs.

"After first stealing them," the dragon on the jury said. But the human jurors had exchanged looks as Ileth spoke.

Dun Huss spoke briefly, emphasizing that as a feeder Duskirk was used to issuing herbs and potions that would help dragons sleep, and that, in the end, he'd come to his senses and tried to atone for his crimes by saving the eggs. He'd confessed fully and made no attempt to offer a defense of his actions.

So Yael Duskirk was spared his poisoner's death, but even an attempt at murder was a forfeit of his existence. He was sentenced to labor in the mines at the Widowsend.

"It is not the end for him," Hael Dun Huss said, discussing it with

Ileth and Preece later over late-night tea in the dining hall. "If he can avoid an accident, after a few years the fact that his crimes came before full legal citizenship, his confession and attempt to make amends by—ahem—saving the eggs by cutting them off Fespanarax, plus influence from a few dragoneers, might get him removed from there and put into the Auxiliaries."

Dun Huss was willing to write a letter in his favor, in a year or two when his crimes weren't so new. He would look up the boy's birth date and plead for some kind of suspension of sentence in exchange for enrollment in the Auxiliaries when he turned eighteen.

The dragoneer poured Ileth a little more tea, carefully turning his body so any accidental splashes wouldn't hit his purple sash. "We all make mistakes when we're young. Provided they're not irrevocable, you can start anew. A bad start is still a start, after all." He smiled at Ileth. "I think you're fond of that expression."

"True, sir," Ileth said. "As I've a-always tried to say."

19

Between the trial of Yael Duskirk and Vithleen's recovery, Ileth met with a jury of unnamed official questioners who asked her, in detail, over the course of two days all that she could remember about events in the Galantine lands. They screened the room in such a way that she couldn't make out their faces clearly, though she had ample light on her thanks to a skylight. She tried to be completely honest. She found the process exhausting. They questioned her closely about the news of Vithleen's clutch. As far as Ileth could tell, there was no way for the Galantines to have learned of the eggs through her; the first she'd heard of them was when she returned to the Serpentine. Yet Fespanarax's returning to the Serpentine with a supply of poison implied that the Galantines released him with the idea of having him steal the eggs. The consensus of her jury seemed to be that since negotiations delayed the dragon's return again and again, the rescue of the children from the plateau gave them an opportunity to return Fespanarax as their agent without questions being asked. Ileth happened to be caught up in greater plots than she knew, which dulled the shine of her Galantine title.

Therefore there was a spy, or several spies, for the Galantines within the Serpentine. It would be easy enough for anyone to communicate with other spies in Vyenn, who could then send secret messages back via courier down the river. A simple boat trip down the river could get you to the border.

When they formally dismissed her from questioning they did so with a promise and a request. A promise that her excellent and useful observations would be noted, and a request to not say anything about suspicions of Galantine spies.

Leaving such matters for the investigators, she finally had her much-delayed appointment with the Master of Novices. She settled on an evening after she'd finished dancing for Falberrwrath, who was still out of sorts over the poisoning and the eggs, so much so that he didn't even regale her with old war stories, but shifted about nervously until the music, motion, and, she supposed, the smell of her sweat soothed him.

She was too tired after that to be nervous. She found Master Caseen alone in his office.

Ileth couldn't think of what she'd done to be called in. It couldn't be that she was promoted to apprentice; Selgernon would be present for that. Had news of her Galantine title caused her some difficulty? Perhaps she'd violated some patriotic rule. Reintroducing aristocratic titles or something like that.

She certainly hadn't put on airs—though she'd been tempted to ask Santeel if a Galantine Lady of Hospitals and Refuges, with Acts, had to perform a courtesy to a Dun Troot first, or if it was the reverse. Hael Dun Huss hinted that he understood the meaning on those streamers hung on Fespanarax for her return. She'd confessed it to the jury of inquiry and showed them the Galantine King's letter. Maybe this was leading to an official reprimand.

"Here you are again, Ileth, in my office. Feels like old times, eh?" Nothing had changed, not even his habit of scratching at his elbows as he filtered memories. He even wore the same decorative mask and tasseled sash. No, there was something different. He had a new lamp. It was on an arm and counterweight that allowed the light to be tilted without spilling the oil, and the light had a shade that reflected and concentrated the illumination. Very clever. It was probably from one of the artisans in Tyrenna. The things they created!

"You have a new lamp."

"Yes, the flame adjusts better for reading. My eyes are getting old, along with the rest of me."

She couldn't say much to that.

"I have an interesting letter here." He gestured to his desk. For a moment Ileth startled, thinking it was from the Galantine King, as it was roughly the same size, but it didn't have nearly the same rich décor of ribbons and seals.

"Does it concern me, sir?"

"I took my time figuring that out," Caseen said. "It's from no less a personage than Governor Raal of your own North Province. Some weeks after your first flight on Vithleen, he wrote me demanding the return of a runaway to the Freesand Lodge. The runaway's name was Ileth. Now, for all he knew, I had six novices named after a Galantine Queen who went to her death with a Directist prayer on her lips, so I wrote back asking for more information. It turns out she stutters and had been seen on dragonback carrying the Republic's mails. That letter I gave to Kess in the archives to ask if anyone of that description had been enrolled, but as chance would have it Kess blundered and misfiled it. It's rare, but it's been known to happen. By the time a personal representative of your Governor showed up at our gate, you were a prisoner in the Galantine lands and there was nothing we could do for him."

Ileth could only say, "Thank you, sir."

"Governor Raal has never been any sort of friend to the Serpentine, so I wonder at him writing us himself. The man who ran your lodge, did Governor Raal owe him some great favor?"

The Captain, in his cups, always insisted that he knew important names who owed him. But then, when drunk, he also insisted that he'd killed sixteen men single-handed and escaped the Rari pirates, and that the moon was always watching and knew if you were talking mutiny, so Ileth had not taken the claims seriously. "I don't know anything about such matters," she said, happy to be entirely truthful.

"I'm glad that's settled. You wish to exert your right as a sixteen-year-old to choose your own path and dwelling?"

"Yes, sir."

"Good. Because I have more news for you."

She braced herself as best as she could and just looked at the mask and his sound eye.

"It is happy news for a change. You are appointed apprentice."

So it was that! She'd made it in, found a place with all these Names. Despite the stutter. Despite the Lodge. Despite the rumors about her mother, which, when she was a child, the whole world held over her, and now they yellowed and faded into sad garden-wall gossip that deserved only a contemptuous snap of her fingers. Despite, perhaps, the demands of a Vale provincial Governor. "Thank you," she said, her voice choked with emotion for a change, rather than tripping on her poky and unreliable tongue.

"Why . . . why isn't the Master of Apprentices here for this?"

"Selgernon's on leave. He's been indisposed since this Duskirk business. He may quit the Serpentine and attend to his health."

"I hope he recovers."

"He's a good man. I told him not to blame himself for Duskirk; you can't know what's in the hearts of hundreds of youths. But I'm sorry this took so long. We should have done it while you were in the Galantine lands, but the thing with Galia stirred things up here a little. We'd lost a wingman to marriage; suppose an apprentice went with her? I don't expect you to understand what some of the fine figures at the Assembly say about us sometimes. There's a faction always looking to get rid of us. The dragons of the Serpentine absorb a good deal of balance sheet ink. We're also seen as a legacy from the King and a refuge of aristocratic feeling. But we've turned the tide in battle too many times for them to get rid of us. The Republic wouldn't exist without her dragoneers."

Ileth clearly wasn't listening. The Master gave her a moment to collect herself.

"You are also the last of your oathed group of novices to move up to apprentice. The rest moved up before you or went by the wayside one way or another. It makes you the tailer of the draft of sixty-six, even if it's not your fault you were a prisoner. I'm sorry, the title will cling."

Ileth thought she could show she cared not how she made apprentice, just that she did, by using a Zusya-like phrase like "better the tail than a . . ." But Caseen's office was no place for adolescent jokes.

"But it's just a name. Names change and are forgotten. Not like this." He tapped his mask.

"Sir, if you don't m-mind me asking, why a party mask?"

"Oh, didn't I ever tell the story? I thought I did. The night before the battle I was at a masquerade ball. I remember thinking I looked intriguing in it and wishing I had more opportunities to wear it. Little did I know. Just goes to show that you must be careful with your wishes as well as your actions. Sometimes they'll haunt you. Still, I was lucky. The surgeon said that if I'd lost more skin and had bone exposed in such a fashion that he couldn't pull some bits together and stitch so it was covered up, I'd have died from a gangrenous rot. Alive and mysterious behind a mask is better than dead and good-looking."

Ileth nodded slowly. She would miss this man.

"So this is it for us, we with our odd speech and lack of distinguished Name. I'm no longer Master of Ileth. The Blue Book turns its page. I've cleared my desk for a new draft. Anything more I can do for you?"

Ileth finally had time to get an answer to a question that had been bothering her off and on. "What does that gesture with the two fists brought together mean?"

"Like this?" Caseen asked, bringing his arms in front of his chest in tight fists joined as one horizontal bar, knuckles out.

"Yes. Please, I've seen it a few times. I even saw Aurue do it."

"Did he? That's good. I've heard he wasn't entirely sure about being here, at least before the whole egg rescue. Well, ask six dragoneers and you'll get six different answers. Some say it's just a reassuring gesture for white-knuckling through difficulty. Another might just say it's a gesture of approval. More nautical types say it means *hold fast*."

"What's your answer, sir?"

"I'd say it means *keep the troth*."

"I like that one b-best."

They smiled at each other.

Oh, there was one other thing she was curious about. "When we f-first met, that first day you opened the door to me, you mentioned a portrait. Before your . . . before your burns. I should very much like to see it. As I suppose I won't be called into this office anymore, I confess I've always wondered. It seems this is my last chance."

"I remember telling you you knew how to flatter an old man.

Anything for the newest apprentice of the Serpentine," Caseen said, smiling. He stood up, stretched a little stiffly, and started rummaging around in a map case. He opened a drawer fully and drew out a portrait.

"You have to remember, Ileth, that portrait painters find they get much better commissions if they flatter up the subject a bit. Many a young man, and woman, I suppose, has been tricked into forming an attachment over a portrait that didn't tell the entire truth."

Even allowing for a certain amount of artistic flourish, the portrait showed a sharp, eagle-faced young man in the most dashing style of dress dragoneer uniform. The young, unburned Caseen left Rapoto Vor Claymass well below and far behind.

"Sir, I had no idea," Ileth said. "You really should hang it, but it might be too distracting for us girls." She wanted to sit and drink wine and take in the picture. She quietly chuckled. For the first time in her life, she wanted to have someone's babies!

That night she couldn't sleep so she walked the walls, enjoying the summer wind until almost dawn, losing herself in the light of the beacon atop the Beehive, looking for the sun coming up over the mountains on the other side of the Skylake and down at the doorstep of the red door where she'd sat and waited and starved almost two years ago. She'd had enough bad moments in life to know that a good one should be lingered over, savored, memorialized. Apprenticed! Even containing her happiness was impossible; she kept alternately crying and laughing. Two Guards pacing the south wall must have thought her mad.

In theory, her place among the dragoneers of the Serpentine was now secure for the coming years of her apprenticeship, six by tradition, and much longer if you were a specialist. Shatha, after all, was believed to be above forty and therefore ancient. Ileth could almost count on rising by default, and, barring an accident or illness, would someday fly on commissions, just as Annis had atop Agrath. If she had money, she'd hire an artist to paint her likeness so that she might always have the moment a childhood wish came true.

Which gave her a thought.

In a bit of a daze from lack of sleep, she begged a bit of early break-fast from Joai, who was already up and at work in her kitchen, having just fed a few Guards coming off their night rounds. When did the woman sleep?

"You're the prettiest tailer the Serpentine's ever seen, anyway," she said, kissing Ileth on the forehead at the news. "I knew this day would come. Provided you lived. Some people are prone to adventures, but not all of them live to write their memoirs."

Ileth thanked her and hurried to the Dancers' Quarter. She needed to retrieve her dancing sheath.

Most were at breakfast. Santeel was washing up a few odds and ends from their improvised pre-drill breakfast. "What are you so happy about?"

"Caseen has seen the last of the draft of sixty-six. The Blue Book is closed, at least on our class."

"Why are you—wait, you've made apprentice?"

"The tailer," Ileth said.

Preen and Zusya entered the washroom with their drill clothes. Preen gave her hair a playful pull; Zusya hugged her. The news would spread through the Serpentine quickly enough now.

"Saw your letter to Falth," Santeel said, casually. "I wasn't aware your friendship extended to my family's servants."

"About that," Ileth began, before she fell into stammering.

"Oh, I know my family. Don't even worry about it, there's nothing to forgive." She leaned in to hug Ileth and pulled her close, pressing her hand into the wash basin and holding it under. "If you ever write a word to them against me, I'll drown you myself as a betrayer," she whispered. Then she was released. "Congratulations on your promotion, appren-tice!" Santeel laughed. "I'm so happy for you!"

Ileth fled the Notch and begged off morning drill to Ottavia.

She was an apprentice now. She could leave the Serpentine, as long as it was daylight—and she returned in daylight. She had that privilege. And it was daylight, just. Though she should be at drills, there was something more important to do.

She dug around beneath her bed and retrieved one item, a souvenir of the Galantine lands, and rushed out to the Long Bridge.

They barely noticed the mad girl in the bad-fitting overdress; those few who were up and about were yawning and heading for breakfast.

Ileth made it to the gate. That monkeylike boy with the long name who'd walked in on her changing was in an ill-fitting Guard uniform and serving as gatekeeper that morning. He called for the Dragon Gate to be opened for her. He watched her pass through with the same bemused, curious expression as he'd had looking at her in Joai's kitchen, eyes peering out from under an ill-fitting fore-and-aft-rigged hat that nearly came down to his eyes. She ran down to the bayside and those old overturned boats. Panting, she made it just as the sun left the mountains on the other side of the lake.

"I've done it, Father. I passed their tests. I've made apprentice.

"Apprenticed!" she shouted, scattering the birds poking about at the edge of the lake. Farther out, she heard a splash. She'd probably startled an otter.

It was time to show him that aerial pirouette he'd once asked about.

As she bowed, centered herself, and began to dance, showing a kindly memory of a dragon who believed love and beauty and knowledge transcended the curtain between life and death, a walking flock of muddy geese appeared on the hill above, moving down toward the far end of the bay.

Two old farmers, grandfathers now who probably had sons and grandsons doing the heavy work and had been left to easier tasks, were moving their geese down to feed at a little creek that fed into the bay. With spring well on, the creek would be thick with bugs and small frogs for the geese and, when they ran out of frogs, young tender grass shoots.

One of the men saw Ileth and switched his long goose-driving pole to his other hand so he could nudge his friend.

"What do we have here, you think?" Ileth leaped and spun, leaped and spun again, one leg forward in the air, another tucked behind, her arms up and out, smiling. Perhaps crying, but then she needed some water to go with the earth on her feet and the fire in her limbs as she spun through the air.

"Don't you know? One of those girls as dances for them dragons up there. Charms them, like, so them that ride the beasts can handle them."

"Tricky stuff, goin' about all raised up on your toes like that. How's she not fall down, I want to know."

"Thinking you'd let your young Annis twirl around like that?"

"Heh, I can just see it."

"Eh, isn't that the spot where they said that old dragon washed up and died?"

"I believe it is, Ewesh, I believe it is."

They passed on with their geese. Meanwhile, the slight young woman pirouetted around an odd black stick. It stood there in the center of her circle of footprints, two red-and-white streamers left to flutter in the breeze. She threw a long shadow in the morning sun. But not so long a shadow that you couldn't see it dancing with her.

CAST OF CHARACTERS

THE DRAGONS

AGRATH, a silver
AURUE, a gray
THE LODGER, an ancient red-and-black-striped recluse
VITHLEEN, a very fast green
AUSPEREX, a male elder
TARESSCON, a senior green
SHRENTINE, patroness of the dragon dancers
CUNESCIOUS, a young copper
MNASMANUS, a mighty purple
FALBERRWRATH, a veteran red
FESPANARAX THE RECKLESS, a prisoner of the Galantine Baronies

THE SERPENTINE AND ITS ACADEMY

ILETH, a novice from an orphans' lodge in the Freesand
ANNIS HEEM STRATH, dragoneer to Agrath
SANTEEL DUN TROOT, a novice from a distinguished family
YAEL DUSKIRK, an apprentice with the feeders
CASEEN THE MASTER OF NOVICES, a veteran dragoneer disfigured by battle
JOAI, a fixer of battered flesh and empty stomachs
THE MATRON, supervisor of the female novices at the Manor
GALIA, an apprentice from the streets of Sammerdam
QUITH, a novice
GORGANTERN, an aging apprentice
KESS, the archivist
JEROTH, a cook

ROGUSS HEEM DEKLAMP, Charge of the Serpentine

RAPOTO VOR CLAYMASS, an apprentice from wealth from Jotun

PASFA SLENG, a wingman from Zland

PREECE, a wingman

GRIFF, an apprentice in the Cellars

ZANTE, a novice under Griff's wing

GOWAN, apprentice archivist

HAEL DUN HUSS, a dragoneer of distinction

DATH AMRITS, a dragoneer often in the company of Dun Huss and the Borderlander

THE BORDERLANDER, a dragoneer from the North

AMONG THE DANCERS

OTTAVIA IMPERENE, Charge of the Dragon Dancers

PEAK, a senior dancer and muse

ZUSYA, a most talkative friend

SHATHA, the oldest dancer

VII, the daughter of a seamstress

TASSA, a senior dancer

FYTH, a new recruit

DAX, a musician of Vyenn

NOTABLES OF THE VALE REPUBLIC

FALTH, servant to the Name Dun Troot

STANTHOFF, an Auxiliary in the Cleft

LEITH, a fishing boat captain

THE DUN TROOTS, concerned parents

THE GALANTINE BARONIES

BARON HRYASMESS, a kindly lord

THE BARONESS, a busy mother

TAF, the Baron's daughter

YOUNG AZAL OF CHAPALAINE, the Baron's son

DANDAS, a Baronet and distant relation to Baron Hryasmess

RANYA, of the Tribals

ACKNOWLEDGMENTS

Novels are Frankenstein creations, dug up out of the author's experiences and stitched together with others passing vital thread. There's Rebecca Brewer at Penguin Random House and my agent John Silbersack, who did the work of getting it out to shelves and warehouses and digital libraries so you readers can buy it. I'd like to thank Miriam-Rose and the staff of the Joffrey Academy of Dance in Chicago, who welcomed a fifty-year-old man who wanted to learn ballet with enthusiasm and encouragement. Rachel Brice, whom I was lucky enough to get to know at various dance workshops my wife attended, first gave me the idea for dragons being calmed and hypnotized by sweaty women. I'm also indebted to barre instructor Candace, who knows what my femur is doing even with her back to me and continually tries to turn the solid matter of my body into liquid or gaseous forms. I'd also like to thank my son's speech therapist, Jenna, who gave me some valuable insight into Ileth's speech and ideas on how to depict it. Speaking of medical people, I give thanks to Peter Grant MD, without whom I might not even be sitting here typing out acknowledgments. I'd also like to thank the fans of the Age of Fire series who wrote asking for more stories of my dragons, and Marylou the Mother of Dragons, who was this novel's first reader with no personal stake in me or the book and provided much-needed encouragement that I still had some game left. My brother Stefan offered his professorial (Go Mountaineers!) erudition in everything from low-frequency audio communication in elephants to the best design for the Dragon Horn. Then there are my three awesome kids, each of whom provided a piece of Ileth, and my wife, Stephanie, who puts up with my frequent trips deep in my mental submarine. Any and all errors of fact, style, or taste are on me.

Photo by Ebert Studio, Oak Park, IL

E. E. Knight was born in Wisconsin, grew up in Minnesota, and now calls Chicago home, where he abides in domestic felicity with his family and assorted pets. He is the author of the Age of Fire series and the Vampire Earth series.